DEMON BLOODED

THE HIDDEN HERITAGE SERIES
BOOK 2
DAN KENNER

For Kathryn and Glen, your love and support has been instrumental in my author career

CONTENTS

I TEACH THE DRAGON BOY A LESSON

"**Y**OU CAN'T BE SERIOUS," I say, folding my arms and leaning my head against the headrest.

Our van rolls to a stop in front of a run-down sign that reads "Park Motel." It consists of only floor-level rooms, the doors so close together that only a bed with a few feet on the other side could fit. I clench my teeth, burning frustration building like a volcano about to erupt.

My demon side stirs within, writhing and twisting to emerge and make me smash a window—or even someone's face.

"At this point, I'll take anything just to get out of this van. My legs are all jittery," David says behind me.

His voice gives me the sudden urge to spin around and plant a fist right on his nose. I don't do it, even though a little voice in my head tells me I'll have to keep listening to him if I don't shut him up. Flexing my hand open and closed, I turn my attention to the motel, inspecting it and thinking of the positives.

David's right. We'll get out of this car, we'll take a rest for a day or two, then we'll be on our way north. I unbend my knees a few inches. My legs feel restless, too. Drawing on that feeling helps me calm the stoking heat within, reducing the desire to punch a hole in the window.

I wonder if I could. I'm constantly surprised by what I'm able to do in my demon form. Not *pleasantly* surprised, mostly terrified-surprised. I shift my jaw back and forth, warding off the newfound anger that spurs at the thought of my dumb demon father and this temperament he forced upon me by siring me.

Mom turns around in the front seat and stares at me. It's like she knows I'm fuming as she raises a questioning eyebrow to silently ask if I'm okay. I give her a nod. I can deal with the anger. It's something I've lived with my whole life. Sure, when I was younger, I may have indulged in the feeling a little bit. More than one bloody nose has gotten me suspended or expelled from schools, but for the most part, I can keep it at bay.

Her clear blue eyes study my neutral face. She sizes me up. I can see the way she's scanning me from head to toe to figure out if I'm about to be a danger to everyone in the car. Does this annoy me? Yes. Everything does. A deep, gravelly tone—the voice of the demon in my mind—tells me that Mom doesn't trust me and doesn't think I'm capable of handling myself, but I push it away.

I don't feel like dancing today, demon, get out of here, I think.

"I'll go grab us a room—maybe two or three," Bob, Jared's dad, says.

"Great, honey," Mom replies, her eyes still trained on me. "I'll stay in here and make sure no teenagers try to get out of the car and escape into the fields."

Her eyes twinkle at her jest. The demon protests at her stupid joke.

Tearing my eyes away from her, I watch as Bob lumbers over to the room on the far right of the motel. A laminated white piece of paper with the word "Office" is taped to the door. His massive tribal tattooed arms soak in the sun beating down from above. I like Bob. He seems to be one of the few people who my demon anger doesn't attach to every second of every day. Something about the big islander man endears itself to the more severe part of my personality. Even though I like him, I can't call him Dad.

He's just Bob.

"Is there any food in this place? I didn't see a single restaurant as we drove in here," Amir complains from the seat over my left shoulder.

"Do you think of anything besides food?" David asks, his tone light.

"Food has literally driven human existence for thousands of years. So no, underneath all my science and math neediness, I don't care much about anything else," Amir responds.

Jared chuckles from his bucket seat. "I've been listening to the kid's thoughts for the past few days and can attest to the fact that he does not think about much more than food. Well, food and how far behind he's getting in school."

Amir folds his arms, shooting daggers from his eyes. "If you had a perfect attendance record and straight A's, you might be more concerned about not missing school. I've already come to terms with the fact that my attendance is ruined, but I can at least keep up with my assignments."

I shake my head. I'm not sure how much more I can listen to before my anger reaches a bursting point. School sucks. That's that. With my vibrant red hair and eyes that practically glow in any amount of light, people often want to talk to me and be my friend. Why does physical appearance make a person popular in school? One glare and they would run away screaming. Jared cares more about being friends with everyone. I just want to live my life—the life my demon father forced on me when he decided to have a child with my mother almost seventeen years ago.

"There is going to be food," Mom says, shaking her head. "I should have guessed that two more teenage boys would have exhausted our driving snacks in an hour flat."

Amir beams at the comment.

"I pride myself on the ability to eat far more food than necessary. Growing boy and all that, you understand," he says, puffing his chest out.

David groans. "I know you said you'd keep us from running away and whatnot, but can I at least get out of the car and stretch my legs? It's been hours since we last stopped."

What a complainer. He tries to shift his legs and bumps the back of my seat. Something primal roars inside my chest. Memories of riding in airplanes with younger Jared come to the forefront of my mind. Other passengers would bump my seat, and it enraged me. I want to spin around and gouge David's eyes out.

But I don't.

Fury comes easier than forgiveness in most instances, but it took only a few infractions to learn that follow-through actions are never worth it.

Mom sighs, then gestures out the sliding door.

"Fine, but stay by the car. The last thing I need is you wandering off and doing something that gets the police called on us," she says. "And that includes turning into a red-scaled version of yourself. It took way too long to explain our way out of that one."

I don't even bother stifling my laugh. David's face turns bright red, and he glares at me. Two stops ago, David was walking across a street toward a gas station bathroom when a car zoomed near him. It wasn't close enough to hit him, or even clip him, but it activated a defensive part of his brain, and his face scaled up like a dragon. Sure, only three people happened to see him like that, but the police were called in a jiffy. We spent a few more hours than we expected to in that city, much to everyone's chagrin.

"You of all people should know how difficult it is to control your powers at first," he says. "At least I didn't smash a register."

My smile falls, the rage returning. I don't often lose control, but that checkout guy deserved that.

"Krista, please keep yourself from going all demon in the car. We can't afford to have a popped tire because your body suddenly weighs four times its normal value."

My eyes snapping to David's face, I see his gaze slip down toward my arm, which feels unnaturally cold. All of my body is unnaturally cold. Something about demons having a lower body temperature. There's nothing like getting freezing cold when it's even sixty degrees outside. Most people would be wearing their shorts and tank tops. I can wear sweats all day every day until it gets near a hundred degrees. Does it turn lots of heads when I go about? Absolutely. Do I care? Not even a little bit.

I focus on my breathing, counting to five, then holding my breath for five, then letting it go slowly. Almost immediately, the stoking fire inside me calms down, and my arm returns to its normal size. When I peer at David again, he looks pale. Did he honestly think I'd go all demon on him and tear his head off?

I need to be better at making friends.

"Sorry, I'm fine," I say, looking at Jared.

He raises his eyebrows and gently taps the side of his head. The message is clear. So, I lower the barriers in my mind, allowing his consciousness to brush up against mine. Having a half fairy for a brother used to drive me crazy, and putting up mind barriers was the first thing I learned as a part of my training. There are times, however, that it can be really handy.

Are you doing okay? You seem to be more on edge than usual, his voice echoes in my mind.

I'm fine. Though it's been way too long since I've been able to punch someone, I reply. *Spar after this?*

Jared's mouth presses into a thin line. He doesn't want to. I try not to sigh out loud.

All right, fine. I can tell you don't want to, I say.

His eyes flick to David, then back to me.

You could always try to get David to fight with you, he suggests.

"Okay, why did everyone get so quiet? Are you doing the creepy brain thing?" Amir asks. "Because I'm not okay with you having secret conversations without me."

Jared's consciousness leaves my mind, and I focus my eyes on Amir.

"Some things are best left private. Not everyone wants to wear their emotions on their sleeve like David," I say.

David growls quietly in the back of his throat. I can tell he's about to tell me off when Bob knocks on the window, flashing a couple of key cards. Mom rolls down the window, hot air blowing into the car and making me sigh in relief. I've already closed the air conditioner vents facing me, but everyone else seems bent on having the inside of the car feel like Antarctica.

"No adjoining rooms, unfortunately, but I figured we would be fine with rooms right next to each other. Boys in one room, Krista with us?"

Joy. Nothing I want more than to hang out with the gross lovebirds.

"Actually, I'm fine just staying in the same room as Jared. I'm sure he'll keep the raging hormonal teenage boys off of me," I say.

David blushes, and I smirk. For some reason, I find it entirely all too fun to tease him. He's overly confident and doesn't embarrass easily, so I'll take any chance to make him squirm.

Leave him alone. He didn't do anything to you, Jared presses into my mind.

I'd forgotten I left my barriers down. I focus on my walls, solidifying the image until I can feel Jared leave my mind.

Bob hops back in the car and drives down the row of floor-level rooms until we get to the corner one. We have two rooms nestled there. I'm struck with the smell of stale cigarette smoke and cleaning products. Apparently, the previous tenants didn't care about the faded "No smoking" sign on the door—or the signs plastered throughout the room. Blue-and-yellow-swirled carpet meets my eyes in a sickening 80s dance room kind of way. Two queen-sized beds sit against one wall, and an old brown dresser with a box TV sits against the other wall. A narrow brown door on the back wall leads to a bathroom that has a yellow porcelain sink, a toilet, and a bathtub shower.

I'd like to say that it's better than sleeping on the streets, but I don't believe it's that much better.

"I guess Amir and I will take this one," David says, slipping his pack off his shoulder onto the bed closest to the door.

"Nope," I say, grabbing his pack and yanking it from his hands. I toss it on the bed closest to the bathroom. "I always sleep closest to the door."

He scowls at me.

"Aren't you going to realize at some point that we aren't going to get attacked? We're *fine* here, Krista. It's been two weeks since we came from Qotan, and there haven't been any other enemy sightings. You just need to chill!" David huffs, moving to the other bed.

I give him a clear "I don't care" expression and fold my arms.

"I am always by the door," I say firmly. "Get over it, dragon boy."

His jaw locks, and I wonder if he'll take a swing at me, but instead, he shakes his head.

Amir whistles. "Tension in this room is hotter than the asphalt in hundred-degree weather. Did I miss something here?"

Jared shakes his head. "Just two cocky teenagers struggling to fit their big heads into the same space."

David spins on Jared, ready to retort. Before he can, I laugh. I'm not sure why this makes me laugh. Probably because I know my brother has a point. I'm cocky. So what? It's easier to mask the fury with a false charisma than hide in a corner. Most people run away from cocky kids.

David trains his attention on me, his eyes narrowing. I shrug in response.

"It was actually funny, that's all," I say.

Before he has a chance to say anything else, I throw a thumb over my shoulder.

"Anyone up for sparring? There's a field across the way with some tall grass. Probably high enough to hide what we're doing," I suggest.

Amir throws his hands up. "No thanks! The first *and last* time I tried to practice fighting with you, I got my butt handed to me. I think I'd rather sit and read."

He moves over to the bed I assigned to David and him and pulls out his e-reader. Jumping backward on his bed, he slips both shoes off and lets out a loud sigh.

"Oh man, it feels so good to lay down. I think I'm done with cars for the next week," he says.

Jared gives me a half smile, then points to our bed. "Actually, I think I'll stick it out with Amir. We're buddy-reading this one, and I can't let him get too far ahead. The only reason I haven't fallen behind is because I can actually read in the car without throwing up."

Amir looks up from his e-reader, a frown on his face. "Hey, I hear that's genetic. Don't poke fun at my inability to do anything but sleep and look out the window while driving."

Jared chuckles and settles in with his own tablet.

I look expectantly at David, who's still glaring at me.

"Actually, you know what? Yeah, I'd like a chance to smash your face in a bit with some sparring," he says.

I grin at him. We may not get along all the time, but some healthy competition will do us some good. Bob has been training David here and there with weapons. Given that we packed enough weapons to last us a while, it's just about finding the right place. A grouping of trees here, a field there. Each time we stopped our car ride, we have been able to find places for us to teach David a thing or two. He's getting better at potentially surviving a real fight.

We all have it in us. At least, that's what Mom says. She used to spar with me, telling me that my Qotan roots gave me the skills I needed. With David, I'm definitely seeing evidence of that. The last time he sparred with Bob, he managed to get some hits in. Of course, he took more of a beating, but his instincts are there.

"Let's do it," I say.

* * *

Twenty minutes later, David and I are squaring off in a field half a mile away from the motel. Mom and Bob made us promise to have our phones turned all the way up, just in case they needed to call us. They also said that if we see any signs of trouble, we're supposed to stop right away.

My fingers rub the wooden handle of the practice one-handed sword. There are weights embedded in the wood grain over the blade and handle to simulate what a steel sword might feel like in a real fight. The sun beats down on my head and face, the heat filling me with a warmth that so often eludes me. David's face is pink, sweat forming on his brow. I have the advantage here because of my years of training.

"First to five blows wins?" I suggest.

He nods curtly. "But only blows on normal skin. I need to practice my scale defense. In a real fight, that would keep me from losing anyway."

I shrug. "That's fine. You can have the handicap."

He glares at me, but I don't let him say anything else. Rushing forward, I swing the sword at his head. His eyes widen momentarily before they harden into resolution. He attempts to block my blow, but his movements are too slow, and he ends up missing, his sword swishing through the air. In a freak set of events, this causes his body to fling to the side, the heavy sword pulling him along with it, making me miss by a hair.

What dumb luck. I rush him again, stabbing toward his stomach, but he dances away.

"Two bouts and I haven't struck you. You're actually improving, Davie!" I tease.

He scowls at me. "Don't call me that. You know I hate it when—"

He chokes on those words as I dive forward, threatening his left side with a feint before spinning and throwing the sword at his right side. It cracks on him, and he lets out a strangled cry.

"That's one," I say, shuffling backward.

Pain reflects in his green irises. I should feel bad—I could imagine a teenager having enough empathy to feel bad for hurting someone—but the demon inside me shivers with satisfaction. It's a terrifyingly realistic part of my life.

Face determined, he steps forward, swinging his sword wide. I can tell there's strength behind it, but it's slow and not precise. I sidestep him, his sword sliding past me. I take the moment to thump him on the top of his head with the flat of the blade.

"Ow!" he shouts, stumbling away from me.

"Respect the weight of the sword. You may be strong from football, but you can tighten things up," I instruct.

My preferred weapon is a two-handed steel sword. I have it stowed away in the back of the van. I wish I could fight with it in my human form, but with my small girlish frame, I can't do anything with it. Even with my lithe, strong muscles, a massive two-handed sword is a bit much for me.

When I'm in demon form? It feels as light as a toothpick.

"Again," I say, taking a deep breath and stepping forward.

David manages to parry my next few attacks, but I'm not moving at my top speed yet. Just as our swords clack, I see his footing get unstable on the uneven ground. He pitches slightly to the side, opening up his left for an attack—which, I take advantage of without any reservation.

Another thwack and cry of pain.

"What about your scales? I thought you were going to practice those?" I say, not necessarily in a goading way. He still takes it that way.

"Shove it, Krista!" he snaps.

I respect that he doesn't try to defend himself. Two weeks ago, when we first sparred, he tried to explain his way out of everything. At least he's stopped doing that.

"Again," I say once more.

When I step in this time, he's ready for me. He parries my stab, then pushes my sword to the side. Evidence of his physical strength transfers through the parry as my arm swings away with the force of his weapon. He tries to use that to his advantage and smack me on the chest, but I dance away.

"All right, we're getting somewhere."

Sweat pours down his face, and I almost feel bad. I hardly sweat at all with my colder blood.

We launch into a good set of attacks, a dangerous dance that would be deadly with sharper swords. This time, when he stumbles on his footing, my sword clacks on the side of his face, but the sound is different. A dull thud reaches my ears, and I'm shocked to see his face scaled over.

He gives me a mischievous grin. "That's more like it."

My gut twists in annoyance. I'm practicing with him so that he gets better at fighting. Why am I bothered that he's actually learning now?

The bout increases in speed, and my neck prickles with the heat of our actions. It feels good to move. My heart pounds in my chest. My breathing comes in desperate gasps as fatigue closes in on me. I can tell David is slowing down, so I get him with the last blow and declare myself the winner.

He grits his teeth. "How about we go until one of us gives up?"

"Or until one of us disarms the other?" I suggest.

He nods, his brows pinched with determination.

A thrill fills my chest. "You're on, Drago."

He grimaces but takes his position.

This time, the fight is of much higher quality. He bends and weaves, focused on my blade and my feet. I land blow after blow, but he scales over every time. Something must have clicked for him. He looks triumphant—and distinctly in less pain now.

Exhaustion creeps in, but I can't seem to best him now that he's using his scales. Maybe I shouldn't have given him the scale clause ...

Gearing up for my final move, I rush him, jabbing my sword forward to get a blow in before he can move. He takes it on the arm, the scales protecting him. Then a sharp pain rips through my head as it's thrown to the side.

I stumble back, my hand coming to my head where purple blood spills out.

Another strange effect of my father's bloodline. Let's just say with the cold body temperature and my discolored blood, trips to the doctor were ill-advised. Mom had to learn a lot of medical care to avoid having to explain my state to doctors.

David's eyes widen, and his cheeks pale. "I'm so sorry! I didn't mean to hit you that hard."

The burning fury in my chest—the demon inside complaining that I've been bested and I'm not enough—accuses me of failure. The human part of me smiles. He actually did something. I wasn't expecting him to intentionally block my sword with his arm. This new skill changes the way he can fight.

"Lucky shot," I mutter.

My arm throbs, the demonic anger threatening to bubble into something monstrous. I push it away, pressing forward and slapping David on the chest before hooking his sword and yanking it away. It spirals in the air before thudding to the ground.

"I win," I say with an evil grin.

"Hey! I was just making sure you were okay!" he complains.

"How many times have I told you not to let your guard down? That's *your* bad."

He grumbles incoherently but doesn't argue. I slayed him once again in this session, but for the first time, I can see he's leveled up. I take a moment to close my eyes, breathing slowly with a therapeutic count and listening to the swishing grass. David stays quiet. I think he's finally learned when I need some cooldown time.

The demonic feelings diffuse enough that I can open my eyes and look at David without going all massive on him.

"You're getting better," I comment.

He smiles at me. Is that relief on his face?

"I never thought I would improve," he says, holding up his bare arm and flexing the muscle there. Red scales flow over his arm seamlessly, like an ocean tide moving in to lap up the beach and pull the sand away. "But when you hit me the fourth time, something snapped inside me. I can feel the burning, the scales."

I watch as he moves the patch of scales under the sleeve of his shirt and onto his face. It ripples like a worm wriggling through his flesh. Then, it disappears.

"I'll go ahead and take credit for that one," I say. "Heaven knows you wouldn't have made progress if I hadn't been smacking you around." I stick the point of my sword into the dirt.

He scowls at me. "You *would* make this about you."

"It's always about me. I'm the life of this entourage, after all."

David doubles over in laughter. Rage and amusement swirl together inside me like a terrifying circus of colors. I want to punch him and hug him at the same time.

No. We're not doing that.

I shove the feelings away so hard that it's almost painful. It takes a whole minute before David recovers and looks at me meaningfully. My heart skips a beat, and I suppress a growl. Stupid teenage hormones.

"Really, though, thank you," he says.

I nod in response.

A light wind flows over my face, and I shiver. David sighs, using his shirt to wipe the dirtied sweat off his forehead. After sticking his sword in the dirt next to mine, he reaches into his pocket and pulls out one of the sectioned stones. I don't say anything. I just watch him. His furrowed brow is enough to tell me that he's processing something deep. A beam of white light protrudes from the stone toward the northwest.

"Did you ever wonder, why you?" he asks me suddenly.

"What do you mean?"

He sighs. "I mean, did you ever wonder why *you* had to be one in billions? A person who is only half human?"

My heart flutters. In reality, I wonder about this all the time. But I don't feel like I could tell David this. I don't know him that well.

"We were born this way. We weren't chosen. That's just how life works. Sometimes you win, sometimes you get smacked in the face with hereditary issues," I say bitterly. "Nothing to do about it except make something of it."

David nods, still not meeting my gaze. "I just wish my dad trained me more. I'm useless. In Qotan, I managed to do nothing but get hurt, captured, and run away."

I shrug. "Yeah, that's kind of true. But it is what it is."

He finally meets my eyes, and I regret agreeing with him. Pain. Lots of pain. Somehow, I managed to forget that his dad is gone—his blood sacrificed for Urothar's teleportation stones. I clear my throat, sucking in a deep breath.

"I'm sure he had a good reason for not helping you. Besides, it doesn't matter anymore. I'm helping you."

Tears brim his eyes, and I squirm inside. Feelings. I hate feelings. There's nothing more awkward than sitting next to someone in tears. The only instinct I have in these instances is to run away. They say females are supposed to be more empathetic—be more keen on how to connect emotionally—but I feel the opposite. I know it's my dad's cursed blood in my veins, but I still wish I could be a little more human.

I understand David's question more now. Why me?

The moment is broken suddenly as both David's and my phone light up at the same time. His ringtone is something chaotic—a rock song that's popular among high schoolers. Mine plays whatever frantic ringtone is the default. I never bothered changing it.

At the same time, I hear an explosion from the direction of the motel.

Blood drains from David's face as he slams the phone against his ear. I do the same.

Jared's voice shouts through the earpiece. "Krista! They're here! Help—"

The phone cuts off.

We waste no time. Grabbing my practice sword in one arm and David's in the other, the two of us sprint across the field toward the now-smoking roof of the motel.

QOTAN INVADES THE SMALL TOWN

D AVID'S ATHLETICISM REALLY SHINES when it comes to running. He outpaces me so easily that the frustration burns in my chest. As much as I want to keep up, his feet are a blur on the asphalt as he vaults toward the van.

Two goblins are beating on the side of the silver car, shouting something in their grunting language. David descends upon one of them, whacking him in the head. The blue-haired goblin slams into the trunk door and collapses. The other goblin, shocked at our arrival but still nimble, dodges David's next blow, swiping with his dagger. It slices David in the thigh, blood spurting out and down his leg. He cries out in pain.

Before the goblin, now baring her yellowed teeth, can lunge at him again, my sword comes down on the back of her head in a precise motion. She falls in a heap before melting away to a black pool of tar. A groan slips from the grimy lips of the goblin David just smashed. He rolls over, sees us, and tries to scoot away.

I don't give him that luxury. Grabbing the collar of his burlap-sack shirt, I allow my fury to flow into my arms, the skin stretching and growing. The process is uncomfortable as the flesh threatens to split on my forearm. Chilled blood pumps through my veins, which now pop out like a children's art book.

"How did you find us? What do you want from us?" I shout at him.

The goblin winces, then spits on my face. It's at that moment that my body explodes outward in anger. My chest grows four times its size. My face expands, the skin pulling and tugging painfully. With an animalistic roar, I throw the goblin like a football. He screeches as he slams into the brick wall of the motel with a crunch. Before he even hits the ground, he's a pile of black ooze.

"What's the point of questioning him if you're just going to smash him to pieces?" David exclaims.

I spin on him, anger pressing me to grab him by the skull and crush it into the ground.

No. I have to keep it under control. He's a friend. A really annoyingly good-looking friend.

I stare him down, measuring the weight of my words before I let them out. A therapist I once saw weekly for anger management told me that the most important place of decision is between anger and action. Fortunately, I have almost mastered this area.

"He was pissing me off. Besides, he couldn't understand me anyway," I argue.

David tilts his head, clearly not remembering that goblins don't speak English. He frowns, then bends back over his wound, which is still oozing blood. I can tell from the bleeding pattern that it isn't a deep cut. With a look of concentration, David's leg sprouts red scales around and over the wound. Blood disappears as it blends into the color of his scales.

He sighs, then looks back at me. "Apparently, the scales curb the pain."

Good for you, buddy. Any pain or injury I sustain in this form hurts like the dickens—though the burning fury inside masks it well enough. That is until I shift back into my human form. At that point, I've mostly healed from the injuries.

Anger masks a lot of sensations . . .

Glass shatters inside one of our motel rooms, and I spin in that direction. Smoke billows out of the office, a fire smoldering somewhere inside. Priorities align in my head. I know the motel manager might be in there, but our friends are more important. Through unspoken agreement, David and I rush toward our room. I pass through the door before him, my demonic legs pressing me forward more quickly now than the football star David.

The moment I'm through the door, I see a wash of greens and blues. Half a dozen goblins and orcs form a ring in the center of our room, blocking the way to the back. A ferocious roar strains my ears, and I wince.

A massive black panther jumps forward and swats its claws at the group of enemies. It's Jared. They dance away from him, swiping with their swords until the panther backs off. I wonder why Jared hasn't ripped all their throats out with his claws, but then I see a form on the ground. Amir's head is bleeding, and his eyes are closed. His e-reader lies on the ground, cracks running through the screen and plastic pieces strewn about.

They were attacked while distracted with their reading.

"Amir!" David shouts.

I curse internally, throwing my hand out to cover his mouth. What happens instead is the back of my hand collides with his cheek. He's knocked to the side, his head crashing into the wall. My stomach drops, fury melding with fear. Have I just inadvertently killed the dragon queen's only son? To my great relief, he recovers quickly, and when he does, I notice that his face has scaled over.

It looks freaky, if I'm being honest. A tad bit ironic, considering what I look like.

Both his words and my reaction have ruined the element of surprise. Two orcs and a goblin spin in our direction. One orc lunges toward me, but I can see his movement before he even makes it. I swipe my practice sword out and crack it on his forearm. My sword shatters to pieces just as he collapses. He screams out in pain, unfamiliar words spilling from his lips. Based on his tone and the context, I can assume what he's saying.

David lunges forward, his own practice sword colliding with the steel blade of the other orc. He manages to parry the attack away, but the orc is faster and more skilled with the weapon. Before long, David is against the side wall, his wooden sword clattering to the ground. The orc leaps and plants the tip of his blade in David's stomach, but it deflects with a clang. David slams his forearm—now covered in scales—against the orc's head.

The orc falls with a grunt, his sword clattering to the ground.

I feel a sharp pain in my back. A blade enters my cold flesh. It's a feeling I wish I wasn't familiar with. Bob and Mom challenged my healing abilities all too often. I'm pretty sure CPS would have been called years ago if they'd known the number of times they'd broken a finger or stabbed me with a hot poker.

Is it psychotic that my parents kind of tortured me? A little, but I agreed to it, so I can't be too mad at them. The training paid off, however, as my healing rapidly closes the wound.

I spin, swiping my arm to the side and catching the heads of three goblins who promptly slam right into David. He curses as he's barraged by the small goblin bodies.

"Sorry!" I cry, my voice down half an octave from what is normal.

A strange goblin and human wrestling match ensues right as I feel something tickle my mind. It's the familiar touch of Jared's ability. I open my mind and let him in.

They came out of nowhere! I can't attack them without them getting to Amir.

As he telepathically communicates, an orc dives forward, slashing his sword downward to distract Jared. The sharp blade narrowly misses the unconscious Amir as Jared uses his massive black paw to bat it away.

Let's give them the blender, I respond.

His panther eyes light up, and his response echoes in my brain without words. David grunts and shouts something, but I can't help him right now. I barrel forward, throwing my hands out to knock aside two orcs to make way for my massive body.

"David, scale up!" I shout.

I can only hope he heard what I said over the noise. Grunts and shouts tell me that more Qotan residents have entered the small motel room. This is really getting out of hand. Before I have time to worry about that, the panther is leaping toward me, claws outstretched. I let Jared fling past me and grab onto his hind legs.

Then, I spin.

The motel room becomes a wash of blood, black ooze, and screams as I twirl the panther around, his claws reaching out and slashing everything that comes in contact with us. I have to tuck my arms inward to ensure I don't accidentally slam my brother's head into the walls of the small room. In moments, it's over. No grunts, screams, or other words in grunting languages sound.

"That was insane!" David pants.

Relief washes over me. Good thing we didn't slash David to death. Jared shifts back into human form, his face and body covered in the orc and goblin ooze. He puts a hand to his head, shaking it slowly.

"You really went for it, didn't you? I think I might puke," he groans, sitting heavily on the ground.

David stands up, covered in goop as well. Just as I instructed, his whole body is shining with scales, which slowly recede as he shakes his head. He spots Amir on the ground and rushes over to his friend, concern twisting his face.

My eyes snap to the doorway, which has been destroyed. A majority of the outer wall is missing, too. No other enemies come in, so I turn back to David. He's slapping Amir on the face, trying to get him to wake up, but it's not working.

"We were just sitting on the bed reading our books when the door burst open. I reacted quickly, but on the defensive. I turned into a beetle to get away from the threat, but I didn't think about Amir. They grabbed him and knocked him out before I could do anything," Jared says.

I press my emotions into his head. Thankfully, he's kept the connection between us open. If I intentionally send him emotions, he can feel them, and although anger comes with it, I force myself to carry comforting thoughts. He relaxes, then slumps against the wall.

How long did he have to defend himself before we got here?

A shrill scream comes from next door, and I freeze.

Mom. Bob.

Jared and I look at each other with wide eyes and tear out of the room. He shifts into a panther once more, his lithe body slipping through the expanded doorway before I can make it out. Skidding to a stop next to him, I see a giant troll hauling the motel owner out of the smoking office. He's screaming, tears pouring down his face as the troll spots us. A familiar looking orc teenager stands next to the troll. He looks like a mixture of a human and orc. Anger smolders in his eyes as he scans my body up and down.

"I'll deal with Orc boy. You check on the parents," I say with a hard tone.

Jared's panther head bobs with approval as he gives a final growl toward Gulran before leaping into the neighboring motel room.

"Take the man. We need more human blood for the teleportation stones," Gulran says.

"No!" I shout, rushing forward, but it's too late. The troll takes out a red stone, then they are gone, their bodies warping into the air.

The half orc son of Urothar meets my fist with the flat of his blade. I grunt in pain as he knocks my attack to the side. I step back, reassessing and putting my fists in the air.

"I finally get to try my hand at fighting the demon mutt," he croons, a thick accent lacing his words. He's speaking English to taunt me—it's the gleam in his eyes. I roar, lunging forward again, but I have to back up when he jabs with his sword. He's fast, and even though I can heal quickly, I can't afford to get sliced too many times. Even healing has its limits.

I curse at myself. Why didn't David and I think to arm ourselves when we got to the van? My practice sword is broken, and I only have my fists to defend me against Gulran.

"You are the filthy reason that I have to exist!" he spits, his mouth twitching. "Father wouldn't have ever tangled with a human if it weren't for that stupid prophecy. He assumed, with my half-human blood, that I could more easily hunt and kill you."

I take the moment to try and get a blow in. My fist hits the side of his head, and he sprawls to the ground. But somehow, he manages to recover quickly, launching to his feet to whack my arm. His weapon cuts deep, and cold purple blood pours from the wound. I grit my teeth, keeping my good arm raised.

"Hasty now, are we? You are not a woman of many words, I can tell," he says.

I spit on the ground. "Words can only get you so far. I usually resort to fists to solve my problems."

He glowers at me. "Undoubtedly, that is true."

Jared roars from our parents' motel room, and I itch to go in and help him. I can't rush in without this guy stabbing me in the back. Gulran's head is bruised and bleeding from where I hit him. He reaches up and touches the blood, looking at his hand with a smirk. Then he licks it. My stomach turns. He closes his eyes, reveling in it for a few seconds before looking back at me.

"As much as I want to kill or capture you, I doubt I'll be able to do that alone," he says. "Besides, I got exactly what I needed anyway."

He holds up his sword, my purple blood dripping from it. Then he sticks his hand into a pouch hanging from his pants and pulls something out. It's one of the stones the elf king gave us. Gulran lets a drop of my purple blood land on the stone, and light flares to life. It's pointing at me. Dread burns my chest..

"There you are," he taunts. "Now I can find the others before you do. Thanks again."

He smiles at me, then his body warps into the air, vanishing.

My chest explodes with fury, my vision turning red. The rage rushes through every part of my being, and my muscles flex with emotion. Images of carnage, destruction, and death tear through my mind. It takes everything inside to hold myself back from running toward the motel and ripping through everything in my way. The building wouldn't stand a chance. Not to mention the flesh-covered beings—human or Qotan creature alike.

I breathe deeply, gathering the humanity I've trained to over-come the beast within. As much as I wish it would go away entirely, it's a part of me. It's in my blood. So, I gather up the emotion and shove it out of my way. Once I size down, it'll diffuse more quickly, so I just have to make it until then.

A simple truth burns my mind. Gulran got away, and he has my blood. I failed yet again. I *hate* failing. I haven't done a lot of it in my life, but those few times I have are still seared into my memory like a parasite, crumbling my confidence.

A panther's roar rips through the air, and I snap to attention. David drags the still unconscious Amir out of his and Jared's room. His head is down, and his teeth are bared as he tries to move his friend through the minefield of shattered glass and debris.

Two goblins form in the air in front of him, both holding small tubes. One of them puffs his cheeks and holds the tube in front of his mouth. Memories of the poisoned darts in Qotan slam into me like a ton of bricks, and I jump to action. I don't have any weapons, but these are just goblins.

"David! In front of you!" I shout.

David's head snaps up, and he furrows his brows at me in confusion. It's too late. The first goblin's cheeks press inward, and a red-feathered dart flies toward David's head. He finally gets my message just in time to see the dart coming at him. Either the goblin is distracted or he's a bad shot because his dart misses David's head by a mile.

My muscles ripple as I rush toward them and throw my fist full-on into the goblin's head. It connects with a deafening crack, and the small creature slams into his companion. They both fall to the ground in a heap, the one I struck melting into the black ooze.

"Urk mgl dravenk Urk frinlti—"

The goblin's otherworldly language curse—or scolding, I'm not sure which—ends abruptly as I pummel him in the chest. My hand comes back covered in the black goo.

"Thanks," David murmurs.

His face is green. Apparently, he's less okay with all the violence than I expected. My eyes wander to my goo-covered hand, and the human part of my mind wonders if I should be okay with what I've just done. Life should have more meaning, shouldn't it?

Now is not the time for questions of morality and humanity. These idiots are here to take us—or kill us, for all I know. There's no time for temperance.

"If you weren't so worthless, I wouldn't have to watch you like a babysitter. Get yourself together, dragon! I can't always be there for you!" I scold.

David's face contorts in frustration. He opens his mouth to inevitably retort in a not-so-diplomatic way, but his words are cut off by another panther roar. Glass shatters as Jared's panther body explodes out the motel room window. He rolls a few times before coming to a stop. He struggles to his feet, but I'm there before he can rise. All it takes is me wrapping a beefy purple arm under his stomach to hoist him up.

I open my mind to him, the defensive part of my fury calling for blood.

Who did this to you? I demand in my thoughts.

Krista, cool it. I'm fine. Three trolls are blocking the way. I killed the orcs and goblins, but the trolls are too strong for me.

Mom? Bob? I ask.

He shakes his head. *Barricaded in the bathroom. I can't get to them, but they are safe as far as I can tell.* He pauses. *I can hear Dad's thoughts. He's calling for us.*

Jared bears his teeth and struggles to his feet.

"I can take them," I growl, my low voice making a chill slip up my spine. I don't think I'll ever get used to the way I sound as a demon.

Jared's form shifts, his black fur arms expanding and becoming more muscular. His neck shrinks and his chest expands. He's turned into a massive gorilla. With a single nod, I get the message. He's ready for round two.

I spin toward David. "If you die, I'm going to be pissed."

David narrows his eyes and scoffs. "I can take care of myself!"

I open my mouth to argue, but Jared impresses on my mind. There's no time for this. Instead, I glare at David and barrel toward the motel room. As I enter, I smell blood.

My nostrils flare as my enhanced olfactory glands process the information. Mythical creatures turn to goo, not blood. The only humans in this room are our parents. One of the unfortunate side effects of becoming a demon is the temper. Another is the inconsolably strong defense mechanism for those I care about.

The human-like control I maintained throughout the fight snaps like a twig as my demon "mama bear" takes over. I hear myself desperately cry out in warning, and fortunately, Jared hears it. He backs away as I tear into the room. True to Jared's warning, three massive trolls block the way. Their heads are turned sideways, their stature too large for the small motel room.

The one closest to me holds a massive wooden club with sharp stones pressed into the wood. Crude angles threaten to tear into any soft flesh they meet. I make a mental note to avoid the club at all costs. Both queen mattresses are upturned, sheets and pillows torn and strewn throughout the small space.

The troll on my left swings his fist. It connects with the bathroom door, splintering the wood. I go for him first, my massive purple-fleshed fist slamming into the back of his head. He grunts and slumps forward into the wall, but he doesn't melt away. Just as I'm pulling back to hit him again, a force punches my gut. All breath leaves my lungs as I crash backward into the wall, denting the sheetrock and knocking the cheap-looking sconce to the ground. The lightbulb shatters, adding to the chaos around me.

I'm injured. I can feel hot blood pouring from wounds on my abdomen. The troll must have used his club to hit me. The human part of my mind shouts in frustration at my stupidity, but the demon part of me doesn't care about the injuries. They will heal.

As the second troll readies his massive club, the third takes a swing at me with a beefy blue fist. I lift my arm to block it, but before he connects with me, the gorilla meets his fist halfway, using his whole body to force the arm back. This pulls the troll off balance, and he lands on the wooden bed frame, wood splintering everywhere as the full weight of the creature crumples the poor piece of furniture.

I guess the motel didn't consider beds for heavy-weight trolls.

Stupid thought, I scold myself.

My mind is firing back and forth between my logical human thoughts to the brute and bullish thoughts of the defensive demon inside. I'm distracted just enough to take another hit on the side of my head.

My vision blurs, and my mouth tastes metallic from blood. An inhuman growl rips from my throat as I recover and catch the club from the second troll. My fist meets his face. I put everything I can into the punch. Thankfully, he melts away into a large pile of black goo.

Jared the gorilla cries out in pain as the troll swings his arm into the wall, Jared's body now crushed between the fleshy blue arm and the sheetrock. The wall buckles, and roofing and insulation rain down on both of them. I curse and bend down, shoving my whole weight into the troll's chest. He must not have seen this coming, because he doesn't block me. Instead, he takes my full weight and dissolves into goo.

Thanks, Jared says in my mind.

I only grunt in reply.

Have you ever woken up from a deep sleep and your mind is still fuzzy, your body still numb from the sleep chemicals keeping you down? That's how I feel when my demon takes over. I've trained the monster inside to identify the ones I love. I won't attack him, but I can't think straight enough to respond using words.

"Krista! Help—" Mom's screams peal through the air.

The third troll holds her up by her head in its huge palm. Her eyes are full of terror. Bob's struggling, too, as he's secured by the creature's other hand. The troll gives me a toothy grin, sharp teeth angled in all the wrong directions, then he vanishes along with our parents.

"NO!" I bellow.

I'm panicking. They didn't come here for our parents. They came here for us. Right? At least, that's what I thought.

Sirens in the distance echo in the broken and bashed motel room. The TV is shattered on the floor, the walls ripped and torn apart. The fluorescent lights inches above my towering head flicker.

Jared, still in his gorilla form, heaves air like he's never had a breath of oxygen in his life. I watch as the muscles ripple, his skin shifting back to its normal brown color. His dark hair lightens up until he's blond again.

Now in human form, he stares at the ground, disbelief written all over his face.

"They—took them," he says hollowly. "But—why?"

I can sense the anger telling me to do things I know I shouldn't. Rip everything apart. Kill anything in the way. My fist clenches, and before I can stop myself, it's punched through the wall into the next room. More building insulation and sawdust puffs up.

David skids into the room, his hand clenched around the broken wooden practice sword.

"Where are they?" he asks, searching the broken room wildly.

Jared looks up at him, tears welling in his eyes.

"They're gone—"

David frowns, and his shoulder slump. All I can think is, what could he have done with that puny sword? Poke the trolls to annoyance? The idiot would have killed himself.

I close my eyes, focusing on reining in the anger. Fortunately, some of it diffused when I vandalized the wall. I use the moment of expelled emotion to pull back my demon form. My skin wrinkles as I shrink, the purple veins receding. I wince, disliking the sensation of my stretched skin returning to normal. It prickles with pain, but I bear it.

"Why would they take your parents? I thought they wanted us?" David questions.

Jared shrugs forlornly.

"They didn't want us," I mutter, my voice hard. "They didn't want them. They wanted my blood. And I handed it right to them."

I HAVE AN UNFORTUNATE RUN-IN WITH MY FEARS

Sirens echo in the distance as the authorities approach the destruction we've left behind. I take in the mess. The only thing that's missing from the crime scene is the bodies. Qotan casualties left no evidence in our world other than black ooze. At this point, we're the only guilty people here.

"We need to leave," David says.

No one speaks as we rush out into the motel parking lot. I spot Bob's keys lying on the ground, so I snatch them up, but before following Jared and David, I have a stroke of genius. Frantic and still angry from the encounter, I start flipping things over, looking for our parents' bags.

Jared pokes his head back into the room. "What are you doing? Let's go!"

"Do you want to get stranded without gas in half a day?" I retort. "We don't have any money!"

The realization hits him, and his eyes widen. He rushes in, helping me to flip over the mattresses, shuffle the bedding, and rifle through the debris covering the room.

"There!" He points to the wall where I see a bit of brown leather.

I snatch up Bob's trifold wallet and stuff it in my hoodie pouch.

On my way out of the room, I barely miss the glass jutting out from the door frame. Getting sliced again is not on my to-do list today. I remember the gashes from the rock-filled club. Twisting side to side, I still feel the twinge of pain. At this point, my demon blood has closed the cuts, but the bruising will take more time to heal.

Smoke continues to billow from the main office, and even though a part of me wants to run in there and put it out, I know that would be dumb. We can't get caught here.

"*Come on!*" David shouts just as three police cars rip around the corner. They're still too far away to see us well, but I know our time is short. Amir's unconscious form is propped up against the silver van, and David is pulling him up over his shoulder.

Frantically pressing the unlock button on the keys, I wait for the flash of the taillights. Jared rips open the sliding door, grips Amir under his armpit, and tosses him. David grunts as Jared shoves him inside, too.

I run around the car, my mind still reeling from the events of the morning. As I jump in, I realize I'm sitting on the wrong side of the car. Rather than the front passenger seat, I'm in the driver's seat.

My chest tightens and my face goes cold as the blood rushes away.

"You didn't have to shove me in like that," David complains, righting himself in one of the bucket seats.

Flashing red and blue lights shine in my eyes through the rearview mirror.

"Krista, move out of the way!" Jared bellows.

"What's going on? Why aren't we moving? Come on, come on!" David exclaims.

A strong hand shoves me to the side, and although the rush of annoyance and fury threatens to pull my demon form back out, the fear of sitting in the driver's seat curbs that.

"Move, Krista," Jared says.

I shuffle into the passenger seat as he sits in the driver's seat and snatches the keys from my hand. The vehicle roars to life, and before I can put my seatbelt on, his foot presses the gas and we rocket forward. Air twists and pulls at me as it rushes through the still-open sliding door, and David curses, reaching over to yank it closed.

"What was that?!" David huffs, his face red. "Why didn't you get us out of there?"

He's looking at me, his wild green eyes sizing me up. My hands are still shaking from the situation in the driver's seat.

"Cool your jets, Dave, Krista just saved your hide," Jared says.

David grips the headrests of both mine and Jared's seats.

"*Cool my jets*? The police would have arrested us in a heartbeat. Why didn't you drive off?"

I lock my jaw, tears welling in my eyes. I won't cry. I don't cry. But the hormones in my body scream at me that I should be bawling. The stubbornness in me, however, forces the feeling away. I can't stave it off forever, but I'll try.

"She doesn't drive, David. She's too scared," Jared explains, keeping his eyes on the road as we pass the "Welcome to Sutherland" sign once again.

David appears confused. I turn away, angling my face so that I can't see him anymore.

"Oh—but—huh?"

My face burns so hot that it feels like a sunburn.

I want to punch Jared for freely admitting that I'm terrified of driving. Not only is it embarrassing, but it's also impractical. One of the main reasons I can't drive is because of my demon heritage. Driving becomes a whole new ball game when the angry part of me suddenly sees the vehicle as a full-scale weapon. I made it through half a year of driver's education before I had a fury storm. The school is *still* replacing the driver's education cars I took out when that happened . . .

I stare into the rearview mirror, amazed that we aren't being followed. I suspect we were seconds away from being caught in a high-speed chase with the cops.

The car lapses into silence. As we speed onto the highway, the events of the morning finally hit me.

They're gone. Mom. Bob. Even the motel owner. They will more than likely have their blood drained to make more teleportation stones. Their lives will be used for the dark race creatures to invade our world. I've failed yet again.

My eyes sting with tears I can't stop. Memories of Mom drift into my mind, causing me to wallow in our loss.

I should have been stronger, faster, and better. What's the point of being a half demon princess with abilities when I can't even protect my family? Through my blurry, tear-filled vision, I glance at Jared, who looks determined as he drives us to who knows where.

"I'm fine," he says, even though his voice wavers.

He lost his dad, too. Bob was a good dad, just like Mom was good to me.

"Stop thinking in past tense! We'll get them back," Jared states in a firm voice.

My jaw hardens, and I shove up my mental barriers. I hate when he gets in my head without permission. Besides, he's wrong. We aren't going to get them back—just like we haven't been able to get David's dad back. It's been more than two weeks since we magically came back from Qotan, and we've barely made progress toward another halfling. We don't even know *which* one it is. I shake my head, trying to pull together my thoughts before I spiral into a negative-thought whirlpool of doom.

That's one thing I seem to be successful at constantly.

"What are you talking about?" David asks.

"Nothing—don't worry about it," Jared responds.

"Easier said than done, buddy," David says. "We were just attacked by a bunch of dark race creatures. You think I can go on as if nothing happened? How did they find us? How did they even get here?"

The searching stone weighs heavily in my pocket, as if David's questions suddenly remind me it's there. Ever since the elf king gave us the stones in Qotan, I've never let it leave my person.

When I pull it out, the beam of light extends toward the front right of the car. It's been on the same setting since we left Kentucky—a strange symbol of what looks like a tree. I'm struck with the recurring thought of how unhelpful the elf king was when he gave these to us. I had asked about the symbols and what they meant, but he didn't offer an explanation. He only said, "There isn't time."

Stupid elf king. It would have taken thirty seconds.

"My guess on how they found us? It probably had something to do with the stones," Jared offers as he flips on the car's blinker to change lanes on the interstate.

I think for a moment that he's reading my mind again, but I sense the mental block I set up. He came to the same conclusion as me. I lift the stone upward so that the beam of light shines out of the window. This draws a glance from Jared.

"They took David's stone right before we teleported back here. We know that the light doesn't work across worlds, so I'm guessing they came here and activated it," I say, thudding my head back into the headrest. "And they probably understand these dumb symbols better than we do."

David scoffs. When he speaks, regret laces his voice. "I shouldn't have let her take that from me."

I spin around, the seat belt digging into my neck.

The weight of Mom's loss hits me like a wave, and I have to close my eyes to ward off more tears. After gaining a bit of composure, I stare at David.

"You couldn't have done anything. We were all trapped by that wench." I glance at Jared to gauge his response. He offers only a hardened jaw. "So stop boo-hooing about it and let's actually make a plan. What are we going to do?"

David folds his arms and sighs heavily.

"Wh—what's happening?" Amir asks groggily from the back seat.

That kid has a way of jumping into conversations at the most inopportune times. I glower down at him, and while I'm ruffled by the timing of his wake up, part of me is glad to see it.

"Why do I feel like my head was used in a batting cage?" he groans, putting a hand to his forehead.

"Amir! You're okay!" David puts a hand on his friend's shoulder.

My jaw relaxes as I witness the interaction. The look in David's eyes is clear enough. They're close friends. I mean, I knew they were, but seeing the relief in the half dragon's face hits home for me.

Jared has been—and most likely will be—my only friend. I've never been good at making friends. There was one time I almost had. I was in eighth grade, and I was sitting at a lunch table. Jodie Miskin. She had light-brown hair in a pixie cut. She wore all sorts of bangles and charms, and her headband sported Hello Kitty.

Was she weird? Absolutely. We'd just witnessed a pointless argument between two girls. There was yelling and hair pulling. My only thought at the time was how easily I'd have destroyed them if I had been their opponent. Jodie looked at me, and I made some smart comment about their pointless argument. She laughed. This girl actually *laughed* at my dumb joke. We sat together at lunch most of that year.

I thought we'd actually become friends. We'd even hung out a couple times at my house. Mom didn't even complain about having to hide the weapons and other training paraphernalia in our backyard. But then, I'd lost my temper. Whether it was teenage hormones or my demon side, Jodie had run pretty quickly from the lunch table when my fork went clean through the wooden surface. Or perhaps it was when I slammed my giant purple hand down and snapped the table in half?

We had to move after that incident. I told myself then and there that friends were not in my future. It was a harsh reality to confront, but a practical one.

"Okay? I would hardly describe myself as 'okay' in this state. My mom and dad would kill me if they knew I was out of a seat belt right now, but I can't think straight enough to be scared," Amir says.

I come back to reality, shaking off my past failure with Jodie. I wish those things didn't stick in my brain like glue, but that's just the way I am.

"You took a goblin dart to the back," David explains. "I got to you before the goblins could take you like—"

He pauses and looks up at me.

"Am I the only one who can finish a dang sentence?" Amir complains, closing his eyes.

I clench my teeth, take a deep breath, and fill in David's sentence.

"They took my mom and Jared's dad."

Amir's eyes snap open, and he tries to sit bolt upright. He pauses with a wince and slumps back into the seat.

"Maybe you should hold off on the bad news until I don't feel like a pile of painful jello," Amir says. "What happened?"

I recount the story, David filling in the bits that I miss. I'm surprised at how few times I snap at him for interrupting me. His eyes lock on me every time he does, a question lingering behind them. Am I going to bite his head off for this? It's a valid question, to be sure, but the fact that he interrupts me regardless makes me admire him in a way.

He's bolder than he was a few weeks ago when we first met.

"And then Krista and Jared rushed out and threw you in the car," David continues.

Amir grunts. "So, I have *you* to thank for some of these new bruises."

He gives me a half grin, and I roll my eyes, turning back around in my seat.

"It was better than getting caught by the cops," Jared affirms. "Besides, maybe I thought it would help you wake up."

"Ha. Ha. Very funny," Amir mutters.

"So, what now?" David asks.

I look down at the stone and the beaming light. Through the whole conversation, I hadn't let it slip from my grasp. The rough-cut surface presses into my clenched palm, biting into my skin. It's a feeling that keeps me grounded, even if it hurts a bit. When they created these stones, they intended on giving them to us so that we could find each other. Why? If it was such a risk to get us together, then why would they want to encourage it?

My mind wanders back to the prophecy—or whatever we learned when we were in Qotan together last time. We're supposed to be sacrificed together as a whole to unlock some power to be used for good or evil.

How appropriately dramatic. A part of me is frustrated that Mom didn't explain this all to me. I'm also not surprised. She didn't spend seventeen years training me to fight, to control my temper, and use my demonic abilities so that I could be a doctor. Does it suck that we were conceived to die for someone else's gain? Absolutely. But life is life. The circumstance of my birth—and the birth of the other half-mythical creatures—wasn't normal to begin with.

"We find them," I say, holding up the stone so David can see it. "We find the other halflings before the orc king does."

David scowls. "But what about your parents? If we go after them, we might be able to get to them fast enough—"

"They're gone, David. There's no point in chasing after them," I say.

His foot comes out and kicks the back of my seat. "Don't be dumb, Krista. Just because you—*we*—gave up on my dad doesn't mean we have to give up on your parents."

My chest burns. I notice the poignant change from "you" to "we" as an attempt to mask the fact that he blames us for not going back to get his dad. Jared read his mind. We all know he blames us.

"Bob isn't *my* parent, for one. And two, they knew the risks when they brought us into this world. They knew they could die." I squeeze the stone in my hand to curb the temper that rises rapidly inside of me.

"Oh, come off it, Krista. Don't be such a noble warrior. We're *teenagers*, for heaven's sake! Do you really think we'll just go out, collect some kids, and end a war between a bunch of mystical creature races? Your parents are savable *now*. If we can just—"

"This is bigger than our parents, *Davey*. If they live, they live. If they don't, then they signed up for it."

My heart breaks even as I say the words. I don't truly want my mom to die. In fact, the daughter in me screams in pain—writhes in agony at the thought of her death. Yet the sense of duty she hammered into me my whole life presses stronger. This is about more than our parents.

Jared heaves a shaky sigh, and with a quavering voice says, "Krista's right. We have to keep pushing forward."

"Are you kidding me? Are you both psychotic? Do you not care about your parents dying?"

The rage explodes inside me. My hands expand into purple monstrosities, and purple veins become visible all over my body. As my skin stretches, the ever-familiar pain burns everywhere. I accept it, as I always have.

"Don't you *dare* accuse me of not caring for them! Mom is the most important thing in the world to me. But I wasn't trained, tortured, and pushed to my limits so that I could teleport to Qotan and land right in the nets of the orcs. Or the goblins. Or whatever stupid creatures are holding our parents right now. Even *if* we teleported back to Qotan—which we haven't proven possible in the first place—we wouldn't be ready for them. *You* aren't ready for the fight!"

My words strike David deep. Tears of frustration well in his eyes, but he doesn't let them fall. He presses his lips into a thin line and looks away from me, his face reddened. I almost feel bad for how I said it, but I push that away. There isn't time for feeling bad. It's true that we teleported back to our world using our human blood, and it's true that we've entertained the idea of teleporting back, but we've not tried it in earnest. I know it's possible. I can tell that we have that inside of us, but we aren't ready.

Jared's hand comes off of the steering wheel and rests on my purple arm. It's hot like fire, my ice-cold skin and blood leeching the warmth from him. He gives me a furtive glance as if to tell me to pull back. In response, I open my mind.

Breathe, Krista. Calm yourself down. We can't afford to have you get us in a wreck.

Shut up, I respond mentally. He nods. We've been doing this our whole lives. I lose my cool, and if he's around, he pulls me back.

As I shift around and do some breathing exercises, Amir pipes up.

"So, where exactly are we going?"

It's clear he doesn't want to address the fact that David and I were just at each other's throats—or the fact that I started to go all demon on them. He doesn't have to say anything for me to notice the way his eyes flick down to my arm and back up to my face. The fear in his eyes? That's the reason I don't want to connect with people. Jodie's terror in that lunchroom comes back to me suddenly, and I resist the urge to shatter the window to my right.

"Well, we have the stone," Jared replies, changing lanes casually and gunning it to pass an old silver "soccer mom" van. "We follow that to find the other kids."

"The other freak shows, you mean," I say.

Clearly, I'm not handling the morning very well. We sidle past the van that's packed with a bunch of kids. The dad drives with his eyes glazed over and his mouth slack-jawed. I stare at him. What would life be like in such a mundane situation? What would it be like to travel with your family and not be chased by bloodthirsty, mythical creatures from another realm?

Whether it's the energy from my stare or fate laughing at me, he turns to glance in our van window and jumps about a mile. He promptly slams on the break, their car disappearing behind us quickly. I flinch and smack my head against the headrest as if it will hide me from view.

"What the—?" Jared says before he catches my thoughts. "Oh. Um, Amir, can you hand Krista the blanket behind you? She needs to cool her jets for a hot second before she causes a wreck. Her features are scaring other drivers."

Amir chuckles, but it's not mirthful. It's more hesitant. Anger roils in my chest. If they don't like the way I look, then they can go off on their own. I could do it all myself. I could probably kill the orc king with my bare hands. Strangle him until his stupid green face turned purple, and he—

I close my eyes and take a deep breath. Emotions can't rule me. Not if I want to survive this whole debacle.

David has apparently recovered. His hands relax down to his ripped jeans. I didn't notice how much damage his clothing had taken. There are claw marks and tears all along his front. Most likely from the "blender" move Jared and I pulled off in that small room. If he didn't have his scales . . .

I force *those* images out of my mind. Something stirs in my chest at the thought of David being sliced to death. Nope. I don't like that. There's no room in my circle of loved ones. Just Jared, Mom, and Bob.

"So, how are we supposed to find these kids? I know we have the rock and everything, but unless you all are made of money, my broke behind isn't going to get us there," David says.

This comment makes me smile. It also helps the demon skin and veins recede just a bit. I relax more, my muscles sore from being tense for so long.

I hold up Bob's wallet.

"Covered. You think I wanted to sleep in the car on the side of the road forever? I have a demon appetite to fill. Human flesh doesn't sate hunger as much as you'd think," I say with a smirk.

Amir chuckles before his face falls. "Wait, you aren't serious, are you?"

Jared and I exchange glances, then I turn and give Amir a flat stare.

"I only eat the annoying ones, so don't get on my bad side."

Amir pales and pushes back in his seat as far as he can. This is the perfect time for Jared to bust up laughing. Despite the anger still coursing through my blood, I can't help but join in. I don't laugh hard—or freely. That's not something I can do after all we've been through, but the situation relaxes me fully, and I feel my human side take over.

Jared senses this and smiles at me knowingly.

Guess you don't need that blanket after all, he says in my mind.

I glare at him. *Shut up*, is my only response.

"Amir, she's just joking. Calm down. Besides, if she tried anything, I'd stop her from getting to you," David says.

Bold comment. Shortsighted and definitely wrong. I could level this jock in two seconds flat. But I don't put him down for it.

"Jokes aside. We have the wallet, and we have the stone, but where do we head next?" David asks.

Amir still eyes me warily, but he leans forward so he can see the stone on my lap.

"The light is still pointing northwest. If we're going to be logical about it, let's assume that the half-blood is in a major city. Northwest from here, I'm thinking Seattle. Or maybe Portland."

David scoffs. "If they are a half-blood like us, they probably wouldn't want to be in a major city. You think we chose to be in Podunk, Kentucky, because I wanted to be there? No. They'll be hiding somewhere. A small town."

"There are thousands of tiny towns in this direction," Amir says, throwing his hands in the air. "How did you want to narrow that down? I'm good at math and probabilities, but not *that* good."

David frowns.

"Not to mention I don't know the way to anywhere," Jared says. "The highway is easy. But at some point, we're going to need directions."

I nod, considering our options. The beam expanding from the stone on my lap has stayed a steady northwest, like Amir said, but the farther west we drive, the more the mystical needle shifts north.

"We need a checkpoint. Somewhere to sit and think for a bit," I suggest.

Amir's cell phone rings, and he jumps so high that his head hits the roof of the car.

"Ow! Dang it!" he whines, holding his head. "Oh man. It's my mom."

He gives David a desperate look, then answers the call. He's speaking quietly, so I assume he doesn't want us to hear the conversation. My enhanced demon senses could pick up on it if I tried, but I decide to give him privacy.

David glances at Amir with an apologetic expression, then folds his arms and looks at me expectantly. I pull out my smartphone and open up a digital map. Tracing my finger along the line, I shift the small screen and find a direct line to a major city.

"Salt Lake City is on the way," I say, opening my fingers on the small display to zoom in.

"Like, in Utah? That sounds—so fun," David says.

Jared shrugs. "I mean, we've never been there before. It's as good a place as ever."

I hit the "Start route" button and watch as the app calculates the time to arrival.

"The faster we get there, the better. Let's trade off drivers so that we can drive all night," I suggest.

David smirks at me. "I guess you can sleep the whole time since you can't take a rotation."

I bite my lip, curbing the rising fury. David sees my reaction, and his smile melts away.

Calm, Krista.

Shut! Up!

I choose not to say anything biting or rude, only because I don't want to offend Jared.

"Can Amir drive?" I ask.

David nods.

"Good. When he's off the phone with his mom, tell him to sleep. He's on the next driving shift. It's a long road to Salt Lake, boys."

I tilt my head and watch the green corn field outside my window. Thoughts of Mom and Bob dance in my mind. My failure still stings. That should have never happened, but I wasn't strong enough. I wasn't good enough to keep them safe. They will have to be okay. And if they aren't, *I* will have to be okay. As unfair as it is that I was born into this situation, it's my burden to carry.

Our burden to carry, Jared interjects.

I glare at him and block my mind off, pushing Jared away. He's not offended by this. Even he can tell when a girl needs privacy.

Now that Gulran has a stone *and* a fresh supply of my blood, the race is on.

We have to get to the halfling before he does.

TEENAGE ANGST ALMOST GETS ME IN TROUBLE

THE DRIVE IS FASTER than any of us expect. It helps that there are a lot of things to do on a smartphone. I watch a few movies when I need to block out the sound of Amir's incessant prattle. He's like a walking encyclopedia, sharing random facts about the places we pass or the natural rock formations. To be honest, the information is kind of interesting, but it gets old real fast.

The only respite we get from that kid's chatty mouth is when he's sleeping, which he does for a few hours here and there. As discussed, we switch off drivers every five or six hours. Jared makes me stay in the front seat for all of it, even though I'd rather Jared take the co-captain's chair when the others drive. Amir doesn't make me uncomfortable. David, on the other hand, makes me squirm.

I can't describe why, but having him drive with me in the front seat makes me want to shrink back into my hoody and pretend I'm not there. The stubborn part of me doesn't want to show my discomfort. So, I watch movies and sit up straight, pointedly ignoring my irked feelings and David's attempts at conversation. Amir resumes his chatty nature as captain, which is all good because it means he won't fall asleep while he's driving.

I can only sleep when Jared drives. Even though the others are friends to a point, my defensive self won't allow me to relax and drift off to sleep. This results in me being bleary-eyed and exhausted by the time we get to Salt Lake.

The highway opens up from two lanes to eight. Despite the wide roads, they are packed with so many cars that a small accident ahead would cause a massive pile up. I'm no stranger to traffic. We'd spent most of our time in the suburbs of Los Angeles growing up. That was before my hormones and demon heritage started fighting with each other. We moved around a lot, escaping school after school because of my slip ups.

"Sheesh. I'm glad you're driving because this many cars would stress me out," Amir says, shivering.

David gapes out the window at the billboards that line the highway and the massive mountains blocking most of the western sky.

"I haven't been around this many cars or people in my entire life. Those buildings are *huge*. I'm thinking it's not smart to go into the city with our—circumstances."

He glances at me, clearly trying to hide the intended message.

"You mean it's not smart to bring me into a public place, right?" I say, my tone hard but a smile playing on my face.

He blushes.

"Well, calm down, Watson. Jared and I survived in Los Angeles of all places without getting caught or thrown into a mental facility. Besides, this isn't even a big city," I say, gesturing out Jared's window toward the tall buildings.

"I mean, that's a pretty big city, if you ask me," David says.

Amir laughs. "He hasn't gotten out much. I visited New York last year. Did you know that over 1.6 million people live in Manhattan alone? Salt Lake's got a piddly 200,000."

David grunts. "It's all too many people for me."

I turn and give him a critical look. His leg bounces up and down so rapidly that I'm surprised I can't feel the whole car shaking.

"It'll be fine," I say. "We're here to rest up and make some plans."

Jared stretches, pushing on the steering wheel to arch his body back. His spine crackles, and he shivers in relief.

"I don't know about you, but I could use an actual bed to sleep in. Even if it's only for one night."

I nod. My body is stiff from sitting for so long. We took pit stops along the way, but "stretching your legs" for ten minutes does very little when you are stuck in the same position for days in a row. The pleasant female AI voice alerts us that we need to exit the highway soon. Jared follows its instructions and pulls off on the next exit. As he does, my stomach growls. It's just past noon. We ate breakfast at a gas station. So, needless to say, we didn't eat actual food—just packaged donuts and pastries.

"Sheesh, those are some wild mountains," Amir comments, his face plastered against the rear window.

Snow capped mountains loom over the small city. From here, they look picturesque, as if they are a painted backdrop on some massive theater stage.

"Did you miss the mountains we've been driving next to for the past half a day?" I ask, smirking.

Amir looks offended. "Did I—are you serious right now?"

No, I'm not serious. He's been rattling off facts about mountains and rock formations ever since the first mountain came into view when the sun rose this morning. Even though I can tell I've bothered him, I don't turn around and indicate I'm joking.

"Dude, you haven't shut up about the mountains all day long," David says. "She's kidding. Just ignore her."

This doesn't bother me as much as it should. It's probably because Salt Lake City is capturing most of my attention. The mountain landscapes behind the city *are* pretty captivating, but more than anything, I'm struck by how empty the streets of the city are. We were just in New York a couple weeks ago. There was hardly even a place for us to walk with all the pedestrians gallivanting on the road. Not only are they empty, but these streets and walkways are also as clean as a whistle. What kind of city is this?

A car to my right blares its horn loudly, and I spin to look at a man shaking his hands at us. He's shouting something through his closed window, and he swerves in front of us and off down the road. Jared slams on the breaks, and my seat belt cuts into my shoulder.

"Stupid one-way roads," Jared mutters. "I hate cities like this."

Reaching over, I punch him on the bicep.

"Don't sweat it. That guy is just having a bad day," I say, trying to console him.

He shrugs but gives me a grateful look. For such a large dude—a person who commands respect by nature of that stature—I'd expect him to be more hardened against feedback. But Jared takes everything to heart.

I open my mind to him and stare directly at his ear, forcing mental energy in his direction. The moment he perks up, I know he's gotten what I sent. He stares forward at the road, opening up his mind to me.

I wish you could drive so I don't have to do so much of it, he complains. His hand quivers on the steering wheel.

You're fine. Forget about that idiot. "We're almost to the hotel anyway," I say out loud so everyone can hear.

Jared's shoulders slump, a small testament to his little relief. We all need the break.

"This hotel better have a good restaurant attached to it," David says. "I'm tired of this packaged crap we've been shoving our faces with."

Amir nods. "I mean, if you'd just *tried* the meal I've been happily eating—"

"No!" Jared, David, and I all say in unison.

The "meal" in question is canned sardines with peanut butter on them. How in the world can that kid eat something so disgusting? At first, I thought he was just joking until he casually combined the two in the peanut butter lid, mixed it, and took a big bite. I told him right then and there that his choice of food made me wonder about his pregnancy status.

He didn't think that comment was funny.

Amir shrugs. "Your loss. Suit yourself."

As he leans down to rifle with something on the ground, my hand snaps back and grabs his wrist. He cries out in surprise, but I don't let go of him.

"We are *minutes* away from getting to a restaurant. I don't want to spend those last minutes dying from the smell of your awful craving," I say with a hardened tone.

Amir swallows hard, then nods slowly.

"When we get out of this car, you can do whatever you want. But not now—"

"In one thousand feet, your destination will be on the left," the map application warns us.

Sure enough, a five-story building comes into view. The cursive writing of the logo is both inviting and relieving. We could have taken the time to find hotels along the way, but we'd decided on a checkpoint, and I wanted to get to Salt Lake as quickly as possible.

"Hang on, I haven't checked the stone in a little while," I say, pulling it out.

Even though the sun hangs high above us to mask the residual light from the stone, I still glance around to make sure no one is watching our car. An older woman and gentlemen sidle out of the car a few spots down and walk slowly into the building, but they aren't paying us any mind. With a deep breath, I flip the dial in the center of the stone to the tree symbol once more. It flashes to life, expanding to point north. The slant on the beam is a lot steeper than it was a day or two ago.

"Look," I say, drawing the attention of the boys in the car.

Amir whispers, "Wow," softly.

"It looks exactly the same as before," David observes.

I don't fault him for not noticing the change since he's less observant by nature, but the savage part of me wants to make fun of him for the mistake.

"No. It's a little steeper. Based on the direction of the car, the beam is pointing less west and a lot more north."

"Agreed. It looks like it's around fifteen percent steeper than when we left Nebraska a couple days ago," Amir notes.

David stares at Amir incredulously.

The fact that we are much closer to this other teen should encourage me, but instead, it gives me a heavy sense of foreboding. Something tells me that having a fourth half-blooded person is only going to make our lives more complicated. Especially since the orcs have one of the stones that can track us.

I wonder how long my blood will last?

The car leaps upward as Jared accidentally runs over the curb turning into the parking lot.

"Sorry! I think I'm reaching the end of my rope," he says, looking in the rearview sheepishly. "I'm exhausted."

I punch him lightly on the shoulder. "Oh, come on, Fairy Boy! Can't you go for days and days without sleep or proper food? Don't get soft on me."

He glares at me, then punches me back.

"I've got a lot more body to take care of than you, tiny."

I feign offense, then glance back at the other two. Amir's mouth has fallen open, and he looks from me to Jared and back again. David looks horrified, like I just said something wildly offensive.

"What?" I say, a rising unease burning in my chest.

"That—was weird. You almost acted like a normal teenager there," Amir says, biting his lip.

David continues to stare at me. I kind of wish I could read his mind to know what those dumb eyes could be hiding. My heart flutters, and I feel nauseous suddenly. This serves to only frustrate me more, so I scowl and turn back around.

No, I will not tell you what he's thinking, Jared speaks in my mind.

I promptly close Jared off again.

Jared pulls the car up to the hotel. It jerks to a stop as he shifts the vehicle to park. My head longs for a soft pillow and quiet place to sleep. When I roll down the window, I can smell the mouth-watering scent of fried oil and meat wafting from the attached restaurant. If it wasn't for the fact that Jared needed Bob's wallet to check us in, I'd have abandoned this shoebox and gone for food right away.

Oh no . . . An essential part of booking a hotel room is ID. My stomach drops, and I snap toward Jared.

"They'll ask for your ID before you can use the credit card," I remind him.

He grins at me. "I didn't forget. I'm not worried about that."

He taps the side of his head. "I'll know if she has any concerns about my appearance before she can voice them. If I have to play the part of an 'impolite guest,' then I will do what I have to."

David scoffs. "For some reason, I can't see you acting like that."

Jared grins. "I've had a great example to learn from."

My jaw hardens, and I give Jared a critical look. His comment makes both David and Amir chuckle, but they shut up really fast when I redirect my glare in their direction.

Jared sighs. "Can you at least try not to kill each other before we make it to our rooms?"

I lean forward. "*Room.*"

Jared frowns, turning back to me. "Don't you want your own—?"

"No. There's no way I'm sleeping in a room by myself with crazy goblins and orcs ready to slice me to pieces in my sleep. Forget decency, just get us one room."

Jared shrugs and leaves the car.

"I'm going with him. I need to stretch my legs," Amir says, leaping out of the car to chase after my lumbering brother.

And that leaves me with the dragon lord. I clamp my jaw down so hard that my teeth start to ache, but I try to act casual. Folding my arms, I lean back and rest my head against the headrest. The last thing I want is to suffer in silence, so I flip on the radio to some hard rock. Base and electric guitars riff wildly as some dude screams at the top of his lungs. I close my eyes and revel in the sound, grateful that I've filled the emptiness that makes me want to squirm out of my seat.

"Wow, you've got a really good taste in music," David says, his tone screaming sarcasm.

I ignore him, hoping that I'll be able to convince him I didn't hear the comment.

"I said, *you've got a really good taste in*—"

I spin around before he can finish.

"Yeah, I heard you, Dragon Boy. No need to repeat it."

Why do I feel the need to tell him off every time he tries to talk to me? It's as if my mind rejects the idea of having any semblance of a conversation with him. Even now as I stare directly at his face, my heart thunders in my chest. I want to run away *and* sidle up next to him. An image from days before as we sparred in the field comes to mind. His sweaty brow glistening in the sun. His light brown hair plastered to his forehead.

And those stupid eyes . . .

"If I didn't know any better, I'd think you were trying to avoid talking to me," he says loud enough for me to hear.

"Well, you are right. I *was* trying not to talk to you."

His feet kick the back of my seat, and a primal fury explodes in my chest. A single purple vein protrudes on my arm. I have to hold back the punch I want so badly to let fly.

When I lock eyes with him again, he's not angry. He's actually smiling. It's not a mirthful smile—more of a vindictive and hostile one.

"Whatever your problem is, you're going to have to get over it, purple. We won't make it very far if we can't even keep from killing each other." His fist is clenched down at his side, knuckles white. They tremble ever-so-slightly. I almost activate my intimidation ability to make him balk. Yet something stops me. His smile is gone. He seems sad and angry.

And suddenly, I feel bad. My purple-veined hand comes behind my back, and I focus internally on the things that calm me down. Green landscapes. The smell of freshly cut grass and laundry in the heat of the summer. Conversations with Mom.

That one twinges my chest, but it helps.

I relax, my teeth unclenching. "You're right. If we're going to survive this mess, we can't keep fighting."

Even though the heroic part of me wants to add something about saving our parents, the negative part of me wins out. They're already dead. Their blood is fueling the next set of stones that will bring the enemy races right to our doorstep.

"Just like that?" David says, confused. "I didn't expect you to give up so easily."

Burning kindles in my chest again, but this time, it's manageable.

"I *do* have more control than you think. I'm not a monster," I say.

He humphs. "Could have fooled me."

"Oh yeah? Well, what about you, scale face? You don't think you have a bit of an ego yourself? Star football player—but only because you have the blood of a dragon to give you an edge. If you didn't have your mother to thank, you'd be a witless idiot like Amir. A little cute, but no social life whatsoever."

I know my words are low, but as the anger builds in me, I don't care. Who does he think he is? He wasn't even the captain of the football team, but he acts like he's the commanding presence in the room. Ever since he discovered—*we* discovered—that he's the high prince of Qotan, it's like he's had a complex.

David grips my shoulder, and my defense system engages. My arm expands to its demon form, and I spin, ready to sock him in the face even if I knock his head off completely.

His face is inches from mine, and I freeze. His hot breath hits my nose, and I lose all ability to think. It's as if my thoughts are scrambled like a blender, and all I notice is the smell of him. My eyes focus on his irises, the soft starburst pattern drawing me in even more now that he's close to me. I can sense my hand shrink to half its size. It's still capable of causing a lot of damage, but now it's not likely to knock his head clean off.

We stay there for what seems like hours, staring. His lips part, and even though my mind screams at me to punch him for how rude he's been, another form of burning mixes with that thought, and I almost lose all faculties of my body. We move close to one another. His hand goes up to grab my head.

Then the driver's side door opens. I react instantly, throwing my outstretched hand into David's face. He grunts from the impact, and my hand starts stinging furiously. He reacts quickly and scales up the part of his face where my hand connected. When did he get so fast with that?

"Seen his face when I told him to respect—"

Jared stops talking when he sees me whack David in the face. Dragon Boy's head snaps into the wall, but his scales protect him. Instead, it puts a massive dent in the plastic shell interior of the vehicle, a crack growing up and down from it. Amir's laughter dies down, whatever joke he and Jared were sharing now completely lost.

"Stop! Krista! What are you doing?!" Jared exclaims, practically leaping into the car.

"The idiot was trying to—"

"I was trying to help her stop being a jerk," David snaps, wiping his mouth and glaring at me. "But she's incapable of taking a joke."

Is that what he was trying to do? He flashes a glance at me, a testament to the lie he just told. Tension tears at my chest, but I hold it back. He tried to kiss me, and now he's backpedaling. The worst part is that I wanted to kiss him back. Desire still tugs at me, but I use the fury from his comment to drown it out now that we have spectators.

"You're incapable of keeping your mouth shut," I retort.

Jared stares at me critically. He's trying to communicate with my mind. Nope. Not letting him in right now. Not while I can't even gather my thoughts. When he fails to connect with me, he gives up trying and looks at Amir.

"Um, I get the sense that we missed something," Amir says.

"No, really, Sherlock." David folds his arms and looks out the window. The scales disappear slowly from his face, his lightly tanned complexion coming back into view. "Did you get us a room, or are we car-sleeping again?"

Jared clears his throat. As much as he wants to talk about what he just witnessed, he's too polite to do so. Bob raised him to be a ninny. All right, that's not entirely fair. He's just a nice kid. I think back to the battle at the motel and the football field weeks ago. Though Jared may be a soft and kind dude in calm situations, he's savage in a fight. We've both been conditioned to be.

"Yes, we got a room," Jared says. "It's on the top floor and near the end. The last thing I want is window access for unexpected goblins to sneak in on us while we sleep."

They get back in the car, and he pulls it around near the right side of the hotel. It doesn't take long for us to gather our things, considering we lost most of it at the other motel. We made a couple pit stops at department stores to get the essentials, but aside from the clothes on our backs, we don't have much. Nothing like off-brand cheap clothes to show off the better side of you. Fortunately, I don't wear anything other than the large sweats I get in the men's section. Sure, I'd love to go shopping for something nice—maybe wear a sundress, or even try on some nice-fitting jeans that actually show off the good parts of my body.

The demon blood prevents me from doing any of that. If my clothes can't expand with my temper, I'd be left with rags all too often. Bitterness twists my insides, but I stave it off. This is the lot I drew, and there's nothing I can do about it.

My nostrils burn with the strong smoke and air freshener scent in the elevator, and I reflect on how hotels all smell the same. The others probably don't notice the smell like I do. They don't smell like animals.

Brightly colored carpet greets us as we step off the boxy metal elevator, and Jared swipes the key card at our assigned room.

"Nice," Amir says.

He flounces on the white comforter of the queen bed nearest the window and sighs in relief. I shake my head, stifling a smile. As annoying as he is with his facts, his non-poker face and easy-to-read emotions are a bit refreshing. Unlike the other company. Images of David inches from my face dance in my mind, and I resist the urge to glower at him. When I'd first met him weeks ago, I could tell he had an ego. I've been to a lot of high schools, and most jocks are the same. Big head. Little self-awareness.

David shoulders past me and plops his backpack on the floor with a thud before sitting on the bed next to Amir.

The plump white pillow practically calls to me from the bed, but with one glance at a lounging David, I decide I'd better cool off.

"I'm going to take a shower. Then I'm going to find something to eat," I say, tossing my own pack onto the bed and unzipping it to find a fresh set of sweats. These are electric blue and will more than likely turn heads no matter where I go, but the department store didn't have many options.

As I walk away, David mutters something about the beacon-like colors of the sweats. I ignore him.

Before long, the hot water is pouring over my ratty hair, and I'm sighing with relief. I should have brushed my hair before I stepped into the water, and I'm paying for it now as my fingers get caught in countless gnarls.

When Jared knocks on the door and tells me it's been thirty minutes, I let my head hang back and close my eyes. The time went way too fast for my liking. Still, I know they are hungry, and my stomach has been roaring at me incessantly for the duration of the shower. Food is definitely in order.

I dry, dress, and brush my hair as quickly as possible. Once my long hair is pulled up in a wet ponytail, I pull the door open to see three pairs of puppy dog eyes staring at me.

"Are you serious right now?" I say, slapping Jared on the shoulder.

"We're hungry, yo! And you were taking your sweet time in there."

I scoff and push past him. As I do, I catch the scent of David's hair.

My stomach is suddenly filled with butterflies. I noticed the smell before. It always had the same intoxicating scent, but I didn't care. Right now? It only made me think of the incident in the car. Fortunately, my poker face is well practiced, and I easily suppress it.

After storing my old sweats and other bathing implements, I turn to the boys.

"So, where are we going to eat?"

5

A FAIRY RUINS OUR MEAL

MY TEETH TEAR INTO a bacon cheeseburger, and it takes everything in my power not to moan out loud. That would be both creepy and disgusting. I can't recall why we didn't stop at drive-through restaurants instead of eating gross gas station food.

The others don't say much as they stuff their faces. Part of me wonders what Bob would do when he gets his next credit card statement and sees that we spent so much money. He's always been a bit of a tightwad. Mom says it's what's made it easier for us to live and move about so quickly. I just think Bob didn't know how to have fun.

Jared flinches and glances at me.

While we walked here, I let him into my mind so we could talk about what really happened in the car, and I haven't closed my mind off since then.

I grimace, remembering that Bob might never see his next credit card statement . . .

I apologize mentally, then block off my thoughts.

"So, another appetizer?" Amir asks, finishing off his second plate of food.

"Dude, where are you packing that stuff? You're like five and a half feet tall and maybe weigh a buck fifty," David says. "You got a hollow leg?"

Jared chokes on his drink and ends up in a coughing fit. As annoyed as I am with David, I crack a smile.

Amir folds his arms and gives David a condescending look. "You can just say you're jealous of my fast metabolism."

David rolls his eyes and takes the last bite of his massive burger.

"I'm not going to pretend like I care about what food does to my body. Being big is kind of my thing," Jared says, grabbing a fresh basket of fries the waiter left for us.

He leans back and stuffs a small handful in his mouth. Seeing Jared next to Amir is quite comical. Jared is at least six inches taller than Amir and probably weighs a hundred pounds more than him, thanks to the Samoan roots of his father's ancestry. Amir, also dark-skinned, though with black hair, looks like a child by comparison.

"And I say, yeah. Let's do another appetizer."

The waiter soon appears, and our group orders another two entrees and a few desserts. I shake my head, knowing that my stomach will be full long before we can dip into the new food. Amir engages in an animated conversation with Jared about competing to see who can eat the most onion rings. Meanwhile, my eyes move slowly to David, who's sitting next to me at the square table. Was it my first choice to sit right next to him? No.

His smell is distracting. But it was either that or run the risk of staring at each other.

After about ten minutes, the new food shows up. I watch in sickening horror as both Amir and Jared dive into the fried chicken strips and wings. My stomach turns as they each down two full strips in thirty seconds. I almost comment on how they need to chew their food before they choke when David murmurs next to me.

"I'm sorry about earlier."

Mouth snapping shut, I turn and glare at him. "Sorry for . . . ?"

I pause. I want to hear what he thinks he needs to apologize for. Guys have an insufferable way of making us girls angry and having no idea what they did. To my utter shock, he manages to apologize for the right things.

"I'm sorry for what I said. You clearly have more of a handle on your emotions than I thought," he explains. "And I'm sorry for getting in your space."

Heat creeps up my neck and into my face. I glance at our companions, but they don't seem to be listening to our subdued conversation.

"Well, color me surprised, you actually have the ability to apologize," I say, leaning back in my chair and folding my arms. He grimaces and looks around as if he'll get in trouble.

"I'm not a complete jerk, contrary to your apparent belief in me," he adds, his tone souring.

"It's going to take more than an apology to get me to believe that," I reply.

He slumps in his chair. Before I can respond, I hear a commotion to my right. Pots, pans, and other banging erupts from the kitchen, echoing throughout the restaurant. It's far enough away that David and the others haven't noticed. A pot suddenly flies out of the open doorway and clatters to the ground. This alerts more people.

My gut twists. Something is wrong. A man shouts—in anger or fear, I can't tell which—then there are more clatters and bangs.

"Something's happening!" I hiss.

I'm mostly talking to Jared, but Amir and David are listening.

Before Jared can speak, a bloodcurdling scream rips through the air.

I jump up from my seat, partially freeing the demon inside of me. Skin stretches and expands on my arms, and my hands take on their massive form. Strength courses through my body, and with it comes the intense furious frenzy. A tingling energy tries to convince me to punch the closest living thing to me, but I push the thought away. Jared disappears, melding into a small creature and scuttling off through the legs of the patrons near us.

"Did he just *run away*?" David asks.

"No, he's getting in position to flank them," I say.

Under different circumstances, I might be more defensive of my brother, but right now, I have my eyes trained on the kitchen door. More people in the restaurant have noticed the commotion. Possibilities of the dangers approaching dance in my mind so quickly that I almost expect a whole army of goblins and orcs to come pouring out.

Instead, a bright flash of blue light almost blinds me. I curse and step back. David stands in front of me, his arms covered in red scales.

"Stay behind me," he says.

"Over my dead body," I reply, shoving him to the side.

The glowing orb of blue light shoots in our direction, and I duck just before it pelts me in the face. Customers scream in shock, and the restaurant becomes a chaotic undulation of noise.

"What is that—?"

"Huge firefly!"

"Kill it! Kill it!"

While my experience with fireflies is limited, I know this firefly isn't normal. It flits to and fro, bouncing off of peoples' heads and knocking over cups and dishes. I ready my fist to take it on; however, it's not attacking anyone. It doesn't even come for us.

I spin back to the kitchen and train my eyes there. Glass is shattered all over the floor, and there is still commotion coming from within, but most of the frenzy is now outside of the kitchen. No other lights or threats appear, so I turn back to the problem at hand.

I'm met with the disappearance of tables left and right. They snuff out of existence in flashes of blue light. The bouncing orb touches a woman's head, and she disappears in an instant.

"What in the—?"Amir shouts, cowering under his napkin as if that will protect him.

Suddenly, a tabby cat comes out of nowhere and grabs the orb in its mouth. Another scream rips through the air, this time coming from the orb itself.

"Let go of me you little rat! I'll—augh!" a woman's voice screeches.

Jared's mind presses into mine, and I let him in. *Outside, now!*

"We need to get out of here!" I tell the others.

They do what I say immediately.

I stare at the table littered with half-filled plates and empty cups. I'd hate to leave without paying, so I fish out the small-fold wallet that Mom gave me for emergencies. It has two crisp one hundred dollar bills inside, which I pull out and toss on the table. I'm sure it's way more than we need to pay, but I don't have time to figure that out.

Now that the orb and screaming has gone from the room, the patrons all whisper and look around. A few of them lock eyes on me and practically fall out of their chairs. While my head remains the same size, my chest, arms, and hands look like a bodybuilder's. Even though I can't see my neck, I can feel the cold purple-blooded veins poking up just beneath my chin.

I can only imagine what these people must be thinking. Before, we were just a normal set of teenagers eating breakfast in the middle of Salt Lake. Now, we're an odd bunch of troublemakers complete with a tabby cat and bodybuilder status girl who suddenly doesn't fit into her clothes.

My head swims with the frustration of our situation. The urge to overturn tables on my way out pushes to the surface of my consciousness, but I control it, focusing intently on leaving. Even though I manage to keep my hands to myself, my bulky size doesn't prevent me from shoving a couple to the side. A woman yelps and says something marginally deplorable, but I ignore her. I don't need this demonic anger redirecting to an innocent bystander.

An exhaust-filled breeze hits me the moment I open the door outside. I don't spot my friends right away, but Jared's voice enters my mind.

Behind the dumpsters, he says.

Two large brown metal boxes line the side of the restaurant with a two-feet gap between them. The tabby cat has its paw on the blue orb, David looks green, and Amir's eyes are wide as saucers. Shockingly, whatever my brother has caught isn't shrieking like it was before.

As I approach, the tabby cat's limbs ripple and grow, the fur shifting into normal brown skin and the legs forming into blue jeans. Once again, I'm grateful for the fact that my brother's shifting powers don't leave him nude. The last thing I need is that image in my mind.

No, we have no idea why that's the way it works, but we aren't complaining. Jared looks concentrated as he inevitably communicates mentally with the thing he caught. Right before I reach them, a woman's voice rings out loudly.

"How dare you touch me in such a way! I never thought the fairy prince would be so unbecoming to put me inside his *mouth,* of all places," the orb says.

Now that I'm closer, I can see tiny fluttering wings and dark brown skin. The fairy has short brown hair in tight curls that look way too quaff and perfect to have been snatched in the mouth of a cat. Based on all the explanations I've had, and all the fairies I'd seen in my life, this is not an unusual feature. I scoff at her perfect appearance. Why are girls so obsessed with their appearance? Even as I think this, I feel the twinge of jealousy. I'll never have that opportunity.

"You didn't leave me much choice," Jared says, grimacing. "You came out of nowhere into this world shrieking like a banshee—"

The fairy gasps, her minuscule hand coming over her mouth. "Don't you *dare* associate me with those—those—*dead* creatures! I'm more sophisticated than one of those evil revenants."

Jared flushes, his next words sputtering out. "It's just a saying. I don't actually mean you're a *banshee*."

I grunt. "Don't bother trying to reason with her. She's incapable of talking about anything but how she looks."

There's a spark of light and a loud crack when suddenly the fairy is a full-sized woman. Her head spins in my direction, her hands flowing and her mouth moving in what is inevitably an incantation or something, but when her eyes land on me, another shriek rings through the air.

"Stop that!" Jared hisses.

Her hands come to her face, and she backs away so quickly that her wings beat against the side of the dumpster. This, in turn, makes her shriek again.

Jared's head falls into his hands.

"Wait!" David says. "It's you. You're the fairy from the tree building."

Amir's face brightens up. "I thought I recognized the timbre of your voice! Rolinda, isn't it?"

"Hmph," Rolinda says. "At least some of you have the decency to remember who I am."

My chest burns, and the image of me squeezing the woman tightly until her head pops off dances in my mind. From spite alone, I hold on to that image longer than I probably should before I shove it away.

"I've never seen you before in my life," I say dryly.

Her eyes flick toward me, and she flies slightly away, as if she's afraid I have a plague that she might catch if she's too close. Her feet are hovering above the ground a few inches, and there's the constant sound of large bee wings. Her blue gown is short, ending just below her knees. It sparkles in the high sunlight, short caps over her shoulders. Now that the threat has passed, and we know it's just a ditzy fairy, I breathe slowly and let my anger gather up inside my chest. My arms shrink rapidly, the skin tingling.

"What are you doing here?" David asks. "*How* are you even here?"

Rolinda looks sheepish as she reaches into the folds of her dress.

"I took this from my captors and used it to teleport here. I did *not* expect to be attacked by savage people with knives and pans. The human world is so cold, empty, brutish, and—"

"Hang on a minute," David says, interrupting her.

Rolinda looks putout at his interruption, but she doesn't scold him.

"Captors. You were a prisoner? What happened?"

Her scornful expression fades away quickly, and tears well in her eyes.

"Ferona, my mistress, she—"

Rolinda doesn't finish before she bursts into a fit of sobs. A family headed into the restaurant stares at us with strange looks. The smallest one holds out her hand and says, "Look she's floating."

My stomach roils. This is not the place for a conversation.

I step in front of the fairy just before the girl's parents can see what she's pointed out. The mother sizes me up, then mutters something about troubled teens skipping school.

I haven't even thought about the fact that it's a school day. So much has changed in the past weeks that I don't even consider myself a school-going teenager any longer. Police sirens echo on the surrounding buildings, and somehow, I know exactly where they are headed.

"She betrayed us all. Orcs, trolls, goblins, and other dark creatures invaded our home and took it over. We were all captured and told to obey or have our blood harvested for teleportation stones," she says, giving a furtive glance toward the stone in her hand.

David goes to ask another question, but I stop him.

"Here and *now* is really not the place to be doing this. Power down, fairy girl, and hide in someone's pocket until we can get to our hotel room," I say, snapping my fingers.

Rolinda's hand comes to her chest, and her mouth opens in a critical O shape.

"Well, I never—how dare you—"

"I said, *power down*! Unless you want us all taken to jail in the next few minutes." Her head cocks to the side when I said the word "jail," so I amended it quickly. "Captivity."

With one more "Hmph," the fairy shrinks down with a pop and flash of light.

Jared grimaces, then points to the inside of his jacket pocket. "Hide here. It's not great, but it will have to do."

To my utter surprise, the fairy doesn't complain as she conceals herself inside his hoodie pocket.

We make our way around the back of the restaurant. The sirens echo ever closer, but soon, we're inside the hotel and the elevator. A sigh escapes my lips as the doors finally close before us. David sighs as well, and we share a look. It's not the most friendly look, but the relief that comes between us is comforting.

Amir shifts from side to side, his hands wringing in front of him. He mutters something I choose not to listen to—mainly because my ears are focused on the space around us. It's unlikely that the police saw us enter the hotel from the back entrance, but the last thing we need is a SWAT team storming up the elevator to meet us on our floor.

Fortunately, I don't hear anything as the doors open.

"Jared, get the door unlocked. I'll watch the stairwell," I say.

David, hearing my suggestion, takes up position on the other side of the elevator, and we both exit, our heads snapping down opposite ends of the hallway. Nothing.

Our hotel room door clicks open. The tension diffuses as we enter the room and yank the door shut.

Jared winces. "Sorry! You can come out now."

I assume he and the fairy were having a mental conversation, and he just voiced the final part out loud for our benefit. Out flies the fairy in a fury, her body spinning. Another crack announces the arrival of her full-sized version.

"Such unbecoming methods of travel for such an esteemed fairy as myself!" She sniffs, inspecting our surroundings with even more contempt.

"Spill, fairy. Why are you in *our world*?" I ask firmly.

With a small squeal, her wings carry her back a few paces as she inspects me fearfully once more.

"We were all taken prisoner. Huron and the other guards. This was mere days after you traveled through and spoke with Ferona in the flower garden. The queen came to visit us on the *pretense* of taking care of political business with the elf kingdom. But when she came . . ." Rolinda's eyes tear up again, and she sobs through her next words. "She had an army of orcs and goblins."

David's jaw hardens, and his eyes smolder. The very woman who lured him into Dranith to flaunt his captive mother and kill his father. He deserves this anger and frustration. If it had been *my* mother and father, I would feel the same way.

But then again, she probably *does* have my mother. I decide not to focus on that. Instead, I mentally encourage David's apparent fury. Let him roil in his anger. Let him build his frustrations. I'll be able to help him harness that the next time we practice—whenever that will be.

"And you didn't even put up a fight?" David asks. "You just let her come and take you all?"

Rolinda's head snaps up, and she points a bony finger at him. "Huron and the other dwarves *fought* as long as they could. But in the end, they conquered us. Ferona even brought a *shade*, of all things. She told us that we had to join the new order of Qotan or be killed. The only reason I wasn't slain was because I'm her trusted advisor and confidante."

Her reddened eyes turn on David, who looks like he's about to punch a hole in the wall.

"She betrayed us all to the orc king."

Jared looks away from her, his eyes trained on the textured wall. I know the motion. He's ashamed. Ashamed to be associated with the woman who caused the downfall of Dranith, imprisoned the dragon queen and nation, and threatened to kill us in a creepy sacrifice for power.

Suddenly, my demon dad doesn't seem so bad . . .

"We know about Ferona," David says.

Rolinda's eyes widen as she considers each of us. "How?"

David sits heavily on the bed, his hands clenched in fists. "We were captured by Ferona in Dranith. In the palace."

He recounts for her how, after they left the Elder Tree, we met up and journeyed to the grand dragon city. The fairy's face grows ashen, and she descends until her bare feet rest on the carpet.

"So, it's true. The queen—Ferona—claimed that the orc king prevailed over the high crown. I didn't think it was true. They said that they were looking for you to fulfill the prophecy and take over the rest of Qotan, but I just couldn't believe it. They dragged us along. Me, Huron, the other dwarven guards. And the whole time, I thought I was losing my mind."

She sobs again, her hands covering her face, her shoulders slumping.

I have to force myself not to grimace at her overbearing show of emotion. She *has* been going through a lot, and it would be inconsiderate of me to shush her.

But boy, does it take a lot out of me. I don't realize I'm clenching my teeth until Jared nudges me and gives me a critical look. He taps his jaw to send me the message. When I relax it and my teeth come apart, they are aching.

The silence draws on for thirty more seconds before Rolinda's sobs slow down.

"But how did you find *us* in this place?" Amir asks. "When we teleported from Qotan and ended up in New York, it was clear that the realms are overlaid somehow. How long have you been in our realm searching for us?"

Rolinda sniffles, then gives him a severe look. "Don't you know?"

She reaches into her pocket and pulls out a roughly cut gray stone. My breath catches in my throat. At first glance, it looks like a jeweler's failed attempt at practicing on a stone to make a brooch—or some other ornament. Yet as I look closer, I can see six sections outlined like a pizza. In the center, a bronze spindle, thin and wiry, points at one of the sections. It's not a perfect imitation, but it's clear what the point of the stone is.

"Where did you get that?" I ask, heat moving up my neck and into my face.

Rolinda cowers away from me, holding the stone out frantically.

"I took it! From the orcs guarding me. They were using it to track you down—or at least, that's what they said they were doing. All I know is that every so often, one of the guards would take a teleportation stone and disappear from the realm with both this and the stone to come back. After they were gone for a few moments, they'd appear back in the same place and point to where we should go."

I snatch it out of her hand while shoving my other hand into my pocket. My palm wraps around the real tracking stone, and I pull it free. It's still set to the tree-looking symbol, the bright beam of light extending to the north. The new stone is much lighter and feels like it's made from a different type of rock; yet when I look closely, I can see that a less-clear beam of light extends from it. A weak and flickering light points right at David. Biting my lip, I gently turn the fragile-looking dial of the new stone to a roughly cut version of the tree symbol. The weakened beam shifts in the same direction as my stone.

"It's like some shoddy artists tried to copy the appearance and function of our searching stones," I say.

Jared moves next to me and inspects it over my shoulder.

"How many of these copies did you have?" he asks the fairy.

Her hands make a waving motion. I take it as her version of a shrug.

"I do not know. In the group of guards and soldiers I was in, I think this was the only stone. Yet I *do* know that there are many groups looking for you. I suspect that they each have a stone of their own to track you."

I'm not sure if I lose control or don't care about maintaining control, but I let my fist expand in demon fashion, slamming it into the wall. It passes through easily, sheetrock snapping like a carrot. Someone yelps in the room next to me, and I curse myself. So much for a hiding place. If the people next door report what they heard, no doubt the hotel owner will be knocking at our door soon.

"How is this possible?" David asks. "I thought you told us only the rulers and their combined magics could create the stones."

"That *is* what he told us," I remind him. "But this copycat was clearly crappily made."

Even as I say this, the weak beam of light flickers and goes out for about ten seconds before flaring back to life.

"It's flickering so much that I bet they can't rely on it much. That explains why it took them two weeks to find us."

Amir frowns and puts a hand up to his chin.

"So, if they've copied the stones, used the blood that they took from you in the Dranith palace, and you popped up in the kitchens of the restaurant, then they are like . . . right by us in the other dimension?"

Rolinda does her shrugging thing.

"That's wild!" he says, shivering.

David's hands are clenched, and his arms are quivering as he glares at Rolinda. It's not the "I'm mad at *you*" type of glare, but more of an "I want to kill whoever is on the other side without asking questions first" kind of look. I've never related to him more. Our eyes lock, and despite our awkward past, we agree.

Jared's eyes go unfocused and his mouth falls open. "Oh no."

We all turn to look at him as he rushes to the window of the hotel and yanks it open. My ears are met with the sounds of a lot of people screaming. My skin prickles.

"What is that?" I ask.

Jared turns to us slowly. "The orcs aren't in the other realm anymore."

6

WE SPAR TO THE DEATH WITH ORCS

T HREE TIMES.

That sums up every encounter I've had with a magical being from Qotan before we met up with David. Only one of those times had been threatening. The first time was when I was eight. I was still experiencing the "My parents are a little crazy and think that I'm half demon" phase. And it was before my hormones caused all the fun changes in my mind and body.

Bob had brought home the smallest man I'd ever seen. He called him a gnome and said that he was an ally of the light races of Qotan. The gnome, despite his size and quirky personality, had fashioned weapons and armor for each of us. The sword I preferred to fight with sat in the trunk of the van parked outside. But since it's impractical to carry around, I don't use it in combat all that much.

I wish I had it the whole time in Qotan, but we'd been sucked in there too quickly.

The second time, we'd come across an elf woman. She was working as a nurse in the hospital I was admitted to. I didn't realize who she was when I was lying on the bed in pain, but she knew me. Her eyes were saucers as she sensed the demon blood flowing through my veins. Apparently, Bob had known about her, which was the precise reason he'd chosen her. During one of our practices, we'd gotten a little too heated in our sparring—so heated that I wasn't paying attention to my surroundings and lost a few fingers. My body can heal rapidly, it just can't grow limbs or appendages back.

Because of my purple blood, the elf nurse was the only person we could trust to sew my fingers back on. When I asked Bob how he knew she was working at the hospital, he'd given me some vague answer. "It's important to know our resources," he'd said.

We were more careful after that, and I didn't have to see the elven nurse again. I never even got to ask her why she lived in our realm. I've been bothered by that for way too long. More importantly, I can't stop kicking myself for not asking *how* they lived here without turning to sludge.

The third and final time comes back to me as we rush down the hall of the hotel, but I shove the memory away, removing its distraction for the coming fight.

We each had seconds to pack our things and be out the door. We won't be able to come back to this hotel after what we're about to do. Shortly after the screaming started, we heard glass breaking and grunts of a foreign language.

My body protests as I stand with my duffel bag over my shoulder. Even though I can heal rapidly, I still suffer from sleep deprivation like everyone else. Without sleep, my body can't fully recover. David looks gaunt, and the purple circles under his eyes are wild. Amir and Jared look just as exhausted, but there's nothing we can do about it.

There are people that need our help.

When the elevator dings and the door slides open, we rush to the parking lot. Jared unlocks the car, and I throw my duffel inside before grabbing Amir by the arm and shoving him inside.

"Hey!" he complains. "What are you—?"

"No humans. *Especially* one that can't defend himself!" I shout.

"You can't seriously expect me to miss all the action! I'll stay out of the way—"

"No!" I reach out for the blue fairy, who has returned to her smaller size. My fingers wrap easily around her body, and she shrieks in terror. Ignoring her protests, I toss her onto Amir's lap.

"You both have to stay here."

Before Amir can say anything else, I slam the sliding door shut. David's mouth presses into a thin line, but I know he agrees with me. My guess is that he doesn't want to repeat what happened at the motel since he had to drag Amir out before he got killed or kidnapped.

My fingertips tingle as I anticipate the battle. More than anything, they long to hold the weapon I've been itching to use all this time. The moment the trunk door pops upward, I spot the broadsword.

Made from a deep gray metal that only exists in Qotan, the blade waves to and fro like a set of seawalls frozen in time. A dark opal is set in the pommel and cross guard. Everything slides into place the moment my hand grips the sword. Though I'm sure it doesn't actually hold any mythical energy, I feel prickles travel up my arm as I pull it free.

Years of practicing with this sword has prepared me for this moment. All of the failures I have endured and the abuse I went through in practice is going to be put to good use. It's not weighted for my human self. It's weighted for a demon side.

"That thing is a beast," David says. "Are you sure you can handle it well enough?"

His question stirs the part of me that is terrified of failure, but I tell her to go away.

"I can handle it just fine."

I let the fury that roils in my chest free. My skin stretches and burns, my muscles flex and grow, and in seconds, my whole body fills out the blue sweats I'm currently wearing. David takes a step back and eyes me warily.

"Okay, then," he says, reaching in the trunk and pulling out a short steel sword.

"Are you sure *you* can handle that sword?" I ask, my voice now a whole octave lower. It rumbles in my chest, the all-too-familiar anticipation of combat tingling my limbs and brain.

He scowls, then looks up at me. The moment he takes in my new visage, he backs away, eyes wide.

"I'll be fine."

David clears his throat, then looks away from me. This stings more than it should. I don't have feelings for him in any way, but for some reason, seeing his repeated disgust feels like a knife twisting in my chest. He's gone before I can try to say anything to make him feel less visibly terrified of me.

Are you sure you're up for this? Jared's voice echoes in my mind. *There are civilians in there. You have to direct your anger away from them.*

Burning rushes up my neck. I've not yet mastered the ability to mind-block Jared while I'm in my demon form. My mental control is flimsy when my emotions root so deeply inside of me. Even remembering this makes me want to cut the whole van in half with the massive sword.

I sense Jared's trepidation even without me using my intimidation aura.

I'm fine. Get out of my head, you fool, I respond.

He withdraws from my mind, then stands at my side—not close enough for me to hit him. I've only lost control with him a couple of times, but that's enough for him to steer clear of me when I'm like this. I glance over at him, seeing the fist weapons the blacksmith made for him. Though he spends most of his time fighting in animal form, the smith recognized his proclivity to fight with claws. Thus, he has human claws.

Screams erupt from the restaurant, and Jared curses, leaping forward and melding into a large panther. I bound after him, a determined smile tugging at my mouth.

David disappears behind the door, and I curse the idiot in my mind for running in like that. He's not a good fighter. Yes, he's made some great progress in the last couple weeks, but his actions are foolhardy and bullheaded. Regardless of my worries, I reach out and tear the door off its hinges. I didn't mean to pull it clean off the frame, but I toss it aside without another thought.

David stands in the entryway, his sword thrust through an orc's chest. His eyes smolder with something . . .

Revenge.

The orc disappears into a puddle.

Two goblins leap at David, their sharp teeth bared and their small knives flashing through the air. I pull my sword back to cleave them in two, but Jared pounces on them first, his claws digging into the chest of one and his mouth clamping down on the other. They turn to black ooze before they even hit the ground.

Oh, come on! That's the most disgusting thing I've ever tasted, Jared complains in my mind. He sends an unwelcome description of the taste. Salty toes and body odor . . .

David turns slightly green, holding his hand to his mouth. "You could have *not* shared that mental experience with us."

I grunt as a trio of orcs stalk confidently through the restaurant window, smashing tables and tossing dishes of food left and right. The heat in my chest transfers to my whole body, and I crash forward into the fray. The orcs stop in their tracks, their eyes moving along my body until they meet my face. I grin the most terrifying and evil grin I can pull off.

Unfortunately, it doesn't have any effect on the creatures.

They shout something in their guttural language, then charge at me with their swords and axes high in the air. Could I take three at once? Probably. I'll likely come away with a lot of cuts and bruises, but I could do it. The ego part of my demon blood wants to show off.

Collecting a cool energy in my chest, I focus on the charging creatures and send the energy outward. Even though it's not visible, their reactions to the wave of power are visceral. One of them stops, his double-edged axe falling to the ground as he puts his hands over his face. The largest of the three hesitates, but not for long. His tusks protrude upward, and he bares his teeth, continuing to run. The woman orc doesn't pause. She's within reach of my sword just as I swing it with all my strength.

Her blade meets mine, and a wild clang rings my ears. Even though she parried my attack, my demon-enhanced strength is too much for her. She growls as her hand flies to the side, her sword going wildly off course. I'm shocked that she managed to hold on to it.

I attack again, and she barely manages to dodge my broadsword by rolling out of the way. Her companion rushes in, but he falls forward in a puddle of foul-smelling sludge. My enhanced senses pick up on it, and my stomach sours. Yet the anger still fuels me.

They endangered these people.

They ruined my normal teenage life.

They took our parents.

I see red as I spin on the orc still locked in place by my intimidation aura. With a cry, I low blow him in the gut. The black ooze pours over my sword and mingles with the syrup and pancakes that litter the floor.

A panther roar sounds from behind me, and a massive thud mixes with the clash of shattering glass. I don't get the chance to assess what's happening with Jared before the orc woman is back to attacking me with wild and quick slashes. It takes all my concentration to block each blow—and even so, she's much faster than me. She dodges or deflects every single one of my counterattacks.

After a few minutes, my heart thunders in my chest, and sweat drips down my forehead. I block and dodge, attack and swing, but the orc is too fast for me. I see the edge of the blade's path before I feel it bite into my side. Teeth locked, I swing my empty hand out and catch the orc on the chin. Her head snaps back, and she collapses to the ground.

The desire to skewer the orc with my sword almost drives me to do so, but I fight the instinct. "Where are our parents?" I demand. "What have you done with them?

Her eyes narrow, and she spits on my feet. My fist tightens around the broadsword, and I envision it passing through her neck to sever her spine.

"Where—are—they?" I grit out, holding off the monster.

"*Uch grintal chk chk brrvan.*"

I lose control of the monster inside, and my sword plunges into the orc. My blade gets covered in mythical creature ooze. When I turn around to check how the others are faring, I see Jared swipe his claws through the chest of a goblin who flies through the air, melting it in the process. It splatters on a group of cowering patrons who didn't make it out on time.

Their fear insights a newfound fury in me, and I rush forward toward a massive blue form. The troll is at least a foot taller than me, its head grazing the ceiling. I bellow and lash out with my sword. This alerts him to my attack, and he catches my hand in one of his beefy blue ones. I grunt in frustration, but I can't pull free.

"Help!" David screams.

I want to look, but the troll's beady black eyes bore into my soul. A smile grows on his face, his yellow and broken teeth a horrific sight. Then his other hand lashes out at my head. I should have anticipated it, but David's shout distracted me. It connects with my face, and I feel one of my teeth come loose. It rattles in my mouth, along with the metallic taste of blood. My vision swims, but I right myself just in time to duck under the troll's next punch.

I unleash a wave of intimidation at the creature; however, it does nothing but make him hesitate for a millisecond.

The big ones never respond well to my aura. Even with my failed attempt to stop him, I'm slightly faster—even if he's stronger. As he throws another punch, I drop my sword and catch his fist in my palm. Bones crack in my hand, and pain radiates up my arm, but I hold strong. My other knuckles connect with his face, the thud so loud that it makes my ears pop.

He falls to the ground in a heap and doesn't melt away to blackness.

My brother is currently circling another orc. The orc dances in, flicking twin daggers wildly, but Jared's panther form is more than a match for the creature.

David needs my help over Jared. At least a dozen goblins have him pinned, their weapons bashing his face and arms. His red scales block each of them, but he struggles desperately, his cries strangled and cut off by the entourage.

His body flares up, fire lacing his whole being, but only a couple of the goblins yelp and jump off of him. My demon brain itches to kill each one of them, and my hand prepares to lob my broadsword at them. I could pick off at least two. As I pull my hand back, Jared's voice echoes in my mind in warning.

Don't throw your sword! You'll kill David!

Yes, I probably will. Yes, I should probably care. But I don't care. The weapon calls to me, telling me to pull my arm back and unleash it. No . . .

"Help! They're—augh!" David cries out.

His scales are about to fail!

Jared's growls turn to whimpers as a massive orc slams him into the wall. He slumps to the ground, his black fur turning back into a t-shirt and jeans. My protective instinct goes haywire. David is about to die to a bunch of goblins. Jared is about to get a sword in the chest. I freeze, my body split in two. I try an intimidation aura wave, which actually causes a few of the goblins to freeze up. They fall to the ground, but there are still too many on David.

The orc approaching Jared hesitates, but then he glares at me and keeps walking.

Failure. I'm failing again. No matter how I calculate my next move, I have to choose.

I refuse to choose. I refuse to fail.

A roar the likes of which I've never heard before erupts from my lips. Coldness collects in my whole body, and I throw my hands outward. Then, everything goes pitch-black.

The electric lighting of the restaurant, the sun, everything is gone. We're in darkness.

The air chills at an alarming rate. Before, it felt like a decent spring day. Now it feels like the precursor to winter. I blink rapidly, trying to figure out why I can't see anything.

For an alarming few seconds, I think I've gone blind from rage, but then the light comes back. My eyes sting from the sudden change, but I recover and spin toward David. To my utter shock, he's flung most of the goblins away and is picking them off with his sword. When I flip to look at Jared, he's finishing off the orc with his clawed weapons.

What—was—that? Jared asks pointedly in my mind.

I push him out and resist the urge to use an expletive.

Somehow . . . *I* caused the weird blackout. I know it. It's a gut feeling that runs deep to my bones. The cold, tingling energy pulled the light into me, expunging it from the restaurant.

I swallow hard. Had I caused darkness across the whole world? Surely that wasn't possible?

Then again, no demons had walked in this realm for hundreds of years. No one would be able to explain what happened to me.

Two more orcs appear out of nowhere and rush me with wild grunts and cries. I raise my weapon and block both of them with a quick swipe. The blow flicks their swords to the side, and I grab one by the neck. With all my strength, I smash his head into the other orc. They crumple to the ground before turning into sludge.

The salty, acrid smell burns my nostrils and twists my stomach. Forget about the broken furniture and shattered windows. The dishes and food scattered everywhere pales in comparison to the mess of black sludge that covers everything. David's clothes and Jared's fur are caked with the corpses of the creatures we've slain.

The demon half of me purrs in delight—the human half wants to throw up.

Whatever power I just used gave us the edge in the fight. I spin to see the last three dark race creatures standing in a triangle. Two orcs and a tall troll woman. Her red-dyed hair is full of bones, and it's matted into a dreadlock style. She holds up her massive blue hands and glares daggers at me.

"*Grrvn itl griffnan yul frrnrr,*" the troll says in a deep tone.

"She told us to hold our weapons," David says, moving to my side.

His scales are gone, and he has a wicked gash on his left temple. It oozes blood down his face and chin. Despite the injury, he stands slightly in front of me and holds out his sword to the troll. When he speaks next, his normal voice is gone. He's grunting and purring like the troll. His translation ability is far more useful than my intimidation aura, but I blast them with it nonetheless. The two orcs flinch and drop their weapons, putting their hands over their faces in fear.

The troll narrows her eyes and says something to David.

"*Brrvan grt vondrr yup frrrnrr,*" David replies.

Stay calm, Jared's voice echoes in my head.

A combination of adrenaline and fury urges me to chop off their heads and reduce them to goo. David clearly has another plan because they continue talking for far too long. My aura blast runs out, and the orcs almost fully recover, their weapons coming to the ready. Yet they watch me with trepidation, their pupils flicking in my direction.

"She wants us to stand down and come with her quietly," David says, contempt in his tone.

"Yeah, not happening!" I snarl.

"That's what I told her, but she keeps repeating herself. Apparently, the room full of sludge creatures isn't enough to scare her away."

Right as he says this, the troll reaches behind her back and pulls out a huge axe. It's made from a dark metal and has a blade on either side. Notches mark the blades along the curves, a testament to the many times the troll has used it in battle. The troll glowers at me still, but she's speaking to David. Each grunt makes me want to scream.

Before she finishes the conversation, her axe swings rapidly in my direction. My instincts are quicker than she expects, and I block it. She scowls, then grunts an order to her orcs, who leap toward me. They're met with a bout of flames from David's hands. The heat is blistering and uncomfortable on my chilled skin.

One of the orcs screams in pain and falls to the ground in a flaming heap of black sludge. The other orc backs away, wildly flapping her tunic, which is burning quickly. She pulls it off and discards it.

Jared roars so loudly that my enhanced ears ache. The orc flinches. The troll holds her ground. In response to Jared's threatening roar, the troll opens her mouth and unearths the most earsplitting and terrifying sound I've ever heard. My eardrums explode, purple blood dripping down my face. I scream in pain and fall to my knees. David and Jared collapse, too.

I can't hear anything but ringing now.

Despite the pain, I force my eyes open and watch as the orc walks confidently toward Jared, who's still writhing on the floor. My protective instincts roar to life once more, and I jump to my feet, swiping my broadsword toward the orc's neck. She dissolves into goo.

The troll's face twists in rage. She thought she had knocked me down and would triumph easily.

Over my dead body.

Ignoring the splitting pain in my head, I slam my blade down toward her head. She blocks it easily with her axe and swipes back at me. It's the type of counterattack that I should be able to dodge, but my depth perception is off without my hearing, and I misjudge how close I am to the wall.

Pain lances up my arm as my elbow connects with the drywall and a hidden stud. I curse and shove my weapon up toward the troll's chest. She manages to dance out of the way and swing her axe at my face. It misses, and my ears start to tingle and itch—a sign that they are healing rapidly.

I wrap my huge palm around the haft of her axe and pull hard, launching myself toward her. My head connects with hers, and we both fall to the ground. In the end, however, the troll is stronger. Her beefy blue arms clamp around my neck, cutting off my airway. My vision blurs, and my head swims. I'm vaguely aware of Jared and David shouting. My eardrums must have healed enough to catch it, though it's still muffled and faint.

Coldness douses my chest again, and this time, I don't hesitate. I accept it and call it into my being.

This time, I'm not surprised when the lights go out. It gathers rapidly from every source and plunges into my body. The troll grunts in surprise, and her grip on my neck slackens. Then she bellows in pain as I feel heat wash over my left side. Her skin melts and hair singes as a flame roars over both of us. She releases me, thudding to the ground.

"What is happening?" Jared roars.

"It's like we're out in the middle of nowhere on a pitch-black night," David pants. "Did I get her?"

I revel in the cold feeling for a bit longer before I let it go. Light rushes from my body and returns to the room. The family we'd seen enter the restaurant from early cowers under their table, whimpering and pointing at me with wide eyes and open mouths.

And then the sirens start up. They're much closer now. But this time, there is a massive purple demon as evidence of the destruction.

WE ALMOST FALL OFF OF A MOUNTAIN

W E RUSH FROM THE restaurant to the van. I'm exhausted, which frustrates me because we didn't learn anything from the creatures who attacked us. When I first heard
the desperate screams, I figured it would be cathartic to knock
some heads in and force some information out of them.

But my demon blood had different plans.

As we reach the car, David slumps on the side, eyeing me
critically.

"What was that?" he asks. "I shot flames at the troll, but I
couldn't see where they hit. Everything was black. I couldn't
even see light from the fire."

I peer down at my scorched skin and blackened hair, and
David's furrowed brow loosens. He frowns, then curses.

"Sorry, I didn't mean to—"

I hold up a hand to get him to shut up.

"Now is not the right time to talk to her," Jared translates, looking warily at the road. "Those sirens are close, Krista. Can you speed up the calming down thing just a bit?"

His comment only makes matters worse. The heat flares inside of me, along with the sudden urge to flip the van over. Amir takes that very moment to pop open the door and gape at us.

"Did you see that? People were running and screaming, then the whole restaurant got sucked up in a massive ball of black smoke."

So, I hadn't blackened the whole earth. Good to know. Hearing this is both encouraging and disappointing at the same time.

"Happened twice. I seriously thought you guys were sucked back into Qotan through a portal," Amir says, sounding more annoyed. "What would I have done stuck here with this fairy? I can't exactly take her home with me."

"Amir! Now is not the time," David scolds. "We need to get out of here."

Jared looks at me desperately, but I can't calm down. I want to smash everything and kill everyone in sight. Holding my actions back is easier for me than calming down. That is something I'm still learning. The troll's demands echo in my mind. Her bellow and subsequent pain tear through my memory and stoke the fire inside.

"We don't have time for this, Krista! *Calm down* so we can—"

I snap. My hand shoots out and shatters the back window of the car. Rolinda screams, her tiny orb of a body leaping behind Amir's shoulder and nestling there.

"Don't tell me to calm down!" I growl.

David crouches down into a fighting position and holds his sword up. His other hand produces a balled-up flame, and the human girl inside of me is impressed at his reaction time.

Three cop cars and a fire engine tear down the street and turn into the hotel parking lot. Jared curses and shouts at David to get in the car. With his eyes still locked on me, David backs away enough to open the driver side door.

"Krista, get on top and hang on!" Jared orders.

I want to argue with him, but the cops have spotted us and are now headed in our direction. With a small leap, my huge body lands on the roof of the vehicle, my stomach down and my legs dangling. I grip the car through the open front windows, and it roars to life. Jared gasses us out of the parking lot with me dangling on top. Running is the smartest thing we could do right now because how are a bunch of teenagers supposed to explain their way out of being at a restaurant on a school day with swords and flaming hands? Not to mention the purple-skinned, red-haired beast who looks like a failed science experiment.

Lights flash wildly behind us and tires squeal on the asphalt as we barrel down the road toward the mountains. Jared maneuvers the car with terrifying and expert motions, and I'm left wondering where he learned to drive so well.

"Hold on!" he shouts as he spins the wheel to the left.

The force of the turn yanks me to the side, and I dig my hands into the metal. Rolinda screams again, and David shushes her, telling her to chill out. I close my eyes, feeling sick from all the motion. The adrenaline from my demon form is wearing off. Since we aren't fighting anymore, my defensive instincts are fading.

Not good.

Jared takes a sharp turn right, and I'm thrown in the opposite direction. My heart isn't thudding quite as hard now, and I feel my body and muscles shrinking by the second. I desperately grasp at something—anything to keep myself from shrinking to my normal size.

Closing my eyes, I think back to the battle at the motel. I imagine Gulran's stupid face as he gloats, practically licking my blood off the sword with his dumb, egotistic expression. These thoughts fuel my anger, and my body swells back to its large size.

That's exactly when Jared slams on the breaks. I'm not expecting it at all, and my legs flip over my head, my back coming in full contact with the windshield. It shatters under my weight, and everyone screams.

Pain rips up my back and radiates into my skull. My hands feel raw, and I smell blood. The metallic salty scent only adds to the tumult currently churning in my gut.

"Halt! You are under arrest for the destruction of private property and the endangerment of civilians!" a voice in front of the car proclaims loudly.

When I open my eyes, I see four cop cars blocking our way. They must have called in a whole squad when they saw us fleeing.

Jared curses, puts the car in reverse, and then stops when he sees more cops in the way.

We're trapped, and the anger fueling me has almost entirely diffused.

My stretched skin shrinks back to normal, and I sink into the hole I created in the windshield. It was stupid of us to intervene at the restaurant and not think about how it would look. There's no evidence of goblins or orcs breaking things and attacking people—only a lot of black sludge and four guilty-looking teenagers in a minivan. Even if any of the creatures were left over, these cops wouldn't believe they were real. They'd think it was all a ruse or some weird gang activity with people playing dress-up.

A woman cop speaks into a megaphone, and she sounds very, very angry. "Exit the vehicle and put your hands in the air, *now*!"

I lay my head back on the broken windshield and try to take deep breaths. My chest hurts, and I'm struggling to pull in air. It's like someone shrunk my lungs, and now I have to figure out how to survive on less oxygen.

"We have to do what they say," Jared says, moving to open the car door.

"Are you crazy?" David hisses. "We can't go to jail. We'll never get out of there!"

Though he says it quietly, my enhanced hearing picks up Amir saying, "I can't have a criminal record! I'll never get into Harvard or Yale. I can't go to jail."

"I said, get out of the vehicle and put your hands in the air!" the megaphone cop shouts again.

Do you have any ideas? Jared asks in my mind.

At this point, I'd like to pass out to get away from this pain, I say darkly.

He's not amused. Jared gets out of the car and puts his hands in the air, David following suit. Amir does, too, and Rolinda, who is still glowing blue, tucks herself into the sleeve of his left arm. The cops see it as some type of weapon, turning their gazes toward him. Five uniformed officers stand with their weapons drawn and pointed at us.

"Get off the vehicle, now!" the megaphone booms.

"Easier said than done," I say, mostly to myself.

Still, knowing that my body can definitely *not* sustain bullet holes right now, I slip off the windshield as carefully as possible. A jagged edge of the broken glass catches my left side and tears a gash. Air hisses through my teeth, but I don't react further. Ghastly purple blood oozes out of the gash. The officers closest to me stare at the wound with their mouths gaping. Just when I think we're done for, Jared's voice rings in my head.

We need to escape to Qotan.

My jaw locks tightly, and my teeth ache instantly.

Are you crazy? We aren't even sure it will work, I respond.

He disappears from my mind for a moment, then comes back.

David's on board. We have no other options. Do you want to go to jail today?

No, I really don't. Mainly because I know I'll become a science experiment the instant we're processed and sent to a correctional facility. I've seen enough movies and TV shows to confirm this. Knowing we're innocent won't do jack squat when there's tons of evidence against us.

We can either try, fail, and go to prison anyway, or not try at all, Jared says in an altogether annoying fit of logic.

Fine, I respond.

Something in my gut tells me that it will work. I can't describe how, but each time I've thought of Qotan—even briefly over the past few weeks—I feel a subtle tug in my gut. It isn't as strong as what I felt about home when we were in the other realm, but it's present. One thing about this plan makes me uneasy. I don't know where we will end up in Qotan once we teleport, but Jared's right. It's our only shot out of this cop situation.

"Officers will approach slowly to handcuff each of you. Please do not resist. We don't need anyone to get hurt today," megaphone cop says.

On the count of three.

Jared starts counting in my head.

One.

"If you cooperate, we can ensure that you have the chance to explain yourselves."

A few officers are almost within arm's reach of me, and all I can think is . . . my broadsword is in the back seat of the van. Being in Qotan without it last time was horrible.

Two.

I refuse to leave my weapon again. When we first teleported realm to realm, we'd accidentally brought some orcs with us. Without bloodstones, they had melted to sludge. They had been touching us when we pulled them through. *Touch.* My eyes snap up to the officers as they approach. If I put my hand down too quickly, they'll shoot me. Instead, I lean my hip into the car to make contact with it.

Three.

Many things happen at once. David scales up and steps backward, grabbing Amir by the shoulder. The cops open fire on him from the sudden movement. Bullets snap against his body and shoulder but ricochet off in sparks. And Amir screams in terror as they warp in the air and disappear.

"What the—?" the cop closest to me exclaims.

Jared's body warps into the air like he's been put in a blender.

All guns point to me now, and everyone starts shouting.

The cop closest to me reaches out to grab me, but I close my eyes and focus on Qotan. I think of the hot desert and the freezing water. I think about the elven city, awash with beautiful flowers and foliage and the smell of the damp forest. At the same time, I focus on my contact with the car on my hip.

I chant the words "Please work" in my head, then everything spins. My ear rings as one of the cops fires at me, but I don't feel the bite of the bullet in my flesh. Instead, I'm falling, the car still rooted to my side like it's stuck with gorilla glue.

Then, all at once, my feet hit hard ground.

Except that ground is on a very steep incline.

My eyes snap open as gravity tugs me backward, causing me to fall. The sky becomes ground, and the ground becomes sky as I tumble down the rocky hill. By the time I'm finished rolling, my stomach turns, and my vision continues spins. I have to close my eyes to control my nausea before I lose that delicious restaurant meal all over the ground.

"Oh, come on," David complains, spitting something on the ground. "Did we *have* to come through on a mountainside?"

Wind whips at my hair and whistles my ears.

Amir lets out another scream, and electricity runs through my veins. I spin over, adrenaline coursing through me.

He clings to a rocky cliff, half his body hanging over the edge.

David staggers back against the steep part of the mountain, his arms shaking. I glower at him, still unable to believe how terrified he is of heights.

"I'm slipping!" Amir cries. His body slides over the cliff.

Determined, I jump forward and grab his wrist just in time. My chest slams into the hard rock ground, and the wind is knocked out of me for the second time in less than ten minutes. I gasp for air but hold on as tightly as I can. Amir, however, is a little bigger than me, and my petite girl form isn't heavy enough to keep him from falling.

He starts pulling me over, and I curse.

"David! Jared! Get your behinds over here!" I yell.

Amir grasps at me desperately, but his hands keep slipping.

A loud cawing noise tears at my ears, and I look up in the sky, startled to see a huge eagle descend upon us, its talons outstretched. Great. Of all the times to be attacked by a bird of prey . . .

The bird's yellow feet speak only death as the sharp claws move to snatch the two of us, but then I recognize the creature for what it is. My brother. Relief washes over me.

Suddenly, a flash of bright blue light blinds me, and Amir's weight is all but gone from my grip. When my head snaps that direction with swimming sunspots in my vision, I see an ebony-skinned woman with tightly curled black hair and a beautiful gown. She's holding Amir in her arms, her fairy wings fluttering and humming.

"You shall not die today, young heroes!" Rolinda says.

Did she just call us heroes? The cheesiness of it makes me want to vomit, but I'm too relieved to focus on it.

Jared lands on the ledge next to me and shifts back into human form, eyeing Rolinda in a grateful manner. The sun high above practically makes Jared's blond hair glow. I have to squint and look away to avoid being blinded. When I gaze off the mountainside, I see a deep canyon with a river at the bottom. It doesn't look familiar, but at the same time, it reminds me of traversing the mountain to get to Dranith—the precursor to getting ourselves in an even bigger mess.

Amir's breathing hard from the ground next to me where Rolinda deposited him. "I'm starting to understand Dave's terror for heights," he grumbles. "I'd be happy never to have that experience again."

I glance toward David. He's still cowering against the side of the mountain. His wide eyes are locked on the edge where we are sitting, and he's entered some kind of trance. I've put people in similar fits before with my intimidation aura, but I can't take credit for this one. I actually feel bad for how terrified he is.

Jared sighs. "I'll see what I can do to help him."

He moves toward David to try to breathe some life back into him.

"Humans really should have evolved to have wings. It's impractical for you to not have them," Rolinda says smartly.

I glare at her. "Humans aren't going to *sprout* wings because it's practical. Besides, we get around just fine with cars and airplanes."

She raises her eyebrows in confusion. "I don't know what those are, but they sound as impractical as humans without wings."

She "Hmphs" and flashes back to her small fairy form.

"Trust me, I'd grow wings if I could," Amir says, lying on the ground.

Peering over the edge, I catch sight of movement far below. It looks like a small group of creatures trekking in our direction—thirty or forty of them. They are too far down for me to recognize what they are. All I can tell is that they have various colors of skin.

A shiver rockets up my spine, and I shuffle away from the cliff's edge.

"Dark races, *get back*!" I hiss to Amir.

His eyes shoot open, and he scoots away quickly.

Rolinda yelps and zips to Amir's shoulder. Apparently, the fairy has taken a liking to the kid. I instinctively reach for my weapon but grasp only air.

The car. It's in the trunk.

I spin to find where the vehicle is and am relieved to see that it's still near us. On the opposite side of the narrow pathway, the car sits suspended on an extremely steep incline. I'm grateful it didn't tumble over the edge. But it's precariously situated. Even if we could make it to the cab doors to get in, we couldn't move it an inch without it plummeting to the bottom. If we didn't die from the fall, the small army below would take us out.

"Did they see us?" Jared asks.

I shake my head. "I don't think so. But even if they did, I would imagine it would take them some time to make their way up here."

"Oh! Please don't let them take me away!" Rolinda squeals, shivering slightly.

My eyes widen as I make the connection. Rolinda mentioned running away from her captors and escaping to our world to find us. If what we learned by popping into New York from Dranith is true, that means that her captors would have been close by in Qotan. We only drove half a mile from the restaurant before we were caught by the cops.

"These are the same goons that had you before?" I ask, my voice steady.

Her glowing blue ball of light bobs up and down in a full-body nod. Great. The only thing that saved us from being ambushed was teleporting to the side of a mountain. If we had been fifteen feet back, we would have phased in at the bottom of the cliff.

Voices drift upward, and I hold my breath, afraid that any sound will alert them to our presence. Somehow, we are sandwiched between danger in both realms. The cops are inevitably wondering where we went, and now we have a bunch of dark-raced goons a hundred feet below us. Could arrows reach up here? I don't want to find out.

We can't phase back to earth for who knows how long. This is the second time we've used that ability. Based on our last experience, it will probably be at least a few days before it'll work.

That means we're stuck in Qotan until then.

Amir's face scrunches up like he's going to sneeze, and I glare at him. He waves his hand in front of his nose and mouths the word "Allergies." I shake my head and stare daggers at him. Rocks shift under my feet as I leap toward him, slapping my hand over his mouth as the sneeze is let free. The sharp sound snaps against the rocks around us, echoing a few times before stopping.

The voices below cease abruptly.

Breathing as evenly as possible, I wait for the inevitable second sneeze. It comes with a passion, and another echo ripples along the cliff.

The conversation starts up below, but it's far away and in a grunting language that I can't understand.

"They heard you," David whispers.

I'm relieved to hear that Jared worked some life back into him. Shaking the thought away, I nod my head in David's direction. Somehow, he catches my meaning.

"I can't catch every word, but they heard the sound and are trying to be quiet to listen." He looks toward the edge, pales, then closes his eyes.

For a few tense moments, we're left in strained silence, both parties being as quiet as possible. My mind flips through scenario after scenario of how we can get out of this mess. Honestly, the only option I see is getting my broadsword.

Tracing the path to the car, I determine how many seconds it would take me to run and snatch my weapon. Just before I make the leap to secure the sword, shouting issues from below. A cold energy overtakes my body. An orc has spotted me.

Rolinda squeals again, which further alerts them to our presence—and Rolinda's.

"They're pretty pissed now," David says. "They know she's the fairy they lost. They want her back."

The grunting language increases as twenty other creatures come into view, moving far enough away from the base of the cliff to see us fully. Goblins and trolls and orcs gaze up at us. One of the goblins nocks an arrow on a large bow and releases it right at me. I gasp, ducking to the ground. Even if I hadn't ducked, the shot would have missed me, but the shattering glass I hear isn't comforting. The arrow struck the back windshield of the car.

I need my weapon, so I charge toward the car. In three steps, I'm grappling with the handle of the vehicle. Locked. I open my mouth to shout at Jared to unlock the door when another arrow slams into the metal next to me. No time for that.

I grip the edge of the window where the glass broke, the sharp edge cutting into my flesh. The pain shocks me into action, the demon part of my brain soaking in the sensation. A glittering black jewel sits within reach—the pommel of my broadsword. I grab it and slide back down the incline as more arrows launch at me.

When I look up, I see one coming right at my chest. My heart skips a beat, but I brace for the shaft to enter me. Before it can, a flash of red streaks my vision, and David plasters himself against me, grunting as we fall against the incline.

"Ouch!" he groans, now on top of me.

He took the full brunt of the blow. The boy quite literally took an arrow for me. My face flushes at the prospect. I should say thank you or something, but my emotions are too much right now, so I shove him off of me. He's much heavier when he's all scaled up. His body thuds to the ground, and he curses.

"Sheesh! A thank-you would be nice!"

Before I can respond, another volley of arrows comes at us. There is a flash of blue, and a few arrows go off course. Some still rain on us, and Amir cries out in pain. An arrow has lodged into his leg, and blood immediately seeps from the wound.

"Jared," I yell. "Get Amir away from the edge!"

Jared shifts into a bear and grabs the back of Amir's shirt in his mouth, dragging him away screaming and wailing.

The goblins below prep another set of arrows, and dread fills me. We're about to become skewers of human meat. But then, something strange happens. The goblins all blink and stir in confusion. Their bowstrings slacken, and they stare up in wonder at us.

"Be silent! At once!" a voice hisses to my right.

I level my broadsword in anticipation of a fight. Blood roars in my head as my skin explodes outward, and my arms and chest expand to their demon form. It hurts—even more this time than earlier. But I accept the pain.

A ten-foot tall, blue-skinned elf stands before me with his hands out. Another elf is behind him—a female with silvery hair and closed eyes. She wears a leather dress, her shoulders exposed, with a skirt that extends to the ground. Her mouth moves as she mutters words I can't understand.

Voices drift up to us from below. The dark-raced army there is shuffling and shouting in anger and confusion.

"She is hiding you from view," the elf man says. "Hold still and *keep silent*."

My heart thunders in my chest, and my breathing comes in ragged waves, but I don't move. The others quiet down, too, except for the whimpers and sobs from Amir. Can't blame the kid for that. An arrow to the leg can't feel great.

The elf says something in a language I can't understand, and a short dwarf appears from behind him. The man's brown and scraggly beard hangs down from his chin to his knees. Brown-black irises stare at us from under bushy brows. He has a thick hammer strapped to his back.

The combative demon blood coursing through me wonders how quickly I could dispatch the little guy. His beefy arms prove he's not weak, but my weapon and height might give me the advantage.

While I'm deliberating thinking about taking out the dwarf, he gives me a severe look and shuffles past me. He pulls out a leaf of something and pops it into his mouth, chewing it rapidly. When he spits it out, it's a glob of green mess that he presses around the arrow in Amir's leg. When Amir tries to shriek, the dwarf puts a firm hand over his mouth. After a few moments, Amir's eyes roll back in his head, and he relaxes.

We continue to stand frozen, and my legs and back start to ache from holding still for so long.

"Lead them away," the elf instructs, his glowing eyes still watching me.

The chanting of the elf changes, as do the sounds from below. A large orc, dressed in dark leather and chain mail, barks an alert and points along the edge of the cliff. My heart stops when I see myself. It's not a perfect replica of me. My hair is a little too red, and I'm a little shorter than normal, but from this distance, it looks enough like me. There's also a bear with a version of Amir riding it, and David on foot with a glowing blue orb hovering over his shoulder. The elf is creating an illusion of us. It feels like I'm watching a movie.

Chaos ensues as the army rushes after the false versions of us. In moments, it's silent below.

I try to relax, but the adrenaline and demon blood still flowing through me make it hard.

"You are blessed," the elf says, raising thick silvery eyebrows. "We saved you just in time."

I grunt. "We would have been fine on our own."

The look the elf gives me reminds me of Bob when he knows I'm lying to him. It's both frustrating and endearing.

"I am Glaverin, and this is Strovan and Mendory." He gestures to the dwarf still stooped over Amir and to the chanting woman next to him. "You are the heirs to the kingdoms."

My chest constricts, and I grit my teeth.

"How do you know who we are?" I ask firmly.

He smiles. "Your blood sings to my mind. I know you."

I want to shout at him and tell him to keep his creepy ears out of my business, but he interrupts my thoughts.

"Come. We have a safe place to speak."

Mendory stops chanting, and even though I can't see the illusion hiding us, I can feel it disappear.

"Follow. We have a message from the elf king."

Despite every part of me *not* wanting to listen to this old elf, I suppress the urge and follow him along the mountainside.

AN ELF GIVES US GRAVE NEWS

THE FLAMES FLICKER AND dance as I stare at them. Heat washes over my skin, but it doesn't bother me. The coldness of my blood soaks it up as if I will never get enough. David sits to my right and Jared to my left. Amir and Rolinda, who is now human-sized, stand near a small shelf of stone talking to the squat dwarf. So far, the dwarf hasn't smiled once or given any indication that he has the ability to be happy. Still, Amir chats with him, his face animated. I could probably listen in on their conversation, but I'm not in the mood, so I shut it out, instead focusing on the crackling of the wood in the fire.

"*Ghurvlanti il vanreuvan nlim yesnin?*" the elf man asks.

"*Rfilsnitlan il reuvan,*" David responds.

I grit my teeth. They've been going on like this for at least five minutes, and I'm losing my mind. After being saved by the elf's illusion magic, they led us to their hidden cave, which turned out to be only a few hundred feet away, nestled behind a rocky crag. Thankfully, the cavern is large enough to fit all of us comfortably.

A set of leather packs and weapons are piled near the edge of the cavern in the shadows, and three bedrolls are there as well.

The elf says something incoherent, and David responds again. Jared listens intently, understanding every bit of it through David's mind. Pent up frustration boils in my chest, and I can't hold myself back anymore.

"Would you just speak English!? Some of us regular people don't have built-in translators in their brain!"

Jared presses his lips into a thin line and gives me an apologetic look. The elf man seems unimpressed. His silvery hair is done up into a ponytail and flows down his back to his waist. The female elf, Mendory, has similarly long hair, but it's left untied. Their eyebrows are long—peaked upward like they've been gelled that way permanently. My comment draws the gaze of the dwarf and Amir, but they soon return to their conversation.

"Forgive me," the elf says, giving me a critical look. "There are things I had to settle in our own tongue. You are the royal halflings of our rulers. Certain truths had to be told in the elven tongue, or else I would think that you were telling tales to get me to trust you. Even if your blood sings to my mind, there are traitors afoot. None can be trusted."

The elf peers at Jared sternly, and my brother winces. He looks down at his hands and pretends to let the comment slide off him. But the poor sap is an open book. My defense mechanism kicks in.

"If you are seriously accusing my brother of being a traitor like his idiotic mom, than you can just shove that right up your—"

"Krista," Jared interrupts. "He has the right to make sure I'm not going to turn you all over to the orc king."

I immediately slap him on the shoulder. "He has the right to keep his suspicions to himself. If he doesn't believe you, then he can talk to my fist."

David rubs his hands over his face and speaks through them. "It's fine, Krista. Glaverin was just asking me normal questions. It's not like I spilled a whole long list of secrets about you. Not that I even *know* any of your secrets."

My stomach twists at whatever veiled meaning his words could have. I choose to push it out of my mind. This demon girl isn't going to be distracted by the dragon boy.

"Look," I say to the elf, trying to keep the annoyance from shifting into anger and making my demon side emerge. "I appreciate you saving us from the enemy out there, but you said you have an urgent message for us. What is it?"

Amir and Strovan promptly fall silent and stare at me.

Glaverin's face maintains a quiet poise as his attention latches on to me. After a moment of awkward staring, the elf looks away, his silver irises landing on the female elf. Mendory glances down at the fire, her face impassive, like she hasn't felt anything for years. I find myself a little jealous. I wish *I* could feel something other than inflammatory anger that is constantly prevalent in my mind.

"He calls to all those who are loyal to the high kingdom of Dranith. The dragon city has fallen. The citizens are missing, lost to the cunning of the dark races. Queen Ferona has aligned with the dark plans of the xfwiforc king. A traitorous act that none anticipated."

Glaverin scrutinizes our faces for a reaction. When none of us burst out or exclaim, he merely nods and looks back to the woman elf.

"The war has begun in earnest, and an army amasses outside the Terovan Forest. Scouts have spied dark races preparing to siege the elven city of Terendrell. In the name of the royals of every light race, and in the name of the half-blooded heirs of the prophecy, all are called to the defense of the elves."

I'm not sure why, but I expected his "message" to be more specific to *us*. The fact that it's a general call for help is disappointing. However, it kindles the burning anticipation of a fight. I think back to my scuffle with Gulran at the hotel and how he took my blood to operate the stone. My failure scorches in me like an unholy flame—the desire for revenge. If Gulran is going to be a part of this war, I want to be there to remove him from the world with my broadsword.

"We were journeying to answer the call and join those who will fight against the enemy. That's when we discovered a small band of our enemies. We've been following them, watching from a distance and waiting for the opportune moment to release the prisoners they have in their grasp," Glaverin says, his eyes drifting over to where Rolinda hovers. "We did not expect to cross paths with the heirs of the prophecy. The Yrivar smiles upon us this day. With you by our side, we will march on the elven city and bolster the hopes of our allies and those loyal to the high dragon queen."

David puts his hands in the air. "Woah—woah, no one said anything about coming with you to fight alongside an army. In case you haven't noticed, we're kind of on our way to do something else."

As much as I want to argue with David and tell him that I'd rather go knock in some orc and goblin heads, I know he's right. And now that Gulran has the stone and my blood, he will be able to track down the other three royal half-bloods.

The elf frowns at us, deep-set wrinkles becoming more cavernous with the expression. "What could possibly be more important than joining your kin in defense of our homeland?"

I mentally will Jared to explain. He's much better at these things than I am. He nods and sits up taller.

"We are searching for the other half-bloods before Urothar can find them. Urothar has the means to locate the others, and we need to get to them before he can."

This draws the attention of all three strangers. Mendory's face shows surprise, and Strovan's face deepens with seriousness.

"But ye've been 'idin' fer many years now. What 'opes does the orc kin' 'ave of findin' 'em befer ye can?" Strovan pipes in.

Jared gestures to my pocket, so I reach in and pull out the lumpy stone. The spindle is still pointing to the image of the tree, but no light beam expands from it. It's another testament to the fact that we are nowhere near our realm. I spin the dial until it lands on the symbol that I know represents David, flames set behind a large, curved claw.. The white light shines out sharply to my right, pointing him out as the mark.

"*Yrivar ghilrish!*" the elf exclaims.

Is that a bad word in their language? Storing that away in my mind just in case, I look down at the stone.

"It works from our blood. If any one of us touches the stone, it points us in the direction of that half-blood. We know what these three are—"

I turn the dial to my image, the beam jumping to me, then I turn the dial to Jared's image, butterfly wings wreathed in a dust like substance, and the light points to him.

"But this is the one we're following right now," I say, flipping it back to the treelike symbol.

The stone goes dark once more.

"We don't know who it is or exactly where they are, but we were traveling in that direction when we . . . ran into some problems," David says.

How perfectly vague of him. Problem is a misnomer. We managed to draw the attention of cops twice, and we were involved in the destruction of a *lot* of private property . . . I grit my teeth, trying not to focus on all the damage we caused—or how much it will cost to put it all back together. Our DNA is written all over those scenes. The only thing that will stop the cops from finding us right away is the fact that none of us are in the system. I shake the thought away. Cops can't get to us here.

Amir scoffs. "Problems. That's the understatement of the century."

Glaverin gives him a questioning look. "And you travel with a human? That is ill-advised. Humans are no longer safe in this land."

I roll my eyes. "Yes, we know about humans and their blood being turned into stones and all that fun stuff."

I ignore the twisting that tugs at my gut as I remember my mom. Is she now powering one of the stones that the dark races used to attack us today?

"You are well-versed in the troubles of our land," Glaverin says. "This is good. I presume the lack of a light beam indicates that those half-bloods do not reside in our realm?"

I nod, and he looks thoughtful.

"May I hold it?" he asks.

I hesitate, my hand wrapping around the rock.

He won't take it. He's a friend, Jared urges in my mind.

I glare at him but open my hand and hold it out.

As the elf's fingers brush my skin, I feel the blazing heat of his warm blood. It is yet another reminder of my freakish state and all the troubles I've had to deal with growing up. I let these memories harden me, closing them inside a mental bottle, never to be opened again.

"The spindle points to the mark of the elves," he says. "You seek the daughter of King Ilvinar. That is this mark here."

He points to the tree image, then moves to the axe and mountain, then moves to what looks like waves of the sea with a music note.

"This is the mark of the dwarves. And this is the mark of the Sirens. These three are still in your realm."

"We have to get back to our realm as soon as possible," David explains. "They stole one of these stones and are tracking down the other half-bloods."

The elf man regards each of us slowly, then without saying anything, turns to look at his wife. He says something I can't understand. She responds, then stares at each of us in turn. My hair prickles at the sight of her emotionless eyes, but then her eyelids droop, and she quiets for a few seconds. "Yrivar wills us to help the half-bloods accomplish their design. They are not yet to answer the elf king's call to war."

Glaverin nods as if he was expecting this all along. Strovan, on the other hand, grunts and casts me a dark look.

"And 'ow do ye propose makin' it back t' yer land? We aren' close t' any o' the portals, in case ye've fergotten?"

The dwarf directs this question at his companion with a very dubious expression. Glaverin doesn't react. Instead, his eyes bore holes into my face as if he's trying to see into the depths of my soul. This agitates me, and I find myself shifting from foot to foot, staving off my frustration so that I don't go full demon on them.

"They came not by portal. Don't you see, Strovan?"

The dwarf grunts again. For a moment, we all sit in silence. It's so uncomfortable that Jared and David start swaying side to side, their eyes flicking around to see who will speak first. I embrace the silence. I love the silence. It means I'm safe. It means that any scrutiny or judgment is kept inside of their minds.

"How did you come to Qotan?" Glaverin asks me.

Does he think I'm the leader or something? Perhaps it's the way I sit with a straight back—or the way I stare down the person I'm talking to, be they enemy or friend. In reality, we don't have a leader. Sure, David is meant to be the high prince, but he's as capable as a little kid.

"Our blood allows us to travel between worlds," I explain.

By the widened eyes of my friends, they did not expect me to be fully honest.

"Yrivar bless, that is remarkable. How is this possible?" Glaverin asks.

"The same way those idiot orcs and dwarves suck the blood out of humans to invade our world!" I practically spit.

Glaverin's mouth parts silently. The way he's looking at me stings more than I care to admit. Countless faces from past years and different schools flash through my mind. Every person who witnessed my anger—or my demon phase—assaults my thoughts.

Not today, anxiety.

I try to focus on the things that will calm and distract me—primarily sword fighting, but also puzzles and watching TV.

"Incredible, yet again," Glaverin marvels.

"They shall walk two worlds to save in tandem or perish together," Mendory says as if reciting something.

The words have an ancient feel to them, so much so that my skin chills, and I resist the urge to back away. A mystical tingling enters my brain and distills along each of my limbs, flowing into my whole being.

"Is that—something I should know?" David asks.

Glaverin looks surprised at his question, then shakes his head. "Oh no. No, that is merely a ditty that I learned from my childhood. A saying, if you will, that children recite for their games and for fun."

This elf has absolutely no poker face. It's obvious that he's not telling us everything, and even though I want to call him out on it, Jared cuts in before I can.

"You know how we can span distances more quickly here?"

Tension ripples through the air as Glaverin's eyes blaze with a fury that I understand altogether too well.

"It is impolite to steal thoughts from those whom you haven't first gained permission," Glaverin snaps. "Just because you bear the royal blood of the fairy queen herself does not give you free rein into my mind."

Jared flushes. "I'm sorry—I just—"

The elf raises his hand, his palm roughly the size of my face. Even though his skin is a deep shade of blue, I can still see wrinkles. Calluses cover his palms just under where his fingers connect, and his nails are quite long.

"It is forgiven, but know that you will be held accountable if you extract sensitive information without my permission."

Strovan folds his arms, holding his angry gaze right on Jared's face. "No pokin' 'round me skull or ye'll find yerself missin' a few fingers after ye wake up in the mornin'."

Jared pales, then nods quickly.

Glaverin continues. "There is another matter that is grave at present, but first, I must understand the direction the stone is taking you. Where is this fourth half-blood whom you seek?"

I say north at the exact same time that David says west. A fresh wave of bother flows through me, but David is blushing, and it diffuses the tension instantly. He looks almost . . . cute with that expression on his face.

Inexplicable horror runs through me at the realization of that thought. Jared coughs, and I know that he caught a hint of it in my mind.

Glaverin's eyes bounce between the two of us.

"Then, Yrivar has aligned your fates. At the time of our king's call, many of the light races answered. Those who have been loyal for their whole existence came without any objections. Through Mendory's mind, we know that many have been arriving to bolster the defenses of Terendrell by the thousands. Yet among them stand none from the demon kingdom."

Even though I don't think he meant it as an insult, it still feels that way. Is he calling my people cowards?

"Why haven't they come?" I question.

Glaverin shakes his head. "Not one soul knows the reason behind their silence. Yet perhaps"—he scrutinizes me from head to toe before speaking again—"if the offspring of said king could petition him for aid, he's more likely to answer the call and assist those he created a treaty with hundreds of years ago. Whatever reservations or concerns he has would surely be swayed by the convincing voice of his kin."

I'm stunned into silence. Did this elf just ask me to grovel to the demon king—my dad—so that he will join the defense of the elven city? Groveling is not something I have ever or *will* ever do in my lifetime. The fact that he even suggested it is offensive, and it draws anger out of me like a full sponge being squeezed.

I grit my teeth, holding the rage at bay to prevent my demon form from appearing. It doesn't stop me from quivering. My body wants to expand and let the emotion flow so I can punch this idiot's head off. Purple veins trace up my arms slowly like meandering snakes going for a slither in tall grass.

"What makes you think he'd even listen to me? I won't beg. I won't ask for help like a child."

Glaverin frowns. "But you are a child. There is nothing to be ashamed of. The help of the demons would ensure our victory in defense against the amassing armies of the dark races."

"Yeah, that's great and all, but we're on our way to save another teen from getting her head cut off and sacrificed to the orc king."

I know it's not likely to happen. The prophecy says he needs us all alive, but I can't fail again. Finding the heirs to the other kingdoms has given me a purpose. It makes me feel like I'm doing something worthwhile instead of hiding in the shadows and keeping to myself. I need this. We *all* need this.

"And the longer we stay here, the more likely they are to get to her first," Amir points out.

I shoot him a glare, and he shrinks back, standing behind David.

Mendory turns to me with a slight smile on her face. "Yrivar's will is known. Their first purpose is wise and true. Finding the other half-blood is important. Yet their journey to the demon kingdom bears more weight to the survival of our realm. You must first accomplish this design."

Glaverin "Hmphs" and sits back on his stool. Strovan looks less than pleased at the idea of having us around longer.

"Thus, it is. My wife is an oracle of Yrivar. She communes with our goddess, and her will must be followed," Glaverin says. "You must first seek the aid of the demons. Then, you can return and find the daughter of the elves."

The mere thought of meeting the demon who sired me and sent me away makes me want to punch a wall. He abandoned me sixteen years ago. He's not exactly "father of the year" material.

"Yeah right, we are not following your dumb goddess's will. We have to get home. After we save the half-blood, *then* we'll see the demon king."

Glaverin frowns, but when he considers each of my companions, they all nod in agreement with me. It's encouraging to see.

"She's right," David says. "We all agreed to save her. We'll come back after and talk to the demons."

I don't miss the wary look David shoots in my direction. He probably thinks that going to the demon capital of Qotan is a terrible idea. I try to brush it off, but it still bothers me.

Glaverin regards us with a critical gaze, then shakes his head. "Do what you must. But know that Yrivar's will is not to be ignored. Fetch the daughter of elves, then return at once to petition for the demon king's aid."

"Fine," I say.

The elf reaches into a leather pouch hanging at his side and pulls out a miniature sculpture. It's a creature with massive black wings, and it has four arms and legs. After inspecting it further, I realize it's a griffin. Tiny red jewels are fixed where the small eye sockets are, making them gleam in the flickering firelight.

"The half-blood you seek lies north, as does the realm of demons and their kingdom. Though few have traversed the halls of their dark palace, many attest to its grandeur and beauty. Return to your world, find the daughter of elves and man alike, then return to Qotan."

His words sound awfully like an order, which makes me clench my fists. I don't like taking orders from people I don't know.

The elf brings the talisman sculpture close enough for me to see it better. The details are impressively intricate.

"Once you have returned to our land, use this talisman to call the griffins to your side. They will bear you up to the palace of the demon king. Though they will dislike the request, they cannot deny the caller of their talisman. Wherever you may be, they will assist you."

He holds it out for me to take, but I shake my head, pointing to David.

"I'm not holding that thing. The last time we were in a fight, I lost my wireless headphones from my pocket," David says.

Jared shakes his head before I even bring it up to him. "I'm not going to be responsible for it. I get just as involved in the fighting as you do."

His point is annoying and valid, and something clicks in my mind. When did I become the queen bee to this ragtag group of half-bloods? Technically, David is the one who should be in charge, but I have to agree. If this talisman is the only way that we can get around, it would be a real rain on our parade if he lost it in the first fight. I take it from the elf begrudgingly.

"I don't know why you think my deadbeat of a dad is going to listen to anything I have to say, but we can't let the orc king take over."

A part of me aches to know what it's like in the capital of the demon kingdom. It's like a compass inside of me is tugging me in my dad's direction. Jared and David both received messages from their mystical parents when they were babies. Me? Nothing. Demon Lord—whatever his name is—didn't give me so much as a letter. Mom tries to tell me he loves me, but if his demon blood is anything like my demon half, how can that be true?

Glaverin nods, then gestures to the opening of the cavern. "Yrivar's will be done. Go forth and find our lost sister."

Before we leave, they outfit us with some provisions, which I tell them we don't need now that we're heading back to our world. They don't listen, primarily because they don't understand the concept of a convenience store. David and Jared ultimately tell me to shove it and just take the food provisions they offered. I sigh, knowing I'll have to eat their hard bread and cured meats. I'd rather just buy a bag of chips . . .

By the time we make it back to the precariously balanced car, the sun has almost dipped below the horizon. It's been hours since we came here, which means it's been about half that time in our realm. We don't know how slowly time passes back home, but if the police haven't given up on trying to find us by now, then they are a different breed of law enforcement. Surely they've found some other problem to deal with?

"All right, I guess this is where we part ways," Amir says, holding his finger up to his shoulder for Rolinda, who is now back to her tiny fairy form, to jump on. I have to hold my tongue not to tell a joke about how she's like a pet bird. Jared shoots me a sharp look and tells me via our mental link to shut my trap.

"What do you mean? I intend to join you in your realm," her tiny voice says.

I start shaking my head before I can formulate a response. But when I do speak, it's charged with menace. "No way. We aren't dragging your fairy behind around our realm. Even in your fairy form, you're too obvious. Plus, how long will that human blood-stone thing last?"

My stomach twists at the mention of how the magic stone was made. I press the feeling away, glaring at Rolinda.

"That, I do not know. But surely you can lend some drops of yours to sustain me? Or perhaps I can survive in your realm, unlike the dark races?" she suggests.

"Are you willing to risk becoming a pile of sludge?" I respond.

Her small face goes ashen, and David glares at me before addressing the woman.

"I think it's best if you stay here. Glaverin and the others can keep you safe. We can meet up in the elf kingdom. That's where we'll all end up anyway, right?"

Rolinda doesn't look pleased with this idea. I can see it in her eyes—she's running through lots of scenarios that end with her becoming a puddle of black ooze.

"It's settled, then! Let's get a move on!" I say, stalking up to the car and putting my hand on it. The metal, which should be cool to the touch, feels slightly warm. My cold blood seeps it in, drinking it like a thirsty child.

Amir gives Rolinda a sad look, and I try not to read into what's going on between those two. She's a fairy. She's gotta be like . . . a hundred years older than him, right? She blows him a kiss, and I roll my eyes. My mind cannot comprehend the oddity of something like that ever happening. The truth is, Amir isn't one of us. Every time I remind him of that, he gets belligerent and offended. But at the end of the day, he can't keep coming to Qotan. He has a life to live.

"All right, everyone stand around the car where you were when we came here," David instructs. "It makes sense for only one of us to take the car, and the other to take Amir. I've got him. Are you good to bring the car, Krista?"

I nod, averting my eyes. I feel strange from all the looks David has been giving me lately. Boys are dumb.

"Okay. On the count of three," David says.

I turn toward the cave. The two elves and the dwarf are standing there watching us. Strovan nods in approval, and Glaverin holds his hands up in a form of elvish farewell. Mendory, on the other hand, stares at me, her silver irises boring into my soul. She mouths something, but I can't read lips. A shiver slips up my spine at the thought that she might be casting a spell or something. There aren't any signs of danger around, but maybe she's putting an illusion over us?

"One," I say to get the count going.

"Two," Jared says, following my lead.

"Three," we all say in unison.

OUR BLOOD FAILS US

SPOILER ALERT. NOTHING HAPPENS.

I grind my teeth together, closing my eyes and focusing on home, but the strange pull I feel is weak at best. I'm not spinning into oblivion, and Salt Lake City doesn't come into view.

"So—uh, you guys going to get us home?" Amir pipes up.

Heat burns in my chest, and I have to hold myself back from yelling at him. It should be working. The fact that it's not makes me want to break the closest thing, which in this case happens to be the passenger side window.

"I can feel the draw there, but I can't pull on it," Jared says.

David swears under his breath.

"Just like when we got back to our realm. We tried coming back to Qotan, but it didn't work. There must be a recharge time," Jared continues.

"Perfect. How stupidly *perfect*!" I shout.

Amir recoils at my outburst. More than likely, he's waiting for me to go all demon on them and start tearing things to pieces.

Come on, I have more control than that. Still, I grab a rock and chuck it off the cliff, letting a small roar escape my lips.

David gives me another one of his looks. I'm tired of those looks.

"What? Are you all calm and happy about this? Our car is on the *side of a mountain*. Even if we could get it off, we can't drive it with no gas. I don't want to sit around and wait until our dumb human blood decides that it wants to help us get back home."

"Chill out, Krista. I'm not happy about it either," David says. "But I can't *make* it work. We're just going to have to change our plans."

Jared nods solemnly.

Blood roars in my ears, and my eyes snap to where Mendory stands.

"She did it," I say. "She did something to stop us from going back."

This time I won't hold myself back. I let the purple veins roll up my arms and into my neck. I allow my skin to expand with burning pain. Something inside me is convinced that the elf oracle tampered with our teleportation magic. Why else was she whispering while staring at me like some evil witch?

Jared's mind connects to mine, my mental barrier falling away with the anger that courses through me. But I ignore him.

Krista, don't! You'll regret it! Jared cries.

At this point, my whole body has increased in size, and I'm ready to pummel some faces in. Strovan reaches behind his back and pulls out his double-edged axe, a determined look on his face. Glaverin takes a step back, his eyes wide, but he doesn't arm himself. Good. That will make it easier to toss the lot of them off the mountainside. The steep drop is a couple feet to my right. With a quick swipe of my powerful arm, I can send them flying.

"Stay back, ye demon wench! Ye ain' gonna do nothin' t' the likes o' us," Strovan roars, his deep voice echoing on the mountainside.

Amir and David join in on the throng, but none of them come toward me to stop me physically. They are too scared to get in my way. My chest aches knowing that, but it's an insignificant feeling compared to the explosive fury. A cold breeze slams into me as I continue down the path. Red strands of hair whip wildly in the wind, slapping me in the face and getting in my mouth. None of that matters.

Mendory must pay for stopping us from getting home.

Just before I reach the two elves and the dwarf, they vanish into thin air, and confusion overtakes my anger. Right then, a falcon drops in front of me, talons outstretched and ready to dig into my purple-veined arm.

Stop this now! Jared's voice echoes in my mind.

The idiotic bird wants to face my might? Cool. He can get thrown, too.

Stop, a human girl's voice echoes in my mind.

Oh . . . that's my voice.

I can't kill them. What was I thinking? I need to get rid of the pent-up anger. Without hesitation, I bend down and lift a boulder the size of my beefed-up chest. Accompanied by a monstrous roar, I toss the boulder off the edge, watching it for every second until it smashes to the ground in a cloud of stone dust and rock chips. Suddenly, the anger isn't so bad. It's there, and it's still pressing, but I can push it away. Like a balloon deflating, my body returns to normal.

"I'm—"

"Sorry" is what I mean to say, but I can't get the words out.

Jared shifts into his human form and stands between me and the elves. He could have been killed, but he did it anyway. Jared's brotherly love astounds me every time. He's always there to keep me from going over the edge. His large arms warp around me, and I feel tears stinging my eyes. Failure. Yet again. It's happened too many times over the last few days. If I can't start succeeding at something soon, I'll descend into a pit of despair, and that's not something I can easily come back from. It's happened before.

I try not to think about those days. *Ever.*

In a rippling wave of light, Mendory and the others appear again. My anger tries to flare up, but it's weaker now. I'm exhausted from transforming into my demon form. It's something I have to worry about whenever I power down. I'm vulnerable. It would be a pretty good time for a baddie to take an easy shot at me.

Jared urges me to apologize, but I still can't get the words out, no matter how hard I try.

"It is forgiven. Your nature is part of who you are," Mendory says in a monotone voice.

I'm floored. The tall and thin elf stares at me with eyes that practically glow in the falling light of day. Her husband doesn't seem as prone to forgive me. He stands with his shoulders back and his hands outstretched.

He doesn't carry a weapon, but this is an elf from Qotan. He's intimidating by nature. The demon part of me wants to challenge him—to burst forth and try to knock his head off with my fists. Fortunately, I don't give in to the temptation.

"Okay," I say.

Getting out of apologizing? I'll never complain about that. I sense Jared's disapproval. Whatever. Good thing he's not my parent . . .

Glaverin sighs and relaxes his posture.

"Yrivar guides you north. Call the griffins to lead you there. They know the way," Mendory says.

With all my past infractions, it's refreshing to have someone *not* want to talk through all the details. I can think of at least a hundred times where I was forced to "talk it out" or tell people about my feelings. Each time that was required of me, I wanted to get more violent.

Shrinks did nothing to help with my thoughts or feelings. Yet that's what every school mandated when I got into fights or said something stupid to a teacher. Those dark days are past me—for the most part—now that I'm older, but every time I'm forced to talk about my feelings, it rehashes all of that trauma.

For the first time since we met the ragtag bunch of Qotanians, I actually feel grateful. Mendory smiles, then gives me a nod. I freeze, wondering if she has the ability to read my mind, but I know that can't be true. That's the power of the fairies, not the elves. Plus, I can feel my mental walls. Even Rolinda can't get past them.

I nod and pull the statue out of my pocket, peering up at Mendory. "How do I make it work?"

Glaverin slumps like he can't believe I actually asked the question. This doesn't help me feel any better. It only makes me defensive.

"Hey, it's not like there was an instruction manual for this thing. You gave us a statue and said, 'Use it when you need it.' What did you want us to do? Read your mind?"

The elf man raises his eyebrows, then glances in Jared's direction. This manages to annoy me even more, but before I can release the words tied up in my tongue, Jared pipes up.

"There's holes in the top and bottom. It's like a whistle that you blow."

I flip the griffin statue around. A small hole is bored into the crown of the griffin's head. The stone feels cold on my lips as I press it there and blow steadily. As the air moves through, a clear and pure whistle fills my ears.

At first, my brain reacts as if it hears a painfully loud sound, but then it washes over me like a wave of pure emotion. Happiness. It's so jarring that I stumble backward to where the car sits on the hill. Mendory and Glaverin close their eyes as if they are basking in the music of the small instrument. Strovan grunts and cleans his ear with his pinky, twisting it left and right with a grimace on his face. Even though I know the whistle is magic, it still surprises me when I'm infused with artificial happiness.

As I pull the whistle away, an animal calls from a distance in the exact same pitch and tone.

"Oh—my—word," Amir whispers.

He points out over the darkening forest below. A few shadowy shapes move in formation toward us, their massive wings flapping up and down. My defensive instincts kick in, and coldness rushes through my limbs, the demon form waiting to come forth to fight.

I fill my lungs with the refreshing night air, letting them expand until they can't anymore and holding it for four beats. It's a technique that a therapist gave me years ago. As much as I wish it didn't work—I hate giving therapists satisfaction for doing things that help me—it calms me down.

Mendory turns and puts her hands up as if to welcome a friend into her embrace. The same screech pierces the night, but it's much louder now as the three griffins zoom into view. Mom used to tell us stories about griffins, saying that they had befriended the elves in Qotan. The elves even had the opportunity to ride the creatures a few times. Apparently, there's nothing like the experience of soaring the skies on such a loyal and magnificent being.

Thick hind legs thud to the ground next to me, the lion fur shaggy and orange. Front talons and claws follow. Mendory moves to one of the griffins and wraps her arms around the creature's neck, burying her face into the feathers and stroking the fur of the griffin's back. She's speaking fondly in a language I can't understand, but based on how David watches her, I know he's hearing everything she says. Glaverin and Strovan stride to the other two, greeting the animals like friends. Are these their personal griffins?

"They're your pets, aren't they?" David voices the question right as I have the thought.

Glaverin pulls back, his large palm still resting on a griffin. "They are not pets. They are companions. Trusted friends and allies who have bonded with us for life."

Amir shuffles next to me, his hand opening and closing next to his body. Glaverin notices the motion.

"Can I—" he says, raising his hand and wiggling his fingers a little.

"He wants to know if he can touch him," Jared says with amusement.

Glaverin smiles broadly and nods. "Of course. They love when you scratch the spot behind their wings."

Amir's face melts into what can only be described as a nerd's dream finally coming true. He steps up to Glaverin's griffin and places a hand on its flank. That's when he becomes a babbling fool, spouting facts about the myths of griffins and their power levels in various book series. Jared, equally as giddy, but less overtly so, steps up next to him and joins Amir in conversation. Rolinda flits over Amir's shoulder, the teen's ever-present companion.

"Why weren't they here when you found us? You've been traveling by foot this whole time when you could have been flying?" David asks.

Valid point. Though, I have to say I'm grateful they weren't here. A quick glance at the five-inch long talons tells me all I need to know about how a fight with these guys would end.

"Why did ye 'ink we'd been travelin' by foot? Griffins gotta rest, too. 'Eey've been out 'untin' and the like. Told ''em we'd call 'em back when we were ready," Strovan says.

"Right," David murmurs.

We exchange a glance, and as our eyes connect, heat flares in my face. I look away quickly. Nope. Not dealing with that right now.

"This is Jervile," Glaverin says. "He will gladly lead you to the demon kingdom."

The creature lets out a growl-roar combination, and it's enough to cause David and me to take a few steps back. Strovan and Mendory tell us the names of their griffins, too, but they sound strange—not something I'll be able to remember. Particularly because Jervile stares me right in the eyes. Even though I can't hear its thoughts, I can tell that it's sizing me up. Can it sense my demon blood?

"He is loyal to a fault. He's been a friend for nearly a hundred years," Glaverin says.

An electric energy keeps me staring at the tall and magnificent creature even though the discomfort of doing so makes me want to look away. After nearly a minute, the griffin bobs its head and turns away from me. It seems I've passed the animal's test—whatever that may be.

"You will not be able speak to his mind like I can through our bond, but he does understand your tongue."

David frowns. "You spent all that time teaching your griffin how to understand English? I mean, I'm grateful for that, but why?"

Glaverin looks thoughtful for a moment. "Humans used to live among us. They are a beloved race here in Qotan, bringing a new set of cultures and minds. Their short lives provided a sweet contrast to the longevity of our own. Now, they are not safe here. Urothar means to end their existence in Qotan by any means. This saddens me."

His silver pupils gloss over me and David, then they move to where Jared and the others are still geeking out over Jervile.

"I wish to see the day when humans can walk safely in Qotan again. I fear that it will not be soon." He pets Jervile's mane. "Have you ventured to the realm of demons before?"

I shake my head. David looks at me expectantly as if I'm about to share a bunch of secrets. And Glaverin doesn't look disappointed in my answer.

"Then, move with caution. Griffins are a friend to all light races and will ensure that you have safe passage into the realm. While Jervile doesn't enjoy traveling into the dark north, he will suffer it for you and for the sake of Qotan. Do you have light with you?"

I frown, looking at David.

"Uh—you mean like flashlights? No, we don't have any of those, but I have this—"

He flares up a fireball in his hand, the flickering yellow-red light creating dancing shadows behind everyone's backs.

Glaverin looks thoughtful, then nods.

"It will have to do. The demon realm is veiled by a deep darkness. Its citizens prefer it. The sun never shines on that land. While I've only ventured there once when the peace treaty was brought forth and signed by Krell, I can scarcely forget the unsettling nature of their world. Demons are a volatile and dangerous race, but they will not harm you unless you strike first or speak out of line. Our dealings with them, while peaceful in practice and nature, are still tenuous due to their nature. Tread carefully. They revere boldness and strength. Any show of weakness will make them lose respect for you and your cause."

David grunts. "They sound about as fun to be around as you."

He nudges my shoulder. I almost sock him in the face, but when I turn to look at him, there's a twinkle in his eye. It stirs the uncomfortable desire in me again. I look away, my anger diffusing.

"How are we supposed to do that?" I ask, folding my arms and leaning into one hip.

Glaverin waves a hand in the air. "I suspect you will know when you arrive. It is half of your heritage, after all."

What an unhelpful and annoying answer. He holds a hand up in what is clearly a farewell gesture and moves to Mendory, who is finally finishing up greeting her griffin. Strovan joins them where they stood before, and the three of them venture back to their cave without a word.

"Okay, I guess they don't have anything else to say," David comments.

The three griffins are notably different. Jervile is the largest of the three, though only slightly bigger than Mendory's griffin. His neck feathers are pure-white, blending into his orange lion's fur coat. Mendory's griffin has white neck feathers, but they are flecked with darker feathers of brown and silver. Her eyes—yes, Jared informed us that she's a girl—have a silver sheen. Strovan's griffin is smaller, but it still towers over us. His head and feathers are a light brown with deep black feathers mixed in.

Amir and Jared finally conclude their geeking.

"That sounds comforting," Amir says. "I wonder what they think about humans." He pales slightly at the thought.

"I guess we'll have to share since there are four of us and three of them," David says.

Rolinda squeaks and flits to David's face.

"*Five* of us, dragonling. How dare you forget about me?"

He gives an apologetic smile, then brushes it off. He's better than me. If she'd said that to me, I probably would have swatted her out of the air.

"Right. It looks like Amir and Rolinda will take Strovan's griffin, which is the smallest. Jared should probably ride alone on Mendory's. That leaves me and Krista."

I scoff. "No *way*, dude. I'm not sitting with you the whole way."

He narrows his eyes, clearly confused at my outburst. I can only imagine what he's thinking. Maybe he stinks or maybe I think he's gross for some reason. Honestly, I don't care what he's thinking as long as he doesn't get the wrong idea about how I feel about him.

"What did I ever do to you?" he asks.

I open my mouth but stop. All he did was look at me in fear. He didn't technically do anything wrong. The culmination of everything everyone has said to me comes back to bite me again. Sometimes I wonder if I'm the one stopping myself from having a healthy relationship with anyone.

"You know what? Don't worry about it. I'll sit with you, and we can get this whole thing over with," I say with a little too much firmness.

David sighs and walks over to Jervile.

Clenching my jaw, I walk up to the large animal and hoist myself up. Even in my non-demon form, I am relatively flexible and strong, in a wiry way. I can't stop my chest from constricting when David slips onto the griffin's back behind me. It slopes down, forcing our bodies to press together. The way my heart thunders frustrates me, but I can't stop it. I close my eyes and pray that David can't feel it in his chest.

"Let's get a move on, then!" he shouts.

I internally curse myself. My teenage hormones are going haywire right now . . .

"Don't you want to grab some things from the car first?" Jared asks.

"Oh, right. Yeah, we probably should," I say, even more frustrated at my flippant disregard for logic. I dismount, pointedly ignoring the hand that David offers me to help me down. He sighs once again, then dismounts as well.

Retrieving things out of the car is not an easy task, but we manage. The first thing Amir does, naturally, is struggle up to the trunk and pull it open. He's promptly bombarded by loads of weapons and gear that smash him to the ground. Aside from a couple bruises and a destroyed ego, he's fine. My broadsword bops him pretty good on the head, so he's got a goose egg that will undoubtedly become a purple patch in time.

David helps him up.

"You should probably just hang out over there for a minute," he says.

Amir sheepishly moves off to the side, Rolinda whispering something like, "Oh, it's okay. It happens to the best of us."

Weird.

"So, what are you going to take with you?" I ask, trying to make conversation to distract from the smell of David's cologne, which is currently burning my nostrils in a good way. It's lost some potency after all we've been through, but my enhanced senses can pick it up still.

"I want the weapon I had before in the restaurant," he says. "But I left it there. Are you bringing your monster weapon to match your mood?"

This actually makes me suppress a satisfied smile. I heft the sword up and rest it on my shoulder over the gray sweatshirt.

"You betcha. Can't be carrying around a toothpick like you."

He rolls his eyes as he moves along the side of the car, his feet slipping on the loose rocks. Just then, Jared slides loudly down the other side of the car.

"Got the wallet and keys. Hopefully it's not a problem if we just leave this here. Not sure what the orcs would do with it if they find it, but the griffins certainly can't carry it with us."

"No duh," I say, punching him in the shoulder. "But thanks for remembering the wallet. The last thing we need is a quick trip back to the human realm with no way to get ourselves food."

We stuff snacks and other provisions into our backpacks, as well as some clothes.

"I guess this is as good as it's going to get," Jared says, shrugging. He presses his lips together, eyeing me. "You doing okay, sis?"

My eyes linger on David way longer than I want them to, but I yank them away and grin at Jared.

"Just dandy. Ready to talk to my deadbeat dad and chop some orcs to pieces."

He narrows his eyes, then taps his head. "Keeping me out a lot more recently."

I keep grinning. "And that's completely on purpose. I'll let you in when I need you."

At that, I stalk over to Jervile and pull myself up again.

"Hey, Dragon Breath, let's get a move on!"

David glares at me but ends up shaking his head, his frustrated expression melting into a more exasperated one. A hand lands on my leg, and my whole body tenses, but it's just Jared looking up at me.

"Don't lock yourself up in there too much, Kris. You don't have to shoulder things alone. I can help you."

"Yeah, yeah, I know."

He holds my gaze for a moment before I shoo him away with the back of my hand. Reluctantly, he moves over to Mendory's griffin and hoists himself up. We're all delighted to see that Amir is able to get on his mount without help. It seems like ages since he first struggled to get on a crelotin's back. That was only a couple weeks ago in reality. Things have changed so much.

David slips back behind me, but my backpack and broadsword are now between us. This, I am grateful for.

"Um, any chance you can get this pack out of the way? It'll be impossible to keep myself on here with that shoving me backward," David notes.

Is he trying to get close to me again? This idea simultaneously makes me angry and annoyingly twitterpated.

"You can deal with it," I say.

"Really? What if I pitch off the back of this thing because your backpack is shoving me back so far?"

I cock my head. "Might not be too bad, honestly."

He takes a deep breath the way a parent might if they were dealing with an unruly child.

"Don't be a jerk, Krista. Just move it to your front. Please," he says.

"Well, if you're going to ask nicely," I huff, letting the shoulder strap slip off my arm. I readjust the sheathed broadsword and the backpack.

"Thanks."

After getting ourselves situated, all eyes lock onto me. Once again, I get the feeling that I'm the leader. I'm far from one, but I'm not going to argue.

"All right. Jervile, take us to the demon kingdom," I say firmly.

The griffin lets out a squawk-roar, and my skin prickles where the hairs stand on end. It's a terrifying and magnificent sound. This provides just enough distraction for me not to panic when it crouches and leaps into the air.

Powerful wings beat downward, thudding in my eardrums so heavily that I wish I had earplugs. I take one last look at the van below, hoping that no creatures will disassemble or destroy it while we're gone.

We ascend rapidly, the mountain falling away from us. A laugh escapes my mouth as I take in the scenery of the night. Amir lets out a whoop and pumps a fist in the air. Even Jared is beaming with delight. David tenses behind me and mutters something like, "Oh my! Oh my!"

His hands suddenly lock around my stomach, and I'm about to curse him and shove him off when I remember his fear.

Right, heights.

My skin chills underneath his grip, but I relent, part of my brain actually enjoying it.

"Chill out, drago! I'm sure it'll be fine," I call out.

He doesn't respond. His fear practically wafts off of him, infusing into me. He'll be fine once he gets used to it.

The griffins turn away from the mountain and fly over the trees. A cool and crisp air flows over my face and into my hair, which waves like a frantic flag behind me. David's grunts and shifts from side to side, and that's when I realize my hair is fluttering into his face.

"Any chance—you can make it—so I don't eat your hair the whole way?" he asks, eventually ducking his head and resting it on my upper back just under my neck.

I suck in a shuddering breath. My whole chest goes numb at the touch, and my brain screams at me to calm down.

"Yup. Sorry about that," I say, reaching into my pocket and work out a hair tie. "Make sure I don't fall while I do this."

"You're going to let go?" he asks.

"Oh, shut up! Do you want my hair out of your face or not? Just keep me up here."

His arms tighten around my waist, and suddenly, I can't breathe anymore. He's shaking like a leaf, and his arms glisten with sweat from his body's response to fear. I've never put my hair in a bun faster than I do now. Once I grip the griffin's fur again, I practically gasp for him to let go. His hands loosen before they slip away. The dual relief and disappointment is jarring.

"How long until we get there?" David asks shakily in my ear.

"Don't know. Unless you can speak to these guys," I reply, nodding to the griffin.

And with that, we soar north over the trees in the moonlight.

WE DESCEND INTO DARKNESS

FLYING SEEMED LIKE IT would be a nice delight the whole way.

Little did I know how hard the back of a griffin would be on my behind. The first hour was incredible, my eyes wide and my mouth open in a smile. Even the grumpiest of humans couldn't deny the amazing beauty of the Qotan landscape, with its rolling hills and trees. A vast body of water—a sea, I'm guessing—covers most of the left landscape in the distance. As the moon travels in that direction, we enjoy the view of it reflecting off the soft waves.

The beauty keeps me entertained for a bit. But then tiredness hits like a wall. My backside aches like we've been on a two-day road trip without any respite. David has calmed down a bit, but I can still feel his tense body behind me.

I wonder if he'll ever get used to the heights. It's better than wondering if I'll ever be able to sit on my bruised butt again.

"Are you doing okay back there, Dragon Breath?" I ask.

He groans. "I don't even have the energy to complain about your stupid nickname."

"You aren't shaking as much."

He grunts. "As long as I don't look—oh my—"

His head thuds down on my back once more, an electric energy waving through me.

"Don't look down, then. It's simple."

After a moment, he blessedly takes his head off my back again.

"It's easy for you to say. You're fearless. Not scared of heights. Not scared of death. You rush into fights like you've been doing it your whole life."

He's wrong, of course, but I won't admit that. There is the thrill of the fight, the demon-blooded urge to smash and crash into anything. But the girl part of my mind is terrified each time. It's not something I'd ever tell anyone, let alone him of all people.

I can curb the fear. But the failure? My jaw tightens almost unconsciously at the thought.

"It's not as easy as it looks. Mom and Bob trained us our whole lives. I went through a lot of pain to practice healing. I've been battered and beaten to make me stronger, but it doesn't make me strong enough."

I grimace. That admission was a little too much, and I can sense an obvious shift in David's emotions.

"What—what do you mean?" he asks.

I curse at myself for opening up. If certain government entities found out about how our parents treated Jared and me, I'm confident we would have been pulled from them quicker than you could say the word "taken."

My mind shifts back to one particular instance when Mom gave me a dagger and told me to draw blood. I close my eyes, willing the images away. Never once did I doubt their methods, and while a bit insane in nature, I can attest that those practices are the sole reason I can persist in fights.

A demon's ability to heal is like any power. It needs to be practiced and developed over time. Where now an injury might heal in seconds, it used to heal in hours. It still doesn't get rid of the emotional pain I feel. For years, I worked to suppress that part of me—to suppress the horrid memories of training.

I just want to be like other kids.

"It's not worth going into details. Let's just say that I couldn't always fight and heal as effectively, and I used to be terrible with a sword," I reply.

The silence that extends between us is uncomfortable—and this is coming from someone who normally *thrives* in silence. It's a great intimidation tactic when you are staring at someone. Most humans can't handle it.

I just used the term "humans" as if I'm not one myself. The thought hurts, even if it was unconscious.

"So—your parents—I mean—your mom *hurt* you to help you learn to heal better?" He sounds horrified.

"In a nutshell, yes," I reply. "Before you can let your mind go all 'horror movie' and 'gore' on me, it was mostly never that serious. She's not a bad parent. *They* are not bad parents. They just wanted us to train so that we could be ready for when we retired to Qotan."

David slumps behind me.

"My dad just wanted me to have a normal life," he says. There's pain in his voice. "I had a hard time believing anything my dad told me until my hands started lighting on fire. It's hard to deny that something's off when you spontaneously combust in anger."

I can't help but chuckle. "Oh, so your powers are tied to your emotions as well? I thought I was the only grumpy one here."

He punches my back shoulder softly. "Hey, being a teenager has its own sucky moments. I can't be happy all the time."

Silence again.

A bird caws loudly somewhere to my right. When I turn, I see a V of birds flying in the same direction as us. They are large and full of black feathers, save for their heads, which have pure-white feathers. It's not difficult to make them out in the darkness, given that I basically have night vision, but when I point them out to David, he gasps in awe.

The sun is coloring the sky with miraculous oranges and pinks. We haven't slept the whole night, but I don't feel exhausted. The thrill of this adventure and the adrenaline from everything has been keeping me alert.

Tall mountain ranges extend up ahead, filling the whole landscape. Below, the forest is thinning out, rocky crags of stone filling the spaces in between. I spot a large cat of some sort chasing after a small pack of deer. The fact that this incredibly beautiful world is somehow overlayed with earth's realm makes my mind twist. Fortunately, David pulls me back to the present conversation.

"I don't understand why my dad didn't want to teach me more than controlling my flames. If he knew that Qotan would need me, why didn't he prepare me the way your parents did you and Jared?"

Regret and bitterness are obvious in his tone. I recognize those feelings, and my own emotions boil in frustration at David's regret.

"You're complaining that your dad didn't put you through rigorous training? That he let you have a life as a teenager and make friends? You actually *have* friends. You have football. You had the opportunity to actually *live*, and now you are *complaining* about it? That's all I ever wanted! To be a normal girl. To have friends and to do makeup and to geek out over stupid girly stuff. You have Amir, for crying out loud!"

I want to shove myself back hard enough to knock him *and* myself off the griffin. Okay, no, the human side of me knows that intrusive thought is incorrect. Yet the demon inside me urges me on.

"You had it all. Just like you'll have it all here, *High Prince.*"

He tenses behind me, and I expect an outburst now. My boiling blood threatens to expand me into my demon form. I sense Jervile tense beneath my legs as if he can feel that something is going wrong. If I shift now, I'll be too heavy for him, and he may fall from the sky. Air rushes into my lungs, and I draw it in deeply, count to four before releasing it slowly.

"I'm sorry, Kris."

His response is so unexpected that I snap my mouth shut. I look down at Jervile's neck, inspecting the transition from feather to fur. I should say something. I should thank him or tell him it's okay.

But it's really not okay. The stuff I went through to make me who I am today, the training, the intensity . . . All of it was so I could come here to be sacrificed for the good of Qotan.

We were literally born to be slaughtered.

"It's whatever. I don't want to talk about it anymore."

David sighs. "Fine. But the last thing I'll say is this: I've never thought about my life that way before. Since we came to Qotan, I've felt like a thorn in everyone's side. I could hardly defend myself, and I needed you and the others to rescue me more than once. It's like I'm a child who knows nothing. At first, I resented Dad for not teaching me to fight. Now, I feel like I'll get you killed if I can't learn quickly enough."

I think back to when David first encountered the dark races in the football stadium. He looked lost and terrified—and yes, I had to save his hide more than once. But in the past few weeks, he's improved a lot.

"Don't worry about that. I'll whip you into shape," I encourage.

There's a pause.

"Thank you."

"You might not thank me when you accumulate more bruises than you can count. But when you don't die in the next fight? Then you can thank me," I say.

He chuckles.

"So, how much longer is this ride? My behind hurts!" Amir shouts from the griffin next to us. "Also, I have to pee."

Admittedly, I'm not sure how much longer the ride will be. When Glaverin told us to fly north, he didn't give any additional details. While I don't think griffins can fly as quickly as airplanes, it's been at least six or seven hours since we left. Naturally, the moment I think of this, my bladder protests that it needs to be relieved. We split the food and water bottles so all of us had something to eat along the way, but now nature is calling.

In the distance, the mountains loom taller as we approach them in the increasing sunlight.

"We may have to touch down if we don't see anything soon," Jared shouts.

Wind roars in my ears as we're buffeted by a crosswind high up in the sky.

"Can't you communicate with the griffins or something?" I ask, gesturing to Jervile with my head.

Jared frowns. "You don't think I've tried? Their thoughts are muddled and full of animalistic words that make no sense to me. I'm not *David*, for crying out loud."

How perfectly annoying. The one half-blood who can understand any language isn't the same as the half-blood who can literally read minds.

It feels like the orchestrator of all this—whoever he or she is—stands somewhere and watches us with laughter.

"Can you—like—try to say what they are saying in their heads out loud?" David asks.

The look which Jared gives David almost makes me proud. It's somewhere between a "Are you stupid?" and "Do you realize how crazy that sounds?"

"Even if I could replicate the noise, which I'm pretty sure I can't, there's no way I'd sound it out properly," he says.

"Why don't we just ask the griffin to speak out loud?" David suggests.

Right. Simple solution. I feel dumb for not thinking of it.

"Jervile! How much longer until we get there?" I holler over the wind.

The sounds which come from his beak are a mixture of grunts and terrifying screeches. My skin prickles when I hear it, images of monsters and other creatures from my childhood dreams coming back to me.

David laughs.

"Okay, that's really weird," he says. "He sounds like Josh Groban when he talks."

And suddenly, I desperately want to know what David hears in his head when other races speak.

"Well? What did he say?"

David doesn't answer me. Instead, he says something that sounds so disturbingly creepy that I resist the protective instinct of going demon. Deep growls, screeches, and groans come out in David's corrupted human tone. It sounds disturbingly like a bird and a lion being tortured.

Jervile responses once more, and David laughs.

"He says we're nearly there and wonders how our human eyes haven't beheld the wonders of the demon capital yet. He also used some pretty derogatory terms for our inability to see the important things right before us."

"Helpful," I mutter, squinting ahead at the growing mountain range.

As far as I can tell, the mountains look normal enough. If I hadn't seen the elves and dwarves and wasn't riding on a literal griffin right now, I might have thought that we were staring at the Rocky Mountains back in Salt Lake City.

Gray stone formations break up the constant greens and browns of tall pine trees. As I pan over the scenery, my eyes get caught on something—a patch of mountain that doesn't look quite right. The coloring is much darker than the rest, as if the painter of this beautiful canvas made a mistake with one of his brushstrokes.

"What's the dark smudge?" Amir calls out.

As I watch the smudge grow, an electric energy slips down my arms and legs. It looks familiar somehow, as if it's a deep darkness I've been to before in dreams. A memory appears in my mind's eye. It's an image of us standing inside the restaurant back in Utah with the light sucked inside of me, as if I was drinking it in. It produced darkness so thick that even my eyes struggled to make anything out.

The smudge turns into a recognizable cloud of darkness, like thick black smoke contained within an invisible sphere.

"That's it," I say loudly.

"How do you know?" Jared asks.

"I just—I can tell—"

And I can. There is a pull in my chest toward the dark sphere. Something—or someone—wants me to enter. Naturally, the idea of someone *wanting* me to do something immediately triggers the rebellious part of me. I want to do things because *I* want to.

"How are we supposed to get in that thing? In all the movies, I'm pretty sure you are not *supposed* to just waltz into a dark ball of death," Amir observes. "That's generally how the story starts with everyone dying and releasing some dark monster into the wild."

"This isn't a movie, Amir. That's not going to happen," David says, his tone firm.

My chest flutters again. Stupid teenage emotions . . .

"He's right," Jared adds. "Let's touch down right outside of it and make a plan before—"

"No," I say firmly. "We can fly right in."

I wish I could say why I feel calm about entering the dark sphere, but I know it'll be fine. Jervile lets out a screech-roar that makes David squirm.

"Jervile says that you're right. They don't plan to stop anywhere for any reason."

I turn to see that his face is a sheet of white. Under different circumstances, I might make fun of the jock for being this terrified. I wonder if I'm a psychopath for not wanting to tug on Jervile's neck feathers to turn him around and get us out of here.

My ears roar as blood rushes there, the demon part of me activating in an almost excitable way. What? It isn't the normal sensation I get when I feel the demon side of me waking up.

"It'll be fine," I say calmly. "The demons signed a treaty with the light races to join forces against Urothar and the other dark races. If that holds true, then we really have nothing to worry about."

"*If* that holds true," Jared reiterates, grimacing. "I don't like working with 'ifs.'"

And he doesn't. While he's incredibly able to deal with my nonsense and emotional outbursts, one might think that he's like that in all unknown situations. Not Jared. He likes things done a specific way. Any variance from the norm makes him get all jittery. He'll never show that on the outside, but we've connected minds. I can tell what goes on under the surface. Even now, as I look over at him, I can see his large hands fiddling with the feathers on the griffin's back. Sometimes I need to be the one to tell *him* to calm down.

My gaze returns to the dark sphere that protrudes from the side of the mountain. It covers a large part of the ground beneath the slope as well.

I think back to the things Mom told me about the races in Qotan. Hundreds of years ago, the dark races rose up in rebellion against the high kingdom of Dranith, demanding that they take control of Qotan. At that time, the demons and the Sirens were notably part of the dark race regime. The struggle was so intense that thousands died in that war. Ultimately, the dragons led the light races to victory and condemned the orc king at the time to death.

I don't recall his name, but I have a suspicion that he was related to Urothar. Fast forward a few hundred years, after the light races exacted control and forced a treatise on the dark races, Urothar took control. That's when a random seer lady predicted the fall of the high kingdom of Dranith and the fall of light races as a whole.

That's where we come in. When the prophecy was supposedly laid out, the demon king and Siren queen shirked their alliance with the dark races and joined the light races. Mom still doesn't know what their reasoning was, but she was there when it happened. And naturally, I was conceived to be a part of this dumb prophecy.

Here we are, stuck in this situation.

"They'll hold to the alliance. I'm living proof of that. They wouldn't dare go back on their pact, especially when I'm here with you. Let's just hope they aren't a 'shoot first and ask questions later' type of race."

Amir looks terrified. "Why did you have to mention that as an option? Now I can't help but feel like there is an arrow aimed at my chest."

I bite my lip. If my declaration of demon alliance is rejected, I'm going to feel stupid. I have to trust the things my mom told me about my dad. He has a temper, but he never hurts those who are innocent or undeserving of violence.

My stomach lurches as Jervile starts to descend, the other griffins following suit. David grunts, leaning closer to me and making my back skin flare up from the heat of his body. The air takes on a colder tinge, like we've moved from spring into the throng of fall, preparing to enter winter. A shiver runs up my spine, but it's not from the chill.

Entering the sphere of darkness isn't what I expect it to be. It's like being on an airplane as it flies through clouds—only the clouds are thicker and much darker. The mountain landscape around us fades away slowly until it's a dull gray color and almost invisible. The air thickens and smells musty, like I've entered a basement that hasn't been cleaned in years. Just as the landscape fully disappears into the darkness, a flare of fire explodes next to my head. I gasp and lean forward, expecting it to slam into me, but David curses.

"Sorry! I didn't mean to do that!" he hisses, his teeth clenched. "I just—hate this darkness. It reminds me all too much of when you sucked the light away at the restaurant."

When I'd pulled the light into me, it felt both wrong *and* right at the same time. My human mind seeking the light. My demon blood seeking the dark. Why can I see David's firelight when I wasn't able to in the restaurant?

Abruptly, my eyes catch purple flecks of light scattered below us in the darkness.

"Something's down there," I say.

"Sis, I don't see a thing," Jared says. "What are you going on about?"

Amir shivers. "I've been here for two seconds, and I already hate it. When can we get out?"

"Move closer to us, guys, so we're all in the firelight," David suggests.

"Uh—this thing doesn't have a steering wheel, Dave. I think you're going to have to do it."

David sighs, likely realizing the fallacy of his suggestion. A series of growls and squawks emit from his mouth, and I grimace. It honestly sounds disgusting to my ears. The two griffins glide inward, close enough that they are bathed in the light of the fireball.

"We're getting close. I can tell," I say.

The specks of purple are now the size of my fist as we descend rapidly.

"I still don't see anything," Amir complains.

David leans into me one more time, attempting to get a better look. I shout mentally at my heart to hold a constant beat. It doesn't listen.

"No, wait. I can see them, too. They're dim, but there's purple lights or something down there."

He barely sees them now? Yet again, I'm grateful for my ability to see within the darkness effectively. I can't see in the pitch-black, but all it takes is the tiniest bit of light—even a pinprick—and I can see everything.

Suddenly, the purple lights flourish and expand.

A massive network of paths and buildings appears out of nowhere. Wrapped around the network is a tall black stone wall made of huge bricks. Set along the top of the wall are massive beings, some looming at least twice or three times my human height. My skin chills at seeing them, but it's not from fright.

Am I . . . pleased?

Demons. Huge purple-skinned behemoths wield axes and bows with arrows the length of my whole body, and they watch at the wall like sentinels. Jervile flaps his wings, pulling us down. I grip his feathers to keep from falling off, and David's arms tighten around my waist again.

"Sorry," he mumbles.

But I'm not paying attention to him.

Beyond the walls, the network of buildings, and the black stone streets, there's a huge palace. Three huge black stone cylinders are stacked on each other like a cake, each tier shrinking a bit as they move upward. Large spikes extend in a circle along each of the tiers, creating a gothic look that matches the darkness of its surroundings.

Purple spheres of light are fixed along the edges like strange flaming lamps. I don't have much time to inspect it before the edge of the wall covers the view.

Jervile slows his descent, air buffeting our faces. The blast knocks pebbles and dust every which way. We land in front of two towering metal gates. Like the stone, it's made from a dark medium that makes it look all black. The gates extend upward five times my height, a monster's maw ready to consume us teens.

"I don't want to think about why those gates are so large," Amir says, leaning into his griffin.

David lets go of my waist and puts a hand on my shoulder. He leans forward and whispers, "So, now what? Do we just knock?"

At first, I find it weird that he's whispering to me, but then, I realize why. It's eerily silent. Considering we came from flying high above where we could see and hear a lot, it's striking to hear nothing. No wind blows into my ears. No animals call or cry out in the distance. The only sounds are the griffins' claws scuffing on the dirt road and our breathing. In fact, there's no sign of even a single demon standing guard on this side of the gate.

"I guess they aren't used to getting guests," Jared surmises. "Any ideas on what we do now?"

He's looking at me with his eyebrows raised. This ultimately leads the others to do the same thing.

"I hate this place," Rolinda says. "There's no light anywhere. It's gross and smells funny. Why did you convince me to come along with you, human?"

Amir looks incredulous as the small orb of light flits into the backpack he has slung on his back. David and I exchange looks of amusement.

"Did the fairy seriously just blame her tagging along on me?" Amir murmurs.

Jared holds back a laugh. "You didn't try to stop her if I recall."

Amir rolls his eyes and gestures wildly to the gate. "Can we get back to the task at hand? What are we supposed to do about those gates? I'm guessing the griffins didn't take us over the wall for a reason."

"Most likely to avoid us getting skewered by arrows or spears. There's a fair amount of demon guards up above," I say.

"Wait, you could see them?" David asks. "I can barely see anything."

I glance up at the gate, noting a few glowing purple stones. They light up the whole area easily for my eyes. David's flickering fire reflects in the shiny metal of the gates. It's odd to think that they couldn't see what I witnessed as we flew down. That means they didn't see the palace. Their nervousness is founded in the fact that they can't see anything. Mine is rooted in the fact that I'm about to see my dad—the dad who conceived me as a sacrifice for this world, then promptly sent me away.

The tugging sensation in my gut draws me forward to the gate. My demon blood sings in my veins, cold energy urging me to let it take over, to pull me into the version that belongs in this dark place. Somehow, I know what I have to do . . .

Slipping off the side, I ignore the warnings of "Be careful" from the others. I'm too focused on the black shininess of the metal gate. My feet crunch on the dirt, the sound not echoing even in the silence.

"Krista, please be careful," Jared says again.

I turn to look at him, his expression full of concern. You know who else looks concerned? David.

Butterflies erupt in my stomach as I make eye contact with him, but I grimace and glare at him. He rolls his eyes. It's for the best anyway because I know what I have to do next. I return to the gate and place my hand there. It's like ice against my skin. I don't gasp or pull away. Instead, I focus on the tingling of my blood. The demon wants to be free.

For the first time in my life, I let it happen despite the complete absence of any anger or intense emotion. The pain of my skin expanding consumes me, but this time, I embrace it. I watch as my fingers go from skinny to fat sausages, purple veins running through them. My wrists double in size, along with my forearms and biceps.

I check myself, waiting for the heat of anger or the urge to kill someone. It's there, deep within me, but it isn't ruling me. I've transformed on demand without rage forcing itself into my world.

I almost *like* the feeling.

The human part of me can't accept this. I'm just a teenage girl. I can't live in this form and have a normal life.

"By Selenti's might. It can't be," a deep voice rumbles in the air. It vibrates through the wall and into my arm, connecting with my brain and ears.

Fear stirs inside of me, accompanied by a bit of anger at why this demon isn't showing itself. I know why I'm here. They should know why I'm here, too. I have nothing to be scared of.

"I've come to speak to my father. The king of demons," I say with my firm and deepened tone.

"So be it. Come, daughter of darkness."

The voice rumbles with every part of my being, resonating in my mind as vibrations slip through the gate.

A loud crack splits the silent air, still absent of the echo that feels natural. Then, it opens slowly, the hinges squealing so loudly that I wonder how many years it has been since they last opened.

"I guess they think it's okay to let us in?" Amir says, cowering once again on his griffin.

Despite being in my demon form, I laugh. Once again, something I've never experienced or heard before. This is new for me. When the demon takes over, I don't feel anything but intense anger and frustration.

I turn to my friends, pointedly ignoring David's face.

Jervile throws his head back, saying something in its language, and David grimaces. "It's the end of the line for us. The griffins say they won't go any farther. Everyone off."

With some grumblings, the others dismount, their feet crunching loudly. Once we've moved into a small group away from the creatures, they toss their wings out, launching themselves in the air with one final farewell caw.

Amir gulps. "Into the belly of the beast, then."

"Let's start a war, why don't we?" I say, a smile creeping up on my face.

WE GET IN A FIGHT WITH SOME DEMONS

I FEEL ENTIRELY AT ease and completely comfortable. It's such an unusual feeling that I don't know what to do with myself. The anger still hasn't come, but I've been in my demon form for at least ten minutes now. The beings before me look the same as me, except that my skin is paler and humanlike. For the first time in my life, I don't feel like a purple-veined freak.

We stand inside the large gates, which close with a massive clang. David and the others hover close to me like I'm the nucleus of our little traveling band. Rolinda mutters something that sounds like a prayer. Based on what David has told me about her, she isn't fond of demons—at all.

Half a dozen large demons stand in a semicircle, blocking us from moving farther into the city. Their squat one-story buildings are organized in a way that doesn't make sense to the human side of me. Each structure is made from black stone, which reflects the purple lamps that line the twisting streets. My eyes allow me to see everything perfectly, but I suspect that my friends can't make out what it looks like.

"So, what are we doing?" David whispers in my ear.

He's standing close to me, and it's encouraging. His past horrific expressions have led me to believe that he'd never feel comfortable being this close to me in my demon form. I press those thoughts away, focusing instead on the group of demons who block our way.

They are all enormous, standing half a body taller than me, though one of them is nearly twice my height. Their purple-tinged skin is covered with thick, dark purple veins, and their eyes are pure black. Horns, formed into all different shapes and sizes, protrude from their scalps like deformed plants seeking sunlight. Though most of them are staring at me directly, one of them scans our group silently.

My anger finally manifests itself. It's both irritating and comforting. I thought for a moment I was learning to control my emotions, but I suspect it's just this place.

"Take us to my father," I say firmly.

The demons don't move.

"What the—?" Amir squeaks. "Krista's gone off the wall. What is she saying?"

I frown, confused at his comment. I didn't do anything differently, and I was speaking English just the same way.

"Abandoned daughter of Krell, you were not to return to this land until you were grown. You are not allowed here—especially with the company you currently keep," one of the demons says.

His mouth is moving in ways that don't match the words he's saying. It's strange, so I bare my teeth like a dog. Somehow, this seems like the right reaction.

"My father doesn't get to dictate when I come back. I was drawn here by my blood. It's not like I want to be here anyway. I'd rather be back on earth finding the next half-blood, but instead, I have to convince my deadbeat dad to help the elves so the whole of Qotan doesn't fall into ruin," I say, heat flaring in my cold-blooded chest. "Take—me—to—him—*now*!"

I punctuate the final statement to make my point clear. It's probably unwise to talk this way to a bunch of demons who could probably snap my head off. But for some reason, I feel like I have power over them. To further my influence, I flare my intimidation aura, casting it upon the demons blocking the way.

They shuffle, and a couple of them actually take a step back.

"Yes. We will take you to him," the nearest of the demons says.

He's shirtless, his pecs and abs accentuated by the purple veins running through them. His round head is bald, the veins easily visible. The other five demons are a mixture of male and female—some with long hair and some with short and stubby hair. While the leader wears no clothing other than pants made from black cloth, the others wear robes over their gigantic frames. They're like bodybuilder monks—some with their hoods up. I can't help but wonder at their choice of fashion. I can't judge them for it, considering I always wear baggy sweats to account for my growth in demon form.

Human-form me actually has a decent appearance, with my long red hair and sharp facial features. I'm slender, like the cheerleaders. Guys have, on occasion, tried to ask me out despite their fear of talking to me. It's usually my unfriendly demeanor that turns them away quickly. Ultimately, I focus on the fact that these experiences have made me stronger, and I pull on this confidence now as I stand up straight and nod resolutely at the closest demon.

When they don't move immediately, I say, "Let's go, then."

"You will follow closely. Do not touch anything, and do not talk to anyone," he says, addressing my companions.

David puts up his hands and responds, "Not a problem. Our friends don't speak your language."

I furrow my brow. It's then that I realize why Amir made the comment earlier. We haven't been speaking in English this whole time. Something tickles the back of my mind—an awareness that wasn't there before.

If this is what David experiences every time he translates, then I can understand why it's hard for him to remember to translate to our friends. I can only imagine what they think I'm saying since they are hearing some odd language.

"Tell your human friend, the fairy mutt and your fairy pet," the demon says, bearing his teeth.

I take a step forward, my defensive instinct flaring up.

"Hold your tongue, demon. That's my brother you are talking about," I snarl, my intimidation aura flinging out of me with everything I've got. "Besides, the *fairy* mutt you are talking about can understand everything you are saying. He reads minds, or do you not know the power of the fairies?"

Once again, I'm surprised when he slumps, his eyes wide as he cowers slightly.

"Yes, Majesty," he says. "Forgive me. I recall their power. But know that even your bloodline and status cannot save them from being tortured in our dungeons for any insolence."

I narrow my eyes. If it came to a fight, I'm not convinced I'd come out on top. The demon part of me thinks that I could take them all and crush them under my fists, except their fists are much bigger than mine.

David turns and quietly explains what has been happening and what we have to do. I keep my body turned toward the demons, holding my intimidation aura up in the hopes that it will keep anything bad from happening to my friends.

"We go," the demon says in a gravelly and thickly accented voice.

"What did he just say?" Amir asks. "He sounds like he just woke up with a sore throat and needs a big drink of water."

I roll my eyes, facing him and shaking my head.

"He wants us to follow him."

My deep voice grates against my ears, but compared to the other demons' voices, it's not so bad. A flare of something positive enters my stomach, but I don't let myself dwell on it. We are in a turbulent situation right now.

The demons either don't understand our English or they don't care what we're saying, for they turn one by one and move up the narrow road. It appears to be made from the same shiny stone material that all the buildings are, making it difficult to track when the pathway ends and the wall of a building begins.

A pressure enters my mind, and I sense that Jared is trying to communicate with me. With my turbulent emotions, I fear letting him in, especially since he has a tendency to poke around places he's not supposed to. I relent quickly, though, and he enters my thoughts.

It's easier to talk about things in our minds where they can't hear us.

Do you think this is a good idea? They don't seem thrilled that we're coming along with you, he says.

Indignation flows through the link, and I press back.

If they don't like it, then they can meet the business end of my fist.

Jared stifles a smile, but through the link, he accidentally lets some of his fear trickle through. In reality, these demons are much bigger than me. Yet, for some reason, I'm not even the slightest bit scared. The only thing I sense within myself is an intense curiosity—a draw forward that drowns out any other emotion. The absence of deep anger strikes me again. Never before have I entered this form without having first been provoked.

It feels more natural than I expected.

I stalk forward, the others funneling in behind me. David makes a point to let Jared and Amir in front of him so that he can be in the rear. The protective instinct both annoys me and endears me to him. He really is the perfect boy, isn't he?

Deciding that it's not worth blowing up over when we're already in a precarious situation, I turn forward and follow the demons. The steady purple torches cast eerie shadows on the twisting structures and pathways. The illumination serves to make this place seem even more unnatural. It's not like they have electricity. Qotan is not advanced by any means.

My weight naturally tilts forward as we begin climbing the steep road leading up to the spiked palace at the center of the city. More demons come out of the buildings as we walk, most of them taller and bigger than me. Their hair is various shades of reds, purples, and grays. Their purple skin soaks in the torch light, somehow deepening the shade. They stare at me with wide pure-black eyes, and some of the smaller ones even point at me, murmuring things that I can't hear.

Even though I'm similar, I'm not the same. My skin is human, pale and pasty compared to their purple. The only thing that matches in color are my eyes, my hair, and the veins that carry the same cold blood. I can never be fully like them.

It's another reminder of how us half-bloods are in limbo, perpetually not a part of either world.

I wish it didn't sting so much.

Focusing on the path ahead, I press the thoughts out of my mind and instead focus on the details of my surroundings. My eyes lock onto a family of demons.

It dawns on me that the smaller ones are the children—or however demons refer to their young. Their hair isn't as grown, and their horns are shorter, too. As we pass one of the kids with dark pink hair and horns about the length of my palm, she shies away and enters the arms of a demon twice her size.

Even this child is as tall as Jared.

Yeah, it's freaking me out that I'm not the tallest one around. How long does it take to get used to being the runt? he asks me.

I force annoyance through our bond. My emotional eye roll.

Don't like being humbled, do you? I think with a smirk.

He shakes his head.

"They're going to kill me," Rolinda says with a shaky voice. "Demons and fairies don't get along, and it's a wonder why. They're thinking about how they can clip my wings and hang me up to laugh at me!"

Amir says something about how she's being ridiculous because honestly, the notion is dumb. Demons wouldn't really think that, would they? I almost respond to tell her to stop being dramatic when Jared shakes his head at me.

Oh, right. She can literally read minds. That must be what they are thinking.

The glowing orb of a fairy descends beneath Amir's shirt and nestles in his armpit. He squirms and tries to pry her out, but she doesn't budge. At this point, I'm just glad that she's attached to him and not me. I couldn't handle that.

I stare ahead, tracking where the group of demons leads us. They turn around a bend in the black stone road, disappearing behind a house. I can feel all eyes on me specifically. Those black eyes bore into my soul.

Every once in a while, I can sense one of them testing me with their intimidation aura. Though it's the first time I've ever been hit with the power, it feels familiar. The human girl in me shrinks in fear, trembling at the demon-created terror. She's small and weak and not entirely in control. I respond with a wave of my own intimidation, the energy radiating out of me in waves that wash over the onlookers. A demon child gasps and rushes into the house next to me. At the same time, the aura disappears.

Guilt enters my chest, but I force that away. I've done nothing wrong. Sure, it was just a kid, but he started it. The two lumbering demon adults in front of that particular ebony house glare at me. I expect for a moment that they'll attack me—or at least slam me with their intimidation aura—but they don't. I'm not sure why they don't. If it was my kid, I'd have probably attacked them outright.

Abruptly, something massive and shiny comes at my head. If it wasn't for my demon instincts and copious amounts of training, I'm sure it would have taken my head clean off. I duck and roll forward. In the same motion, I reach behind my back and grip the handle of the broadsword. With a quick tug, I roll upward with the sword in my hand.

Two demons, one with light gray hair and another with deep black hair, stand with their teeth bared and their eyes wild.

"No putrid human dares enter the halls of Etherek. Human flesh is not welcome within our walls," the gray-haired one spits.

I recognize these two as the demons who were leading the group. The others are nowhere to be seen. Either they were overwhelmed or they went to wash their hands of what these two demons very clearly want to do with us.

The black-haired demon's eyes go wide, and I'm slammed with his aura so strongly that it makes me step back. Still, I can overcome the effects of the artificial fear and return with my own wave of emotion.

Krista, Jared says weakly, and I make the mistake of turning to look at him.

His eyes are wild, and he cowers in place. Amir and David are shaking, too, but their bodies are frozen, and their faces hold pure terror.

This lights a fire in my soul. Anger explodes internally, the heat stoking so hot that all conscious thought is lost in instinct. I snarl at the two demons, who look very surprised that I haven't succumbed to their mental attack.

"Let my friends go!" I spit.

The gray-haired demon bares her teeth and points a long spear at me.

"Your vermin human friends aren't fit to be anything but food for the darangkin. You will die alongside them for your human corruption," she hisses.

Then, she leaps.

She's much larger than me, and I can see her muscles rippling with a strength that I undoubtedly could never match. One blow will shred me. Even my demon healing might not save me from taking such a powerful hit to the skull.

In the end, it doesn't matter because I'm much faster. Rather than back away, I step into her swing, ducking under it so that her spear swishes overhead, the tip connecting with the black stone of the house behind me. It clacks off of it harmlessly.

I don't hesitate. If I do, my friends could die. The tip of my broadsword enters her stomach and slips through easily, the thickness of her flesh being the only thing that keeps my weapon from going all the way through. Her eyes spasm, and she shrieks in pain.

Her companion takes a swing, and this time, I don't have the ability to dodge it *and* pull my sword free. I leave it embedded in the demon and duck away, and the spear swishes dangerously close to my head. Weaponless, and now a little desperate, I rush toward him ready to tackle him to the ground. The one disadvantage of spears is that they aren't great for close combat. His mouth drops open, and he shouts something in his garbled language.

My shoulder connects with his chest, and he grunts as we tumble to the stone pathway in a heap. As we roll, I see that my friends have started moving again. I can't keep my intimidation aura on when I'm distracted by fighting. It's comforting to know that normal demons can't either.

My blood burns in my body as I continue to wrestle with the large demon. His powerful arms press me away, and I start to lose the fight. He's much stronger than I am, and it shows as he tosses me to the side. I fly through the air and into the building closest to us. Something cracks in my back and my shoulder as I collide with the hard stone, and my vision blurs. I have to shake my head to keep from passing out.

The other demon, my sword still planted in her gut, stands with her teeth bared. Her foot comes down, landing a kick in my side. I gasp, pain consuming me momentarily before I roll away and get to my knees.

"Your weakness shows, human filth!" she says, gripping the broadsword and tearing it free. She winces and falls to her knee for a few seconds. It gives me satisfaction to see that I've hurt her and put up a good fight. The wound in her stomach starts closing rapidly, the flood of purple blood stanching itself as her body heals. The male demon I tackled is on his feet again, and he holds his spearhead at my chest.

"Death is your only future, vermin," he growls.

I can sense my demon blood healing me. My shoulder pops back into place, and I grit my teeth. Bones knit together just as fast as I witnessed this demon's healing.

With a vicious roar, he dives at me. A torrent of flames washes over him, the heat singeing my eyebrows and making my cheeks sting. The demonic roar that comes from the onslaught chills my bones, but it also excites me. When the flames clear, the demon is cursing in his guttural language.

A hand rests on my shoulder, and I flinch, ready to sock whoever's touching me.

But my gaze is met with soft green eyes and raggedy brown hair. Human Krista sighs in twitterpated glory, and demon me resists the urge to crush him.

"Get up," David says..

His whole body is covered with red scales. In all honesty, he looks a bit terrifying. That pretty face all marred up with dragon skin.

And yet my stomach still fills with butterflies. For a moment, the directional anger that drives me spins in circles, the teenage girl hormones making me lose the ability to think. A roaring sounds in my right ear, and my focus snaps back into place.

"Stay out of my way," I instruct with my deepened demon voice.

David scoffs. "'Thank you' is a more appropriate response."

I would roll my eyes, but the demons bear down on us again. My broadsword flies through the air to block the spear that's directed at my head. When our weapons collide, I feel the brute strength of the demon. Yes, he's stronger than me, but with gritted teeth, I manage to keep him at bay.

David attempts to parry the spear that comes at his chest, but he's nowhere near strong enough to take it. The blow throws him off his feet, and he tumbles to the ground with a gasp. With my own roar of indignation, I shove with all my might. The demon I'm fighting is forced to shuffle backward, and I take the moment to move in, my speed giving me the advantage I need. My broadsword slices into his stomach, and he cries out in pain.

Jared now joins the fight, transforming into a lion. His golden mane flicks through the air as his paw connects with the demon's face. Claws rake against purple flesh, and the she-demon screams. Her fist slams into Jared's chest, and he grunts, flying twenty feet and slamming into a building.

David's back on his feet at this point, flicking his sword left and right. I'm impressed with his form, even if it's not perfect. The only problem is that these moves are better used against an opponent who isn't three times as strong as you—and one that's not using a spear. David takes the spear tip to the chest and flies backward to join Jared on the ground. My brother's body ripples and returns to his human form.

My chest tightens, and my mouth runs dry. Vision turning red, I sense the defensive part of me activate. All human rationalization and thought are swept away in a frenzy. I don't think, I just move. I bear down on the she-demon so quickly that she hardly has time to react. The broadsword is through her chest in a flash. Her mouth falls open, revealing her sharp yellow teeth before she groans and collapses.

Pain erupts in my stomach, and I pitch forward. When I look down, I see a spearhead sprouting from inside me. The human part of me comes back alive, and it's full of panic. Purple blood flows over the spear and drips on the black stones.

A force shoves me to the right, and I stumble, but I don't fall. Then a blast of heat washes over my back, and I shy away, my icey skin rejecting the inferno that's exploding behind me.

David's fire disappears quickly, and the charred remains of the demons who attacked us is all that's left.

"Jared," I gasp as I fall to my knees.

David curses and runs to my side. "He's fine—he's just knocked out—oh my—"

His face pales, and he puts the back of his hand to his mouth. "You're bleeding really bad."

I nod as if this is a normal piece of news that I would get on any day. Demons watch us from the doorways of their darkened homes. When my eyes glaze over them, they look away from us as if they are ashamed. A few still watch me with interest. One of them even looks a little impressed, most likely thinking that this vermin demon shouldn't have lived through that. I bare my teeth at him, and he grins back.

The spear is heavy in my gut, and I know we have to yank it out, or I won't make it.

"Pull—it out—now," I grit out through clenched teeth.

David goes from pale to green. "Are you kidding me? I'm not going to—"

"Pull it out!" I plead, shouting at him.

David recoils, but his jaw hardens. I shouldn't have yelled, but he's being dumb. Just because his dad didn't teach him basic first aid like our parents doesn't mean he gets off easy. My demon blood is trying to heal the wound, but it's struggling to keep up with the spear's damage. Even though I'll be able to heal, my energy will be fully expended. If another demon decides to get bold and attack us like these two did, then we're done for.

"I'm sorry," David whispers.

I feel a tug on the spear, and I throw my head back, a visceral roar escaping my mouth. David swears again, but it's done as quickly as it started. The spear clatters to the stone pathway. It's a hollow sound, almost musical alongside the pounding of my heartbeat in my ears. The untamed anger fades, and I know it will force me back into my human form—at least that's what it is supposed to do. Fortunately, when the anger diminishes, I don't turn back into my human self. It's not like I can't heal when I'm out of my demon form, it's just a lot more efficient when I stay in it.

Are you okay? You can't die on me, Kris, Jared's voice echoes in my mind.

The panic in his mental tone makes me smile. Despite how I've treated him all these years, and despite him having to put up with me, he loves me. And as much as I will never admit it, I love him, too, even if he's not really my brother.

I'll live. Are you alright yourself? I return.

His relief comes through the mental link, then it quickly turns to pain.

Aside from broken ribs? Sure.

Even after all this, I can't help but laugh.

"What are you laughing at? You just had a spear shoved inside you," David says, still hovering behind me.

"Nothing. Don't worry about it."

He huffs, upset. "You sound like a raging lunatic."

"Demon. Lunatic. Tomato. Tomah-to."

I'm struck once again by the fact that I'm still in my demon form with no apparent anger. Energy seeps out of my soul as the wound heals. Blood stops flowing, and the immense pain dissipates until only a dull ache remains.

"The other demons that were guiding us, where are they?" I ask.

David shrugs. "My guess is that they're hiding like spineless dogs. This was clearly planned. They probably didn't want to get involved. How noble of them."

Rage stokes up in me once more. Nope. I can't let it catch hold. Not right now. Even if I wanted to fight them, I know I couldn't without a good rest.

The sound of large wings beating against the air draws my attention up. I tense, raising my eyes to see what evil is descending upon us now. An electric energy raises the hairs on my arms as I spot three enormous black creatures coming in our direction. Demons murmur and cry out around us. Whatever is coming, they clearly know what it is.

"That doesn't sound good," David says.

"He's coming!" Jared shuffles over to us, his hand wrapped around his midsection to support himself. Amir rushes over, too, cowering behind me. Seeing Amir makes me feel guilty. During that fight, I'd completely forgotten about him and Rolinda. She's twittering something in her high voice under his shirt, but I can't quite understand her. Something about "brutes" and "not fit for the light race pact." In the aftermath of my first real fight with a full-blooded demon, I'm inclined to agree with her. Before this, her disdain for demons was just annoying.

Now, I can understand why she feels that way.

We knit ourselves together in a tight group, David and myself in the front, and my injured brother and Amir in the back. I look over at David. Even with our differences, I can't help but feel relief that I'm not the only one here. I'm getting tired of being the one who has to step up and defend the others with reckless abandon. For the first time in a long time, I don't feel completely alone.

David meets my gaze and gives me a nod. Then, he does something I'm not even close to ready for.

He grabs my hand.

Butterflies come to life in droves in my stomach, and I swear my blood pressure doubles. I stop breathing. My brain screams at me to pull away while another part of me is filled with joy. It's such an exhausting feeling, on top of the literal mortal wound I just healed from, but I'm frozen and can't pull away from him.

"Whatever this is, we'll face it together," he says.

"It's the demon king. He's heard the disturbance and is coming to find out what's going on," Jared says.

Dozens of demons around us angled their gaze upward. As usual, Jared is sourcing his information from their minds. How unlucky of me to be born with half-blood powers. While Jared is gallivanting around as a gecko and reading everyone's minds,

I'm trying not to hulk out and smash someone's face in. Oh, and I can suck light away from spaces. I'm a kid's worst nightmare.

The creatures descend quickly, their powerful legs slamming into the stone. They have doglike bodies and heads. For all intents and purposes, they look like short-haired black dogs, except with humongous bat wings that sprout from their backs. And they have no eyes or eye sockets. Instead, there is furred flesh over where their eyes should be. It's so unsettling that I force my gaze away. The demon in the front slips down from his mount, his heavy demon body thudding on the stone.

"What in heaven's name are those?" Amir whimpers.

Rolinda speaks up from under his shirt. "Darangkin. The horrific mounts of the demonkind. They're the most unnatural and dark creatures I've ever laid eyes on. They feast off the fears of their enemies, as well as magic of any kind. Oh, I'm a flitting meal for them! They can sense me! I can hear it in their minds. Don't let them near me. Please!"

I shush her, and she falls silent. In all, there are three darangkin with three demons atop them. The demon at the front of the pack is the largest by far. His vibrant red hair falls over his shoulders in waves, and his horns are mighty and curved upward. With powerful shoulders and a bare chest, he wears nothing but leather pants.

But the most terrifying part of all? He's familiar. He looks kind of like me.

David steps back, his eyes becoming saucers. His hand pulls out of my own, leaving me with both relief and disappointment. "It's—you. I—I know you."

I frown, looking at my friend. "You recognize this guy?"

The demon king's eyebrows furrow, and he glares at me.

"Yes, I saw him just before Rolinda took Amir and I through the traitor's curtain."

The demon king sizes David up with his black eyes, then nods.

"It was but an aspect of my soul sent forth to determine the true heir to the high throne. I sensed my kin entering this world and wished to investigate her. However, when I searched, I found *you*—a more apt subject of interest," the demon king says.

I tense. Teenage angst mixes with the awkward fact that I'm standing before my dad, the very man who abandoned me to earth. Now he's just admitted that David was more interesting to watch over than me.

"You knew I was here, and you didn't try to help us? Best dad award goes to—you," I say with disdain.

His dark eyes train on me. "Krell. My name is Krell. I sense that, as expected, your volatile human emotion rules your every word and decision."

Did he just blame my human half for my outbursts? I open my mouth to give him a piece of my mind, but he speaks over me before I can.

"What has happened?" he asks, pointing to the two dead demons lying on the ground.

This only serves to flare my anger even more.

"Are you *kidding me* right now? Your daughter, who you sent away to another realm to keep safe, just came back home, and you don't care one bit? Why did you have me if you didn't want me!?"

Tears well in my eyes. I know I'm being unreasonable, but the burning inside me doesn't care. I grit my teeth to ensure that no tears fall. I'm strong enough. I won't cry in front of him. For some reason, I feel like I need to prove something—prove that I'm not a human ruled completely by emotions. What I feel inside paints a different picture.

Krell inspects me from head to toe.

"There is time to discuss your grievances later. For now, tell me what has happened."

I deflate inside. Whatever I was expecting from my father, this was not it. With how often my anger issues get out of control and cause me to shift into demon form, I just assumed my lack of composure was inherited from him. All along, I blamed my demon side for my inability to control my emotions. I shouted at the demon king himself, and the only sense I'm getting from the man is apathy.

Pure apathy.

"It is against the demon codes and our pact with the light races for anyone within the conchords to slay a demon. You've broken the code, dragonling," he says, his eyes locking on David.

David shrinks back for a moment before his eyes narrow, and he steps forward again. Krell looms above him, easily twice his height and at least three times his weight. I have to give credit to the football star for his gall.

"Is there anything in your *pact* that says we can't defend ourselves? Your demon subjects threw the first fist. They tried to kill Kris, and I stepped in to save her. Maybe you should keep a better watch on your own," David replies boldly.

There, that has to get the guy riled up. Surely he's about to explode and cut us to pieces. I crouch slightly, allowing the burning heat to fuel my fight instinct and prepare me for a battle.

Instead, Krell does nothing. His face remains impassive as he scans David up and down. He then turns to a small group of demons that have gathered and bowed their heads in reverence.

"Is this true?" he inquires.

I recognize the demon he addresses. It's one of the door greeters who disappeared around the bend before we got attacked. He bows his head low and speaks in a gravelly tone. A pressure in my head and the confused groan of Amir indicate that he's not speaking English anymore.

"Yes, it is true. I regret to say that I, knowing the intentions of Illgrit and Troit, removed myself from the situation," he says.

Krell regards him quietly before raising his hand.

"Thank you for your honesty. In direct violation of the con-chords of the light, you will now die for your mistake, along with the others who fled and did not raise a hand in support of the heir of the demon, dragon, and fairy thrones," he states in a flat tone.

My mouth falls open. Did he just condemn his own people to death?

His attendants clap their hands, and guards materialize seemingly out of nowhere, grabbing the four guides who left us to die. My skin chills at seeing their emotionless response to being taken to their deaths. I'm expecting a fight—or for one of them to at least seem a little angry.

But they are blank. I never thought that seeing emotionless demons would be so terrifying. I would rather deal with the alternative. At least enemies in fury are more prone to make mistakes and have their weakness exploited. I don't know how I would handle an enemy this emotionless.

Krell regards me once again, then gestures to the creatures he and his two followers flew in on.

"We shall continue this conversation elsewhere," he says, turning to David. "If that is alright with you, High Prince."

David squirms where he stands. "Um, did you just ask for permission?"

Krell's gaze is measured and unbroken. "As high prince of the accords, your status cannot be ignored."

The accords . . .

I'm even more curious to know what that means. When the demons and the Sirens—or so my mother told me—entered a pact with the light races, they swore their fealty to them as their allies. Based on how Krell is reacting, whatever was written must be comprehensive. The curious part of me wishes I could get my hands on a copy of these accords, but the practical part of me knows that I don't like reading. This is the exact type of thing I would look up on Wikipedia...

Since that doesn't exist here, I'll take the "it's on a need-to-know basis" approach.

David puffs up a little at the mention of his status, and I resist the urge to roll my eyes. He's still an egotistic high school boy.

"Then, yes, I agree. Somewhere we aren't prone to get attacked again," David says.

Krell nods. "Btindon and Grilvan, return to the palace on foot. Our guests will take your darangkin alongside me."

The two attendants nod and gesture to us to mount the strange creatures.

Since coming to Qotan, I've encountered lots of creatures that have made me uncomfortable. Between the crelotins, the griffins, and these, the odd bat-dog creatures take the cake.

We hesitate, staring at the things with plenty of discomfort. In the end, I know I'll be the first to move and do something about it. I stalk over to the larger of the two creatures and examine it closely. The fur on its eyeless face and neck is coarse and black—so coarse that it looks like there are little needles everywhere. The wings look like bat wings, all veiny.

The others follow my lead, staying far enough out of reach from the sharp and jagged teeth of the creatures.

Amir asks the question we're all thinking. "How do they know where to fly? You know—without—without eyes?" He swallows hard.

Krell doesn't answer right away. He moves over to his darangkin and slips easily up on the creature.

"The blood pact. They see through my eyes," he responds frankly.

I'm not shocked to hear that it's something creepy like that.

Amir waits for more of an explanation, but it's clear that Krell has no intention of giving any. So, in the midst of an awkward silence and a lot more pure-black eyes watching us, we pull ourselves onto the strange mounts.

This time, Amir ends up with me, my massive demon form and his slight frame a better balance for the creature. He starts spouting random facts about birds and flight patterns based on wing size, but I ignore him. I've noticed he gets chatty when he's nervous.

"We fly," Krell says.

His darangkin leaps into the air with powerful, flapping wings, and my stomach drops as our darangkin follows suit, launching upward.

And just like that, we're on our way to the place I originally came from.

12

WE HAVE AN AUDIENCE WITH THE LORD OF DARKNESS

I T TURNS OUT THAT flying on a weird bat-dog is nothing like flying on a griffin. My powerful legs grip its body as we barrel through the sky. While the griffins had a more smooth and direct approach to flying, the darangkin seems determined to knock us off its back.

We pitch and roll from side to side, the creature occasionally doing a barrel roll when it feels like it. Amir's arms are firmly around my huge waist, but his hands can't meet on the other side, so his fingers dig into my flesh—even through the baggy hoodie that is stretched to its limit. His face presses into my back, and his whole body trembles. At first, it made me uncomfortable to have him hold me this way, but it's better than listening to his horrified screaming.

I choose to ignore the sensation and focus instead on where we are flying. The palace looms larger as we get closer. Referring to its appearance as a cake is both appropriate and oddly hilarious. Each stacked cylinder gets smaller—much like a wedding cake. The spires that ring the main structure are spaced evenly around, their bases connected to a decent-sized wall.

Now that we are closer, I can see that a winding staircase twists up each of the spires. The same purple torches that line the rest of the city also line the palace. About twenty feet from the top of the spires, there's a platform of black stone jutting out. A single guard sits watching atop each platform. Though I can't quite make out what weapons they are holding, I suspect they are the projectile shooting kind—unless my father intends on his defenses jumping off with their axes or spears flying through the air wildly.

Knowing how emotionless my father is, I wouldn't put it past him.

My heart twinges, and I shake my head. No, he's not worthy to be called my father. He's just the demon king. Nothing more.

Can you believe that you might have grown up here if we weren't sent to earth? Jared's voice echoes in my mind.

No, I can't believe that. This place looks like something from a gothic horror film, I reply.

He chuckles.

I look over at their darangkin weaving side to side and doing rolls every once in a while.

I wish they wouldn't do that, Jared complains. *At least give us a warning.*

I laugh. I can't help it. Then, I let my eyes shift back to David. His arms are also wrapped around Jared's midsection, but he's not screaming and doesn't have his face pressed into Jared's back. He stares blankly at nothing, his face whiter than a ghost.

Poor thing. What a bummer to have such a fear of heights given all we've been through. It's probably a good thing that one of his powers isn't flight, or he might lose his mind.

My stomach drops as the darangkin descends rapidly toward the palace. We pass one of the spires, the demons atop raising their weapons in greeting. They shout something I can't quite hear. Soon, we land more gracefully than I expected on the outcropping from the second level. It's a sort of balcony formed from the tiers of each of the stories of the building.

Krell dismounts without a word and starts walking toward the black wall of the palace.

"I guess this is our stop," Jared says, giving me a look that says, "What's this guy's problem?"

I shrug, extricate myself from Amir's iron grasp, and slip off the darangkin's back. Coaxing Amir off is a much longer process than I expected, but eventually, with David's reassurance, he comes down.

"It looks like you hated that even more than I did," David comments.

Amir only grunts. He's sitting on the ground now, his head bowed between his legs like he's going to throw up.

"It's a shame you can't all get used to it like me," Jared adds. "Flying like an eagle isn't that different from how these things fly."

I glower at him. "Careful, Jared, you're sounding like a crazy bird enthusiast with a strange fixation."

David shakes his head. "I think he's lucky. The only thing I can think about right now is the fact that we're going to have to ride those things again to get out of this place." He looks around warily. "*If* we get out of here."

I fold my arms. "Are you saying you don't trust my people?"

My stomach squirms. Saying "my people" out loud is a lot weirder than I expect it to be. For some reason, I feel the need to defend the demons, even though I don't have much experience with them. If Jared or Amir had said the same thing, it might not have stung so much. I shouldn't dwell on this. I might spiral out of control.

David peers at me with his eyebrows raised. "Well, 'your people' haven't exactly given us the most welcoming arrival." He pauses. "I'm not scared of you, Krista, no matter what you look like. I hope you know that."

His hand wraps around the sausage that is my pointer finger, and he gives it an encouraging squeeze. Did his face just turn red? He shuffles away before I can validate if what I spot is true. My stomach feels like it's full of nothing but air and a frenzy of fluttering wings.

"You will follow me to the throne room, and there, we shall discuss the plights of demonkind," the demon king instructs.

Amir raises his hand. "With all due respect, Your Demon-ness. I think we'd rather not enter the death gate of darkness."

He gestures to the dark portal of a doorway. The only light present is the same steady purple light that comes from the torches throughout the black citadel.

Once again, Krell shows virtually no emotion. Maybe a minor amount of annoyance? If Amir talked to me that way, my anger would have flared up. The demon king shakes his head, pointing again to the doorway.

"Only those loyal to the house of Ivan are allowed within the halls of the palace. There are none you cannot trust under this roof. I swear on my life," he says. "Come. We have much to discuss."

I hesitate. It's not from fear or any sense of unease. I'm confused. No matter how hard I've tried to return to my human form, I've not been able to revert back. It's as if something in this place is drawing the demon out of me. It's an energy that I can't push away. Yet at the same time, I don't feel myself. For the first time in a long time, I'm calm. Sure, phantoms of volatile emotions come and go, but I've managed not to smash anything except out of defense.

What I thought was an experience common to demons turns out to be me—just me. Watching the demon king walk so calmly—even if a little intensely—into the doorway makes me feel like I'm at home and also unwelcome at the same time. My whole life, I assumed I'd finally feel at peace when I made it back here. It turns out I'm still an enigma, unable to fit in on earth or Qotan.

It stings. Really bad.

"We should follow him," Jared says, pulling me out of my thoughts. "We either follow him into that place or try to survive out here where there are any number of demons who might want us dead. That is, if we can get the darangkin things to follow our directions."

The creatures let out a barking wail before pushing themselves off of the roof in a rush of air. My hair flips wildly around my face, slapping my cheeks and tangling in my eyelashes.

"Or—not. I guess we only have one option now," he says, gesturing with his head toward the doorway.

I square my shoulders. "We're here to get them to join the fight, and we won't leave until they do."

With that, I lead the motley crew of half-blooded misfits, a human, and a strangely silent fairy across the balcony and through the doorway.

The moment I walk into the palace, I catch sight of two figures, one on either side of the doorway. They hold their spears high. I react, throwing my fist to the side in surprise. A heavy palm wraps around my wrist, stopping the attack. When I try to pull away, the demon holds on to me tightly. Before I can sound the alarm, I hear Krell's voice.

"As guests in my kingdom, I would suggest not attempting to slay any of our kind," he says dryly. "Release her."

The demon follows the command, flashing me a grin of sharp white teeth.

"Princess Karistana, welcome home." The same demon guard bows his head slightly.

Blood rushes to my face, and it feels different from when I blush as a human. My skin prickles with the concentration of cold blood as it pools there. Being called princess is already not my favorite thing. Maybe if I had a father who played with me and called me his little princess, I wouldn't be so averse to it. Bob did what he could, but he was just a stepdad, there to help train me when Mom couldn't do the heavy lifting. Literally.

"Don't call me that," I say flatly, turning my back to the demon.

"Yes, Princess Karistana," he replies.

I spin around, ready to knock some sense into this idiot, but David and Jared are there, each lacing an arm around one of mine.

Calm down, Krista! He's not doing anything wrong, Jared says in my mind.

"Cool it, Krista. Your dad—uh, Krell—already told you that we're in hot water for killing the demons out there. Do you want to get us thrown into a dungeon?"

I growl and pull my arms away. They don't let go. My anger comes hot and fast, but it ends quickly.

"Fine," I respond, yanking against them again. They ultimately release me.

Krell hasn't paused, suggesting he wasn't truly worried about me attacking his guards. That, or he doesn't care.

The pathway descends enough to make my calves burn by the time we walk through another doorway. It's strange not having to duck through doors—unlike in the human realm. Here, there's plenty of room above my head, making me once again feel small compared to the other demons.

We enter a hall that forks to the left and right. Krell lumbers to the right, and while my curiosity tugs me to go the other direction to see if I can figure out a way to escape this place, he calls me.

"Krista, to me."

Krista. He actually used my human name. Mom told me that Krista is a nickname of my actual name, Karistana, but she only told me to inform me. Never once has she called me that. I've always just been Krista.

It feels important and meaningful that the demon king addressed me that way, but I can't grasp why.

A steady, warm breeze rushes past my shoulders, stirring my hair and bringing a sour and salty scent from outside. It smells like blood, and it makes my stomach turn.

The floors here are smooth black stone. The purple-fired sconces reflect off of the shiny floor. The wall, on the other hand, is mixed with other forms of stone and holds images. While they aren't the most intricate of carvings, they depict clear enough pictures that I can at least tell what they are.

"It's giving major Greek sculpture vibes, except with a more horrific element," Amir comments, coming up to my side.

He traces his hand along the wall over the face of a snarling demon. It's fighting a smaller muscular orc. I turn, looking at the opposite wall. There's a dragon carved there. Enormous wings overshadow fighting figures below. Trolls, goblins, and other unknown dark races are locked in an endless battle with winged fairies and armed dwarves.

A looming presence prickles my skin, and I recoil.

"The war after the accords," Krell says quietly. "These were the dark days immediately after the demons and the Sirens left the ranks of the dark races and swore fealty to the dragon kingdom and all the light races. The battle was terrible and many died. In the end, the light races were triumphant. We were the turning forces in that battle. The Sirens secured the seas, and we helped secure the lands."

He stops as if he's about to say something else. Instead, he stands silently like a sentinel, inspecting the artwork before he turns and moving through double doors that lead into a bigger room. His every step reverberates back to my sensitive ears.

The throne room is vast and wide, but not nearly as tall as I might have thought. Unlike the throne room in the dragon capital, the ceiling is only a foot or two higher than Krell's head. It's a strange design choice for such big creatures. Pillars hold up the large stone roof throughout the room, but they don't seem to be organized in any specific way. They're scattered everywhere, casting shadows on the floor and over our faces as we pass by them. I spot a pedestal that looks like an altar with a large metal urn in the center.

"What do you think that is for?" Amir asks.

"Sacrifices. Definitely sacrifices," Jared murmurs.

I flinch. While it's entirely unlikely to be the true purpose of the altar, it still makes my stomach twist at the thought.

"Not enough blood," Amir surmises. "That bronze urn looks *way* too clean to have been used for sacrifices."

"Unless they burn them alive," David adds.

This elicits a whimper and more babbling from Rolinda, who is still hidden beneath Amir's shirt. I can tell he's joking from the way he says it, and a quick glance at his grinning face confirms this. Amir, on the other hand, looks amazed and starts writing invisible text in the air like he's taking notes for his next best-selling book series.

"Oh, there's two," Jared says, pointing in the opposite direction. Sure enough, a second altar is set up on another black stone pedestal. "It's for a ritual of some sort, to be sure."

A demon stands at each altar quietly with one arm behind their back. In their free hand, they grip huge spears. Krell climbs a couple of stairs to a raised pedestal with a bronze throne atop it. The throne is shaped like the palace grounds, spires protruding from the back in spikes. The metal extends above his head, fusing with the low ceiling. It makes the whole piece of furniture look like a stalactite and stalagmite met in the center of the space.

"Light the everlight," Krell says, his deep voice reverberating throughout the cavernous room.

The two demons standing by the large urns turn and walk away from their posts. They are so in sync that I find myself looking back and forth between them to see if their movements are matched. It's like watching a mirror as they approach two different sconces and stick their spears inside. The purple fire leaps to the spearheads and ignites them. With the blazing spear tips, they march back to the urns and stab inside. Purple fire erupts from the urns, creating an inferno. Oddly, the light coming from the urns is steady. It doesn't flicker like a normal fire.

Amir leans closer to us and whispers so only we can hear him. "What's with the freaky fires?"

David shrugs. Jared watches the demon king with a critical eye, no doubt trying to perceive his thoughts. Whether he's successful or not, I can't tell.

"You assume I cannot hear every word you utter, human. Demon ears have little trouble picking up even the smallest sound from afar. Your whispers leave an ill perception of the skills of your race," Krell says flatly. "But to answer your query, the ritual fires are required for an audience with the king. Such has been our practice for eternity, and such will it be for the rest of all time."

I shake my head. Who knew that my father was such a stick in the mud? On top of that, he just insulted my friend. I step forward, letting the heat return to my chest. It's a welcome, familiar thing in this sea of unfamiliarity.

"Watch your tongue, old man. We didn't come here to be insulted by you," I say.

Jared's and David's eyes snap to me, and they both look like they're about to pass out.

"Are you kidding me? Do you want to get our heads cut off?" David hisses.

Jared doesn't say anything, but his expression suggests that he agrees with David's assessment.

I keep my attention trained on the red-haired demon, waiting for an outburst of anger. For some reason, it's what I want to see. I *want* to hear him yell at me or even descend from his weird bronze throne and threaten to kill me.

I'm disappointed yet again.

He leans back against the tall backrest and smiles slightly.

"While your insolence is not appreciated, I have to admit, the fire in your soul likely makes you a formidable opponent. I was concerned about blending the royal bloodline with a human. Your emotions are more unwieldy than an imbalanced blade. Any incorrect movement can send it so far off course that it's detrimental to those close by."

Great. He just compared me to a dull sword.

"But based on the way those demons were slain in the streets, the combination must be a decently good one," he muses.

I bare my teeth, trying to hold my anger at bay so I don't rush forward and try to strangle the dude.

"We didn't come here so that you could admire your breeding decisions," I bite back.

It stings to hear him talk about me that way. My perception of a father-daughter reunion is, unfortunately, skewed from all the movies I've seen. Cinema is by no means a realistic indication of how life actually works, but I can't help but think about all those daughters running into their dads' arms with tears in their eyes. You know? The slow-motion experience.

His smile falters, and he peers at me more intensely.

"Then, tell me, daughter, why have you come to my realm? You are not due to arrive in Qotan until you have reached twenty years of age. Based on your size—and that of your companions—I would guess you are more near fourteen by human standards."

His words shouldn't bother me, but after enduring years of abandonment—and witnessing how he's treating me and my friends—I can't keep things together.

"Sixteen. And if you were around more often, you would know that," I say. "We're here to figure out why *you* have left the rest of the light races high and dry. Why enter an agreement with them if you aren't going to help them when they are falling apart to the dark races? Dranith has fallen to the orcs, and the dragons have disappeared. Yet you sit here on your throne chatting away like you don't even care!"

These are assumptions—I know they are—but it doesn't make sense. I'm expecting him, once again, to get angry and begin shouting, but his cool demeanor stays the same.

"I have problems of my own," he replies. "Problems which I am working to overcome before I can lend aid to others. You would do well to show respect when you have little understanding of the whole picture. Such is not the nature of one who is heir to rule a kingdom."

I want to scream. My fists clamp so tight that my long nails cut into my skin. One more comment like that, and I'll explode. Heir to rule before we're sacrificed for our blood? I keep these words inside, figuring they are unproductive.

"Then, what, pray tell, is the problem you're dealing with?" I ask.

His eyes leave my face and hover over my head. They remain there for a few seconds, and I grit my teeth, speaking through them.

"What—is—the—problem?"

For the first time, emotion flashes in his eyes. Even though it's fleeting, I recognize it immediately. Sadness. That is definitely not what I was expecting from him.

Abruptly, someone pounds on the door behind us, the echo reverberating against the low ceiling and expansive walls. The two attendants shift and point their spears to the back of the throne room.

"Someone seeks entrance to converse with the king," they say in unison.

Amir whistles. "That is wicked creepy."

"Agreed," David responds.

Rolinda mutters something from within Amir's shirt, but it's not in a language I understand. It sounds like a curse of some sort.

"Do not yet bid them entrance," Krell says.

The two attendants put their spears to the ground and slam them in three successive bangs. As the echoes die down, I raise my eyebrows at Krell, reminding him that he still hasn't answered my question.

His black eyes fixate on me, and he sits back, his hands gripping the armrests tightly.

"There is a coup to seize the throne from me. While I have won the love of most of our people, there are some who wish to dethrone me and take Etherek for themselves. This palace is my home—our home—and I will not relinquish it. There is contention within, and I fear that leaving in such a state would be unwise. As long as I remain within the city, our laws prevent it from being taken by force. I know not the extent of the forces wishing to dethrone me, but I recognize that they may have sizable numbers. If I bring an army to defend the light races, my dissenters may overwhelm any forces I leave behind to defend this place."

I slump when I hear his reasoning. I'm unsure if it's from disappointment or anger. When we traveled here, I fully expected to have to put up a fight—or at least to have to convince him to stop failing the light races.

Now, I don't know what to say.

Krell stares at me with an intensity so deep that I can't help but shift on my feet. The purple light casting on his face deepens the lines that crease his forehead. I have no idea how old this demon is, but he looks like he's been dealing with the burdens of a thousand years.

No, I will not feel bad for him, I scold myself.

Try to keep an open mind, Jared says.

Shut up! I shout at him.

In our current situation, it's probably unwise to close the mind link between us. For all I know, we could have jumped at any moment. Demons could decide to kill us, or Krell could give the order. Sucking in a deep breath, I don't let the fight instinct rule me.

I pause. I *could* shove Jared out of my thoughts. Flexing that muscle internally, I marvel that, despite being demoned up, I have control of my mental wall.

Intense emotion truly does shoot me in the foot.

"While I can say that I am pleased to see you again, daughter, I have to admit, your timing is both perfect and terrible," he says, his hands clasping together and moving to his bare chin.

Without facial hair, he looks younger than someone who could be my father. In fact, none of the demons have beards or mustaches. I can't imagine them having to shave every day. Their anatomy must be very different from human anatomy . . .

Hearing Krell say he is pleased to see me stirs something in me that I don't want to deal with. So, I focus on his complaints instead.

"Oh, *forgive me* for not showing up at the exact time you wanted me to. I didn't choose to get sucked away to this place and almost taken prisoner by Urothar and his idiotic son. I didn't ask to be pulled into this realm and attacked left and right—or told that my whole existence was to be sacrificed for some cause that I'm not sure I actually care about. The last thing I want to be is an inconvenience to you and your perfect life in Qotan. You, and your wife and other kids, and whatever life you've built without me!" I seethe.

The sarcasm is so thick that it practically drips on the floor. Tears threaten my eyes again, but I still refuse to give him the satisfaction of making me cry. Years of trauma and abandonment try to escape me. I can barely hold it all back.

His gaze hardens, and his clasped fingers come apart in a flash. I react, my hand grabbing the hilt of my broadsword in defense.

The pounding echo on the door resumes, this time more frantic. The attendants' spears rise again, but this time, they indicate that they should not be left waiting.

"This is not the time for such conversations. My decision to send you away was not different from that of the other rulers. Though I am content with my title and my kingdom, I am not content with the fullness of this life. You should have been here. Of that, I have no doubt. But the prophecy cannot be thwarted for the survival of all Qotan. We will discuss this later," he says, then he nods to his attendants. "Show him in."

Metal scrapes against stone as the throne room doors open.

"So you are aware, demons mate for life. I loved your mother more than any demon. There is no other to which my heart belongs. You have no siblings. Thus is the weight of your birth. I never expected the prophecy to select us," Krell says before turning away from me to watch the newcomer.

I feel like I've been hit by a tidal wave. I'm unsure how to process this new information. All these years, I assumed he had moved on, hooked up with another demon to be the queen, and had tons of little demon babies. I've been wrong all this time. What else am I wrong about?

"Sire, what is the meaning of this unexpected audience? The urns were not meant to be lit for another day, at least? Who are these strangers in our citadel and what need have they of the prestigious demon king?" a deep and clear voice shouts from behind us.

We all turn to regard him. A demon the size of my father strolls in with his chest puffed out. He wears an open crimson robe that swishes on the ground. His hair is deep black with stripes of gray, wrapped in a long ponytail that flicks side to side as he stalks. Underneath his robe, he wears plated armor made from a dark gray material that seems to absorb the purple light from the fires.

Krell appears hesitant to answer the question, but he ultimately relents. "My daughter has returned."

What happens next, I'm not prepared for *at all*. The demon's mouth twists upward in a sly smile, and his eyes descend on me. He scrutinizes me with a hungry look, his fingers fiddling at his sides. It's so creepy that it makes me want to slash him with my sword.

"I hereby challenge the throne with a death match between heirs," the new demon says.

I frown.

"Peace, Bahresh Khan. There is no need to be hasty—"

The demon scoffs, raising his arms in the air. "There is *every* need to be hasty. For years, I've been attending you, watching as you fail our people left and right. Never have I been able to truly remove you from the throne, what with your single heir conveniently exiled to the human realm until she reaches twenty. That is no longer an issue. We battle this very night."

With that, he turns and stalks out of the room. Krell looks crestfallen, his face now stricken.

"I feel like I missed something important," Amir chimes in. "Why did we stop speaking English all of a sudden? And why does Krista look like she's going to be sick."

My tongue is tied as I process what just happened. As much as I want to pretend like I didn't understand it, I can't deny the inevitable.

"Sounds like I'm about to have a fight to the death," I say, my stomach dropping.

13

I OWE DAVID, AGAIN

A CROWD ROARS, THEIR cries, jeers, and cheers echoing off the black walls. Heavy armor weighs down on my shoulders, and my palm aches as I squeeze the broadsword in my right hand. The air smells of sweat, dirt, and something metallic. As much as I want to tell myself it's not blood, I can't think of any other smell that is similar to it.

An iron gate with thick bars is the only thing that stands between me and the arena. The only solace I have right now is that Krell, the dad who has failed me over and over again, actually took some time to show me the arena from above.

"The crowd sounds really pissed or way too excited for this," David whispers from behind me.

I turn, taking in his armor and sword. He still holds the short sword we took from the car. The demons thought he was ridiculous for choosing it as his weapon, but he insisted, mostly because the alternatives were swords, axes, or maces that were too heavy for his arms. Even with his toned football muscles, only a demon could wield their weapons.

Jared, clad in leather armor, looks resolved.

"You know, this is one of those times I wish I didn't have the ability to read people's thoughts. Some of these demons have really dark images going through their minds," he says, wincing as probably another macabre scene flows through his consciousness.

David grimaces. "I didn't realize you could read *images*, too. How do you manage to keep it all straight?"

He shrugs. "I don't. Most of the time I have to ignore it. Right now, though, there's too much going on to fully ignore."

I turn back to the gate and close my eyes. My friends are trying to keep things light so I don't lose my mind standing here waiting for my inevitable death. What's-his-name, Khan's son, is behind another gate across the black-sanded arena. Though it's dark inside, I have an idea of what monster lies behind it. If he's the same height as his father, then he's got a lot of height on me—not to mention David and Jared. Some would say it's insane for a sixteen-year-old to be facing their death so early in life. For me, it's the norm.

I grit my teeth to pluck up my resolve. I'm stronger than they think. I'm not going down without a fight. Looking at my pale hand, I focus on the purple veins. It's evidence of my royal blood. I'm a demon, but I'm a human as well, and that counts for something.

"Look, man," David says. "I'd trade the ability to understand languages on most days, but right now, I have the pleasure of hearing what they are shouting. Who knew they had such clear equivalents for curse words?"

Jared scoffs. "Most days, I can *understand* what they say through your mind. Right now, I'll take it as a win that your thoughts are drowned out by theirs."

I turn around and fix my gaze on each of them.

"I'm sorry to drag you into this mess," I say. "I . . . shouldn't have asked you to be here."

David raises an eyebrow. "Are you kidding? You think we'd let you go in there alone? You can bet your bottom that he's going to have his backup dudes, so why shouldn't you have yours?" He grins and points a thumb at his chest. "I may look minuscule compared to those demons, but I pack a punch."

His bravado, in this moment, is welcome, and despite the fact that I can see how pale he is, I appreciate it. Jared, on the other hand, appears apprehensive and resolved. The way he holds his shoulders and the way his jaw is set tells me what I need to know. We've trained for this our whole lives. This isn't our first rodeo.

Just before we entered this waiting area, Krell had to give us a crash course on the match. The challenger would send in their representative, and the defender would enter the arena for a death match. He explained that we could choose our *krivnan*, which essentially means two back up fighters in case someone breaks the rules. Apparently, the laws necessitate a level of honor in one-on-one matches, but it recognizes demons' propensity to break or bend rules. Thus, the two additions are kind of "physical referees" to intervene if things aren't kept within reason.

When I asked him what the rules were, he only gave one. No head shots. Something about "honor"and it being "weak to go straight for the source of life and thought."

Don't take the easy win. How helpful.

If one of the backup fighters sees a play at someone's head, it becomes a three versus three match instantly. From what my dad says, that's almost a guarantee. Demons apparently don't like one-on-one. But I'm determined to keep it that way. Maybe I'll be the first not to accept help.

I shake my head, pushing the thoughts out of my mind and returning to our present conversation.

"Still—thank you," I say.

David smiles. "Don't tell me you're getting all soft on me, demon girl. Normally, when you're all hulked up, I have to watch my back in case you knock my head off. You can't lose that drive now!"

I scoff at his comment, a bit of annoyance flaring inside me. I let it fuel the fire in my soul.

"Shut up, scale face," I say, but I smile at the same time.

He smacks his fist into his palm and squints at the gate with determination. As if in response to his comment, a hideous squeaking sound echoes off the walls as the gate rises slowly. Blood tingling in all of my limbs, I prepare for the bout. Across the way, the other gate opens as well.

"Remember, don't be the first ones to get involved unless you absolutely have to," I say. "I'm not going to be the weak one here."

David mutters something I can't hear because I'm moving out into the arena, armor clanking. Though I've practiced fighting with armor before, most of the time, I've relied on my healing more than anything else.

Your best advantage is your ability to be fast, Mom's voice sounds in my mind. My heart twinges as I imagine her face.

Demons may be strong, but their speed isn't something to be de-sired. Be faster. Be smarter.

Sadness throbs my chest, but I don't let it take over. I miss her more than I want to admit to anyone, even Jared. The idea that she's probably dead—her blood used for one of those teleportation stones—fills me with deep longing and fury.

I can use those emotions . . .

When I glance at the other gate, my jaw drops. I was expecting a demon much bigger than me, but what I see across the arena is more than that. He's almost twice my height, even in demon form. His black- and gray-streaked hair is cut short and pasted upward in a weird, spiky afro. His sharp teeth gleam in the dull purple light that comes from above. His chest is bare, save for a few straps to harness his weapons. He has a decent-sized gut and pectorals with huge arms.

"That's one big dude," David comments.

"Understatement of the century," Jared huffs.

His two companions stalk in behind him, one wielding a wicked-looking double-bladed axe. The other has a spiked mace with a ball that is bigger than my expanded head.

My opponent reaches back and pulls out a broadsword that is bigger than mine.

So, it's going to be like that, huh? I think.

Even though the sword is clearly balanced—or looks to be so, based on his grip on the handle—he still looks a little awkward with it. I focus on it for a moment longer before glancing at his black eyes and sharp teeth.

"He's not used to fighting with a sword like that," Jared in-forms me. "He's doing it out of pride. Man, he's a cocky dude."

Despite the terror standing before me, I smile. "Well, we'll have to take advantage of that, won't we?"

Krell stands up in the high seats and spreads his arms wide. "We are here to witness the momentous event, a challenge for the throne by none other than the house of Khan. This tradition has been held for centuries, and while we rarely have the pleasure of witnessing such an occasion, we are blessed to participate. The outcome of this battle will determine which family holds the throne for the next five score years. Before we begin, let the words be spoken. I, Krell of the house of Ivan, do so accept the challenge of dominance within our fabled halls of Etherek."

"I, Bahresh of the house of Khan, do answer the acceptance. Let the weaker of the bloods be razed in the halls of Selenti and forever tormented."

David whistles. "That's dark, man. What kind of culture is this?"

I grit my teeth. Even though I know he's not meaning to insult me, it feels like that somehow. Neither Jared nor I say anything. Instead, we all watch my father, waiting for the customary hand drop that tells us to start fighting. Time slows as Krell looks down at me, and what I see is not encouraging.

Pity. He pities me because he thinks I'm not going to make it out of this alive. Resentment grows hot and fast within me, so much so that when he drops his hand, I don't hesitate. My powerful legs push me forward as I launch into the arena toward some towering stones buried in the sand. Scattered black monoliths of stone sprout from the ground, providing places to hide during the fight. The Khan challenger doesn't have a bow or anything, but I still decide to use one of the stones for shelter to get my bearings.

Loud footsteps thud in the thick black sand. For someone who's supposedly great at fighting, he's sure loud when he runs.

Be careful, Kris, Jared's voice slips into my mind.

I curse myself for forgetting to close him out. Even though he could give me pointers and tell me where the Khan demon is, I refuse to win without it being truly *my* win. I suspect Jared is disappointed with this decision, but I don't care.

Taking a deep breath, I filter out the senses that are distracting. Roars and shouts from the crowd above become nothing but white noise as I focus on the thuds that are now directly behind the stone covering me. The metallic scent of the arena stings my nose, threatening to make my eyes water, but I filter that out, too.

Hot sand radiates through my shoes, and my cold blood drinks it in like it's never felt anything like it before.

A sword comes flying at me from the left. I dodge it easily, the metal clanging into the stone where my chest was seconds before. I spin around the stone so that I'm hidden from Jared and David. I can now see the sneering demons who are backing up my enemy. One of them bares his teeth at me, waving his massive axe in the air with a loud bellow.

This lights a fire in me. To see demons, half of my heritage, rooting for my death annoys me. Heat flares through my chest, and I decide to face my enemy head-on. With a quick glance toward my father, I pivot back the way I came, ready to face Bahresh.

This catches him off guard. With his rear exposed to me, I leap forward, aiming my broadsword right at the small of his back. Somehow, at the last second, he blocks my sword with his own. Vibrations reverberate up my wrists and into my forearms. My bones protest slightly, even though I'm used to the sensation.

I grunt and jump backward, tossing my intimidation aura in his direction. He flinches, but then answers with his own. It smacks into me like an invisible wave, causing my pulse to spike and my heart to throb. At least I don't feel fear from his aura, like he undoubtedly doesn't feel fear from mine.

"The mutt is quick on her feet," Bahresh muses. "Your human instinct to run away must be strong."

I growl and take his obvious bait. The moment I'm within reach of his sword, he steps back and swings wide toward my side. I duck, the sword cutting some of my flyaway hair clean off before it clunks into the wall. Within an instant, I'm inside his defenses. My broadsword comes into contact with his plated shoulder, the metal clanking loudly before it slides off of him.

His dang armor . . .

Teeth grinding, I kick a foot out to push him back until I can figure out what to do.

He's much heavier than me. The push causes him to stumble a little, but it forces me to go flying off balance. My foot catches on a rock buried in the sand, and I tumble. Fortunately, I roll over my back and onto my feet again.

This causes the crowd to lose their minds, their cheers and jeers increasing tenfold.

Bahresh grins at me, his teeth soaking in the purple light from above. "You can't beat me, little human. Demon blood or not."

I raise my free hand and give a very poignant "I can't understand you" gesture. Bahresh's smile falters, and his eyes turn to slits. He rushes toward me, and I parry his attack, but I'm not strong enough to take the full brunt of his weapon. Instead, I tilt my blade every time our swords connect to redirect the force off my person and into the air. As his frenzy continues, my heart thuds in my chest and sweat forms on my brow.

I don't sweat very often, so I know that this is going to be a challenging fight. My arms are already tiring from this bout. I have to come up with some more ideas to survive this.

Another death blow slams down on me, and I don't tilt my sword enough this time. Rather than redirecting the force, I take most of it head-on, and my feet slide in the sand as Bahresh's sword clangs into my armor.

I dance away, determined to give myself some time to think. Focusing on the movement of his weapon, I get a good idea of where it's going, then I step forward. He's clearly not expecting this, but he's already committed to his attack. The sword narrowly misses my leg as it thuds into the black sand. I leap up onto his sword like it's a ramp. Then I plant my foot on his shoulder, leaping into the air. This gives me enough momentum to vault myself up onto the nearest black stone monolith.

He shouts in anger, then sheaths his sword. With a horrifying roar, he leaps up and catches the edge of the stone. Naturally, I take the opportunity to slam my sword down on his hand. Unfortunately, his gauntlets protect him, but the plating on the outside bends inward. It's not enough to injure him, but it's enough to be uncomfortable. He may have a hard time getting it off.

Despite the move, he doesn't let go. I frown, pulling back for another blow when he suddenly vaults upward, his powerful arm yanking him through the air. I gasp, trying to shuffle back, but there isn't much room up here. He throws a blow with his sword, which I deflect, but then his foot crashes into my chest, and the world is a blur around me. The fall isn't that far, but it seems to take forever before my back slams into the sand.

I groan, opening my eyes just in time to see him leap off the monolith with his sword tip coming down at my chest. Kicking my left foot, I flip my body over to dodge him, but his foot comes down on the armor covering my shins. It buckles, the metal pressing into my skin, and I scream.

I use my other foot to kick out, slamming into his legs and making him trip. I scramble to my feet, holding my broadsword aloft and at the ready. Something pricks my mind—a reminder of the new power I discovered at the restaurant. Satisfaction bleeds into my chest, mingling with my anger as I tap into the power to absorb light. Prepared to plunge the whole arena into darkness, I ready my sword. He'll move toward me, which gives me a good prediction of where his chest will be. I can't risk taking a headshot at him. Sensing the power within, I tug on the purple flames surrounding us.

Nothing happens.

I'm so surprised by this that I don't move in time before his sword crashes into my midsection, throwing me back. The air leaves my lungs. The world is a blur, and before I know it, I'm staring up at the ceiling. Long black stalactites taunt me from above as if to say, "Hold still so we can skewer you."

Bahresh bellows a laugh.

"You do not understand the nature of everlight. Our darkness cannot affect it. That is why we use it. It's also the only light that doesn't burn our eyes and skin," he lectures. "But you don't know anything about that. No, your vermin skin protects you."

Until now, I haven't heard anything of the sort. Light burning a demon's eyes and skin? Is that why we can absorb it like that?

I pull myself to my feet, readying my weapon.

"You can just admit you're jealous that you can't sunbathe like me," I say with a jeering smile. "And you're a slow piece of—"

I don't get to finish my sentence before he roars and dives at me.

Okay, so they do have *some* emotions if you pull on the right strings.

We go into another set of attacks and parries, but this time, I can feel my arms starting to tire. Stamina hasn't been a problem of mine for years, but I've not had to fight a demon of this size or strength before. One wrong move, and I'm dead.

I decide to make use of one of his attacks to get away from him. We dance in near perfect unison. His attack. My parry. My attack. His block. Then, his sword comes right at me. Rather than deflect this one, I take it on my sword, placing the blade in front of my chest. The force rockets me backward—and slightly upward. Of course, I'm ready for this, so I land easily, slipping behind another monolith.

Without thinking, I reach down and grab a handful of black sand, ready to throw it into Bahresh's eyes.

"Head shot!" a deep rumbling voice cries from above.

I look up to see Krell shaking his head and pointing at my hand.

Oh, right. Sand in the eyes is still part of his head. I curse, leaning to the side to avoid Bahresh's sword. To my shock, the attack doesn't come. I furrow my brows, peeking around the edge. I hear heavy breathing, but it's not coming from behind the monolith, it's coming from above me.

He comes thudding down. I slip away, but I'm not quick enough because his sword scrapes my back. I trip forward, my vertebra aching from the blow. I barely manage to recover as he swipes his sword at me one more time.

All right, kiddo, time to end this, I think.

As we enter into another bout, I position myself next to a pillar. I have a plan. Just when he thinks he's going to back me into a corner, I turn and rush at the pillar. He follows, which is perfect. I pull a samurai move, running up the pillar, kicking off, and back flipping toward him. My timing isn't perfect, and it's not easy to get the momentum I need to fully clear his large form, but I come within inches of him. Instinctually, I grip the visor of his helmet and tug, the full weight of my demonic body yanking him until he falls on his back.

He has a space in his armor between his shoulder and his chest. I don't hesitate. I slam the blade into the crack, feeling the give of my blade in his flesh.

He roars in pain. When I yank it free, I find another space in his armor and thrust toward it. He knocks my broadsword away with his gantlet and throws his free hand out, catching my legs. I gasp as I fall to the ground.

He rolls over on his side, and using all fours, he launches himself on top of me. His weight plows into me, and I lose all air once again. My vision swims as he pushes off of my chest, his large legs pinning me down.

"Right where you deserve to be!" he growls, spitting into my face.

"Get off me, you perv!" I screech, panic rising in my chest.

I'm stuck. Every time I try to attack with my weapon, it's too large to get a good angle. I push up with my body, but he's too heavy.

"Let's see how quickly you really can heal, why don't we?"

He lifts his sword high, and despite my attempt to fend it off, he drives the tip right into my shoulder. White-hot pain explodes in my body. I scream and start to struggle more frantically.

"If I was a patient demon, I might draw this out," he taunts, his sharp teeth baring down on me. "But I'm not patient."

A cold and wet substance fills my armor and seeps out the cracks where he stabbed me. I look at my friends, and Jared is as pale as a ghost. I can tell he wants to defend me, but I made him swear that he would not intervene. David is enraged, his hand clasping the handle of his sword. The human girl in me cries out in terror, but I suppress her. I'm going to die. I'm going to live up to my father's expectations. It stings, but it also feels relieving in a terrifying way.

Will my death mean the end of Qotan? Perhaps. But that's too big a thing for me to ponder.

I don't close my eyes. Instead, I focus on Bahresh's face.

"Do it, then!" I spit, putting up a brave façade, even though my voice falters. At least he won't get to see my fear.

He leans in and whispers something. "Shod these ridiculous rules. Your head is mine, you vermin."

Abruptly, I open my mind to Jared. *Bye, Jared. Thank you for everything.*

Bahresh raises his sword, ready to end me. The tip of his weapon comes right for my neck . . .

Wham!

A force, heavy and strong, shoves Bahresh off my body. His legs are still clamped on mine, so the sudden movement tugs me onto my side. The only thing I see is a gray mass of something settling on the ground next to me before it shifts into a golden lion.

Head shot, Jared says to me, a gleam in his eyes.

Just then, a wave of fire floods over Bahresh, and he screams in agony.

I spin in the direction of the flames. David is there with his jaw locked and a fierce protectiveness in his posture.

"Let's rock these demons," he says, extending a hand to help me up.

WE SAVE KRELL'S THRONE

DAVID TUGS ME UP. He's strong, but not "pull a half demon much larger than him up easily" strong. I end up doing most of the work, but it's a valiant effort.

Relief and annoyance twist into a cacophony of confusing emotion. "I told you not to intervene! I wanted to kill him myself," I say through gritted teeth.

David rolls his eyes. "A simple thank-you would suffice."

I open my mouth to protest as Jared lets out a rumbling roar. He flies through the air and rolls to a stop. The other two demons have joined the fight now.

"How did you get here so fast?" I ask as we face the oncoming threat.

"Jared read the dude's thoughts. He knew the head blow was coming."

Typical brother—butting into my business. Despite the frustration roiling inside of me, there is gratitude buried there.

"Plan?" David shouts, raising his sword.

Bahresh gets to his feet, his cronies coming to a stop behind him.

"Outsmart them. It's our only shot," I say. "They hate light and heat, by the way."

David's eyes twinkle. "Perfect."

He steps forward with his sword raised, but I grab him by the shoulder and hold him there.

"What are you doing, Krista?" He turns and glares at me. "Do you want to survive this or not?"

"Do *you* want to survive this? Bahresh alone could snap you in two. What do you think will happen when you try to block one of his sword attacks? Unless you deflect the strength of it, you'll be halfway across Qotan."

My words distill into his mind, and he gulps. "All right, good point."

At least he's not arguing with me.

Jared roars again, but this time, his body leaps close to where we stand. He lands hard enough that he melds back into his Samoan teenage form.

"I'd prefer not to get my face smashed in alone!" he grumbles, struggling to get to his feet.

"Coward! Calling your friends is a sign of weakness. Your weakness will be your undoing," Bahresh shouts, his fist banging his chest.

This strikes a chord in my soul—not a good chord. Logically, I know I would be dead if Jared and David hadn't stepped in. I still hate the fact that they had to join in this fight. It's a failure in and off itself. I grind my teeth and look up at the towering demon.

"Coward? *You* are a coward for relying on your armor. In fact—"

In a burst of frustration—and most likely stupidity—I tear off my helmet. When the weight of it leaves my neck and shoulders, I almost sigh in relief. My training with the broadsword and other forms of combat rarely included armor. Mom and Bob ensured that we had *some* practice with armor, but they largely taught us how to fight without it. Removing the plate chest and arm pieces takes more work, but the demons are so perplexed by my actions that they simply stand there and watch.

As the last piece falls with a thud into the sand, I take a deep breath. My body comes alive again in the wake of the ridiculous armor being shed. My shoulder wound is fully healed at this point—as is Bahresh's, I assume.

"If you believe you can truly beat me, then you'll do so without your armor," I challenge.

Bahresh gnashes his teeth. "You are a fool, vermin. My sword will shear right through your flesh!"

I hoped to pull on his vanity to get him to remove his armor. It doesn't seem to be working. Instead, he lifts his headplate and smiles wickedly at me.

"My place at the head of Etherek is sure now. Kill them!"

The two demons rush at us, their weapons held aloft. I open my mind, allowing Jared to enter. I'd locked him out momentarily to focus on banter with Bahresh.

It's about time! I've been trying to talk to you—

No time! You distract Mace Face, and David and I will worry about the other two.

At some point, I'd like you to admit that you owe me, he replies.

Jared shouts and rushes forward, his body melding into a gray rhino. Based on the reaction of the demons, they've never seen a creature like this before. Fortunately, this gives Jared the opening he needs to slam his horn into the armored chest of one of the demons. Despite the size difference, Jared's momentum is enough to knock the demon from his feet.

"Krista!" David shouts.

The other demon is bearing down on us. My muscles flare to life, energy coursing through them as I watch the path of his axe. He is fixated on me. David shuffles back preemptively, which is better for him considering he doesn't have extensive fighting experience. I hold my ground. Without the armor, I feel alive again. I know I can easily avoid the swing. Sure enough, the swing is fast, but I'm faster. I jump in the air, the axe zipping beneath my feet harmlessly. As I land, I swing my sword into the demon's head. He grunts in pain as it clangs against his helmet. No doubt he'll have a headache after that one.

"You die, false princess of the throne!" Bahresh shouts, now joining the fight again.

Before he makes it too far, David blasts him with another bout of flames. Bahresh bellows, staggering back. Then his intimidation aura washes over David.

Eyes wide and arms trembling, David falls to his knees, and his fire stops. I curse, whacking the axe wielder in the face with my sword once more as hard as I can. He falls to one knee but starts rising fast. I leave him, barreling to where Bahresh is now focused on the cowering David.

"Hey!" I scream as I jump into the air.

My sword is aimed at Bahresh's head. He raises his weapon to block me, and the vibrations of the blow go up my arms and into my shoulders. I grit my teeth and spin, aiming for his head again. Bahresh blocks this easily, so I speed up, jabbing and swinging left and right. Even though I'm making no progress, my goal is to distract him from David.

Thankfully, it works. I glance at David, who's finally coming back to reality.

I dodge Bahresh's attacks and take a few steps back. Shouting and thuds drift from the other side of the arena where Jared is still scuffling with the other demon. He hasn't called for help yet, so I can only hope that he's holding his own.

Fire flares behind Bahresh, and the flames meet his backside. He roars in pain, diving away from the heat. Naturally, the moment he is no longer blocking them, they come right at me. Cursing, I leap to the side of the flame column and roll to a stop.

"Sorry!" David cries, relinquishing the power.

"Watch it, scale face! I'm the wrong demon to barbecue!"

David jumps to his feet and rushes to my side. Just then, the other demon is there, his axe raised high. I try to shout a warning, but the axe is a blur as it comes down on David's back.

David's whole body goes red with scales, but the loud thud that echoes off the monolith next to us is sickening. David goes down into the sand hard and doesn't move. I can't tell if he's alive or not, but my protective instinct goes into overdrive. My vision turns red, and my battle sense activates.

I see everything. Hear everything.

Jared growls and takes a fist to the face. Bahresh lumbers toward me with a burning hatred in his eyes. The demon who knocked David down raises his axe to strike again—most likely the final blow.

My feet move before I fully understand the plan. Motion. That's all I can rely on at this point. I barrel toward the raised axe and jump in the air. With my free hand, I grasp the demon's wrist and slip under the weapon, pulling on it with all my might. I yank it off course as I land on my back, and the blade hits sand instead of David's body. Leaping to my feet, I slam my broadsword down on the demon's neck. He groans, muttering something before stumbling away.

He left his axe.

I grasp his weapon quickly, aware of how much heavier it is than my own. Still, I can make use of it.

"Weapon thief. Return my prize or—"

I don't let him finish his sentence before the axe blade thuds into his chest. He gasps and lands on his back. I drop my broadsword so I can raise the axe with both hands. I'm not thinking, only reacting. My eyes focus on a chink in his armor between his shoulder and upper arm. The axe moves almost of its own volition. I grunt and swing hard, the blade entering the space and cleaving his flesh. It cuts clean through, his arm falling to the black sand next to his body.

The demon wails, and I sense Bahresh. Ducking, I feel the swoosh of his weapon just over my head. I roll away, trying to stay clear from the onslaught that I know is coming. Jared lets out a strangled roar, and I hear him call for me.

Krista! Help!

I roll away and jump to my feet, facing Bahresh. Jared is in a chokehold, the demon restraining him squeezing harder and harder. David stirs to my left, and he twists his head to look at me. Where I thought I'd see terror, instead, I see a smile.

He can heal fast like me. Whatever damage that axe did to his back, even while scaled up, must be on the mend.

"Help Jared!" I shout, then I jab toward Bahresh.

He easily parries my attack and takes a step forward. I take a step back in response.

"One good blow. That is all I need to find victory this day," he muses, looking me up and down.

The hunger in his eyes is frightening. David jumps to his feet and rushes off toward Jared, who is starting to turn blue. All I hear is a torrent of flames and a scream.

We're okay here, Jared says, his mind-voice much clearer than his oxygen-deprived vocal cords could manage.

Bahresh's attack comes, and it comes fast. The sword flicks and twists, coming at me from every angle. My armorless body is more agile and easy to move. Each deflection comes easily as I learn his patterns and strategy. Even though I can only see his black eyes through his helmet's visor, I can tell that he's getting frustrated. So, naturally, I turn up the heat.

"When did you get so slow? You must be getting old," I tease. At this point, my low and grumbly voice is starting to sound less strange.

"Silence, half-breed!" he shouts, attempting a new volley of attacks.

It's like he's moving in slow motion—that's how easy it is to avoid him.

In a show of confidence—and yes, a little ego—I slam my broadsword down on his back. When he doubles over from the attack, I jump on his back and vault onto the closest monolith again. Without him as an immediate threat, I check to see that David is hiding behind a pillar and spouting flames around the corner. Jared sits on the ground with his head between his legs trying to get his bearings. They are out of danger. For now.

The monolith trembles underneath me suddenly, and I almost lose my footing. When I look down, Bahresh is backing up. A shout echoes all around the arena as he drops his shoulder and collides with the stone. It rocks to the side, and I crouch to steady myself.

"You sure you don't want to take off that pesky armor?" I suggest.

Bahresh raises his visor just enough to spit on the ground and replace it.

"All right, fair enough."

He backs up and body rolls the monolith once more, but this time, I don't bother trying to stay on. Leaping off, I rush toward David and Jared. Bahresh follows.

I feel the heat on my face and arms long before I get to them.

"Sheesh, hot rod, you're going all out," I say.

David gives a hesitant smile, then peeks out from behind the pillar, sending another wave of fire. The heat prickles my skin and makes me shiver from the intense difference in temperature from my blood.

I crouch down, putting a hand on my brother's back. "Are you okay?"

He nods, but with his head hanging down, it's more like a diagonal head shake.

"Even my lion form can't throw them around that much. These dudes are huge, Kris," he pants, finally looking up at me.

His pupils are slightly dilated. That's not good.

"Did they hit you in the head? You look like you're going to be sick," I say.

He laughs and bows his head again, his next words a little mumbly.

"I've been hit everywhere. While you two were chatting, I was busy getting my face smashed in."

My heart sinks. I didn't intend to leave him fighting without us for so long.

It's fine, just get us out of this. My guess is, this won't end with just Bahresh's death anymore.

He's right. Even though Krell said nothing about when the match ends, now that the extras are added, I know what he means.

We have three demons to kill.

"Rest. David and I will figure something—"

Bahresh's shouts interrupt me, and I duck as his sword swings overhead and smashes into the monolith. Black stone fractures and showers debris over us. I reach down and grab Jared by the lapel, leaping to the side to avoid the next attack. Khan's blade hits the stone pillar again, causing more dust to rain down. David tries to jump away, but Bahresh grabs him by the neck and flings twenty feet, straight into another pillar. His skin is scaled up, but his face still twists in pain as his body collides with the stone. He slumps to the ground, breathing hard.

"No more fire, vermin. Your dragon blood may have sway with the rest of the races, but here, it means nothing!" he spits.

His companions move around the pillar and flank Bahresh. The one who's arm I severed grips his weapon in his other hand. I pray that he's not ambidextrous. Each demon looms over us, my friends looking like runts next to them. I puff out my chest and send out my intimidation aura. As expected, it does nothing to them, but they can sense it. Bahresh's eyes redirect from David to me, a fire smoldering there.

"Leave them out of this! Your beef is with me," I say, holding his gaze.

He flashes his teeth, turning his whole body toward me.

"No—no, *you* brought your friends into this. You are the one to blame for their deaths. They die with you. That is the way of the *krovat*."

You were the one who went for the head! Jared's voice echoes in my mind.

Bahresh roars, tearing at his hair. "Get out of my head, you fairy fool! You have no right to enter my thoughts!"

I smile a little. Even in his weakened state, Jared can still affect the demons, and this gives me satisfaction. I use that moment to rush them, my broadsword at the ready. I manage to land my weapon on the axe wielder's remaining arm while kicking the other demon in the chest. They stumble away, but not far. Bahresh's sword is on me before I can get another blow in. I deflect his attack and dance backward, sending my aura out once more. His aura slams into mine, and I feel it. Though I don't feel the fear, I can sense the power behind it.

It tells me all I need to know about him.

Jared, keep pestering them, I urge through our mind connection.

I feel his mental nod, but I can also sense his trepidation. The auras are affecting him. Even though I resent having to do it, I turn mine off, hoping that Bahresh will follow suit.

He does.

"You use your aura like a child," Bahresh sneers. All of a sudden, his face falls, and he puts a hand to his head again. "I said, *get out of my head*!"

He pulls his sword back like he's going to chuck it at me, but my face falls when I watch him fling toward Jared. My heart skips a beat, and time slows as it flies directly at his chest. I barely have time to shout before it reaches its destination. It strikes the monolith behind Jared, narrowing missing him and splintering more black stone into the sand.

A raven beats its heavy wings and flies up in the air.

I sigh, my arms shaking from nearly witnessing my brother get skewered.

Abruptly, Bahresh's fists pound into the small of my back. My bones crack, and my vision goes blurry. I skid across the sand, rolling to a stop by David, who's still on the ground.

"Kris!" David shouts.

The concern in his voice makes my heart skip a beat. I can't deny what I just heard. He used my nickname.

"Don't—call me—that," I groan.

I push myself up on my hands but collapse. My demon blood rushes to knit everything back together. David gasps and throws his hands up, pouring flames into the air. Bahresh and his companions roar in anger, retreating.

"Are you okay?" he gasps, letting up on the flames.

The heat singes my hair and makes me wish I could get away from it. It isn't until the last bone pops back into place that I can finally move again. I shuffle away from the fire, gulping the air.

"I'm fine, but we have to do something! We're getting destroyed out here!"

He frowns.

Jared, in his raven form, lands on top of a pillar right next to a sconce of everlight. My eyes widen, and I look at David. He releases more flames towards them, the demons backing up again.

"Any ideas?" he asks.

My whole body aches from exertion, and my head is sloshy. David seems like he's about to pass out. But an idea is forming in my mind that I let run on its own. I reach out and use my newly discovered ability on his flames. The heat doesn't change, but all light and color drains out of the portion of the flames I'm focused on. The strip of flames goes gray-black, like a vein of smoke. He turns off his fire, and it disappears.

I scan the black sand and then the monoliths. They're probably hiding behind the black stone. The demons hate heat . . .

"Jared!" I shout, almost revealing my plan out loud.

Knock the sconces off the wall in this section here! I nod toward where we are pinned in the corner of the arena. Demons roil and shout from the seats above us, beating their hands on their chests and stomping their feet. I can't tell if they want us to die or live—they cheer loudly whenever anything happens. I wish I could deny them their show and suck all the light away so they can't enjoy this ridiculous match.

And keep shouting in their minds, I add.

His confusion bleeds through the link, but he does what I say, flapping down to the sconce on his pillar and knocking it loose. It falls with a crash, the flames snuffing out when it lands.

Bahresh's growl makes me jump. He's barreling down on us with the axe he must have taken from his companion.

"Split!" I shout.

David rolls one way, and I roll the other. His axe clips the pillar with more stone chipping off. Then, he follows me.

"Come here, vermin!"

He swings at me and misses again. I respond with a quick swipe of my broadsword, which clangs on his helmet. He grunts. After a quick recovery, he swipes at my midsection. I spot the other two demons going for David, but they pause, putting their hands to their heads and roaring in frustration. Bahresh slashes again, but I dance away.

Flames shoot out from the pillar, warding the demons off.

Another sconce falls with a loud crash, and Bahresh doesn't seem to notice what's going on. He follows me into the now-deepening darkness.

Jared! I need you to—

My thought message is interrupted when Bahresh attacks in earnest. His axe moves quickly as rage builds in his eyes. So, demons *are* capable of feeling. You just need to prod them long enough. The weapon catches me on my upper arm, tearing into my flesh and making me cry out in agony. I dart around the pillar and use it to block the next blow. I have to close my eyes to keep black dust from entering them.

Bahresh comes around the other side. I duck and throw my shoulder into his gut. Pain erupts in my shoulder as I throw my weight into his armored chest. It knocks him off course, and he stumbles away. My broadsword clangs on his arm, sending him to the side.

I know what you need me to tell him, Jared says.

Well, that's one perk of your brother reading your mind.

Two more sconces fall with thuds, and we're now in such dim lighting that my eyes are struggling to make out where Bahresh is.

"Darkness will not save you from my blade," Bahresh spits.

In my peripheral vision, I see David dash away from the other two demons. One has his hands over his ears like he is hearing something extremely unpleasant.

In a moment, David is hiding behind the pillar opposite me. Even with a fully lit room, Bahresh wouldn't be able to see him easily. But in the dim, it's near impossible.

"What will you do if you kill me, Bahresh?" I say, panting. "Do you really think the people will follow you? Do you think your family won't be a massive mess-up like my father?"

I can't see Krell's reaction, but I hope he can hear what I'm saying over the crowd's chaos. If this stings him, then he deserves every moment of discomfort. For this, and for my whole life.

"Do you want to betray the light races and join the orcs again and be a spineless worm?" I taunt.

Bahresh's anger builds. I can hear it in his breathing and the low growl that emanates from his throat.

"*Burvv* them both!" he shouts.

The word doesn't translate exactly into our language, but I have enough sense to understand that it's a demon form of a curse. It seems like one of the more serious ones.

"I'll pave the way for the demons to rule! We deserve to be on the top, not answering to weakling dragons who have no heart to slay their enemies."

I step out from the pillar and put my hands to the side. "Then, come get your victory, *burvv* head."

Apparently, the word is *really* not nice. Though I can't make out his features, I can hear the roar that comes from his mouth. I see the vague form of his body rushing toward me, and I fixate on where I estimate his face plate will be. Imagining his size and height from our fight, I focus on where the slit should be. It's a long shot, but David is tired, and even Jared has stopped flying around. He isn't knocking over any more scones because of exhaustion, and his feathers are fluffed up with his head bowed low.

This is our only chance.

I take a few steps back to make it look like I'm trying to get away, but this serves to stir Bahresh into more of a frenzy.

I count to three, waiting until he's within range.

"Now!" I shout.

I tap my light absorbing ability just as David pours flames out of both hands. Dark clouds of smoke flow from his palms toward the spot where Bahresh steps. He flinches, but doesn't shy away, thinking that the appearance of the smoke declares what it really is. By the time he realizes that it's as hot as a normal fire, it's too late.

He screams, stumbling back, his hands trying to cover his face. David's fire stops, and he falls to his knees, his face gaunt and pale. I leap onto Bahresh, wincing as I feel the heat of his armor. The sole of my rubber shoe melts into his breastplate, but I don't focus on that. I slam my weapon into his faceplate.

And I miss the slit. My sword glances off the metal harmlessly and goes into the dirt.

I wince, and wait for him to buck me off, but he doesn't. He's writhing and clawing desperately at the armor wrapped around him. The metal is literally cooking him alive.

"Augh! It's—burning!" he screeches.

My stomach twists as I watch him try to remove what was once his protection and now is his death trap. With a nauseous stomach, but a hardened resolve, I pick up my sword and move closer. My eyes have adjusted enough to the light that I can see my target.

"No! No! *You* are supposed to die! This is not—"

His words are cut off as my blade finds its destination.

"Krista!" David shouts, forcing me to look away from Bahresh's lifeless body.

The other two demons have recovered from their reverie and are advancing on him. I keep my face impassive and stand in front of David, shielding him.

"Bahresh is dead!" I snarl.

The two demons pause, staring at me with confused expressions.

"You lie!" one of them spits, raising his fists up in front of his face. This was the former axe holder. I can tell by his completely missing arm. The wound has since healed, but even demon healing can't regrow a limb.

"Light us up," I say quietly to David.

He raises an eyebrow, and with a hesitant glance toward the demons, he lets out a small jet of flames in the area where Bahresh lies.

The demons' eyes widen, and one of them falls to his knees. The other lowers his hands, his mouth hanging so wide that his teeth reflect David's flamelight.

"It can't be," he murmurs.

I feel sick. There is something about fighting with what I *thought* was demonic rage before. Every fight, every injury, every kill is drowned out by the emotion. It masks what is actually happening so I don't have the option to think about the battle.

Right now, I feel hollow.

"We have won. Back down now, or meet his same fate," I challenge.

To my utter shock, they both bow down and put their faces in the dirt.

"Princess, by your command," they say.

David laughs, but it's not a mirthful laugh. He buries his face into his hands and lets out a couple of laugh-sobs. I peer down at him, wishing I could collapse, too. I wish I could let out my emotions, but I need to hold them in. This was by far the scariest thing I've ever had to do.

But it's over.

The declaration causes the crowd to explode into the loudest cheers I've ever heard in my life. I'm overwhelmed by the tumult, but I take the moment to reach down and grab David by the arm. When he looks up at me, he's not crying. He has the biggest smile. I pull him up, and his head barely comes to my chest. Then he wraps me in his football-player arms around me and squeezes.

All breath leaves my lungs as I feel his embrace. It's strikingly close to the numerous times I've had the wind knocked out of me. Except this time, the flutters in my stomach make me want to vomit. My brain wars with my heart, and I almost push him away, but I let him stay. Jared flies down to us and turns back into a human. He wraps his arms around my back, joining the weird hug.

You did it, he says in my mind.

And I did.

"Victory goes to the Ivan House! Karista has won the *krovat*!" Krell declares.

The weird three-person hug reaches peak awkwardness, and I shove them both away. They don't fight it; instead, they choose to embrace each other in an adorable man hug. I watch with a little bit of envy at how easily they seem to be able to let go. With a glance up toward Krell, I see something that not only catches me off guard but strikes me more deeply than I expect.

His gaze is filled with pride.

AN ANNOYING MYSTERY IS REVEALED

I ADJUST MY CLOTHES on my freshly bathed body and sit down heavily on the stone chair in my quarters.

My actual quarters.

After we were pulled out of that arena, I almost collapsed from exhaustion. Needless to say, the moment my head hit the pillow, I was out cold. It didn't matter that the bed was made from the same black stone as everything else in this dark place or that the pillow itself was just a bit of burlap fabric filled with straw. Definitely not my first choice of sleeping arrangements, but demons seemed to like roughing it.

All in all, our accommodations aren't too terrible. While I slept, Krell had his servants wash all of my clothing. Even though they don't smell anymore, there are rips on the arms and legs from me shedding my armor during the battle. Most of the holes have been sewn together with bits of dark blue string. I can't judge the repair job too much considering I don't know how to sew anything.

I frown, fingering one of the tears for a moment before scanning around the large room. It's roughly three times the size of my room back on earth, but it's filled with even less furniture. Only a bed, a large wardrobe, a vanity, and a chair furnish the space. A thick rug of hide is in the center of the room. I don't recognize the animal it could have come from. It's spotted, like a leopard—brown spots on reddish fur. More than the color, the size of the thing is incredible.

Krell offered me new clothes, which I declined for now, only on account of us needing to go to the human realm at some point to find the half-blood. The last time I was dressed in torn medieval clothes, we turned far too many heads.

A pounding on the door pulls me from my thoughts, and I move quickly to open it.

Krell stands on the other side with two looming demon guards behind him. He looks . . . hesitant.

"Karistana," he says. "I came to see if there is anything else my attendants can offer you."

I stare at him, taking him in. His red hair is more vibrant than mine, contrasting with the deep purple of his skin and veins. He's wearing a robe of deep blue, left open to reveal armor beneath it. My silence clearly makes him uncomfortable because he's shifting on his feet ever so slightly. It isn't the kind of shuffle that makes him look weak or impatient. This being looks like the strongest and most powerful creature I know.

But he *does* look like an awkward father.

My heart twinges at the thought. I don't want to feel bad for him. I have no reason to. His reaction somehow brings a smile to my face, even if it's just a slight one.

"Food," I say shortly. "That's about the only thing I want right now."

He nods, then steps back and gestures behind him. There stands half a dozen more demons with trays and platters of food. A full array of fruits, meats, breads, and cheeses appears as if it came out of nowhere.

"Oh—I guess you already thought of that," I mumble.

He nods, putting his hands behind his back and lifting his chin so it's pointed at the ceiling. It only adds to his regal appearance. He is a king to be respected.

And I'm his daughter—a princess.

My stomach twists, but I tell myself it's from my hunger.

"Demons have very large appetites to fill. After your victory, I guessed you would need sustenance," he says.

I nod, moving out of the doorway to grab a bundle of fruit that looks like a mixture of grapes and peaches. They are small and green and have fine hairs along the skin. When I pop one into my mouth, it's not like anything I've tasted before. It's like a mixture of oranges and strawberries.

Saliva explodes in my mouth as if my brain finally woke up to how hungry I am. It takes a lot of willpower not to shove the rest of the bundle in and chew it all at once. I suck in a deep breath to ward off the animalistic instincts.

"I've prepared the same selection for your companions, though in smaller portions," he adds. "Would you prefer that they eat with you? Or in their own quarters?"

I pop another berry onto my tongue and chew it quickly before responding.

"I think I'm good to hang out with them again. Don't you have a banquet hall or anything that we can use?"

He regards me with his dark eyes, then nods.

"We have a ballroom in which I normally eat my meals."

We. These words carry more impact than Krell even realizes. I clear my throat and nod.

"Right. Let's go there, then," I say.

He nods, giving an order to the servants to bring the food. They shuffle off quickly. It looks almost comical to witness their large forms shuffling down the dark hallways filled with light the same color as their skin. In movies, servants are usually smaller and seem more subservient. Witnessing hulking demons react and behave like those portrayed in the media makes my brain hurt in the strangest of ways.

He turns and lifts his arm for me to grab on to, and for some reason, this makes me want to cry and yell at him. After all these years of abandonment, he expects me to hold his arm like a debutante? My brain wars with my heart, but ultimately, I shake my head and stalk off, ignoring the gesture. It's rude, yes, but I can't accept this person into my life because he's suddenly here.

I don't see how he reacts, but he doesn't complain or say anything rude. He simply walks next to me, not attempting to say anything more.

We wind through the black stone hallways, rugs of various sizes, patterns, and colors covering most of the floors. Every so often, we pass a large window that is as dark as the materials of everything else in this place. My sense of time is being affected. There are no clocks here, but there is also no sun. The black cloud of mist covering the city makes it feel like an eternal night.

The servants carrying the food enter through a set of double wooden doors into a ballroom. Before I can follow them, a rough but gentle hand grabs my arm to stop me.

"I understand your reaction, Karistana. You do not need to care for me now or ever," Krell says quietly. "But you must know that I care about you. You are the only heir to the Ivan House. For this reason, I must ensure that you are safe and ready when the throne is to be yours."

I grit my teeth, shoving him out of my way. "Don't profess to care about me. *You* sent me away to another realm because you couldn't bear the thought of having a half human daughter to taint your image or your name."

His jaw hardens, and there is a flare of what looks like anger in his slightly narrowed eyes. Meanwhile, I feel like I'm going to explode with the heat building in my chest. It's taking far more willpower than normal to not smash anything. I fight it for a moment, but I decide I don't care about this place, and I don't care about the damage. I throw my hand outward, not even thinking about how much it will hurt my fist and fingers. My hand hits something much softer than stone.

Krell's palm.

My skin chills, and I pull my fist away, turning so he can't see my face. Anger has quickly shifted to an ominous discomfort at the physical touch. This is the first time he's ever touched me. As if to add to the awkwardness, his arms wrap around my shoulders and pull me in.

I break. It's about the most embarrassing thing that has ever happened to me, but I can't help it. The last time I was hugged like this was when Mom was comforting me years ago.

Since then, I've gained strength and hardened my resolve. There haven't been any hugs.

Only fighting. Training.

I sob into his shoulder. He says nothing. He just holds me. I hate him for it, but I also feel safe for the first time in a long time. I'm not the strong one right now. No other person is leaning on me or depending on me to defend them. It's both terrifying and incredibly relaxing.

"I have always loved you, Karistana. You and your mother," he says quietly.

This only serves to bring a new wave of crying from me.

"I voted to keep you here, with me. But when we allied with the light races, and when the prophecy was fulfilled in you and your other half-blooded counterparts, all the parents voted on where to keep you safe. Only myself and Thorin, king of the dwarves, voted to keep you with us. The other four rulers voted to send you away. I had no choice."

I push back from him, breaking the most glorious hug I've ever had. Hearing this explanation doesn't necessarily make me feel better, but it doesn't make me more upset.

"You always have a choice. That's what Mom taught me. You could have at least sent a message, like the others did for Jared and David," I say, my bitterness evident.

He nods, but he doesn't appear sad. He doesn't even seem like he feels bad about that.

"I could have. For this, I am full of regret. But you have returned, and the war is at our doorstep. It is up to you whether you wish to hold contempt and anger in your heart. Whatever you decide, I will still defend you and love you," he says.

And with that, he nods and walks away.

I'm stunned. I just chewed him out once again for being a terrible father, and he doesn't seem to care. My human emotions boil and twist inside my whole being, a testament to how different I am from every other demon. I can't decide if I want to yell at him again, let him go, or rush and get one final hug.

I decide to let him go. He and his guards walk with directed steps and straight backs, disappearing around the corner.

"Krista?" David calls from down the hallway.

He's back in his now-cleaned T-shirt, jeans, and hoodie. Even his Converse shoes have been washed up so they seem almost brand new. The short sword hangs from his waist on a new leather sheath. The mixture of modern clothing and more ancient weaponry gives me cosplay vibes. He grins at me and walks right up, his head tilted back so he can peer into my face.

"Oh, good, you've taken a bath. I was wondering how I was going to hang out with you again if you smelled like you did when we left the arena," he teases, folding his arms and grinning at me.

I scowl at him. "You weren't a bed of roses yourself."

He shrugs. "I'm well acquainted with being stinky. Long football practices don't exactly make you ready for a date."

I shake my head, glancing past him down the hallway. "Where are the others?"

Another shrug from Dragon Breath.

"Not sure. I think they're in their rooms, but this place is so big and dark. I'm not sure where anything is." He pauses for a moment before making an exaggerated sniffing sound. "But rumor says there's food around here."

I nod, my stomach growling at the mention of the feast.

"In there. I guess we can get started without them."

David nods but doesn't move. He continues staring at me, scanning me from head to toe. "You know, despite the tight sweats and hulking form, you clean up pretty well."

I'm stunned.

He gives me a half smile, pushing through the large dark wood doors. Now that I know the emotions writhing within me aren't from my demon heritage, I feel like I should own them more. Right now, I don't know what to do about that boy. My heightened senses catch the scent of his clothing, clean now from whatever soaps were used to wash them. I also smell him. Just him.

I shake my head as I follow him.

On the other side of the door is a cavernous room with a ceiling fifty feet high. Wide windows extend from floor to ceiling and line the walls on either side all the way to the end, where a massive set of copper pipes fill the back wall. It looks like an organ you'd see in a church.

"You should not have put yourself in such danger! Your mother would not be pleased to see you get yourself killed!"

Rolinda's voice echoes across the ballroom so loudly that I'm honestly shocked to see that she's still in her minuscule fairy form. David and I exchange looks of "Oh great, this should be interesting."

"Rolinda, please calm down! I wasn't in any real danger—"

"Not in any real danger? Freya bless me, that is the most foolish thing I've heard you say, and it's still early!" she proclaims. "More than once, I saw your life flash before my eyes and wondered how I was going to explain to the queen that her son and heir to the kingdom got his skull bashed in."

Jared frowns, then averts his gaze.

"Let's be honest. She wouldn't care," he says.

My heart twinges at seeing his reaction, and I almost turn around to get away from the intense emotion. I'm not the "comfort a sad person" type. This is probably why I don't have a lot of friends. Whenever I would start to get close to someone, I'd either scare them away with my intensity or wouldn't be there for them when they needed to talk.

And Jared looks pretty down . . .

The sound of my shuffling feet pulls the attention of the group.

"Will you tell him that his mother loves him, no matter what?" Rolinda says, exasperated.

I scoff. "Are you serious? First off, why do you need *me* to say anything? Second, as much as it sucks, I think Jared's right. That lady's gone psycho. Do you really think she cares about him? About any of us? She tried to enslave *you*, Rolinda. Did you forget that?"

A puff of air and bright flash almost blinds me. Fluttering my eyelids to clear the spots in my vision, I'm finally able to focus on her now-human-sized face.

"She is being compelled to do those things. Did you not see Urothar's marking on her? He's controlling her and her actions. Deep down, she doesn't want to do what she's doing," she says.

I fold my arms, gearing up to lay into this idiotic fairy.

"Rolinda, sit down," Amir says.

I didn't even notice him sitting there with the confrontation going on between Jared and Rolinda. Amir squirms in the high-backed chair, his sweet bun pastry half-eaten. A bit of frosting sticks to the side of his mouth. The poor kid looks exhausted. I know David didn't intend to suck him into all this, but I wonder if it would have been safer to leave him back in the human realm. Thoughts of returning back to our realm twist in my mind. It's been some time since we last tried to pull ourselves back there. I wonder if we've rested enough to try again?

"*Sit down?*" she shrieks. "You're doing enough sitting down for the both of us! Don't you care about your friend? You did nothing to stop them from going into that horrid arena to get nearly killed. You could have volunteered to go in with Karistana instead of Joiron. Have you ever think of that?"

I squeeze my fists tightly at her mention of my real name.

"Don't use that name for me. I'm *Krista*. And he's Jared. Nothing else. And don't be dumb. If Amir had gone in there, he'd have been killed in about ten seconds flat. No offense," I say, shooting him a look.

He shrugs, but I can tell my words hurt. What would it be like to be the only human tagging along with a bunch of half-bloods and an overactive fairy?

"What's the point of the prophecy to save Qotan if you are all going to throw your lives away like nothing matters?" she shoots back, her upper lip quivering.

It takes everything in me not to roll my eyes or shout at her. Before I can formulate a response, David speaks up.

"Rolinda, calm down. I know you don't want to hear it, but Ferona wasn't being controlled. Did you not see my mom? She also had that nasty tattoo thing on her body, but did you see her going all dragon and biting our heads off? No. She was actually *fighting* for control. Unlike Ferona. She was going along with it like it was what she actually wanted," he says firmly. "If you don't like that, too bad. She doesn't care about Jared. She doesn't care about us. In the end, I hope she gets what she deserves."

I turn to him, my mouth slightly ajar. I didn't realize he had that in him. Somehow, it makes me even more impressed.

Rolinda huffs and folds her arms. The door thuds open behind us, and the echo reverberates through the room. I spin, reaching for my broadsword but cursing when I realize it's not there. I left it in my quarters with the rest of my things.

Krell and two guards stand in the doorway. Though I can't be entirely sure, these two guards look different from the ones he had with him the first time we met. One of them looks like a female demon. She is slightly shorter than Krell but has equally large and powerful arms. Her hair is in a thick black braid down her back, and she carries a tall spear. She looks distinctly familiar, but I can't place why I feel that way. The other guard is a male demon. His weapon of choice is a mace that hangs from his side.

Krell sweeps into the room and stands in front of me and Jared. After an awkward moment, his massive hand thuds on my shoulder. I flinch, but not from the weight or the strength of his grip—mainly from the touch.

I hate touching.

"Karistana, I am proud of you," he says, his gaze lingering on my face before shifting to David and then to Jared.

Jared sits up a little straighter, most likely in an attempt to hide the despair he feels from Rolinda's words.

"And thanks to her friends for ensuring her success."

The air takes on an extremely tense and awkward energy, which pushes me past the point of "I need to get out of here." I step back so Krell's hand falls off of where it rests. I liked hearing him say that, as much as I hate to admit it.

"I owe my life to them. And I'm glad it's over," I say. The fighting adrenaline I experienced still leaves an impression on my mind. It felt amazing to let go and become a storm of fury and skill. "But I don't get the sense that this Khan family is going to leave you alone."

The soldier I recognize clears her throat. Her pure-black eyes exude hatred, something that, so far, has been relatively absent from all the demons up to this point.

"My family will no longer vie for the throne. It is rightfully with the house of Ivan for at least the next ten years. Father is not a fool and will vie no more for the throne," she states.

It's then that her appearance clicks in my mind. She has similar features to the demon I downed in the arena. She is also a Khan. I take a step forward, my hands readying themselves for a potential fight.

"You are trusting one of the enemies to follow you around? Are you stupid?" I say to Krell.

No reaction. He merely watches me with a fixed gaze.

"She was part of my retinue before the debacle with her father," Krell replies. "He's been exiled for the requisite ten years. Only then can he return to us. Though, I doubt he will be interested in coming back here."

I pause, taking that in. I don't trust her, and I make that clear by my stiff posture and my dirty looks. She seems unaffected.

"We did not come here to talk of the past, even if we are celebrating your victory," he says. "But of the future. Terendrell is soon to be under siege. I have already organized my soldiers, and we are ready to march to the elf kingdom as soon as possible. I must make good on my promise to defend the kingdoms of the light races."

Amir clears his throat. "Great, but we still haven't gotten the elf girl yet," he reminds us. "Also, thanks for speaking English. It's been annoying not to understand what everyone is talking about."

Krell regards him with a furrowed brow. It's the kind of look you give someone who is mildly annoying, but you can't tell them to go away because they came with one of your good friends.

"Yes, your errand to retrieve the girl," Krell continues. "King Ilvinar and I have spoken. He still urges you to continue your trek to find her with all haste. You are then to return to us and help defend Terendrell. With his daughter back, King Ilvinar believes it will rally the fractured elven tribes together in defense of their freedom."

I frown. Part of me wishes I could stay here. Even in my forced demon state, my emotions are the calmest they've ever been. Not to mention that I also feel like I have a place here. The demons standing behind my father seem to revere me. It's a good feeling after everyone only giving me scared or uncomfortable glances. I feel the need to prove myself to them—to join them right away and fight for the elves' defense.

But I know what we have to do.

"We will leave here as soon as we can," I say.

Krell nods, then peers behind at the table full of food. There are at least thirty chairs around this thing, and it's large enough for a ton of people. Only half of it is covered with the feast.

"First, you must eat. Then, we can discuss how to get you back home," he says.

Jared perks up. "Right, slight problem there. We don't have a way to get home. I tested my connection to our realm before we came here. I can feel the link, but I can't pull on it. I think we need to recharge for longer."

David curses quietly. "Then, how are we supposed to get back to earth?"

"That should be the easy part," Krell says, his loud voice echoing off the walls. "For we have one of the portals secured within our citadel."

"Wait, are you serious?" Jared exclaims. "Ferona didn't say anything about a portal being here. She just said there was one close to Dranith and one that Urothar has captured."

Face still impassive, Krell asks something that stops all arguments. "And why would she have any reason to tell you the truth with her alliance to Urothar?"

Jared looks down again.

"Good point," David says. He awkwardly shuffles to the table, sits, and starts munching on something.

"You must eat. Enjoy your celebration feast for a time. But you must leave here to find the heir to the elven throne. Once you have her secured, find your way back. Join us and fight for the freedom of Terendrell."

It all sounds like the perfect plan. Except it's not going to be easy to find the girl. I reach into my pocket and pull out the tracking stone. I spin the dial until it lands on the symbol that represents me. The beam of light leads right to my chest, absorbing into my body.

"It's going to take us some time to figure out how to find her with this," I comment, showing Krell the stone.

"What do you mean? It should show you the exact location of the heir," he says.

I stare at him. "Right. *If* we're in the same room. Otherwise, we're just on a wild-goose chase, jumping from town to town until we happen to find her."

"Why would you chase a wild goose? I fail to understand how this is relevant. The proximity beacon is only meant to be used when a more detailed map is not available. Why would you follow the beacon in such a way?"

Amir clears his throat. "With all due respect, sir, just ignore the goose thing. What do you mean about the detailed map?"

He sizes up Amir as if he's never seen the boy before. "It is common knowledge that you pair the stone with a map so the magic can work properly."

Snapping his fingers, an attendant appears. I flinch, looking around the edges of the large ballroom. There are stewards dressed in smart-looking black robes with white undershirts.

"My king?" the demon asks, his face flat.

"Retrieve a map of Qotan."

The attendant leaves in a hurry.

"When we used your blood to create the stones, we ensured that they would always be attuned to your essence—your souls, if you will. Most stones can only locate one person or place. It becomes increasingly challenging to infuse more than one essence into a stone with each new soul. We had to put the will and magic of each of the rulers there, as well as blood from each of you. To make six? We were sick for days after creating them. Yet, we knew that it would be imperative for you to be able to locate each other when the time came."

My mind soaks in the information like a growing child entering school for the first time. There is something that bothers me about the whole thing.

"If you planned for us to find each other, why didn't you send the stones with us from the beginning?" David asks.

It's like he read my mind.

Krell's brows knit downward.

"For you to come together before you were ready would be too risky. You were meant to be safe from the dark races in your realm. The combination of your blood—of your magic in one location—would make it easier to find you. We wanted to remove the temptation that you—or your fallible human parents—might have to locate the others. The stones were meant to be delivered to you upon reaching your twentieth year."

"Yeah, that worked out well for us," I say sarcastically.

Jared grimaces. "I don't think they expected Ferona to betray them and lead the enemy to us."

"Quite," Krell says, looking thoughtful. "But we move forward with what we have. You are young and ill-equipped to fight for your homeland; however, you have no choice."

The attendant runs back with a large scroll held underneath his armpit.

"The map, as you requested," he says.

Krell takes the scroll and gestures to the table. The attendant snaps into action, clearing a place for the large scroll. Amir continues eating, his jaw bouncing up and down with his unhurried pace. The demon king rolls out the parchment, pressing it flat, and his movements make me tense. Lines and landmarks indicating different locations in Qotan extend upward instantly like a pop-up book for kids.

"Dude, that's so cool!" Amir exclaims through his bite.

Krell ignores the comment. "The stone," he says, holding out his hand.

I hesitate. I don't know why. It isn't that I don't trust him, but after losing all our other stones, I'm afraid to lose this one as well. He eyes me, an eyebrow raised. After a sigh, I relinquish the rock.

"Just ensure that the spindle is pointed to the correct heir," he instructs, inspecting the beam which is still pointed at my chest. "Then, place it on the map."

He sets the stone down on the parchment, and a pinprick of light appears in the top left corner. I'm not familiar with Qotan geography, but the black circular smudge that houses the pinprick of light definitely represents the giant black cloud covering this place.

David whistles softly, and Jared shakes his head.

"You've got to be kidding me," I say, annoyance flaring in my belly. "All this time we could have just put it on a dumb map, and it would have shown us exactly where they are?"

Amir curses, his face paling slightly. "Rolinda," he says hesitantly, "did you know this all along?"

She flits off his shoulder where she was sitting and playing with her hair.

"Of course I knew it. Why else would I ask if you had a map when we first met? You told me that people don't use maps in your world anymore, so I assumed we could only use the beacon."

We all groan collectively.

"Just because no one *uses* maps doesn't mean we don't *have* them!" I shout.

She shrugs. "I know nothing of the human world. What did you expect from me?"

Krell fixes his gaze on me. "Well, the information is available now. You must leave at once. Please eat your feast, then prepare to go."

16

THE PATH TO EARTH OPENS

W E STAND OUTSIDE THE palace with its terrifying black spires shooting upward into the sky. I gaze at it, wondering what it might have been like to grow up here with attendants and guards, among people who look like me. *Almost* like me . . .

The garden around us has strange plants with brown leaves and stalks. There is absolutely no greenery here. It makes sense, considering this place will never see the face of the sun. Though there's no green, there are flowers and fruits of other colors, such as whites and vibrant yellows. It's the most color I've seen since we got here, save for some of the rugs and tapestries within the palace.

"I have mobilized my armies and have sent the first wave toward Terendrell," Krell tells us. "I will join them shortly as soon as you have set off on your journey."

"You could have just gone with them," I say.

What I *want* to say is that we don't need him and that he doesn't have to hover like a guilty parent who realizes he's been absent for all the wrong reasons. Jared eyes me, likely reading my thoughts. I wall him off right then and there.

"No. This is more important at this moment. Besides, a darangkin can bring me to the army very quickly."

"Creepy dog-bat thing for the win," David jokes unenthusiastically, pumping his fist into the air.

Krell looks unimpressed. "Once you have located the elven princess, return immediately, by whatever means necessary. Guards watch the portal both day and night for any who may stumble through or come with ill intentions. I suspect it is well-hidden in the human realm, for we haven't had unexpected visitors in a while. Still, once you have returned, they will ensure you have safe passage to Terendrell and the coming fight. I hope that you make it in time to help bolster the armies' morale."

I grunt. "I wouldn't mind sticking my sword in a few orcs, so hopefully the fight isn't done by the time we get back."

David lets out an awkward chuckle, but otherwise everyone is measuredly silent.

"How barbaric," Rolinda says, clicking her tongue.

A silence falls on the group, and suddenly, I feel like an outcast again. Always wanting a fight. Always wanting to prove myself. Jared has told me before that he doesn't understand it. The misconception that my urge to fight comes from my demon side makes me feel awkward. It's been upsetting to learn that my fight instinct is exaggerated from my human emotions.

I hate being reminded of that . . .

"Your sword would be welcome in the fight," he says. "But your safety is the most important thing. No soul knows what would happen if one of you were to die. It is a risk we are unwilling to take."

"All right then," I say, trying to push away the awkwardness I just caused between all of us. "How do we get this show on the road?"

Krell stares at me, blinking slowly. Dumb English idioms always seem to go over these demons' heads.

"How can we get to the human realm?" I clarify.

"Ah, right. It's through there."

His long purple finger directs our attention to a wide and low black stone building. The structure has vines running up and down the outside. With the vines' brown and sickly appearance, it looks more like an abandoned crypt than anything else. My imagination runs wild, and I suddenly have an image of a skeleton or zombie attacking us the moment we walk in.

David moves closer to me as Krell leads us through the winding pathway to the building. Two guards stand on either side of the door, one with a spear and the other with two swords strapped to his belt. Their armor glints in the purple everlight that shines from the sconces above their heads.

"Can you believe this place? It's like something from a gothic music video," he says, chuckling.

I get where he's coming from, but it's not funny. Even if I don't feel much of a connection to this place, it's still technically my home. And as much as I hate to admit it, I kind of like the dark aspects of it. My demon blood attunes to what it likes most: the darkness.

"Maybe you should write a song, record it, and post it to YouTube," I say flatly.

He looks thoughtful. "Amir *does* have some pretty good video-editing skills."

I watch him pull out his phone, lifting it up just high enough to snap a picture of me. "Had just enough battery for that beauty," he says, slipping the phone back into his pocket.

"You'll be deleting that," I say.

He shrugs. "Only if you make me."

Before I can respond, I catch Krell telling the guards to let us through and watch carefully until we return. At this point, I'm not sure if we'll make it back. We don't know how far away the elf girl is, but hopefully by the time we get to her, we'll be able to zap ourselves back into Qotan. I reach within, sensing the human half of me and thinking of home. The tug to our realm is there, it's just a little too weak. It's still recharging. After all, last time we waited weeks before we pulled ourselves back.

I can only hope it doesn't take that long to recharge again.

"Enter the building, but do not enter the portal yet," Krell instructs, gesturing for my friends to enter one by one. I take up the rear, but before I can go through the dark gated doorway, Krell's hand grabs my shoulder.

"A word," he says, ushering me away from the door.

I nod and let him lead me out of earshot of the guards. He puts himself between me and the building, his huge form blocking it from my view. We stand there in silence for so long that I start to get uncomfortable. His black eyes are fixed on me, and I can tell he's mulling over exactly what to say.

"I am proud of you, Karistana," he murmurs finally. "When you were born, heir to Etherek, I hoped that you would grow to become a great queen. Never did I expect it to be so difficult to let you go. But now that you have returned, I want you to take this."

He reaches into a pouch at his side and pulls out a necklace. The chain is made from a dark gray material, and at the bottom hangs a beautifully cut black stone. I don't move at first, I simply stare at the piece of jewelry. Krell's hand grips my wrist, his touch not blazing hot like that of my friends. Our temperatures are the same—as cold as the dead. He opens up my hand and drops the necklace onto my palm.

"I know you are unhappy with me—with my choices," he begins. "But know that I want nothing more than for you to be successful." He appears pained. "And I'm sorry. I'm sorry for what your life stands for and where it is going."

Oh. He means the sacrifice. Somehow, in all our journeying and fighting, I forgot that little part of the prophecy. The irony of them wanting to keep us safe only so we can be slaughtered for this prophecy forces a dark chuckle out of me.

"To have children only to send them away until they are sacrificed. Really nice one," I say sarcastically.

He doesn't back down, his posture straight and his eyes smoldering. I've definitely struck a chord.

"I wish it didn't have to be this way, but it does. We all have our duties to perform," he says.

Then, he does something that I'm not expecting. He takes my face in his hands and leans forward to kiss my forehead. My instincts kick in, and I punch him in the gut. He grunts, taking a step back, but he doesn't look angry. Instead, his eyes twinkle. My insides squirm from what I've done, but when I open my mouth to apologize, he holds up a hand to stop me.

"Well deserved. Take care, my daughter."

And with that, he turns and walks toward the building that houses the portal. I stand there watching him for a few seconds before I hear Jared call my name.

"Krista, are you coming?"

I nod, taking one last look at the pendant before slipping it over my neck and down into my hoodie. Nausea settles in my stomach from the confused human emotions swirling everywhere. Validation. Love. Of all the things I expected to feel when I met my father, these two were not on the list.

"Coming!" I shout, trotting over to the doorway.

I duck through the entrance—an instinct more than anything else. Of course, it's built to allow demons to stand inside, but I'm still used to trying not to hit my head on every door jamb.

Light assaults my eyes, and I pause, covering my face until I can adjust. Just inside the doorway, there's a set of blazing everlight torches that line all four walls.

"Someone clearly doesn't like the dark," Amir comments.

I blink rapidly, getting my pupils used to the new lighting.

"It's the first time I've felt safe in this dark and horrible place," Rolinda says, emerging from Amir's shirt.

Krell slides past me and into the well-lit room. He holds an arm over his eyes to shield himself from the torches. When I'm finally able to make out what's in the room, I see that it's completely empty. Roughly fifteen feet by fifteen feet, the black stone walls and floor hold no furniture, art, or rugs.

"We've kept this portal safe and hidden for many years now. I know not where it ends in your world, but you must remember the location of the portal so that you can return to us when you retrieve your quarry," Krell says.

"So, you've just sat on one of these portals for years, and you've never been curious to step through yourself and see what it's like in our realm?" David asks, raising an eyebrow.

Krell folds his huge arms across his chest.

"Curiosity never belies the risk of death—unless it is for the benefit of all. Your world is a darkened place, unfit for any Qotanian."

I have to keep myself from pointing out the irony of a demon from *this* place calling *our* world darkened. I have a sneaking suspicion that he wouldn't take that joke well.

"Right, makes sense. For some reason, I guessed you would all be adrenaline junkies after meeting Krista," David says.

Krell looks even more confused now. "What is a junkie?"

I chuckle. "Don't worry about it."

Krell's eyes flit to mine, and while I can see he's not actually going to take my advice to forget about what a "junkie" means, he doesn't press the question any further.

My gaze wanders to the far wall where I spy movement, and my breath catches in my throat. The center section of the wall is swirling, the black stone warping inward like a whirlpool to reveal the portal.

"So, we just walk right through?" Jared asks. "Did the fairies create this portal?"

"I know not the origin of this particular point, yet I know your kind are capable of such things. Other races are not. It is likely that they had a part in the formation of this portal," Krell admits.

I look closer at the swirling wall. It looks like the ooze that Qotanians melt into when they step into our realm. This doesn't make me feel any better.

"Are you sure it won't close itself off when we get through?" I ask.

Krell doesn't respond right away. "I do not understand the nature of all portals, but it should remain constant, as it never changes on our side. Not for centuries."

Somehow, that guess doesn't make me feel much better. Also, knowing that the fairies were involved in making this portal makes me reluctant to dive through it. What if Ferona somehow redirected the portal to take us to her instead of back to our realm? Another couple of demons enter behind us, their weapons at the ready.

"Sire. The warriors you sent before us will undoubtedly be awaiting your arrival. I recommend leaving as soon as possible," the female demon says.

Krell nods.

"And now we're back not to speaking English," Amir complains. "Why can't I just have "magic dragon Google Translate" in my head?"

We all largely ignore his comment except Jared, who cracks a smile.

"It is as they speak. I must soon fly with my darangkin to join the armies. It is both my duty and honor to lead our ranks to bolster those of the light races," he says, looking at me again. "Fly true, and fly safe. Return to us as soon as you can."

With that, he reaches out, gripping my shoulder for a moment before nodding to each of my friends. He settles on the small orb of a fairy and makes a concerned face.

"Rolinda, will you be joining us on our journey to Terendrell?"

She scoffs, stamping a small foot on Amir's shoulder. "I will *not* be coming with you. The last thing I need is to be stuck with a whole group of you brutes!"

Krell doesn't seem to mind her insult. "Do you care so little about your life to throw it away to death?" he asks. "You have no protection from the darkness that is their realm."

Rolinda scowls, reaching into a pocket hidden in the folds of her gown and pulling out a red-colored stone. "This will protect me, as it always has."

Krell frowns. "Yes, I can sense that magic was once a part of that stone, but it has since expired."

Her face falls, and she scrutinizes the stone more closely before muttering something in fairy that sounds like it wouldn't be allowed in a kid's book.

"No—no—I can't go with all the demons! I won't make out alive!" she complains.

Krell opens his mouth as if to refute her claim, but with a slight shake of his head, he decides otherwise. I suspect he realizes she's not worth reasoning with at this moment.

"Unless you have a way to infuse that stone with magic once more, you will need to stay in Qotan. Our palace has plenty of rooms and things for you to do. You would be well-fed and taken care of among us."

"Well, I *do* know the magic to infuse this stone, but I need a human's blood in order to do that. If you haven't realized by now, humans are in short supply, and I haven't got any close to me."

It's as if a weight drops from the sky and lands on all of our shoulders collectively. My eyes drift to where Amir's purplish everlight-infused complexion pales slightly.

"He's human though," Jared says.

Amir shoots him a look of annoyance mixed with intense frustration.

Rolinda's eyes go wide, and she throws her arms in the air. "Right! I have the means to infuse magic into the stone."

She turns and regards Amir with a hunger in her eyes that I find particularly terrifying.

"Nah, I hate needles and sharp things. I'm going to go ahead and opt out of the blood thing," he says, waving his hands in the air as if to keep us all away. "Plus, I thought you said that humans were killed in the process."

Rolinda scowls. "Now, where would you get an idea like that? Of course, we *can* take all of your blood for a longer living stone, but I won't do that here," she says, flitting to his face and caressing his cheek.

I want to vomit. This is a sixteen-year-old who has managed to catch the fancy of a fairy who is obviously quite a bit older than he is. They've been pretty much inseparable ever since Rolinda stumbled upon us by the restaurant, but this is awkward on a whole new level.

"Come, I just need a bit from you," she whines, moving closer with her tiny hand splayed out like she is going to scratch his face.

I step forward, putting a hand out to stop her. David does the same thing, and our shoulders end up smashing together. I recoil, letting him take the lead to intervene.

"You won't be taking anything by force," David says, the palm of his hand now acting like a wall between the fairy and Amir. "If he doesn't feel like bleeding for you, then he doesn't have to."

David and Amir both flinch at the choice of words. They sound like something from a cheesy romance movie. Jared stifles a laugh as Krell watches on.

"Yes, if the human is unwilling to relinquish any of his lifeblood, to take it by force would be against the laws of our citadel. You would be subject to incarceration and further punishment," Krell says flatly.

Rolinda rolls her eyes. "There's no need to be dramatic. I won't do anything."

In a puff of smoke and a blinding flash, Rolinda stands before us in her full-sized form. She's turned on her puppy dog eyes.

"Please, O noble Amir. Don't leave me with the demons all by my lonesome," she begs. After a moment, her eyes widen and she adds, "Or you could stay with me! Send your companions through, and you and I can continue onward with the demons."

Amir's face turns ashen. "Yeah, fun as this has all been, I'm not staying here without them."

She whimpers, her face falling as she shoves her hand in the folds of her dress. Amir looks pained. Just before I can step in to tell the fairy to shrink up and buzz off, he sighs and holds out his hand.

"Fine. Take it."

"You don't have to do this," David assures him.

"Yeah, the whiny fairy would probably be better off melting the ears of the demons with her complaints," I say.

Rolinda glares at me. I feel the pressure of her trying to access my mind, but she's unable to breach my defenses. I grin at her and point to my temple.

Setting up mind barriers has taken me many years of practice, and I'm glad I took the time to learn. And this "relaxed" demon state allows me to uphold the barriers. Bob said it was a skill he had to learn when he first lived among the fairies. He told us he had fallen through a portal by sheer accident and found living with the fairies to be far more enjoyable than he had expected. More than once, he almost came back to our realm, but something kept him there, though he could never say what it was. I shy away from these thoughts, focusing back on the moment.

"I'll do the honors," David says, pulling his sword free.

"Probably better than the human-sized cleaver," Amir says, nodding to me.

I shrug. "This cleaver doesn't normally need to do small jobs like this."

David holds the sword over his forearm and presses the tip gently there. "Ready?"

Amir looks away and nods.

Baring his teeth, David presses into the skin, blood oozing out of the fresh cut.

Amir curses, peeks at the cut, then squeezes his eyes shut. His body starts swaying slightly, and Jared is by his side quickly, his arms wrapped around Amir's chest to hold him up. David pulls the sword away, and the blood oozes, dripping in a small puddle. He's done a really controlled job, the blood neither stopping nor trickling in a dangerous stream.

"Yes! Perfect," Rolinda says.

She places the stone directly in the puddle of his blood and starts chanting. The stone glows, and the blood starts to absorb into its surface. After a minute, the glow dies down, and she pulls the now-cleaned stone away. More blood springs up, but David grabs Amir's hand and slaps it on the cut.

"Pressure on it while I get a bandage."

It doesn't take long to get it all fixed up. Soon we're standing in a group facing the swirling doorway back to our realm. For some reason I can't explain, I'm nervous. It feels strange being in my demon form and feeling other emotions still. The nervousness, however, takes the cake. Jared is to my right, and David is to my left. Amir and the now-shrunken Rolinda are behind us.

Krell waves and bids us farewell, heading toward the exit. Just before he ducks through the doorway, he pauses and turns around.

"Return to us safely, halflings. Farewell."

Then, he's gone. My heart sinks a little knowing that there's a chance I won't see him again. I shake my head, not wanting to entertain that possibility. We'll return here before the battle happens. I have to believe that.

As if I'm going to be the sole reason he isn't killed in a fight, I think.

"Well, who's first?" I ask.

David squares his shoulders. "I'll go."

As he walks toward the swirling portal, his hands flex in discomfort. With one final sigh, he steps forward. His body twists and warps as if he's being drawn in. Then, he's gone.

"Okay, he didn't scream or anything," Amir says. "That's a good sign. I guess I'm next."

He steps up to the portal and is drawn in the same way.

"Let's do it," Jared says. He moves to the portal and is gone in an instant.

I pause, peering back at the doorway to the home that was never a home to me. A part of me wishes I could stay and realize the dream of having a constant home where I don't feel so isolated and out of place.

Even though I know it will never be my reality—what with the prophecy and our impending sacrifices—I pretend it might be possible. I turn, pushing any sadness of leaving out of my mind.

Then, I step forward. I feel my body being tugged by the force of the portal, and then the world, along with my head, spins rapidly.

17

WE STUMBLE ACROSS ANOTHER HALFLING

My stomach churns as my field of vision blurs. I'm vaguely aware of the others screaming, but the sound is moving in and out of focus so quickly that it's causing me to feel vertigo. Just when I think I'm about to lose my lunch, I fall toward a ground that was definitely not there moments ago. Instinct makes me throw my hands out to break my fall. A pain fires up my arms as my wrists connect with the cement of a cracked sidewalk in an alleyway. I hold myself up for just a moment before my elbows buckle, causing me to land on my face with a grunt.

"Well, at least she didn't fall right on top of me," David groans.

"Dude, it's not like I chose to land where I did. Plus, you didn't have to lay there for so long," Jared comments.

"Teleportation travel is not that difficult. But you humans somehow manage to make it look ridiculously challenging,"

Rolinda says. "It's all about mental fortitude more than physical control."

Amir huffs. "Can you please spare us your lectures, Rol? It's not like we can create portals out of nowhere to take people places. You have a lot more practice than us."

"I second that," David says. "Also, we're *half human*, so get that right."

Rolinda rolls her eyes.

I'm just stuck on the fact that Amir called the fairy "Rol" like she's been a lifelong friend. The thought is soon lost to the pain that continues to radiate in my wrists. That's when I notice that my body is no longer massive with purple veins. Somewhere in the journey, I switched back into my human form. I squirm uncomfortably at the recognition. How is it possible that I started to feel so comfortable in my demon skin in such a short amount of time? It was as if I was coming home, realizing the reality of my life and discovering something that was a part of me.

"Hey, at least if Kris had landed on someone, it wouldn't have been a demon crushing," David jests.

My stomach flutters again at his use of Jared's nickname for me. Jared eyes me, gauging my reaction before continuing.

"I have to admit, I was kind of getting used to calm demon Kris. Do we at least get calm human Krista?"

I nod. I can't tell if it's my spinning head or the overwhelm of what just happened, but I feel calm and collected.

"Yeah, I'm not the "bite your head off" Krista right now," I say.

A wafting smell of urine reaches my nose, and I cough, covering my face with the sleeve of my sweatshirt, which now hangs loose on my arm. Movement to my right draws my attention there.

I reach back and pull the broadsword free from its sheath, my arms straining a bit under its weight. After having spent the last couple days in my demon form, it's strange to actually feel the weapon as a human.

"Woah, what the—" Amir says, following my gaze.

A homeless woman lies in a pile of old blankets. She cowers there, her arms raised high in a pleading action. Though she's speaking, I can't understand what she's saying. It's English, but it's jumbled.

I frown, allowing my sword to fall to the ground.

"Sorry," I mutter, placing my weapon back in its sheath and grinding my teeth to overcome the awkwardness.

Jared eyes me cautiously, his gaze trailing down my body.

Why is he looking at me that way? I didn't shift to demon form. I scowl, wondering why my intense shock didn't transform me into my larger form. Jared taps his head, and I oblige, letting him into my mind.

You didn't shift. Are you feeling okay?

I scoff. Did he want me to go all mental on this poor woman?

I shake my head. *I'm fine. I can sense the demonic form in the back of my mind, but she's more subdued for some reason.*

He nods. *Let's hope she's not subdued forever.*

That would really rain on my parade.

The homeless woman continues babbling, her arms waving wildly in the air as she tries to back away from us.

"No—no, we won't hurt you," I encourage, but the woman's eyes are fixated on me like she's facing a serial killer. In the midst of her tirade, I do catch one word that hits me hard.

"De—demon!" she screams. "Girl—ick—dem—augh!"

Jared grimaces and gestures for me to go away. My chest aches. For the woman, and for me. Her wide, terrified eyes are burned into my brain. All harbored emotions and frustrations from my childhood come to the surface.

I'm a monster. I'm terrifying.

"We won't hurt you. You're seeing things," Jared says, kneeling by her side.

It takes him a moment, but he manages to get her attention. I turn to leave the premises as quickly as possible. As I emerge from the alleyway, I see vehicles on a busy roadway and people traversing the sidewalks. I get a few odd looks, but most people ignore me as they pass.

A hand touches my shoulder, and I flinch, spinning around to plant my fist into the attacker. Instead of hitting flesh, however, my hand smashes into what feels like an uneven rock wall.

"Ow!" David complains, stepping back and putting his hand to his scaled-up cheek.

Knuckles burning from the impact, I suck air in through my teeth and look closer. I more than likely broke a finger, at least based on how hard I punched him in the face.

"Well, don't go sneaking up on people like that!" I almost shout at him. I feel the anger and annoyance boiling in my stomach, but I'm somehow holding the demon form of me at bay. I furrow my brow, reaching for her and readying her to come out and smash a brick wall. I know I could pull her out. Did going to the demon city cure me of my lack of control?

"Sorry," I say absentmindedly, too focused on what is going on inside my head to say anything else.

"Sheesh, you still pack a punch even when you aren't all beefed up," he says, rubbing his face.

"Just be glad I didn't go all demon on you," I mutter, shooting him a "on't press your luck" kind of look.

He shrugs. "Honestly, I *am* curious to know who would win in a fight. Demon fist? Or dragon scales? Sounds like a Mortal Kombat battle to me."

"Oh, please don't tell me you're a gamer. That would make you so much worse."

David grins. "Nah, don't have time for that. I'm too busy with football and helping Dad out with the horses."

His smile falls quickly at the mention of his dad. We still have no idea if he, Bob, and Mom are alive or not.

I scan our surroundings. The road we're on is relatively packed, cars zooming this way and that. A couple people glare at us for being in their way as they walk by. A few stand and stare at us as if they've seen a ghost.

Right. If they just saw me sock a kid with red scales on his face, that would look pretty freaky . . .

Even though we were only in Qotan for a few days, I some-how managed to forget that it's weird for humans to see us. They aren't familiar with our unusual shenanigans. Or, of course, they could be wary of the broadsword on my back. Kids don't generally walk around armed like soldiers from the Middle Ages.

A cool breeze picks up and blows my hair across my face. I spit a few strands out of my mouth and go to put it in a ponytail only to find that I don't have any elastics. I curse, searching for anything that I can use to keep it up.

David frowns at what I'm doing, then pulls his backpack off his back. He rummages for a bit before pulling out a bright pink hair tie.

"You seriously have an elastic band in your backpack? That's really weird."

He blushes. "It's not mine. It's my girlfriend's. Or—whatever she is to me now. She used to make me carry one all the time, just in case. I have bobby pins, too, somewhere."

I stifle a laugh and take it from him. "No need. I'll just use this. Not exactly my color, but I'll take what I can get."

He looks away from me, probably thinking about his status with the girlfriend. During the two-week stint of us being back in the human realm after our first escapade to Qotan, he called her to apologize for disappearing. She didn't take it well. Apparently, she said they might need a break. I suspect David didn't have a chance to process any of it, what with his dad being captured by Urothar.

Something whispers in the back of my mind that them breaking up would be a joy.

I should probably change the subject . . .

"Where are we? Any ideas?" I ask.

Across the street from us, there's a body of water that looks like a lake, and the breeze that wafts through the buildings ripples across its surface.

"Not sure. Riverfront. Lots of big buildings. We're in a city. If traveling North in Qotan is the same as traveling North in our realm, then maybe Canada? What city is on the west coast of Canada?"

I shrug. "Geography was not my best subject."

David levels a glare at me. "Did you even have a favorite subject? You seem like the kind of girl to hate every subject."

I punch him in the shoulder, and he flinches. "PE. That was my favorite."

Jared and Amir emerge from behind us. The slight glow of fairy wings is the only evidence that Rolinda is hiding in Amir's shirt.

"Well, that could have gone south pretty quick," Jared says. "She saw Rolinda's wings and about lost her mind. The only way I managed to get the homeless lady to calm down was by having Rolinda disappear and offer her some cash."

Amir grimaces. "While I get that we can't have a fairy flitting around us, either in small or large form, I don't think I can keep going with you under my shirt. It's kind of weird, Rol."

"No, what's weird is you calling Rolinda 'Rol,'" David says. "Are you two dating or something?"

Amir takes a step back, his eyes wide. "My parents would kill me if they thought I was dating someone. No! We are just friends."

At least I'm not the only one who thinks their relationship is weird.

"Do you have a disguise or something?" Jared asks.

Rolinda's head pokes out of Amir's shirt, and she glowers at me as if I'm the one that she hates the most. Oh. She probably read my thoughts about their relationship being weird. I wall up my mind and return her fiery look with more passion.

"If you must know, yes, I can disguise myself," she says, flying out of Amir's shirt and hovering near the ground.

"Get in the alley!" I hiss the moment one of the pedestrians sees her and starts staring.

She moves into the darkness. There is a little flash and a small pop and out comes a gorgeous woman. Her ebony skin looks perfect, and her afro is styled in vogue magazine fashion. She's also wearing a set of maroon sweats.

"Wow," Amir says. "You look great."

"Keep your tongue in your mouth," I say, noticing Jared and David staring, too. I smack them both in the chest, and they snap out of it.

"Sweats aren't fashionable. I can't even pull them off. I just wear them out of practicality. Can you change your clothes to whatever?" I ask.

Rolinda nods. "What did you want me to wear, then? Nothing? I could—"

"No!" we all shout at once, and she furrows her brows.

I look around and spot a group of stylish-looking women walking down the road.

"Like her," I say, picking one of the taller women.

Rolinda snaps her fingers, and her clothes blur for a moment, settling on a nice set of riser jeans, a tank top, and some flats.

"Better," I say. "Also, if you could have done this all along, why didn't you say something?"

She shrugs. "You didn't ask."

I wonder if all fairies have this much attitude. Thankfully, Jared isn't like Rolinda.

"So, back to the question. Where are we?" I ask.

Jared pulls out his phone. "I only have like 2 percent battery left, but if I do a quick location search"—He types on his screen furiously and then taps the search button—"Portland," he says shortly.

"Not Canada. I was close though," David replies.

"Congrats, Dragon Breath. You got close. But we need to find a map of the US to use with the stone," I say, pulling it out of my pocket.

Jared crosses his arms. "Where can you even buy maps these days? I could look it up, but my phone just died."

David and Amir confirm theirs have no battery either.

"We don't need a physical map, right?" Amir points out. "Can't you just look one up on the internet?"

I almost slap myself with how obvious that is. Why didn't I think of that? Yanking my phone out of my pocket, I note that the battery percentage isn't totally depleted. I haven't ever been much of a phone junkie, so my battery usually lasts longer.

"Pulling up the app now. Zooming out," I say, giving them a play-by-play.

I get a sinking feeling in my gut, though I can't describe why. Is it because I don't know what we'll find when we locate the half elf girl?

My thoughts dance to Gulran and my intense desire to shove my broadsword right through his face. We don't know this girl's personality—or if she's even alive at this point. None of the Qotan monarchs clarified if the stones directed us to the person alive and well. I wish I could say I didn't envision us following the map to find only a grave site.

"What are you waiting for? Do it," David says, pulling my attention back to the situation.

I shoot him a scowl, then flip the stone to the treelike symbol. The light blazes to life, a beam shooting coincidentally through my stomach and out my back. A bit weird, but magic is strange enough, so I'm not too bothered. Amir, on the other hand, can't help himself.

"Woah," he breathes. "For light to behave that way, it can't be based on true waves and particles. If only I could set up a couple of tests to see how it works and—"

"Later, nerd. Right now we have something to figure out," David cuts him off.

Amir shrugs and leans in closer to the small map of the US on my phone.

With a deep breath, I slowly move the rock and my phone closer until they lightly touch. The beam shrinks inward, as if the power is being siphoned by the map on my phone. At first, nothing happens, then a blazing light pinprick appears to the southeast of our location. I grin, unable to believe that we've been sitting on the key all along. My elation soon falters when I watch my phone percentage drop from 34 percent to 0 percent in about ten seconds. The screen goes dark, and the beam of light extends outward again.

"I guess they didn't teach the stone to play nice with technology," Jared comments. "Did it fry your phone?"

I press the "on" button for a long time. When the screen flashes, I sigh in relief.

"We need a charger. Anyone have theirs?"

After a lot of backpack rummaging and more grumbles of irritation, we discover that the answer is no. What is it about phone chargers and not having them when you need them?

The next step is obvious, and we are soon wandering the streets of Portland for a convenience store that might have a charger that we can purchase. We have to visit three gas stations before we finally find one with the right kind of plug in. We grab more than one, just to make sure, and ask the cashier where we can charge our phones for free.

He looks at us like we're aliens and suggests the public library. Fortunately, it's only a few blocks away. The moment we enter the building, my nose is filled with the scent of books and musty old carpet.

"Yes! I love the library so much," Amir exclaims. He balls his fist up and raises it to his chest, eyes gleaming as he scans the shelves.

"At least now I can get something to keep me entertained for the long car ride," Jared notes.

Before the two nerds can walk off to go book hunting, I grab their sleeves and keep them close. "You can't prove your residential address is in Oregon to get a card."

Amir slumps. "Oh, right. Hadn't thought of that."

A group of students passes us, a few making comments about us being in the way.

"Watch out, geeks," one of the boys snaps, giving me a snooty look.

Heat flares in my belly, and I take a step forward, my fist clenching to the side. I sense the demon inside me stirring, asking to be brought forth to give this guy a pummeling. My slight reaction is enough to get him to turn and raise an eyebrow at me.

"Wanna fight, babe? I'm sure I'd enjoy every minute of it, even if you'd be easy to knock down," he taunts. "It's too bad your fake sword isn't going to do you any good. You could always *pretend* to throw a fireball at me. Might make you feel better."

My anger disappears almost immediately. I'd forgotten about my broadsword strapped to my back. We've been waltzing all along the streets of this big city with dirty clothes and actual weapons. I'm tempted to pull it free and slice his hand off to show him it's *very* real, but I know that would be *really* dumb.

Instead, I pull it free and slice a bit off his pant leg.

"Are you kidding me? What the—?" he shouts, backing up.

This alerts a few of the other patrons and library staff. One of them picks up a phone with wide eyes and starts typing what I assume is 911.

A firm hand clamps over my bicep.

"This is not helping us, Kris. We need to get out of here before the police arrive," Jared says.

Shoot. I've messed up. This is really bad . . .

I sheath my weapon, but not before cutting a chunk out of the bully's backpack. As we rush out of the library, I hear something about stopping us before we can get away. We run full tilt down the street and around the corner. At which point, we stumble to a stop to catch our breath.

"Gee, real nice one, Krista. Now we'll have the whole of Portland PD looking for us," David chides.

"I think they had it coming," Rolinda says. She seems completely unfazed by our mad dash and not even slightly out of breath. I notice the humming sound of her large wings and curse.

"Please don't tell me you pulled those things out before we were out of sight!" I scold.

She shakes her head. "Why would I wait? I'm not as comfortable with running as you *humans*. Wings are more practical."

We all groan collectively and decide it's time to move on. Sirens sound distantly. We've gotten impressively good at getting the cops called on us. Picking a direction, we leave as quickly as possible until we're able to ask about another library. The next gas station attendant is more helpful and less critical of our weapons. She says that she likes to role play, too, and can relate to what we're doing.

We just go with it.

Soon, we're walking up to another library several blocks away.

"We can't just waltz in there with these weapons again," I say. "So, who's going to guard them?"

In unspoken unity, Jared, David, and I look at Amir and Rolinda.

"Oh man. Are you seriously going to do all the fun stuff without me? That's lame," he says.

"Rolinda can keep you company," David suggests.

She nods, then pulls out the red pulsing stone that keeps her from melting into a pile of ooze. "The stone is absorbing your blood much faster than I anticipated. Your world is so wasteful, full of dark auras and evil thoughts. I'll need to extract more of your blood."

Amir pales, shooting me a desperate plea. I return with an apologetic look.

After some more arguments, Amir finally gives in. We find a spot in a dark corner of the street and pull off all our weaponry, setting it on the ground with the jacket Jared always has packed in his emergency pack.

Finding an outlet inside the library is relatively easy, but it's not comfortable. I crouch by the wall, ensuring the connection between the outlet and my phone is constant. When the phone has enough of a percentage to turn back on, I hastily hold down the power button, chanting for it to hurry up.

This time, without our weapons, we blend in. Nobody in the library pays us any attention. A few more minutes pass, and my phone only gains two percent.

"We can't wait for this thing to get full," I say.

"Then, just do it now," David says. "If it's plugged in, it will probably be fine."

I sigh. "Did you not see what happened last time? It's going to suck my phone dry and possibly fry the chip inside."

David's eyes train on me. "Then, I'll buy you a new one."

I look around the place, noting a few librarians milling about. The phone percentage goes up one more tick, and stays there for what feels like forever.

"Okay, okay You're right. We'll be here all day. Let's hope this cord can take it," I say, glancing up at a librarian who suddenly catches my eye. She gives me a strange look, like standing here huddled around this outlet is weird behavior.

"Can you distract the librarians or something?" I ask.

David follows my gaze and smiles. "Oh, easy-peasy. Just get that location so we can get a move on. It's my first time to Portland, but I can tell you I already don't like it here. Too big, too many people."

He winks at me, then saunters over to the librarian, leaning on the desk and engaging her in a conversation. Whatever he's saying to her is perfect because she seems to forget all about us.

"Here goes nothing." I reopen the map application and hold the stone closer. The beam of light goes into the wall, which is good because I figure it hides it well from the other patrons.

When the stone touches my phone, the same thing happens. The beam gets smaller and a pinprick of light shines to the southeast. I watch anxiously as my percentage dips down, then pops back up. Flashing draws my attention downward, and I see the plug sparking where I've inserted the new charger. Jared curses and uses his large body to block the view from anyone.

"Zoom in! Quick! Before it causes a fire or something," he hisses.

I pinch my fingers on the map and watch as it zooms in closer.

"It's in Bend, Oregon. That's only like three hours from here according to the direc—"

My words are cut off as the power suddenly flickers in the whole library. I yank the stone away, and it all stops immediately.

"Hey! What are you doing over there?" the librarian calls from behind us.

"They're not doing anything! They're just looking up what books they want to get while we're here—"

David's attempts to keep the librarian away are futile as she storms up to us.

"I'm not stupid, young man. Plus, I can read you like a book. Teenagers like you are only trouble in these parts!" Her dark hair is cropped short and she's wearing a pink sweater over a gray-striped T-shirt. Her denim skirt ages her more than she'd probably like to admit.

I open my mind up, giving Jared a knowing look.

She's a psycho. Any ideas to sweet-talk us out of this since Dragon Boy didn't do well enough?

We could always run.

"I would call the police faster than you could get away," the librarian says.

My mouth falls open, and I stare at her. "Did you—just—"

"Read your mind? Yes. But more importantly, who taught you to wall off your minds like that? Most humans are an open book like this kid here," she says, nudging over her shoulder at David. "You're not fully human. That's obvious. Half fairy, I'm assuming?"

She raises her eyebrows at Jared.

He takes a step back. "How did—"

"You just have that look about you. Plus, I sensed your thoughts going to her. If you're going to be so outward with using your mystical heritage, don't do it so obviously in the open. Not everyone in Portland is keen on our kind."

"Wait," David says, shuffling toward her. "You're . . . half-blooded, too?"

The librarian puts a finger to her mouth and shushes him.

"Don't go around saying that out loud. Most of us have lived in hiding since things went downhill nearly twenty years ago."

This librarian feels threatened, and something about her is weirding me out . . .

She shakes her head as she continues her rant. "I know that you have a pile of weapons outside hiding with your human and—" She pauses. "Wait—you brought a *fairy* with you? How is she still alive? Our world is too toxic for her!"

Jared gives me a withering look.

"How are you even here?" I ask. "I thought we were the only ones like us."

She narrows her eyes at me. "Why would you think you were so special? What would have given you that idea?"

"Because we are the—"

The librarian gasps, her hand going to her mouth. "You are *them.*" Her head snaps back and forth through the library, and she gestures for us to follow her. "Here is not the place to discuss this. We need to go where people can't overhear us."

18

WE RACE TO THE HALF-BLOOD

THE WOMAN LEADS US through a narrow hallway extending behind the attendant's desk. She must be the head librarian or something because despite the scene we've caused, the other librarians don't question her. One of them gives us a curious look, but she returns to her work without saying anything.

"In here," she says, pulling open a wooden door with a big window in the top half of it.

It's some sort of workroom. Laminate counters line the walls, and white blinds are drawn down over the windows.

"First off, let's get your friend and the"—she clears her throat nervously—"fairy in here."

Jared and I instinctively look at David. He slumps.

"Okay. I guess I'll go get Amir," he says, standing up and pointing to the other door. "Does this lead outside?"

The librarian nods.

I inspect our new friend as critically as I can. Her hair is perfect, and her makeup is clean and well done. She doesn't appear to have any weapons on her person—at least any I can see. That doesn't give me any comfort though. Crafty people don't make their dangerous tendencies obvious right off the bat.

"You can keep looking for weapons or threats from me, but you won't find any. I don't have a reason to hurt you. Even if I did, I don't get the sense that I would do very well against you in a fight," she comments, looking me up and down.

"Stay out of my head," I say firmly.

"Don't leave your mind open and on the table, then," she snaps back.

Fair enough, I think, knowing she can hear.

I erect the barriers in my mind, knowing that I'm closing off the lifeline between me and Jared. He'll have to be okay with that. Nothing will be kept private anyway, so we will have to navigate this together as best as we can.

"How are you here?" Jared asks.

She gives him a half smile, then dips her head toward the door David just exited through. "Let's just wait a moment until he and the others get back. I don't want to have to repeat myself."

"Okay, fine, but at least answer this. Why didn't you bust us when David went to distract you?" I ask, folding my arms.

She snorts. "Because his mind was full of thoughts about how attractive I am. Plus, he was nervous. Flattery tends to be a great distraction, even if his spoken words took a different direction. It was only when the power went out that I decided to act."

Even *I'm* embarrassed for David now. We fall into silence, waiting for him to return.

We sit there awkwardly for a minute or two, our only companion being the books in various phases of being repaired, labeled, and barcoded.

Blessedly, David doesn't take long to get back. He walks through the door with his arms full of our weapons and gear. Amir follows with the extra packs slung over his shoulder, and Rolinda follows with nothing in her hands. I scoff. She probably put up a stink about holding anything that might ruin her beautiful nails.

The librarian sucks air loudly through her teeth when she sees Rolinda.

"An actual fairy," she says with reverence in her voice.

Rolinda looks from her to Jared, then back again.

"Oh. Another half fairy. Your Qotanian aura is weak though. I could hardly sense you until I was through that door," she says, eyeing the librarian.

This comment offends the librarian. Her face falls, and she leans back, folding her arms. "My mother wasn't the most powerful of fairies. But I have other skills that are useful."

Her defensiveness disarms me even further. She's so genuine.

"Let's get to it," I say. "We have places to be and someone to find. Bend isn't exactly a ten-minute walk from here."

The librarian eyes me, and then flicks her gaze back to Rolinda, who has apparently moved on from the conversation. Rolinda's gaze lingers on the various things in the room, her mouth moving silently as she takes it all in.

"Right. How am I here? It's simple. I was born to my fairy mother and human father thirty years ago. Like most of the other half-bloods I've met here in Portland, we lived in Qotan until the forced exodus. Humans and mystical beings have coexisted for many years until the orc nation decided they hated our kind mixing. They want to kill off all half-bloods like us. For our protection, and in an effort to avoid conflict with the orcs, we were sent away. I was only eleven. But there are thousands like us. Most have spread through different parts of the world, but a lot of us have stayed close to the portal we came through. Then, they took the portal away."

Her eyes glaze over as she undoubtedly remembers details from having to leave Qotan. My gut twists at the thought. This person, this half fairy, spent more time living in Qotan than Jared, David, and me combined. There is a war of questions in my mind. Part of me wants to ask her what it was like living there for so long, and another part of me wants to drill her for all the details about Qotanian politics.

"Yeah, the portal's not gone," I say. "It's still here. How else do you think we got here?"

She looks hopeful. "Oh! Are they allowing us back in, then?"

Jared shakes his head. "No, and I wouldn't recommend trying. Unless you want to deal with demon bodyguards."

She pales, looking down at the ground.

"This realm is not nearly as lovely as the fairy kingdom," she says. "I hope one day I can return."

Rolinda chimes in. "I don't believe there is anything that could be more lovely than our kingdom."

They share a disgustingly sappy look, and I step in.

"Except for the fact that your queen betrayed the other races and is now working to overthrow them all. Real winner."

The librarian gasps. "What? That's not possible! Ferona would never—"

Rolinda pointedly looks away, not wanting to address the truth.

"She would, and she did," I say, my voice hardened. "That's why we're here trying to find the other half-bloods. Well, the other *royal* half-bloods. Urothar is after them. If we can't get to them fast enough, then it's going to go downhill really quickly."

"But why would Ferona do that?"

I shrug. "Had a bad day? Feels sad she's not the high queen? She's just a wench overall?"

Jared flinches at my words but speaks up. "Mind if I ask your name? It feels weird talking about this without knowing each other. I mean, I know your name, but it's a breach of privacy to—"

She waves her hand. "I'm an open book, honey. No hard feelings. But the name's Susie."

We exchange names, much to my frustration. It's all un-necessary pleasantries. We briefly discuss the history of what happened to us and how we got into this situation in the first place, but this only serves to make her dislike me even more. Once Susie learns that I'm half demon, it's like she can't look at me anymore.

"So, David is the heir to the dragons, and Jared is the heir to the fairies," she says, considering Jared more closely. "Ferona is your mother."

"Astute observation," I say. "Can we get to the part about how you can help us? We need to drive to Bend as quickly as possible—we don't have a vehicle. The car we had—we left it back in Qotan. How are we supposed to get to Bend?" I continue.

Susie chews on her lower lip. "I'd offer to take you, but I can't afford to leave work today. We received a large crate of new books that need to get processed as quickly as possible. Lending my car is not an option, so—"

David shrugs. "Why can't we just take an Uber?"

I level a flat stare at him. "You want to pay an Uber to take us three hours away? That would be so expensive."

"We could rent a car," Jared suggests. "But we'd have to be older for them to let us."

His shoulders deflate at the futility in his suggestion.

"There are buses that go in that direction. You can probably catch one leaving this afternoon if you hurry," Susie suggests. Her eyes wander to the pile of weapons, and her jaw tenses. "Except they probably won't take well to weapons being brought along. In fact, how did you make it here without someone questioning you?"

"I think they assume we're role players," David answers.

Amir puts a hand to his chin. "I mean, it's not as weird as it sounds. I've tried it before, and it can be kind of fun."

Susie shakes her head. "Regardless, these are too intricate and real to casually bring on the bus. Let me help you disguise them as best as I can. Or, at least, Kelven can."

"Who is Kelven?" I ask, exasperated. The last thing we need is more people to know about us. Even though Susie is a half-blood, she still hasn't earned much trust from me. "I don't love the idea of telling *more* people who we are. We're not exactly in safe waters, if you know what I mean."

Susie nods. "I understand. But Kelven is half gnome. He is very crafty with his hands and can undoubtedly put something together to veil your weapons."

It turns out that Kelven is a middle-aged bald man who is about a foot and a half shorter than me. It takes a lot of willpower for me not to say something about his size, which I'm assuming is a sore subject for him. Then, there's the confusing notion of how a human and a gnome managed to be together, but that delves into details I don't want to know.

He spends the next thirty minutes doing exactly what Susie said he would. For the most part, we leave him alone as he works on our stuff. Rolinda and Susie spend most of the time chittering and reminiscing about how things used to be in the fairy kingdom while We all zone out for a bit on our phones. We're trying to charge them up as quickly as possible so we can keep using them for maps. I'm hoping that when we get to Bend, it will be easy to find the next half-blood.

"That should do it," Kelven says, stepping back from my broadsword.

I have no idea how he did it, or where he got the materials for it, but my large sword is now encased in black plastic. It looks like I'm carrying a volleyball net that can be set up anywhere. He's even managed to print an official label. David's sword is now in a guitar case, and Jared's fist weapons are in a newly sewn bag.

"How did you do that so fast?" I ask.

The small man grins at me. "My gnome heritage makes me very crafty. I can fix almost anything and use whatever resources I have."

After bidding him farewell, we gather our things and head for the door.

"Wait, aren't you just going to teleport there?" Susie asks, looking between Rolinda and Jared.

"I would have no idea where to send us. This world makes no sense. And it smells horrible. I would inevitably put us in the wrong place," Rolinda says.

Jared looks stunned. "I can't do that."

Susie stares at him. "You can't? But you are the son of Ferona. Surely you would have the ability to transport by now."

Jared seems a bit hurt.

"Nope, just the mind reading and the animal shifting," I say, trying to spare him. He doesn't owe an explanation to this librarian who thinks she can pry like that.

"Sh—shift into animals? But that's not a fairy ability," she says.

Jared scrunches his eyebrows. "I hadn't considered that. So, you can't shift?"

I can see the cogs working in his mind, and I almost suggest a mind link before I glance at Susie. Privacy is still key. Before we can spiral out of control with this weird revelation, I shoo them out the door.

"We have a half-blood to find. Let's get on it!"

I can tell Jared wants to discuss Susie's comment, but our situation's urgency takes precedence. We've been here for too long. With that, we stumble through the door and search up the closest bus station on our phones.

***

The station isn't as far as Susie made it out to be, and we arrive quickly. Before I have a chance to approach the tender and buy us tickets to Bend, Susie pushes her way up and buys the tickets for us. I give her a quizzical look, but she shakes her head.

"That tender has had a bad day already. Some grumpy man gave him a hard time about a failed payment method. I'm pretty positive he wouldn't let you use a credit card without your ID. I figured since I can't take you there, I might as well help you get tickets. You can just Venmo me the amount," she says.

I have to hold back my laughter when I see her profile picture. It's an image of a gaudy, porcelain fairy figurine.

After we're all settled, we sit down and wait until it's time to board the bus. I would be fine getting on it right away, but Jared and David both insist that they don't want to be cooped up for so long. Susie, Rolinda, and Jared move farther away from us in the station waiting area and have a hushed conversation about who knows what. Part of me wants to open up my mind to see if I can get Jared to talk to me. I want to know what they're discussing, but the slump in his shoulders tells me that he won't be in the mood.

At least not yet.

"So, does anyone have any idea what we'll do when we get the elf girl? I'm pretty sure we can't just zap ourselves back to Qotan. We did it a couple days ago, and the recharge rate is much slower than that," David says. "We didn't mark the portal, and if it moves like what's-her-face says, we may be in deep trouble."

Amir grimaces. "We probably ought to have doubled back to check and see if it was still there."

"No time," I say. "Besides, even if it is still there, what would we do? We can't force it to stay in one place. This whole journey has been an on-the-fly operation. I figure we'll just have to wing it when we get her."

"I hate winging it," Amir grumbles.

David throws his hands up. "Works for me."

I give Amir a flat stare. "You don't have to come with us if you don't feel comfortable. I'm sure your parents would probably be thrilled to have you back home from this impromptu 'study abroad.'"

He pales suddenly. "I don't think I'm ready to find out what they'd do to me when they discover I wasn't actually studying abroad."

I frown. "They wouldn't have to find out."

David chuckles. "That's one thing you must not know about my buddy here. No poker face. His parents would learn the truth in about half a second flat." His smile falters. "Yeah, you can't go home, Amir. Not until we sort stuff out. Either your parents would make you go to a mental hospital for being insane or they'd blame me. I think it's probably best to keep them in the dark."

This decision doesn't appear to make Amir feel any better, even though the color in his face returns. I wonder what it must be like for him—the only regular person in this ragtag band. I can imagine, to some degree, from times I tried to fit in as a younger kid. No matter what I did, the other kids knew there was something wrong with me. Only once did I accidentally go into demonic form. It was my first and only sleepover. Let's just say sleepovers were banned for the rest of my life. Though my masking reaction was to pretend I didn't care, I did.

"You have the type of parents who would hire detectives to find David and convict him of something, don't you?" I ask.

Amir's complexion takes on a slight green tinge. "They just really care about me, okay?"

I gape at David. "How did you hang with this kid for so long without him knowing about your dragon blood?"

David sighs. "A miracle. That's the only explanation. On that note, sorry for dragging you into all this. I—"

David stops when he spots a figure from across the waiting area. I follow his gaze to something green and clad in leather armor. Someone who makes my blood boil and my eyes burn instantly.

Gulran.

I leap to my feet, reaching for my broadsword. I curse when I feel the wrapping around it. Not only is it inaccessible at the moment, but if I were to pull it free, we'd have the cops on our tail. This time, we don't have anywhere to run.

The half orc flashes his sharp canines at me, then holds up his sword and a tracking stone. A beam of light points in my direction. My failure at losing the stone and my own blood, which Gulran is using to fuel the stone's magic, haunts me yet again. I want to scream and cry at the same time. Memory flowing, I can't stop the anger that explodes inside of me. Demon me emerges. My skin stretches and burns, and suddenly, my sweats are tight against my body.

Even though fear flickers in Gulran's eyes, it's gone in an instant.

There aren't a lot of people waiting for a bus on a Tuesday afternoon, but there are enough. The first woman who sees me lets out a shriek that puts everyone on high alert. David curses and grabs his guitar case. Amir mutters something about jail time, but I'm too focused on the snide-looking orc kid. He waves at me, then uses two fingers to turn the dial on the stone. The light flashes to his right, and my heart sinks. I start to rush over to him, ripping the package off my back, but he's gone in the blink of an eye.

Krista, Jared's voice echoes in my mind.

I shout internally at my inability to hold mental blocks in my demon form. I don't *want* to be an open book, but I have no choice.

He's gone, back to Qotan. Come with me to the restrooms. We need to calm you down.

I want to tear up one of the chairs bolted to the ground and throw it at him. The onlookers are what keep me from doing it. I shoot one more glare at the spot Gulran vanished and then stalk off to the bathrooms. I'm not even halfway there when I feel a hand grip my huge palm. I recoil, raising my fist to punch the person away, but my heart stops when I see who it is.

David looks terrified but resolved. His hand is shaking like a leaf, and I sense the flight instinct in him as he shuffles his feet.

"Calm," he says.

It actually works. I can't be sure if it's because of what he says or because of the fact that my hormones can't get enough of this jock boy.

I close my eyes and take a deep breath. Adrenaline courses through me, but it starts lessening immediately. He pulls me toward the restrooms, and I give in. The door swings open and a teenage girl comes out looking at her phone. She almost runs right into me, but stumbles away, her eyes wild and alarmed. David shoos her away, and she lets out a shriek before slipping between me and the wall. Moving in front of me, David shoves the door to the bathroom open and pulls me in.

When the door closes, I still can't breathe.

"You need to chill, Kris," he says.

"Don't call me that," I snap, even though my brain eats it up.

He sighs. "What would you rather be called? Karistana? Demon Breath? Demo-Demo?"

I can't believe what happens next. I laugh. I laugh so hard that I'm embarrassed for myself. The anger disappears, and I shrink to my normal size. David watches for a minute before looking away like he's witnessing something private. His face flushes slightly, but I won't let him off that easily.

"Are you embarrassed to be alone with me? Or are you embarrassed that you came into the girls' bathroom?"

His cheeks turn beet red. "I didn't—no, wait! Don't get the wrong idea. I—oh no," he sputters, looking around frantically.

One of the stalls opens and a little girl comes out. She turns, sees David, and shrieks. I'm pretty sure he's about to die from embarrassment. He's out of the bathroom so fast that he becomes a blur.

David has rarely looked so flustered or uncomfortable. Somehow, seeing him this way makes him more human—for a half dragon, at least. I don't follow him right away, choosing to let him diffuse his embarrassment. Instead, I take a moment to use the restroom and slap my face with some water from the sink. When I get out, the fairy crew has joined the others.

"Bus will leave soon. Knowing what that half orc is thinking, they're going to be on the move. Let's hope this bus gets you there quickly. I have to get back to work, but if and when you get back to Qotan, can you find my mother for me? She's there. Name's Virola. I wish I could say that I don't miss her, but I really do."

Before we set out for our bus, we promise to at least look for her mother. On the way over, I give Jared a questioning look. He seems like he's got the weight of the world on his shoulders. When he notices me, he shakes his head.

Nice try, bro. I know it's not nothing.

The fact that he didn't mentally communicate with me, which I've pointedly opened up for him, is telling. He needs time to process whatever their conversation was.

The bus seats are narrow and covered in blue- and white-striped fabric. From the outside, the vehicle didn't look all that old, but the seats tell a whole different story. I feel like I've taken a trip into the 70s and forgot how to get back to modern times.

Unfortunately, the bus isn't empty, but there are a lot of seats near the back. By the way Jared is feeling, I don't sit right next to him when he picks a window seat and stares out silently. David and Amir sit next to each other, and Rolinda stretches out on the set of seats behind them. I take up the rear, sitting in the second to last row right behind Jared.

Rolinda gets upset when the ticket checker makes her put her feet down, but she hoists them back up again without hesitation when the bus starts rolling. A little over three hours in the grand scheme of traveling is not *that* bad. However, knowing that Gulran and his cronies have a head start makes it feel like forever.

I take out the stone and glance around me. No one sits close, save for an older woman and a kid in the back corner. The boy is asleep, and the grandma is reading a book. To be safe, I lean toward the window and flip the dial toward the elf girl's symbol. The beam blazes to life, pointing through the window to the right of the bus. As if on cue, the driver turns us in that direction, and the beam flows through the seat into Jared's back.

The ride is uneventful except for a mini showdown I have with the kid and the bathroom. I was there first, but he pushed his way in. I wish I could say that it didn't make me almost go demon on him, but it did. Jared had to intervene to keep everyone alive. I attempt to talk to Jared again, but he shuts me out each time. Message received. Amir and David sleep for a bit, and Rolinda stares out the window.

Soon, the bus pulls through a gorgeous forest at fifty-five miles per hour. The slow speed limit of this dumb state frustrates me to no end. Ultimately, though, we arrive, and the bus comes to a stop. I practically leap off the bus, narrowing my eyes at the boy who sticks his tongue out at me.

"We need to get somewhere private to activate the stone," Jared says.

"No time," I say.

I already have an image in my mind of Gulran tugging a bound and gagged girl through a portal to Qotan, kicking and screaming.

I draw the stone out and activate it. The beam points to our right. This bus station is a lot smaller than the one in Portland with only two people milling about. They don't seem to notice what we're doing, so I walk out of the building and onto the street.

Ripping my phone out of my pocket, I activate the map application and tap the stone to the side of my phone's screen. It flickers, and the beam gets smaller. A pulsing light shines on my phone on a part of the map outside of the city limits. It's in the middle of the forest a couple miles away. We get a few seconds of sight before my phone blips and the battery dies.

"It's that way," I say, following the beam of light.

My heart sinks when I see a column of smoke in the distance. It's directly where the stone is pointing.

"We're too late," David says, dejected.

"No! We can't be too late!" I shout, my hands clenched tight. I feel the demon in me rising. "We have to run there! *Now!*"

The command is almost barking, but I turn to rush off. A hand catches my arm, and I spin, ready to sock David for stopping me yet again. But it's not David. It's Jared.

"She can take us there," he says, pointing to Rolinda.

"Are you *kidding me*? You said you couldn't teleport us here. Why can you suddenly do it now?" I practically scream at Rolinda.

She flinches, scowling at me.

"Maps aren't enough, fool. I need a reference point. That smoke," she says, her curls bouncing as she shoves into the air, "is enough. Now hold on to me."

Jared and Amir grab her shoulders with one hand, and David and I hold her bicep.

"No, like *hold on*. This is not going to be fun," she says.

I grip her arm like she's a lifeline.

Just like when we stepped through the portal, my stomach twists as the world spins into a blur of color. I clench my teeth, nausea overwhelming me, and my head goes instantly foggy. Then, colors form back into images. It's a lot of pine green and brown. We stand in the middle of a beautiful forest, and my nostrils are assaulted by acrid smoke. A wooden cottage burns a hundred feet away.

And it's surrounded by goblins and orcs.

THE WARRIOR PRINCESS SHOWS US UP

MY BLOOD BOILS WHEN the first goblin comes vaulting toward me. With my chest and arms expanding, I'm in full demon mode when he reaches me. I swipe with my powerful fist to make him go sprawling to the ground. Rolinda disappears in a shower of dust and sparks, shrinking to her small form and flying up into a tree to bury herself in the leaves.

"Gee, thanks for taking me with you!" Amir hisses, cursing as an arrow crashes to the ground near his feet.

David's skin melds into pure-red scales prepared to ward off any attacks. Jared shifts into a hawk and launches into the sky as arrows fly toward us. One of them cuts through my pants and slits my thigh. It burns, but not nearly enough to make me pause.

With one motion, I yank the package off my back and plunge my hand inside. It brushes against the blade, slicing into my palm. I wince, but I tear it free and flip the weapon so I can grip the handle. A few more arrows swish by me, missing me by inches. My sword cleaves clean through two goblins, melting them into black goo before a massive troll swings his club at my head. It's slow, fortunately, so I'm able to dodge, but I feel the power of it through the gust of wind that makes my hair fly.

The heat from the fire prickles my skin, a blazing inferno that quickly consumes the wooden cottage. Despite the flames, the structure is still relatively sound. It's two stories and contains more windows than walls. I don't have time to inspect it before I'm dodging another blow from the club. Two orcs advance from my left with axes in their hands, but they don't reach me before Jared flies down and shifts into a rhino, landing right on top of them. One melts away, but the other screams out in pain, swinging her axe up to try to get a hit on him.

The rotten scent of the troll's breath combines with the smell of melting plastic and burning wood. Bob said he hated trolls—not because of their angry disposition but because of the way their breath smells.

He wasn't joking.

I open my mouth to breathe through that instead, but I recoil when I taste the potent scent of this creature's spittle. The troll growls and swings a couple more times at me, its club knocking up dirt and weeds. I avoid its next attack and slip my broadsword right into its shoulder. The thing howls in agony and yanks its arm back powerfully. The club narrowly misses my head, and this time, I stab it in the chest. The ground rumbles as it thuds down heavily. Pain erupts in my back, and I fall to my knees, looking down to see an arrow through my stomach and purple blood flowing over the shaft.

"Kris!" David cries out.

An orc lands in front of me, her bicep bleeding from a deep gouge. I don't even hesitate, melting her to black ooze with one blow to the face. This time, when David puts his hand on my shoulder, I know it's him.

And it feels amazing. He slips his other palm under my armpit, human me having a momentary panic attack that he'll smell my stinky sweat. Embarrassment pushes that thought away, and I lock eyes with him.

"Thank you," I say.

That's all I have time to say before we're hit with another volley of arrows. David steps in front of me and spreads his arms out wide. A few arrows clatter harmlessly off his back but one slips by and slices my cheek. I growl, shouting to Jared.

"We need to kill the archers!"

He sends a mental affirmation, then shifts into a hawk again, speeding off in the direction of the archers.

"Well, well, well, what do we have here?"

The voice sends a chill down my spine and fills me with the purest form of hatred. I turn to see Gulran there, his broadsword extended. He wears a stupid grin on his face, and he's flanked by four orcs and another massive troll.

"Where is the girl?" I snarl.

Gulran scowls. "Not here. We've stripped the place and burned everything to drive her out. She must have slipped away."

I think back to the map and the direction of the beam. She's here. The stone can't be wrong—not based on how it's connected to her blood.

"Shame. I guess you better leave," David suggests, maintaining a defensive stance.

I want to scream at him to shut up. This orc mutt isn't going anywhere. I want to gut him and send his head back to his father. Before I can dwell on how macabre and truly terrifying that thought is, Gulran responds.

"If only it were that easy. See, I'm running low on your blood," he says, holding up his sword. "Mind offering another donation?"

"Over my dead body," I growl. "David, you take the others. I'll kill the half-blood."

He opens his mouth to protest, but I'm flying forward, my weapon slashing through the air. Gulran parries my attack and jumps backward through his cronies. My ears pick up David commenting on how I'm "psycho" and that "I'll be the death of him someday," but by that point, Gulran, me, and two of the orcs are locked in battle. Fending off three at a time is not easy, but I manage to keep them a safe distance with my longer weapon.

Kris, something's not right, Jared calls in my mind. *I took care of one of the goblin archers, but the other three have arrows in their chests.*

I dodge one of the orc's attacks and kick her in the chest. She grunts and falls to the ground as the other one leaps forward, fending me off with quick swipes.

That sounds like a good thing! Why are you complaining?

Where did they come from? he asks.

I get sliced in the chest and curse, landing a kick in the gut of the second orc. He falls to the ground, and I leap over him, slamming my broadsword into his chest. He oozes before Gul-ran can come forward.

I wince, now registering a sharp pain. I've been fighting with an arrow in my stomach this whole time, and my mystical blood has been attempting to close it. My energy is waning, most likely from all the attempted healing. I reach down, break the head of the arrow off, and pull the shaft out. Even a demon can't resist gasping at the pain.

Gulran doesn't hesitate to attack me. I parry his first couple blows before taking the flat of his blade on my head. My vision blurs, and I fall to one knee.

"See, it's so frustrating that I can't just kill you right here and now. No, my *father* needs you for some magical ritual. This would be the second time I've bested you in a fight. You're a sorry excuse for a warrior," he spits.

Rage rushes through me, and I jump forward, landing a fist against his abdomen. Gulran grunts, falling backward but re-covering in haste.

"But—you—pack a punch," he gasps.

I give a crooked smile. "More than a punch."

I'm the wind. My arms move in a blur. I flip my large sword through the air, attacking left and right. I can tell that Gulran is struggling to keep up. Even though I'm pressing forward, I know I'm losing energy too fast. If I don't end him soon, I'm going to be in trouble.

David calls out for help, and I risk a glance in his direction. There are only a couple of warriors left, but David is pinned between them both. I'm about to call for Jared when the hawk lands on the troll's face and gauges out his eyes. The blue creature bellows blindly.

I return my focus to Gulran, my chest buzzing with anticipation. We're relatively equal in speed, but I'm stronger. I press that advantage, throwing more ferocity into my swings to try to knock his weapon free. Unfortunately, I'm unable to. Our swords clash, and we press against each other, sliding away so that we are forced to face off again.

"Seems I didn't bring enough friends," Gulran pants, nodding to where David and Jared are finishing off the enemies. He grips a red stone in his hand and whispers something into it. Suddenly, more enemies materialize. There are two more trolls and at least ten more orcs and goblins. I grit my teeth. I'm running out of stamina.

"Oh, come on! That's not cool!" David huffs. He sounds exhausted. I step back slowly until I'm between them both.

"What are our options?" I ask.

Jared grimaces. "Go out with a bang? Unless you have something that we can blow up."

"You think I'm packing a grenade?" David says. "It's a shame the fairy had to run away and hide."

I'm unsure if Gulran can hear us or not, but he grins evilly and shouts something in a grunting language. His new army rushes toward us with bellows of war. I tense, crouching low to prepare for the impact.

Two goblins and an orc melt into ooze on the way over, and I frown in confusion. Before they fell, I thought I saw arrows in their chests. A trilling yell sounds from above me, and suddenly, a tall figure wearing a T-shirt and jeans lands between us and the army. Her hair is raven-black and her skin is blue. Pointed ears poke out of her hair, and she wears a determined expression. For a moment, the army pauses, but then they rush at her. She nods, then leaps above them. All I see is a flash of metal as she clears the troll's head from its body. It falls forward into a huge ooze puddle.

Watching her leap and twist through the group is wild. She's moving so fast I can't keep up with my eyes. Before long, she drops another four of them. The troll catches on, swinging his club to the ground and sending debris everywhere. This stops the girl, and he lands a fist on her face. She spirals out of the group and rolls to a halt.

"No!" I shout, launching myself forward.

My wounds are all healed, but I can feel my demon form faltering. The human me is about to come out. David and Jared are at my side, David's scales now only concentrated on half of his face and arms. He's running out of steam, too. Jared turns into a tiger and pounces on an orc, his teeth coming down on its neck.

"*Urk ghrulan frtlangr!*" David growls at the troll.

I assume he just called the troll something very offensive. Whatever he says, it works. The troll roars in fury and chases after him. I glance at the girl, but she's not there anymore. Gulran and I engage once more, but this time, I press harder, giving it my all. He's backed into a corner, and for the first time, real fear lights in his eyes.

Then, there is a stabbing pain in my back, and I feel a toxin coursing through my blood. I growl and swing back, my hand smacking into a goblin and sending him ten feet away. The moment he lands, the blue-skinned girl is on top of him, a dagger melting him away. She dashes back to the trees and is gone instantly.

What is with this girl? I think.

The poison is moving to my brain, and I feel foggy.

"You've—lost—" I say.

Gulran bares his yellowing teeth. He reaches to grab me, and I swat his hand away, but my strength is waning.

"Not anymore. You're coming with me—"

His hand gets thrown to the side, and a gasp of pain comes from his slightly open mouth. The gasp shifts into a scream as we both realize at the same time that his palm has an arrow through it.

"Curse you!" he shouts, then he vanishes into nothing.

I collapse to my knees. My head is spinning . . .

A hand presses over my mouth, and something spicy erupts on my taste buds. Immediately, alertness returns to my head, and I breathe out heavily. My hands come up in a frenzy, brushing my tongue to try and ward off the uncomfortable spice.

"It's just cayenne pepper oil. You'll live. Let it keep you alert and awake."

It's her. The blue-skinned girl kneels in front of me, her silver irises trained on me. She looks Asian, but an elf version of an Asian. I blink in confusion, but she disappears. There are a few more shouts and grunts, but then the sounds of fighting cease.

"They ran away. Bunch of ninnies," David mutters.

I smile despite the fact that, even though I beat Gulran fair and square, he still cheated and got away. Saved yet again by another half-blood.

The spiciness of the cayenne is lessening now, but I still feel like I need a big glass of milk.

"So, the elf princess can fight. Why am I not surprised?" David says.

I shift my legs and turn around to face them. David's clothes are tattered and ripped all over. Jared's eyes look heavily bagged, and he looks gaunt.

"That—was—insane," Amir squeaks, his voice coming from the forest behind me.

The elf girl regards him with a critical eye, then speaks with an even voice, her tone much higher than I expected.

"You brought a human with you? Are you trying to get him killed? He shouldn't even know about us," she says flatly.

David steps forward. "Hey now, that *human* is my friend. And no, we didn't expect to drag him into all this."

She inspects Amir up and down, then turns to look at David.

"You must be the half dragon." She regards me critically. "And you must be the half demon. But you"—this time, she faces the raggedy Jared—"I don't know what to make of."

He nods, clearly not offended by her words. "I am half fairy."

There is a moment of surprise in her expression before she's hardened and impassive again.

"You are the largest half fairy in the history of our time, surely. Can your wings even pick you up off the ground?" she asks.

I choke on saliva at her comment.

"Um—what? I don't have wings. Also, did you just call me fat?" Jared asks.

She scrutinizes him once more. "I didn't say anything like that. You did."

The girl turns to me and stares for a moment longer. Then, to my utter shock, her skin ripples and turns into a normal color. Her irises shift into a dark brown, and where there once was a tall elf princess, there now stands a very tall Asian girl. I gape at her, not sure how to respond. Fortunately, David has no filter.

"Woah. That's some wild chameleon action you have going on there."

The girl is unimpressed by his antics.

"Elves have skill with illusions. I have to use it to fit in. Though I have stayed here most of my life, being homeschooled. My elven appearance is too attention-grabbing," she says.

"Oh—homeschooled. That explains it," David says.

She folds her arms across her chest. "Explains what, exactly?"

He clears his throat. "You know what? Never mind."

The girl seems irritated by his lack of answer.

"Based on the look of you, I'm guessing you're a jock? Soccer? Football?" She leans into one hip, glaring at him. "Ah, that's it. You switched weight in your feet right as I said that. Learning is more than just sitting at a desk and doing what your teacher tells you to do."

David crinkles his nose and begins to protest, but I step between them and throw my arms out.

"Now is *not* the time to argue about homeschooling versus public schooling. We need to get out of here before more orcs and goblins show up," I say, shooting a furtive look at the burnt cottage.

The half elf girl turns toward the burning building. "I should probably call someone about that."

I'm perplexed at her nonchalance toward her home going up in a literal inferno.

"Aren't you upset that your house is on fire? Or that you just got attacked by a bunch of freaky creatures?" Amir asks.

She gives him a quizzical look. "Not really. I've been preparing for this my whole life. It's why we don't stay in a house for more than two months at a time. I have to say, this was one of my favorites, but it isn't the one that felt most like home," she admits.

"You have more than one house?" David asks.

She nods. "Twelve, actually. Accounts for two years' worth of moving around the globe."

"Wait—*twelve?* That's—how did you even afford all that?"

"Oh. Mother is a stock trader. She's very good at what she does. It's not that big of a deal."

We regard her with mixed levels of confusion and shock, but I break out of it first.

"I'm Krista. You are?"

A genuine smile grows on her face, and she extends her hand out a bit awkwardly. "I'm Lily."

I take her palm and shake it firmly.

"That's David. Jared, my brother. And Amir. There's a fairy around her somewhere, but—"

Rolinda takes that very moment to emerge from the trees with a confident look on her face. Somehow, she always manages to look like she's the boss of the whole situation, even though she literally ran and hid during the conflict.

"Rolinda. Pleasure to meet the daughter of the elf king."

Lily dips her head. "You look too normal to be a fairy."

Rolinda looks taken aback. "Well, this is just my disguise. Waltzing around with large wings would turn too many human heads. Most have forgotten about our kind since our worlds closed off to each other."

Lily shrugs. "Fair enough. So, you came. After what I saw on the news, I expected at some point for someone to come knocking. Mother was sure that we'd be secure here in the forested area, but they found me after all. She'll probably flip a lid when she sees the smoke."

A phone rings loudly from her jeans pocket, the light showing through the thin material of her pants. "And there she is. She probably just saw it."

We stand there awkwardly as she answers the phone and has a strained conversation with a very panicked-sounding woman on the other side.

She is entirely nothing like I expected her to be, I think to Jared.

Agreed. We expected to find a damsel in distress. We found a literal warrior princess.

Who seems unfazed by anything.

Lily ends the call and sighs. "As I expected, she's losing her mind. I told her not to come here just in case more creatures show up. Let's take one of the cars and meet her in town."

"Did the homeschool girl just say *one of the cars*? I'm suddenly regretting my parents' life decisions," Amir says, shaking his head.

No one protests as she leads us to a detached garage through some thick trees. The sirens we heard from a distance show up at the house, and firefighters start working on the fire immediately.

"Aren't you going to go talk to them? Tell them it's your house?" Amir asks.

Lily looks perplexed. "Why? They don't need my help to put out a fire. Besides, I thought you said we had to get out of here as soon as possible."

"Well, I did—but—" he sputters..

She waves off the comment. "It's fine. Mother can file a report about it later if she decides to. More than likely, we'll just call it a wash and move on to the next house."

"Um—they're not going to just let us drive away. They're going to think that we were the ones who lit the fire and we're running away," David points out.

I didn't even think about that. Thinking about the scene from their perspective makes it obvious that they'd assume we're the perps. At this point, there isn't any other option but to go talk to them. The last thing I need is *another* almost-jail time experience.

Lily stares at him incredulously. "But they won't see us."

Annoyance slips through my body, but demon me doesn't emerge yet, even though she really wants to.

"What do you mean they won't see us? Unless one of your powers is to make us invisible—"

I realize it right as the words leave my mouth. She *does* have that ability. "Oh, right."

Even though I've handed her the perfect ammunition to make fun of me or say something rude, she simply smiles and gestures through the open door into the fancy garage. It's wide enough to fit at least six vehicles, and there's exactly that many nestled inside. Most are two-person vehicles. Some are sports cars that I don't recognize. There's even a pair of motorcycles. It's ridiculously clean—more clean than any garage I've ever seen in my life. Ours was always full of boxes, weapons, and traps.

Lily leads us by the vehicles until we reach a white-colored Escalade SUV. She jumps in the driver's seat and tells us to hop in.

"Dude, you have a Lamborghini!? How much did that cost?" David asks, his face plastered against the back window as he tries to get a better look at it.

"I don't know. Mother doesn't share information like that with me," she says, reaching for the ignition and turning on the car.

"When did you get the keys?" I question her, confused.

"We just leave them in the ignition," she replies. "Isn't it normal for people to do that?"

I shake my head. "Definitely not normal. Aren't you worried about people stealing your things?"

"We have a state-of-the-art security system and gates blocking the road out. If someone tried, they wouldn't make it far."

She pauses then, turning with a confused expression. "How did you get past all of that?"

"Fairy teleportation," I say flatly.

Raising her eyebrows, she frowns, nods, then turns back to the steering wheel. She has zero issues with processing what I just said. Who is this girl?

The car roars to life, and she artfully backs it out of the garage onto the road. I can't help but hold my breath as we move closer to the fireman and ambulances, but they don't even spare a glance at us.

"That's so weird," Jared says with a grimace. "I thought it would feel different to be disguised."

Lily peers into the rearview mirror. "From the eyes of those affected, the illusion is hidden. Because I'm using it on us, you won't feel or perceive anything differently. I suspect it's because I'm not altering reality. I'm simply deleting information from the brains' of people around us. It's a very interesting thing to consider from a neural network perspective. I can even alter things such as smell and touch."

David shivers. "So you could . . . make me feel like I'm in a tropical jungle?"

Lily shrugs. "Probably. But I couldn't do it while holding up this illusion—or at least, it would be tricky to do so. Showing more than one person different things at the same time is challenging."

The teenager artfully maneuvers us down a winding driveway until we reach the road. A fortress-like gate sits at the bottom with the metal gates open.

"We're going to meet Mother at Starbucks, and then we'll go from there."

It doesn't take long before we're pulling into an almost-empty parking lot in front of the coffee shop. I spot a fancy-looking convertible with its top down and a short Asian woman sitting in the driver's seat. She leaps out of the car and rushes to us the moment we roll to a stop. She tears open the driver's side door and throws her arms around her daughter.

"Lily! You're alright. What happened?" Her eyes scan the rest of the car, and she frowns. "And who are these people?"

"They are other half-bloods. Like me."

The woman says something that sounds distinctly Chinese, but I can't be sure. She takes her time looking over all of us, then speaks a bit more Chinese.

"Any chance you can translate that?" I murmur back to David.

"Nope. Apparently, my translating brain only works on non-human languages."

"Pity," I reply.

The woman throws her hands out in the air in a welcoming way.

"Finally, my daughter might be able to make friends with people that are like her! How did you get here? Where are your parents—the human ones, at least?"

My face falls, and she notices immediately.

"Are you all . . . orphans, then?"

I shake my head wildly.

"No. Our parents were . . . it's a long story," I say.

She looks concerned. "Let's get inside and you can tell me everything."

David, Jared, and I exchange glances. Would it be smart to stay close by after what just happened? Probably not. But the smell of that coffee and food makes me pause.

"Ma'am, with all due respect," Jared says. "We don't have a lot of time. Your daughter and home were just attacked by the enemy races of Qotan. Urother, the orc king, is marching on the elf kingdom as we speak. We were hoping we could grab your daughter and get going."

The look of consternation on her face is enough to make me want to run. What is it about moms that make them so scary? I want to get away from her critical expression as soon as possible, but I know she's not going to let us.

"You will not take my daughter anywhere until I learn what is going on. None of you were supposed to even meet each other until you were twenty. No arguing. Get inside," she says firmly.

David, Amir, and Jared just say, "Yes ma'am," and shuffle out of the vehicle. I sit there perplexed at how terrifying this small Chinese woman is. She's maybe four foot ten? But she has an intimidating air about her. Her raven-black hair is pinned back away from her face and tied in a tail behind her head. We make eye contact for a moment, and I am tempted to meet her intimidation with my *actual* intimidation aura, but think better of it. I get the feeling that I don't want this mom on my bad side.

Despite how terrible of an idea this is, I exit the car and follow the others inside. She leads us to a specific table in the corner where people are unlikely to overhear us. David offers to give an account of everything and how we got here, but I want this over with, so I tell him to let me. Even though he's unhappy, I'm positive my five-minute breakdown will be better than his theoretical thirty-minute one.

"Wow. I can't believe it," Lily's mother, Jing, replies. "So, the stone you lost to them is how they found us so quickly? Do they still have the stone?"

I nod. "Which means we're on a time crunch. We need to get to Qotan through the portal and rush over to the elf kingdom to help defend it."

Jing grimaces. "They shouldn't be allowing children to do such things. But at least Lily is capable."

Lily smiles and nods. "Let's get things straight. What can you each do?"

I shake my head. "Nuh-uh, we're not going first. You tell *us* what you can do. Then, maybe we'll feel comfortable telling you."

Even though I've laced my voice with enough venom to put the point across, Lily doesn't appear to pick up on it. She shrugs then tells us.

"Illusions, as you've seen. But I can also run very quickly. Roughly five times the average human speed, and I don't tire easily. I also have a natural ability with any weapon, even without extensive training. For example, I've never had any lessons with that bow I shot earlier. When I hold a weapon, it's like it speaks to me and tells me how to use it."

"That's both eerie and kind of cool," David admits.

"Okay, your turn," she says, smirking.

David holds up his hand and scales appear across his skin. "Scales. Naturally."

It doesn't take long for each of us to run down what our abilities are. Jing is more than a little shocked to hear that Amir is just human, and he gets a whole lecture from her about why he should be in school keeping his grades high. I actually feel bad for the kid. Knowing how his real parents have high expectations for him and his grades, I suspect he's endured similar scoldings most of his life. Even though he seems to quell under Jing's words, he looks like he feels better, in a way. Like the scolding was familiar and welcome.

"We need to go," I say, reiterating my earlier point.

Jing nods. "Yes, you must go. I will move to our next house in Montana."

"Wait, you aren't going to come with us?" David asks, surprised.

She shakes her head. "I have work to do here. Plus, I'm no use with weapons. Lily learned all on her own. Very bright. I have work to uphold."

Jing levels a hardened stare at David, then gestures for him to move closer.

"You won't let my daughter die, will you, Dragon Prince?"

David recoils as if the title leaves a bad taste in his mouth. "Uh, no—I won't."

Jing narrows her eyes, then looks him up and down. "You better not. Or you'll get the wrath of Mama Jing faster than you can breathe fire."

David flushes. "But I can't breathe—"

The Chinese woman waves her hand in the air to dismiss his comment. I stifle a laugh. Up until now, most of the people we've interacted with have assumed that I'm the ringleader. Lily's mom knows better. She knows that David is the high prince, and technically, he should be in charge.

I pause, contemplating the fact that this woman was a part of this from the beginning. Did she meet my mother? Were all the humans brought together in a meeting with the rulers where they decided what to do with us half-bloods? My tongue tingles slightly as I feel the urge to speak up and ask her, but I hold back. For some reason, I get the sense that hearing about it will only make the loss of my mother sting more.

She's probably dead. Pull yourself together, I think.

"Why are you still here? Get back to that portal and save Ilvinar's kingdom!"

It's a bit odd to hear her using the elf king's name so loosely, but given her circumstances, it makes sense. I chug down the last few swallows of my drink, knowing full well that I'll regret it later when I need to rush to the bathroom. Still, I can't waste it. Jing was generous enough to buy them for us. The last thing I want is to leave a bad impression on her, given that she seems like the wrong person to cross.

Jing stands with us and embraces her daughter. It's a spectacle of a sight, seeing a mother hug her teenage daughter who is so much taller than her.

"Keep them safe, too, eh? I didn't raise you to let your friends down," Jing says.

Lily nods and looks at me. "So, where's this portal?"

OUR PORTAL DISAPPEARS

THE BUS RIDE BACK feels a lot faster, even though I'm not remotely familiar with this area. Jing insisted that we take the bus on account of the crime rate in Portland. Something about "fearing for her beautiful car's safety" if we were to leave it there the whole time. I mean, she has a point, since we don't know how long we'll be in Qotan, and we might not make it back to Portland soon. Not to mention that the *last* time we tried a vehicle, it ended up stranded on the side of a mountain in the other realm.

Jing really didn't like the sound of that possibly happening to her Escalade.

Lily opts to sit next to me the whole bus ride despite the fact that there are some empty seats. Our conversations are light and shallow, but she seems like a really nice person. Her confidence levels still astound me for someone who hasn't had nearly as many human interactions as me. It's because she was homeschooled, but I'm still impressed. At one point, I lean my head back and snooze for a bit. I can't relax fully knowing that there is a stranger sitting next to me, but I do manage to get some shut-eye. It's when she closes her eyes and starts breathing evenly that I can finally let loose. At least then I'm relatively confident she's not watching me sleep.

When the bus jolts to a stop, I'm pulled out of my snooze. At first, my thoughts direct me right to "We're being attacked," which causes me to stand up and smack my head on the overhead compartment. I curse loudly, garnering a few looks.

"We're here already?" I ask.

Lily shrugs. "I guess so. I've never been to Portland, but based on the fact that people are standing up and getting their things, I would say it's the right place."

At first, I think she's being facetious, but she was literally stating what she observed. I squirm at the misread situation, then shrug it off. My brain is still a little affected by the fog of my recent doze. I close my eyes and focus on my senses to pull myself out of the stupor.

"You'll have to thank your mom again for getting us tickets," Jared says. "I know my dad will appreciate her sacrificing that money given that we've spent plenty of it up until this point."

Lily nods. "So, you two aren't truly siblings, but you were raised that way, correct?"

I furrow my brow at her.

"I just noticed, you called him your brother, but you are both half human, half mystical race. It's unlikely that your human parent is the same given that your ages are the same. Therefore, different parents altogether."

David looks impressed. "I mean, great logic, but all you have to do is look at them to tell one of them is adopted."

He flashes his teeth at me, and I roll my eyes.

Lily responds with a smile. Her considerate nature makes me a little uncomfortable, especially with how polite she seems to always be.

"Technically, they are both adopted, if you think about it," Lily points out. "By the other parent. So, your assessment is both wrong and right at the same time."

David blinks, a perplexed expression on his face. "Uh—yeah, I guess so."

Lily promptly stands up, gathers her large bag, and moves down the aisle.

I exchange a glance with David. I don't think either of us knows what to do with a response like that, so we silently grab our things and follow her. Though our packs are small, Lily has brought a whole suitcase full of stuff. After we left the coffee shop, we stopped at a "safe house" of theirs, which ended up being a storage facility. And here I thought *we* had an arsenal of weapons. But no. It's nothing compared to what Lily and her mother have. On top of that, it's only one of twelve—a safe house for each of their actual homes.

"How far away is this portal?" Lily blurts out.

I shush her, my finger coming to my lips. "You can't just go around saying things like that."

She raises an eyebrow. "Why not? Are you afraid of people thinking ill of us?"

I gape at her. "I mean, it's not a normal conversation, and we don't want people overhearing us."

Lily still looks confused, but she relents, lowering her voice. "Where is the portal?"

Amir calls us an Uber with his phone, and we find ourselves sliding into the seats of an SUV. Jared takes the front seat, while we shove Amir and the hidden Rolinda into the back. Unfortunately, I get stuck in the middle of Lily and David. My arm rests against his, and I can't help but notice how good it feels. And his smell . . .

I grit my teeth the whole car ride. I suspect he's equally affected by the close seating arrangement because he doesn't say one word, and he doesn't look at me. Ten minutes later, we're filing out of the SUV and standing at the entrance of the alley with the portal.

"We're sure this is the right place?" David asks.

Jared nods, turns around, and gestures to the riverfront. "I recognize this place. Plus, that's the way we went to get chargers for our phones."

"He's right. I remember it, too. That means the portal should be just in there," I say, pointing.

"It's a good thing we're almost there. My stone is running out of blood, and I don't think Amir is keen on me borrowing any more," Rolinda says.

Her glowing orb flits into the alley, reflecting off the brick walls. With a puff of smoke, she's back to her stylish human form, though this time she's wearing a striking red top and a different shade of jeans. I wonder what it would be like to have such a convenient ability. Maybe I could wear something that actually looks nice and have it expand with me.

Amir gags, shying away and holding his bandaged cut. "Don't you dare poke me again."

Lily blinks, looking at me quizzically, but I shake my head. "I'll give you a rundown later. Right now, we need to get back to Qotan."

I lead the group into the alley to the spot where I remember coming through the portal.

"We just—walk through it, right?" I question.

Amir shrugs. "I think so. David, how about you go first, since you're the leader?"

David glances at me as if I'm going to save him from this conversation by volunteering to go first.

I won't, though, so I just smile.

"Ugh, fine. If I die or something goes wrong, then you have to explain to the monarchs of Qotan how your idea got me killed," he mutters bitterly.

With a heavy sigh, he steps up to the wall, takes another deep breath, and walks forward with his hands out. They hit the wall, and he pauses.

"Um—yeah, that's not working."

I frown. "Did Krell say anything about how to get the portal to open again?"

Jared puts a hand on his chin, looking up to the sky in consideration. "No. I don't remember him saying anything like that."

"Oh no! I need to get back soon, or I'll die," Rolinda says, a little panicked. She glares at Amir. "Or I'll just get what I need."

"Hey! Not without my consent, you crazy—"

"Stop it!" I shout. When they fall silent, I step forward and press my palm to the brick wall. Even though I don't know what I should be feeling, the fact that it's a normal wall tells me all that I need to know. "Try down the wall each way. Maybe it just shifted a few feet."

We split up, moving up and down the alley but coming up short.

"No portal," Lily observes. "And you are sure this is the correct spot? Could we be in the wrong alley?"

That last part was unnecessary, but at least the girl speaks her mind.

My stomach twists. The sun dips so low over the horizon that we have to use Amir's phone to light up the way.

"I'm sure of it. We all are, but if it's not here, it must have moved," I say, cursing. "We weren't even gone a whole day! Why can't it stay in the same spot?"

David slams the side of his fist into the wall, wincing slightly. "To make it difficult for us, apparently. And even though I can feel the pull of Qotan, I can't teleport there. It hasn't recharged enough."

Lily tilts her head to the side. "Did you say you can teleport there? What do you mean by that?"

My eyes widen in realization. "Wait, you are a half-blood, too! That means you should be able to draw us there if we all hold on to you."

"Yes! This should work. All you gotta do is beam us into another realm that you've never actually been to!" David says, his voice dripping with sarcasm.

Jared nods. "As annoying and negative as David is right now, he has a point. How is she supposed to know what to feel if she's never been there before?"

I look Lily straight in the eyes. "Do you feel anything inside you? Like something or someone tugging on your gut?"

Lily shakes her head. "I mean, I'm a bit hungry, if that's what you're asking."

She promptly slips her bag over her shoulder and pulls out a protein bar, ripping it open and stuffing a bite in her mouth. I gape at her.

"No, Krista means like a warmth or a feeling of coming home," David adds.

She closes her eyes, opens them, and shakes her head yet again. We all slump against the wall.

"Wait, I might be able to help," Jared says. He closes his eyes, and Lily jumps about a mile.

"Woah! Did you just invade my personal thoughts? First off, that's wildly awkward, and second, that's way cool. Where did you learn how to do that? And can you teach me?" Lily asks.

"Unfortunately, no, that is just a fairy thing," he responds. "But here—"

Lily flinches. "That's so weird."

"Yeah, I'm going to need a play-by-play," David suggests, leaning in closer. "Not all of us can know what's going on in someone's head."

"I'm just—going to—you know what, no, you don't get a play-by-play. I can't speak out loud and in her head at the same time," he says.

David folds his arms and rests against the wall. Amir shrugs and looks at Rolinda. I'm surprised she doesn't feel the need to comment. She notices my gaze and gives me a half smile.

"Don't look at me," Rolinda says. "I can hear everything that's going on between them."

The silence draws on, and I start to get antsy, shifting from leg to leg so that I don't end up screaming from the awkwardness.

"Oh, *that's* what you're wanting me to feel," Lily says, nodding. "Yeah, I actually do feel that a bit. So do I just—tug on it?"

My stomach drops as her body starts to fade from existence, and we all panic.

"NO!" David and I shout at the same time.

She jumps, forming back into herself.

"Did I do something wrong?" she asks.

"You almost left us behind," I explain. "How would you feel about trying to figure out how to deal with the demons in the other realm? They'd probably shred you to pieces."

Lily shakes her head. "You really underestimate my abilities. I'm pretty sure I could hold my own."

"Well, you probably aren't holding your own with a suitcase like that. Unless you plan to throw it at them," David comments.

She sighs. "I only brought the whole arsenal because I didn't know what I'd feel like using at the time. Can't I figure out what I'll bring along *after* we make it there?"

"It's getting late," Amir says, his head bending back to look up at the darkening sky. A cool breeze flows through the alley, and I suck in a breath. Because our realm is overlaid with Qotan, and this is where the portal was before, I suspect we'll end up in the same spot as we were when we left. I frown.

"Wait. The portal can't *move* can it? It should be in the same spot as it was before. That building was pretty permanent in the demon kingdom," I say. "So, if it didn't move—"

I feel the blood drain from my face.

David curses.

"Then, that means they closed it," Jared says. "And if they closed it—"

"Then, they had a good reason to do so," I finish.

Lily looks confused. "I feel like I'm missing something."

"It means you better pick a weapon now. We're probably diving right into trouble."

The fact that she doesn't seem worried is odd to me. Her face hardens into something impassive, and she bends down to unzip the hulking suitcase. She pulls out two scabbards with short swords and fastens one on each side of her belt. Then, she affixes daggers to each of her ankles and draws out a bow and quiver, which she strings on her back. The rest of the suitcase is full of random things, like throwing knives and stars—like real ninja stars—as well as other swords, daggers, and a crossbow.

"Sheesh, you mean business," Amir notes, his eyes dipping to the suitcase, then back up to her face.

"Well, I don't know what kinds of things I'll be fighting. Gotta be ready for anything," she says.

"So, you can use all of those weapons like an expert and everything?" David asks.

She nods. "It's in my blood."

I want to test her out right now to call her on the dumb bluff, but we need to get going.

"Because there are so many of us, we'll have to hold hands in a chain," I say, making sure my broadsword is secure.

David holds out his hand to me, and my stomach clenches. When I meet his eyes, there's something there that makes me want to shrivel into a corner. Is that satisfaction? Amusement? I know I could refuse to hold his hand and instead hold Jared's, but the last thing I want to do is draw attention to it. I wish the electricity flowing through my hand when he grabs me isn't real.

Amir grabs David's other hand, and Rolinda holds Amir's. Jared reaches out and takes Lily's hand.

"Hold on tight," Jared suggests.

David's fingers squeezing mine makes my chest leap.

"All right, here goes nothing," Lily says.

I close my eyes and ready myself for the teleporting sensation. It comes fast, and it comes hard. Even with my eyes closed, I can feel the spinning sensation tingle in my belly as momentum tugs at my right side. It feels like I'm being pulled away from Lily. My arm extends all the way, and my shoulder strains. A desperate scream escapes my lips as I open my eyes to see that we are spinning in a lopsided circle. We should have evened out, putting the same number of people on either side of our teleporter. Instead, Jared and Lily's faces are hardened in determination while Amir and Rolinda scream wildly, their legs and heads thrashing.

"Hold—on!" I try to yell, but they can't hear me.

Time slows down as I watch David and Amir's hands slip apart.

"No!" David screams, but Amir and Rolinda disappear into a cloud of darkness, their screams silencing almost instantly.

Heart thudding in my head, I struggle to pull David closer. I have no idea what happened to Amir and Rolinda, but I will not lose David the same way. Even though I tug with all my might, he stays at a distance. Then, all of a sudden, he gets lighter and lighter. The skin on my arm burns with the growing sensation. I'm turning into my demon form. I smile, accepting the boon of my demon side's homeland. By the time the world stops spinning, I'm fully grown and holding David in a bear hug.

"Let go of me!" he shouts, pushing away from my body.

Regret and hurt pangs my chest, but I hold my impassive expression.

"That was insane!" Lily exclaims, gasping for air.

"What happened?" Jared says. "Where's Amir and—"

He stops when he sees David.

"No—I had them! They were in my hand! But he just—he just let go—I can't—" David falls to his knees and buries his face in his hands. "They're lost."

We're inside the portal room, lit by dozens of everlight lanterns. The first thing I notice is that the portal wall is decimated. Rubble from the stone around it is piled up where the portal once was.

Someone destroyed it.

An explosion and screaming echoes outside the room.

"Guys, I don't think we have much time to chill in here," Jared says.

Just then, the room shakes like an earthquake. I bend my knees to steady myself as rock dust and chips rain down from the ceiling. Urgency consumes my worry for Amir and Rolinda.

Wherever they are, I hope they can last until we figure out what we just landed ourselves in.

"Jared—" I begin, but I'm at a loss for words.

David is at my feet, and I want to bend down to comfort him, but I hear the battle outside, and my brain is conflicted. Comfort or chaos. My human brain wants one, the demon wants the other.

Jared rushes to David's side and places a hand on his back. He's whispering something to David about how we'll save them and not to worry.

Another explosion shakes us.

"Oh man, I thought I'd be ready for this—but I'm not sure," Lily says.

"You'll be fine," I encourage.

When David doesn't move right away, I decide to try something else. I stoop down and pick him up by his upper arms. I hold him right in front of my demon face, and my chest burns with passion. Of what type of passion, I'm too afraid to analyze at this very moment.

"I swear on my life, I will find Amir," I promise. "We will get our friend back, wherever he is. I swear it."

I have no idea where the words come from or why I say them, but I see a shift in his watering eyes. He nods, then gestures for me to put him down. After wiping away his tears, he looks pissed. Like, next-level angry. I feed off of that anger, and we stand next to each other.

"Let's kick some dark-raced behinds," he says.

I shake my head at his cheesy comment but respond by only bellowing a battle roar. For the first time in seventeen years, four of the six half-bloods are together, and we're going to save Qotan, starting with my home.

I take the lead, throwing my shoulder into the door. It bursts open easily, flying off its hinges. We emerge into chaos. Fires burn, buildings are smashed, and beings are fighting everywhere. A goblin screams out in a grunting language, his weapon raised over his head as he rushes toward a tall elf woman. She spins and smashes a shield into his head, crushing him into the ground. A troll swings his club and throws a few dwarves into the air, their bodies crunching into a wall.

There's no thinking. There's no decision-making. Only battle. I rush the troll, tearing my broadsword from my back and swinging it in a wide arc. He's not expecting me, so I cleave right through his head.

He doesn't melt into ooze like he would have in our world. Instead, I use his fallen body to leap up and land down in the middle of a group of orcs. I engage them, but before one of their swords can bite into my flesh, it's blocked by two short swords. Lily looks determined as she pushes upward, sending the orc weapon away. She flips and turns, her body like a karate prodigy and a master swordsman all at once. Within seconds, the orc is dead on the ground.

I take down the other two, earning myself a cut on the shoulder in the process.

"Sheesh, girl, you weren't kidding," I say, looking Lily up and down.

She doesn't even pause, spinning and launching her sword in a throw to the left. It impales a goblin's neck, and he falls to his knees.

She stops, regarding me with a single peaked eyebrow. Not even a little scared, she nods in approval. "Like I told you, it's in the blood. Apparently, *yours* is in your blood, too."

I flash my teeth at her. "Like you wouldn't believe."

David shouts, and I spin to see him slamming the butt of his sword into an orc's head. After the orc falls, David stabs him in the chest. My lungs tighten at seeing him this way. It's—unnecessarily hot.

No. Don't you dare, I warn myself.

I sense Jared's presence retreating from my mind and panic.

He heard that thought. Before I can curse again, Jared is launching himself up as an elephant and crushing a few goblins under his large feet. When he turns back to normal, he stumbles and holds his side. I remember his injuries from the arena battle just the day before. He hasn't even had a chance to recover. He swipes with his clawed fist weapons and fends off a few orcs.

I rush toward him and put an arm around his waist.

"You don't heal fast like us," I remind him. "You need to get somewhere safe."

He starts to protest, but I urge him mentally.

You aren't useless, you just need a different role. Can you fly?

Yes, I'm not that hurt.

Good. You need to find my father. Search the minds of the other demons, and if you have to, leave here. Go!

He looks stressed, but he doesn't protest. Even a good warrior knows his limits. He shifts into an eagle and shoots off into the sky.

Lily slides on the ground and settles next to me. "These guys are surprisingly resilient."

She has a slice on her head that seeps blood down her cheek. Her bare arm already has a purple-black bruise, and her teeth are bared.

"Shame I don't have scales like that one," she says.

I turn to see David taking a blow to the arm like a champion, his scales preventing a laceration. Even though he doesn't get cut, I know it still hurts. After he finishes off the enemy he's fighting, he stalks over to us.

"This is insane. We need to get out of here, call the griffins, and fly toward the elf lands."

I scowl, all twitterpated feelings lost at these words. "I'm not abandoning my home," I say firmly.

He scoffs. "What if this is a distraction? What if this is just to prevent the bigger army from getting to Lily's dad's kingdom?"

I shake my head. "I don't care. I'm not letting Etherek fall to the enemy."

David sighs heavily, but he nods. "I get it. And I'll stand with you." He frowns. "Wait. There are dwarves and elves. If they're here, then that means . . ."

My eyes shoot wide open. The battle distracted me so much that I hadn't noticed. "Then, the other races are here. Did the army redirect to us?"

We decide to make for the palace and higher ground to get a better look around. Halfway there, we meet a group of light-raced people battling with a large collection of enemies. After we aid them, I grab the shoulder of one of the elven soldiers. He scowls at me, recognizes my pale, human-colored skin, then stops fighting.

"Where is my father?"

He steps back, swallows hard, and points a long blue finger toward where the palace looms.

"He's mounting the defense in the center with our king," he answers, his eyes drifting to Lily's tall frame. His mouth falls open. "My princess!"

He drops to his knees and puts his forehead on the ground.

Lily looks both embarrassed and honored at the same time.

"Oh—wow—um, yeah it's me," she says a bit awkwardly. "At ease, soldier."

His silver irises fix on her. "Allow me to escort you to your father."

"That won't be necessary," I begin. "We can take her—"

Lily's hand slaps my shoulder, and I glare at her. She has goo-goo eyes for the elf boy. I roll my eyes, allowing the elf to stand up and grab his sword.

Just then, a massive stone covered in flames smashes into the roof of a building a couple streets away. Screams erupt from the area, and we're pelted by rock debris and dust.

"Mind the stones," he says coolly.

"Yeah, no kidding," David pants.

He looks shaken still from the fact that Rolinda and Amir are nowhere to be found. I personally hope that they have been shipped somewhere else close by, but there has been no sign of either of them. As much as it stresses me out to think about that fact, I'm glad Amir's not alone. Amir alone in Qotan would most likely result in him being the next teleportation stone for Gulran. I shiver at the thought, glancing at David. I'm grateful he isn't the one who can read thoughts.

"Come, quickly!" the elf urges us.

He moves swiftly around the building that just got smashed moments ago. We shuffle after him, me gesturing to the others to go first. Jared and Lily oblige. David, on the other hand, engages me in a silent argument about who should be the one to take up the rear. I don't know if it's a chivalrous thing, or if he has a death wish, but we have to rush to catch up when I finally win the staring contest. He ends up rolling his eyes and moving forward.

We pass battle after battle. In some places, the enemy has fallen. In others, our allies are struggling. More than once I almost break off from the group to come to the defense of our allies, but I hold to the group, remembering that this war is much bigger than the individual conflicts. Fortunately, there seems to be more of our numbers than theirs. Still, the city is in ruins. My heart aches for each house I see destroyed—for each demon lying dead on the ground. I wish I had been here. I wish I could save them all.

A rush of comfort comes from Jared into my mind. It's the type of thing a friend does when they put their arm around you and say they understand. Even if I won't admit it verbally, I accept the comfort. Though he's never experienced this type of pain, his mother, the very person who brought him into this world, is to blame for much of this destruction.

We round the final corner, which gives us a perfect view of the large path up to the front gates of the palace. A group of warriors of various races defend the palace. Among them are my father and Ilvinar. I see another armored dwarf who looks regal enough to be royalty, but I don't recognize him offhand.

This is going to be another big fight.

21

THE TIDES ARE TURNED

E VEN BEFORE TURNING AROUND, I recognize Gulran and his father, Urothar. Ferona flits in the air, her body armored with a cured leather breastplate. She's also surrounded by armed guards. My anger burns so hot and fast that my vision blurs. I rush forward but stop when David stands in front of me.

"Don't be an idiot, Kris. Do you see how many of them there are? It looks like they're negotiating or something. Chill," he whispers.

Normally, someone standing in my way telling me to chill would make me go into a frenzy. Strangely, however, David's words calm me. I take some deep breaths and focus directly on David's eyes, letting the heat in my chest dissipate.

"Should we try to sneak around?" Jared offers.

Lily shakes her head. "I don't think that's going to be as easy as you think. Plus, it'll be better if they feel surrounded."

"We're *not* attacking them. That would be dumb," David says.

I falter, looking at each of my friends. "You're right, but if they're surrounded, it may give them pause."

Air hisses through Jared's teeth. "Doesn't matter. They know already. Ferona—"

The hair on the back of my neck raises as we look up to see Ferona. She has a look of deep satisfaction on her face as she raises one of her hands and gives a cheeky wave.

I want to cut her hand off so badly.

David swears and holds up his sword. "Move close enough that we can hear but not so close that they could attack us quickly."

For the first time since we've been here, I am relieved that he's giving orders. It's not that I don't like leading, it just wears on me. To see him step up and command is a breath of fresh air. Part of me wonders if he's acting this way out of regret for losing his friend. Even if that's true, perhaps it was the right thing to kick him over the edge. He should be leading more anyway.

Though . . . if Amir is dead, the cost would not be worth the reward.

We move as a close group, the elf and David leading us closer. I notice the elf has positioned himself in front of Lily as if he thinks he'll be the best bodyguard for her. Either she doesn't notice or she's too focused on the enemy before us. We look like a ghastly bunch. Even the short time we've been thrown into this battle, our clothes are dirty and torn, and the only one without a wound is David.

"And just like that, the half-bloods deliver themselves right into our hands," Ferona coos, her voice carrying on the wind. "Despite the failures of your fool of a son."

Urothar growls at her. "I told you that I'd address his failures later. For now, secure our prizes, and I'll deal with the kings. Etherek will be ours this day."

He bellows the last part and holds his axe up into the air. The enemy soldiers nearby scream in triumph and raise their weapons in response.

"Over my dead body!" David shouts. He mutters two words to me. "Black flames."

Satisfaction rockets through me in a chilling way as a contingent of orcs, goblins, and trolls breaks off from the group and advances on us. Among them is also a ghost-like creature I only recognize from the throne room in Dranith weeks ago and another blue-scaled man. A glyph pulsates on his neck. It's the blue dragon who led the ambush on us.

David holds up his hands and yells at the top of his lungs. Right as the burst of flames shoots out, I focus my energy on pulling the light from inside them. Rather than red and orange fire, a black and gray smoke-like substance comes out in a rush. Naturally, the advancing enemies don't even pause. To them, it looks harmless, like a smoke screen which will only blind them. Then, the screams of pain come. David stokes the flames, and I watch black fire catch on.

When he stops the torrent, I release my power. Light returns to the flames, and the enemy writhes in pain, screaming from the surprise attack.

"Jared, take Lily to her father!" David orders.

Lily gives him a withering look. "No way, dude. This is *my* fight, too. I'm not going to—augh!"

She screams as Jared, now a massive eagle, grips her in his talons and launches into the air. Of the enemies, only the ghost-creature and the dragon advance.

David curses. "I guess fire doesn't hurt them."

The dragon man wears a green military-like uniform with bangles and golden cuffs. He bares his teeth at me, then shifts before our eyes. What was once a smaller man becomes a full-sized dragon with wings that beat so hard and fast that we're buffeted back.

Jared, dragon on your tail!

He affirms my warning, but I can feel his stress through our link. He darts with Lily dangling below to the left, but the dragon's maw snaps at him, and he's forced to dart away.

"To their aid!" my father cries from behind the chaos we've created.

"The ruler's heads are mine!" Urother screams.

David, without even the slightest bit of hesitation, rushes the dragon hovering in the air. I hold out my hand, telling him to stop, but he ignores me, vaulting past the ghost-like creature and leaping up. With his free hand, he grabs onto the dragon's toe and hoists himself up on its large foot. I gape at him, unsure of where his recklessness came from. Yet the uncomfortable part of me burns with a desire I wish didn't exist.

I level my gaze at the creature and walk forward steadily. It looks roughly like the shape of a man, but it wears flowing robes of gray that are frayed and ripped at the bottom, as well as around its sickly white hands. I can't see its face. Only a deep blackness fills the hole beneath its raised hood. Not wanting to move closer until I know more about it, I launch my intimidation aura at it. Naturally, it does absolutely nothing. Instead, I'm met with a similar aura, but it feels . . . so wrong.

My skin chills, and my throat locks up in fear. I blink in confusion as the power overwhelms me. The hand holding my broadsword won't move. In fact, nothing will move. Desperation and terror rush through me as the creature slowly approaches me and reaches out a hand toward my face. Just then, a yell comes from my left, and a sword slams down on the creature's arm. A sickening crack fills my ears, accompanied by a high-pitched and ear-splitting screech. The creature's hold on me vanishes, and I shuffle backward.

At least it can be hit by physical weapons.

The creature rears up and faces the elf who was leading us here. With one swipe of its clawed and gnarled hand, it slashes into the elf's face. He screams in pain but jumps forward and slashes at the wraith. Meanwhile, David shouts unseemly things and swings wildly at the dragon's foot, who is waving it side to side in an effort to throw him off. The elf continues to battle the wraith, and I rush forward to give him aid. Before I can get there, however, the wraith snatches him by the neck and raises him up to its hood. A shimmering light rushes from the elf's eyes and mouth and into the black hole beneath the wraith's hood.

"No!" I scream, desperately jabbing my sword into its back. Even though it flinches, it doesn't relent, pulling the life out of the elf.

What can stop a creature like this? The head. Nothing can live without one. I don't think, I just react, swinging my broadsword quickly toward where its neck should be. As angry as I am and as acquainted as I am to death, I still squeeze my eyes shut when my sword cuts through. The shriek enters my mind, and I fall to my knees, my free hand coming to my ear as if it will help anything. Two thuds pull my eyes open.

Despite my efforts, the elf lies there, skin gray and eyes blank. The wraith's body melts away to dust, flowing with the wind.

I wasn't fast enough. Still shaken by the terrifying scene I just witnessed, I stand and avert my eyes, focusing back on David. I'm broken inside, but I hold it in. This elf isn't even my kin, and yet, I feel responsible for him—for all of this.

David screams out in fear, and he tumbles through the air as the dragon finally kicks him off. I barrel forward, throwing my arms just in time to catch him. We both grunt as we fall to the ground.

He thanks me. After recovering ourselves, we stare up as the dragon leaps, flames erupting from its mouth toward where Jared is desperately trying to escape.

"Any tips on how to kill a dragon?" I ask.

David grimaces. "Why would I know how to kill my relatives? You have *way* more experience with this place than I do. Why don't you—"

I hold my hand up to interrupt him.

He scoffs. "Don't give me the hand. Are we in third grade?"

A scuffling sound draws my attention, and I shove David out of the way, lobbing my weapon in that direction. My throw isn't quite right, so my blade doesn't stick into the enemy aiming his bow at us, but it's heavy enough to knock him off balance. The goblin tumbles to the ground, and I head in his direction. I yank the blade off the ground and end him with a quick blow. My stomach turns if I focus too much on the gore, so I avert my eyes.

More arrows snap against the wall next to me, and I duck into the ally, screaming for David to follow. He runs, but not nearly at the breakneck pace I do. An arrow hits his shoulder and bounces back, knocking him forward. He stumbles but doesn't fall down.

"Sheesh! They need to chill!" he says as he slips into the alley with me. "I'm running out of steam."

Even as he says it, his skin turns back to normal. I take a quick stock of how I'm feeling. My bones ache from all the running and unexpected fighting, and the arrow wound is still healing up, but underneath it all, I'm in the same boat as David. How much longer can we last?

"Remind me that we need to work on endurance," I say, rushing back out onto the street. More volleys launch in our direction. David stands in front of me, grunting as another arrow hits his scaled side instead of sinking into my flesh.

"I didn't ask for you to be my human shield," I say firmly.

"Yeah, because you'll never ask for help!" he spits back.

This strikes me deep. He knows me way too well. Before I can give another quip, the dragon roars, flames spouting all over and blasting us with heat when it comes too close. The archers across the street scream out in agony and dive away from the dragon's flames. Screeches of metal hitting metal come from where my father is fighting Urothar and Ferona.

Kris, I can't keep this up. I'm going to pass out, Jared thinks to me desperately.

I stare up at him, watching him fly left and right to keep the dragon's focus. He's discarded Lily. I can only hope he's dropped her somewhere safe.

"Lily's with her dad. Look!" David says.

I gape at him, wondering if Dragon Boy has somehow learned to read minds. He glances back at me and furrows his brow.

"What?"

"How did you know I was thinking about Lily?"

He points to Jared. "Jared had a girl. Now he doesn't. You gasped when you saw him. I put two and two together. Besides, that was my first thought as well."

Another bout of flames forces us to duck behind the wall.

"Can you make a break for it?" I ask.

David nods. He holds up a hand and summons a fireball. "Worst case, I can clear a path for us."

The burning passion flares again, mixed with the heat of anger and my defense instincts. I have the sudden urge to kiss him. I press it away, averting my eyes from his face and nodding to the main road.

"Run as fast as you can and don't stop. We'll have to push through Urothar and his band," I say.

He cracks his neck, then silently counts to three with his fingers.

On the last number, we rush from the alley, expecting arrows but seeing none. The archers were either killed by the inferno or retreated from the dragon's might.

We rush headlong to where Urothar is engaged in battle with Krell. They slash and weave, attacking each other with reckless abandon. Despite Krell being nearly twice Urothar's height, the orc king is keeping up. Ilvinar fights next to Lily, their swords raised as they fend off a group of orcs and trolls.

David throws his ball of flames toward the fighting. It misses everyone, instead landing in the midst of everything and exploding outward. Enemies and allies alike react in surprise, backing away from the explosion—and each other. We take that moment to leap through the flames like a cheesy action movie. And it gives me a thrill, as embarrassing as that is to admit.

We come to a skidding halt next to Lily and her father.

"Nice pyrotechnics," she says.

Ilvinar regards me with a hardened expression, then eyes David. "High Prince. At last, we finally meet."

Even though it's not my first time seeing the elf king, I'm still struck by how he looks. He wears no crown. Instead, he has a metal helmet that comes down on his nose and chin. His brilliant silver hair pokes out from beneath it, framing his sharp jaw and powerful neck. He stands at my height, and though his frame is slight compared to my brute demon form, I know he's lean and strong. He wears a mixture of chain mail and leather armor, all adorned with dark paint in the pattern of leaves and trees.

"Uh, yeah. Nice to meet you—"

Another flaming rock smashes loudly into a building behind us, interrupting David's response. By now, the flames have receded from behind us, and the enemy is approaching once again.

"No time for this," I say, holding my broadsword up. "My brother is in trouble. How can we get this dragon off his tail?"

Ilvinar looks up and shakes his head. "There is no way. The might of the dragons is one best not trifled with. Your brother is doomed."

My heart falls.

"No way!" David pipes up. "If that dragon wanted him dead, he'd have snapped him up already. Urothar knows he can't kill any one of us, so he's probably keeping him busy so Jared can't get away."

He's right. Urothar wants us alive.

"Fools! I will take Etherek and have your heads for my palace!" Urothar roars.

He rushes forward through the now-dissipating flames and slashes at me. I parry his blow, but it has much more weight behind it than I expect. I'm thrown backward, landing hard on my butt, and pain radiates up my spine. My skin prickles, and I look for my father. He's fighting a group of orcs a little way off.

"You can stay down, demon mutt," Urothar says, rushing in and swinging the flat of his blade at my head. I duck and roll away, giving Ilvinar enough time to dive in and engage him.

My body feels light all of a sudden, and I'm thrown to the side, my skull smashing into the wall.

"Kris!" David shouts.

I watch as his body is thrown back in the same way.

Ferona hovers in the air just in front of us, a wicked smile on her face.

"You came right back to where we wanted you," she says.

One hand extends toward David and one toward me. I can't move my body no matter how much I try. It's as if there is a massive boulder being shoved into my whole being. Air can't enter my lungs, and for a moment, I think I'll black out, but then the sensation eases up.

"What are you talking about?" I gasp with the new relief.

Ferona raises an eyebrow. "I've been tracking you ever since you picked up that foolish daughter of mine."

My skin chills.

"Wh—what?" I manage. "Daughter? Last I checked, Jared's not a girl."

Ferona grimaces and shoves David harder into the wall. He gasps in pain, his head lolling to the side as he coughs and sputters.

"Not him, you idiot! Rolinda," she says. "I've had a bond with that girl mentally for years. Though I can't see every one of her thoughts, I saw enough. The instant I knew you were headed here, we redirected our army. No longer was the elf kingdom our priority. In the end, *you* are the ones we need."

I seethe. Not once since we've been traveling with Rolinda did she ever mention her relationship to Ferona. I shake my head, but I can see it now. Her pain. The way she couldn't believe her queen's betrayal . . .

"You were tracking us the whole time," I murmur, my voice empty.

Ferona scoffs. "Not the *whole* time. When she escaped to your world, she went dark. But then, she was back and headed toward the demon kingdom. You have her to thank for our timely arrival. Where is she, anyway?"

Oh no . . .

Amir is in big trouble. He's walking around—wherever they are—with a living beacon calling for this crazed ruler to come take his blood for one of the teleportation stones.

"Dead," I say firmly. "Killed her when she admitted that she was betraying us."

Ferona purses her lips. "Nice try, fool. She doesn't know that I can track her thoughts and location. No, you feel foolish for not seeing it before. You feel resentment for not sending her out of your presence right away. I wish I could say that she was aligned with my views of this land, but that is simply not the case. Now, stay where you are while I procure my other prizes."

The weight crashes down on me harder, and my vision blurs. I can't breathe. I can't think. David also writhes and struggles against the wall. Just before I can black out fully, I close my eyes and go limp. As I expected, the weight disappears immediately. David's body thuds to the ground across from me. It takes everything in me not to breathe a sigh of relief. I hold as still as possible to make it look like I'm out cold.

Even though I can't see her, I hear Ferona order a couple soldiers to stand near us and keep guard. Their armor clinks right up to my feet. The moment Ferona flies away, I peek open my eyes. David is face down on the ground not moving. Two orcs stand over him, grunting and saying something I can't understand.

I count to ten, hoping beyond anything that Ferona has moved far enough away. Gauging my body, I know that I can take these two out. With one quick swipe, I snatch their heels in my large palms. Yanking inward, they fall to their sides with cries of surprise. I stomp on one of their hands, making him release his hold on the axe, which I spin up and lodge into his chest. He falls back to the ground, and I aim a kick at the other orc's face. She catches it and twists my foot. I almost fall to the ground, but instead, I redirect the motion to land right on top of her. My body crushes her, and I immediately throw my elbow into her neck.

She's down and out pretty fast.

David's guards realize what's happening and start to run toward me. They don't make it far before they're blasted in the back with fire. Their hair and clothing flickers with the hot fire, and they sprint around screaming.

"Oh man, my head is pounding like nothing else," David groans, struggling to his feet.

"You faked passing out, too?"

"I guess great minds think alike," he says with a wink.

Kris! Jared screams in my head. I panic, looking up to where he shifts into a smaller bird and flies into an alley. Right at that moment, Ferona turns around, and her eyes widen when she sees we've dispatched our guards.

"Time to go!" I say, grabbing David's hand and yanking him into the alley.

I am guessing we make it out of range of her telekinetic blast because I don't fall to the ground in a heap.

Kris, I'm about to fall over. I can't keep doing this, Jared says desperately.

The dragon roars, and a wave of heat shoots down from the space between the roofs above us.

"Sheesh, that dragon needs to chill out!" David says.

"Jared needs our help. Do you think you can take out the dragon?" I ask.

It's a ridiculous question, honestly, but he's half dragon, and his scales can actually keep him from being bitten in half or fried. My skin? Well, I know I couldn't heal through that.

He grimaces, looks up at the smoldering stones above us, then levels his gaze with me.

"I mean, why not? But what are you going to do?"

I crack my neck, imagining the enemies I have to engage to give my father a little more time.

"Krell needs help. I can't help you with the dragon, so I might as well provide support."

There's another screech from the sky and another desperate call of help from Jared. I shout at him mentally to hide somewhere small where the dragon will struggle to get him for a minute while I think. Adrenaline rushes through every fiber in my body, making me jittery.

"Right. Suddenly, I'm not sure the dragon sounds so bad," David says. "But you better have some pretty great ideas of what I can do to stop that thing. It's only a hundred times my size and ferocious and—oh, wait!"

I pause, furrowing my brow. He's staring off somewhere behind me so intently that I almost follow his gaze. Then, his worried look grows into a half smirk.

"He's being controlled by Urothar," he says. "With that symbol on his neck. Remember?"

I widen my eyes, urging him on to the point.

"If I can ruin the symbol, the orc's control on the dragon should break," he says.

Oh, that's clever. My thoughts drift momentarily back to the moment in Dranith when we were first confronted by our enemies. The symbol pulsed on the necklace around the dragon queen's neck, but it was also on the blue dragon—and on Ferona. Ferona's submission was voluntary, so it's hard to say how much control Urothar has over her, but as for the dragon . . .

"Worth a try," I say, swallowing hard. My heart pulls me in two directions. The will to fight and take down the enemy wants me to bum-rush the group of leaders, but my defensive instincts shout at me to save my brother. I grit my teeth and nod at David.

"Save my brother." It's a plea that bleeds shame into my chest. Gratefully, my demon face is unable to blush. David flashes me a grin, then nods toward the opening of the alley. The fact that Ferona hasn't come after us suggests that she's otherwise engaged, but I know our time won't last long.

"Mind giving me a boost?" he asks.

"Happy to," I say.

We peek out of the alley. Sure enough, Ferona swipes a long staff around in a circle and blocks an attack from the elf king himself. I don't know why it's weird to see the fairy queen with combat experience, but my mind struggles to comprehend how she spins and parries Ilvinar's sword so effortlessly.

"Now!" I shout.

We rush out of the alleyway toward the dragon, which is nestling its head into a crevice in the side of the palace. No doubt Jared is shoved deep inside unable to escape. I match David's pace as he jumps forward. I reach out and grab the back of his hoodie. He scales up right as I spin in a circle and throw him upward with all my might. A strangled scream of thrill erupts from his throat as he launches into the sky. My follow-through is perfect. A shot put thrower might actually be proud of me. I watch as he soars up and lands right on the flank of the dragon.

"Good luck, Dragon Breath," I say quietly before sprinting right at the person who's pissing me off the most.

Qotan's favorite fairy queen. My broadsword vibrates in my hand, my brain tuning out the sound of everything else around me. The explosive rocks destroying my home left and right, the clangs of steel, the shouts and cries of fighting and death . . .

She is my only goal.

Before I can reach her, she catches a glimpse of me and throws her free hand out to stop me. The force hits me, and I freeze in place, a growl escaping my lips. Burning fills my chest at my failure to slice her in half, but my distraction is perfect. Ilvinar takes the opening to swipe his blade at her chest. She curses and twists, but his sword still catches her arm and cuts deep.

"NO!" she screams, and her hold on me releases. I fly at her in a rage.

Have you ever had a moment where you've been trying something your entire life, only to fail over and over again even after practicing hundreds of times until one day, you succeed? That's how I feel when my weapon slices right into the back of the fairy queen. She's wearing armor, so it doesn't cut her flesh, but watching her neck snap back as the force of my blow hits its mark fills me with satisfaction. She goes down to the ground hard. Right as I raise my sword to chop down on her neck, Ilvinar commands me to stop.

"She doesn't deserve death, not until she's tried for her betrayal!"

I curse, deflated but knowing he's right. As much as I want to kill her, it's not my right. She groans and rolls over to look up at me, then her eyes glow an eerie white, and she smiles. My skin chills, but I hardly notice it when I'm thrown off my feet toward the elf king. Ferona flies up in a fit of rage, but it's not her.

Urothar's control must have taken over.

"Go. Help your father," Ilvinar urges me.

"But *you* need help—"

"No," he says. "I have help."

Just then, Lily slips into place next to him. Her hair is a wild mess, and her face is covered in scrapes and bruises. Yet, despite it all, she's grinning.

"This—is—incredible!" she pants, looking directly at me.

A girl after my own heart.

"Good luck," I say, turning on my heels and running toward where I see Krell battling Gulran, Urothar, and a set of trolls. He's been backed into the wall of the keep with two demons at his side. They stand tall and proud, holding their massive spears to the sky. I let the thrill of battle enter me as I rush toward them.

Distantly, I hear the dragon roar in pain and pray that David is making progress with him. Jared hasn't called out in so long that my throat constricts as I imagine him unconscious or dead. Before I can let that thought overcome me, I vault up on the back of one of the trolls and slam my blade down into its shoulder. It only enters a few inches, the troll's muscles preventing it from entering deeper, but it's enough to make the brute howl. Strong blue hands grip my whole body and throw me toward where my father stands. I hit the ground hard. All the air rushes from my lungs, and the world blurs for a moment until I catch my breath. Krell's face appears above me, his hand held out.

"Karistana! Are you all right?"

I take his hand, shaking the blurriness from my vision and jumping to my feet. I wobble for just a moment, and one of the demon guards steadies me.

"Now, it's even. Can you two take the trolls? Dad and I can take the father and son," I say.

Krell furrows his thick brows. "Normally, the king gives the orders."

I shrug. "Sorry."

His face softens. "I'll get over it. You called me Dad."

I pause. I actually did. My lip slides between my teeth so I can nibble on it.

"Yeah—an accident. It won't happen again."

There's somehow a twinkle in his pure-black eyes as he shakes his head, and we face the enemy. Gulran seethes, his chest rising and falling in rapid succession.

"Your daughter won't save you from your fate, Krell!" Urothar booms.

In all reality, he looks a lot bigger than he did when we first met him in Dranith. This is not a fact that makes me feel better about this fight. But if Krell can distract the king, I can take out his idiotic son. There's nothing I would enjoy more than ending his bloodline right here and now.

"You will fall under my control just like Ellistra and her dragonkind," he says. "My mark will land on you and all of yours."

Krell bares his teeth. "Demons do not fall to anyone."

I can tell he spoke in the demon tongue by how my brain fizzes slightly.

This infuriates Urothar, who comes roaring with his massive iron axe. Krell rushes forward, and his weapon clashes easily with it.

"Let's do this, Orc Boy," I taunt.

Gulran bares his teeth and attacks.

22

DAVID CONQUERS HIS KIN

W HEN I GREW UP, training just became a regular part of
my days. It was a way that I could forget the troubles of
my strange personality. I didn't turn into a demon starting when
I was a baby. Those fun moments didn't start happening until
I was a preteen around the age of ten. Most of my childhood,
I had to deal with my temper and ill-advised decisions. I could
never explain why my outbursts were so often or so embarrassing. Mom was always incredibly patient with me when I broke
her things. We had to replace our furniture so many times that
I couldn't count. All for what kinds of things? Well, once she
opened my applesauce packet without letting me do it myself.

I shrugged those moments off more often than not. They
were the reason, however, that Mom began our training. Jared
had already started shifting into animals, so they decided at the
age of four that we could begin. Sometimes I hated her and Bob
for the obstacle courses and strength training. They were long,
hard days, and all I wanted was to play with my Polly Pocket.
But I didn't have any friends. I wasn't old enough to understand

that my temper would make having friends all but impossible. Whenever I asked Mom why I couldn't be out playing and why I had to train and focus and work so hard when I was so tired, she would only answer with, "It's for your own good."

As I rush toward Gulran, the flaring anger within filling me with energy, I realize yet again how wise she was. My intense emotions needed direction—or else something truly horrible might have happened to someone innocent.

My broadsword slams into Gulran's axe with a clang, and he slides back a few inches. I'm honestly surprised by the resistance of the half orc. He's only half a foot taller than David, but I can see his bulging muscles through his armor and shirt.

"Where's my mom, Green Face?" I growl, my arms struggling to push him away.

"About to be turned into a teleportation stone!" he spits, shoving with all his might.

I use his momentum to jump backward and ready myself. This time, I come flying at him, fury at his words fueling each of my attacks. He dips, dodges, and parries easily. I don't relent. Each and every one of my attacks keeps him from counterattacking, so I keep flinging them. Ultimately, he spins out of one of my blows and is able to swipe in at me, but I dodge it and back away.

"You were lucky last time," he says. "Don't expect the same luck this time."

His axe is a blur, but I can track each motion. Our weapons clang as they clash over and over. Two orcs come from out of nowhere and try to join our fight, but I fling my intimidation aura at them as strongly as I can. They drop their weapons and cower in fear. It won't last long, especially if I have to focus on the fight with Gulran. I turn my back to them and let Gulran push me right into where they cower. Then, rather than parry his axe-blow, I dive to the side. His weapon comes crashing down on the helmet of one of his own. The orc goes down in a heap.

Gulran screams in frustration, leaving the other cowering orc and charging at me. My aura slips, and the orc shakes his head and comes out of the stupor. Before he can pick up his weapon, a group of very small men leap all over him, stabbing and hacking at his exposed flesh. I blink in confusion. Brownies—little palm-sized people decked out in armor and holding swords like knives—overwhelm the orc. I'm only forced out of the shock of *that* image by Gulran advancing on me again.

The world blurs around me as I focus on the only thing that matters right now. We both sync into a beautiful rhythm. To be fair, I'm unsure if his goal is to kill me, considering that would ruin the whole ritual thing, but I can't let off just because he isn't *supposed* to kill me. Accidents have always happened in duels throughout history.

Gulran's face contorts into fury as he presses me back into the wall. Chest heaving with every movement, I slip out from between him and the wall and kick him. I catch him in the leg and buckle his knee. Even though he dips a little, he doesn't fall to the ground.

"Stop playing around!" he snarls at me.

I flash my demon teeth at him, which only serves to annoy him more.

"Get out of my home," I shoot back.

"This isn't your *home*," he spits. "You don't even belong in Qotan. You may be half demon, but you never lived here."

He roars and slams his axe down hard on my broadsword. The blow rockets up my forearms and makes them ache. With a grunt, I shove him away and swipe at his midsection. Even though the tip of my sword catches him, it glances off the chain mail easily.

The dragon roars, making me and Gulran both flinch. I count my many blessings that I haven't had to confront a dragon until now. As much as I want to check on David, I keep my eyes trained on Gulran. His free hand opens and closes rapidly, a sign of either nerves or just agitation. How much I wish I could use Jared's mind reading to see what is going on in his head. I notice his eyes flick to my feet, and it gives me just enough of a heads up to be ready when he feints an attack at my face.

I spin and land an elbow on his neck, which knocks him to the ground with a loud thud. My broadsword comes down on him decisively, and satisfaction blossoms inside me, but he rolls away at the last moment. Then, he disappears from my view. I stand there, blinking for just a moment, before he reappears and slices a deep gash in my upper arm.

Cursing, I leap away and drop my weapon, plastering my thick hand over the cut to stop the bleeding. Gulran grins evilly and readies himself to rush forward. I hit him with the strongest aura I can. His eyes go wide, and he starts shaking, his axe dipping to the ground. I close my eyes, keeping the aura going so I can let my body heal. Fortunately, I haven't sustained many injuries, so it works relatively quickly. But I can feel my energy waning. I need to rest soon.

"New trick?" I say, opening my eyes and glaring at him. I release my aura and snatch my broadsword up.

"Learned it recently, yes," he admits before melding into our surroundings again.

This time, I won't let him get me. I focus my hearing through the din. The music of fighting is loud, with the shouting and the clashing. Among it all, the dragon huffs and growls as it tries to deal with whatever David is doing.

There...

I hear the shuffling of feet to my right and the subtle swish of Gulran readjusting his grip on his weapon. My eyes close, and I focus on the sound. It's slow but steady. All of a sudden, it speeds up and comes quickly toward me. Even with my eyes closed, I know where he'll be, so I hold my place. At the last moment, my eyes snap open, and I dodge to the side. It's not the most effective way to escape his attack, for I couldn't know the actual position of his axe, but he still manages to miss me. I don't hesitate to sprint behind him and thrust with my sword. The tip hits his chain mail and pierces right through, my blade going into his back just to the right of his spine.

A strangled cry comes from his mouth before he lands on his knees and falls forward.

"Die!" Urothar roars from behind me.

All bloodthirst for ending Gulran's life leaves me, and I spin to where Urothar has my father pinned down. One of the demons at his side fell to the troll. His corpse is on the ground near the closest building. The other seems to be winning his troll fight, but the newly freed troll holds my father from behind in a headlock. I taste blood in my mouth, and the air smells sour and smokey. Fires smolder in the surrounding rubble where flaming rocks have destroyed too many buildings to count. Bodies lay strewn among the streets of my destroyed home.

My focus hones in on Urothar approaching my father with his axe raised high to end his life. I don't think, I just run. Even as I do, I let my aura fly toward the orc king.

It alerts him to my attack. I don't realize this mistake until his fist comes flying out at me and catches me in the chest. The air is knocked out of my lungs. For the third time? Fourth time? I've lost count. I fall to my back and gasp as Urothar smiles down at me.

"You really thought you could rush me just like that? I look forward to draining your blood for the ritual. Stay down, demon mutt," he says before turning back to my father.

I try to scream, but I still can't breathe.

Jared! Jared! Help! He's going to kill my dad! I scream desperately with my mind.

But my brother doesn't answer. I still haven't been able to save him. It takes all of my energy to roll to my side, my lungs still seizing and my eyes going foggy. There my father watches with determination as Urothar approaches and prepares to cut him down. Air finally enters my chest, and I choke on it, tears exploding from my eyes. I tremble and try to rise from the ground. My ribs scream at me because his punch broke a few. Urothar ignores me, stalking up to Krell and resting the axe blade on his chest.

"This is the day I conquer the demon kingdom. Etherek is mine," he says proudly.

"You may end my life, but as long as my daughter lives, you will never conquer our people," Krell responds, a satisfied smile on his face.

I want to shout at him to shut up and not provoke the orc king, but it's not in my nature. That's the human girl in me whimpering and whining for her long-lost father. No, he should fight to the end. Stare at the eyes of his killer until he can't anymore. That's a warrior's death.

His determination angers Urothar, who pulls back the axe to give the final blow. Everything goes dark very quickly, and I blink in confusion.

Then, the sky comes crashing down . . .

I'm literally crushed to the ground. I twitch and squirm in a panic as I realize I can't move anything, but it's fleeting as the weight lifts off of me.

"Sorry, Kris!" David's voice sounds from a distance.

"What the—?" I say, rolling over to see David's head poking out from on top of a massive blue mountain.

Not a mountain.

He's on top of the dragon, who is currently on top of me, Urothar, the troll, and my father. David slips down from the huge beast and lands on his feet, stumbling a moment but ultimately recovering. His left arm hangs limp from his shoulder as if it's been broken or dislocated.

"I did it," he says, coming to my side and collapsing. "I broke the symbol and the dragon went wild. Just when I thought I'd get bucked off, I yelled at it to stop and it did. Apparently, the dragon just needed to hear his prince's words. He obeyed me like a trained pet."

Do not refer to your subjects as pets if you intend on getting them all to follow you, High Prince. I was not compelled by your voice; I am merely loyal to your throne, a big booming voice echoes in my mind.

David flinches. "Right. Sorry, don't mean to disrespect." He gives me a withering look, then holds out his free hand. "My left arm's not doing well, but I still have a good arm."

I take his hand, and we both stumble as he helps me up.

"Where is Krell?" I ask frantically.

"Oh, they are just pinned under the dragon's foot, right over there," David says. "Did you want us to let them go?"

"Dude, if you killed my dad, I'm going to—"

"Calm down!" he says, holding his hands in the air. "They are just pinned. Let them up."

The huge dragon foot lifts enough for me to see my father on the ground next to the troll and Urothar. I shuffle forward and drag him out from underneath. I'm beside myself as I pull him toward me and bury him in a hug. He starts laughing.

"This is more the reaction I hoped for when we first reunited," he says.

I shove him away, embarrassed. This only makes him laugh more.

He resists. His strength is beyond my own, the dragon muses in my mind.

Skin prickling, Krell, David, and I back away from the dragon's foot as Urothar roars and shoves it upward and away.

"*Trivlan r'ur grk lavnist eht—*"

"He's trying to put the domination magic on the dragon once more!" Krell shouts.

"Over my dead body," I say, pulling back my arm and flinging my broadsword as hard as I can.

Whether my anger helps me aim or I've just gotten better at throwing, the butt of the sword hits the orc king square in the chest. He grunts and goes down to one knee.

"Curse you fools! This isn't over!" He gasps, reaching to a pouch at his side and pulling out a glowing red stone.

"No!" I cry out.

The orc king fades away into thin air as the teleportation magic takes him. His soldiers disappear quickly, each pulling stones from their pouches. I hear cursing and turn to see that Lily and Ilvinar are staring at nothing. Ferona must have rushed away. We're powerless as the entirety of the living enemy army disappears. I spin to see where Gulran lays dying and find him gone. My arms shake. I didn't get to end his meaningless life before he—yet again—escaped my clutches.

The dragon's body quivers above us, shivering and shrinking until the dragon is no more. In its place stands a tall and buff-looking man. He wears a uniform and has his long blond hair tied back in a ponytail. His clothes remind me of the fancy ones that military men and women put on when they go to functions, though he has no medals or adornments.

"My lieges," he says, bowing deeply in the general direction of all of us. "Forgive my offenses. The influence of the orc king was difficult to resist once he put his glyph in place. If I am to be punished for my crimes, I will accept it without complaint."

His accent is odd but kind of nice, like a combination of British and someone from South America.

My father puts up his hand, but Ilvinar speaks up first.

"That is not necessary. Your deeds were not your own," he says.

I furrow my brow, wondering why *he*, of all the monarchs, is the one who gets to speak and pass judgment. I don't get to say anything snooty because my father catches my eye and shakes his head. Don't rock the boat. I get it.

"It appears that we have won the day, thanks to our young rulers," Krell says, smiling at me.

To my utter shock and surprise, David blushes.

Lily raises her hand and pumps a fist. "Finally got to see some action! My affinity to any weapon felt completely wasted my whole life. This made waiting so worth it."

Krell exchanges a glance with me, then holds out his hand to shake hers.

"You must be the half elf princess. Welcome to Qotan. I wish that I could have welcomed you under more calm and considerate circumstances, but this was a surprise attack, after all," Krell says.

Ilvinar seems cold toward his daughter, which is a bit strange to me, but I notice he's looking around the group of people for someone.

"Where is the fourth? The child of Ferona?"

My blood runs cold. I look frantically for the landmark where I last heard him call out to me. A hand grips mine, and I flinch, almost pulling away. It's David, so I don't yank my hand back.

"I think I know where he is," he says. "We'll get him." David then turns to the uniformed handsome man and nods. "Garvir, mind giving us a lift?"

"Certainly," he says, spreading his arms and expanding in a strange manner until he's in his dragon form once more. David leaps on the dragon's leg and starts climbing up, but I'm not patient enough to wait for him. I pick him up by the midsection and toss him over my shoulder. With one powerful leap, I scale most of the dragon's height until I can grip a spine on his back.

"Okay, sheesh. I get it, you're much stronger than I am," David complains.

Even though he's red from me throwing him around like a rag doll, he looks in good spirits. The dragon leaps off the ground, and I'm sucked downward as my body's momentum catches up to that of our escort.

My mind runs through all the terrifying possibilities. What if we don't find Jared? What if we find him in pieces? I call out to him with my mind. There's no response. I'm kicking myself for not remembering him the moment the fighting ended, but seeing Urothar and his soldiers escape like that distracted me. If Jared's gone, then what would that mean for the ritual? What would that mean for the prophecy everyone keeps talking about?

This day was supposed to be about finding and saving Lily, but it turned into a nightmare.

Hold on tightly, Garvir's mental message vibrates in my mind.

I grip Garvir's spines, and David ducks lower to adjust to the momentum of the sudden drop. The dragon dives toward the palace's second tier. When he lands, it's much softer than I expect. I slide off his back before he even settles, rushing toward the place where I last saw Jared fly to get away from the snapping dragon. This section of the palace is relatively intact, though the roof and wall have been completely smashed in by a flaming rock. Two black stones making up a portion of the third tier's wall are gapped just enough for a small bird to be able to fit in.

My heart thrums as I run to the crack and peek inside. There, I see a creature that would terrify even the most horror-numb individual. Anytime Jared falls unconscious or goes to sleep, his body attempts to shift back into its human form. But there's no room for him to shift. So, what's left is a half bird, half human monster quivering and shaking from the failed transformation.

I grab the sides of the large stone block and start tearing at them. Chunks of rock and dust cover me as I rip and tear as quickly I can.

"Kris!" David shouts at me. "Stop! This will be faster!"

I don't listen. I have to get to Jared. I have to save my brother.

My vision blurs as tears fill my eyes, but I keep tugging and punching, shattering as much rock as I can. Though I'm vaguely aware of the pain in my knuckles and the smell of blood as I work, I don't stop until David's hand grips my arm and tugs me away. Heat flares inside my belly, and I almost attack him, but when I see his expression, I stop.

He's worried about me. "Garvir can get him. Just *move*, okay?" His voice is hard and heavy, but it quavers, betraying his emotions.

As much as I don't want to leave the space, I allow David to lead me away.

Brace yourselves, Garvir says.

With one of his forefeet, he crushes the rocks in a decisive blow. The palace rumbles and shakes beneath us, almost knocking me off balance. David and I steady each other. Where his hands hold my skin, I feel a tingle. More than anything, I'm glad he's here. I feel a lot less alone.

Dust from the blow fills my nose and mouth, and I cough, trying to clear my airways. David coughs, too, but he's covered his mouth and nose with his shirt, so his fit is less intense.

Before I can recover, a huge blue dragon paw extends through the mess toward me. Jared is nestled inside, his body now fully human.

"Jared!" I say desperately, leaping onto the dragon's paw. The dragon scolds me off of him. Something about demons being really heavy.

Jared is pale and sweaty, dust sticking to him like glue. I put my huge hands on his chest in preparation to do CPR, but David stops me.

"You'll crush his ribs," he says. "I know how to do it."

It's a strange thing watching the boy you've fallen for put his mouth on your brother's. Watching David work frantically as he tries to revive Jared numbs me to any other sensation. The world seems dark at the thought of not having my brother there to help me—to guide me through my emotions. After the third breath, I feel hopeless.

Then, Jared sucks in a quivering breath, and I fall apart.

I shove David to the side and pick Jared up easily, cradling him in my arms and bawling. I'm vaguely aware of my surroundings, but at this moment, I don't care about anything else. I don't care how dumb I look. I don't care how embarrassing it is that I'm crying or that I'm covered in dust and blood and look like a ragged monster.

"Sheesh, Kris," Jared says, trying to shove me away. "You're smothering me. I only recently"—he pauses, a series of deep and wet coughs coming from his mouth—"remembered how to breathe. Do you want me to stop doing it again?"

"Sorry," I say, putting him on the ground softly and wiping my tears away.

"What happened? Did we win?"

I nod. "We did. They're gone."

Jared smiles, laying back and letting his head rest on a large piece of rubble.

"And what about the dra—?"

His eyes wander over to where Garvir sits regally and he yelps, rolling awkwardly away from the giant creature.

"It's fine!" David shouts, holding up his hands to calm Jared down. "He's good. He's on our side. Now that Urothar's controlling glyph is gone from him, at least."

I apologize for my unseemly actions. They were beyond my capacity of control. I was following orders and nothing more, the deep voice resonates in my mind.

"Right—uh—forgiven, I guess," Jared murmurs, but he's still inching away from the dragon.

David plops to the ground and sighs. "I guess it's a good thing I remembered my CPR training, huh?"

He gives me that goofy old grin that I hate and love at the same time. Then, without even thinking, I grab him by the arm and kiss him right on the mouth. His lips feel hot and wet compared to my cold and stony ones, but that makes it feel all the better. It takes me a moment to realize what I've done, and my eyes shoot open. I drop David to the ground with a thud and back away.

"Thanks—for saving him."

David sits there with a grin on his face. "Now *that* is a proper thanks. You are more than welcome."

It's about time, Jared muses in my mind.

Shut up, is all I say.

WE'RE SENT TO THE ELVEN KINGDOM

I SIT IN FRONT of the mirror, intentionally trying *not* to look at myself. The mirror is a large oval-shaped bit of glass wrapped in tangling branches like what you'd see in the *Snow White* movie. Overall, the whole vanity is an incredible piece of furniture, as if someone coaxed a tree to grow it. A porthole-type window lets sun filter through, casting the early morning light onto the only other furniture in the room—a four-poster bed and nightstand.

My fingers trace the obsidian crown that sits on the vanity next to me. Krell had it fashioned before we left Etherek. Despite my protestations, Krell and Ilvinar agreed that the demon palace needed to be repaired and that we should be sent to live with the elves until we are fully recovered. I smile, observing the seven spikes that poke up from the crown. It's entirely too large for me, considering I'm in my human form. My demon form isn't stuck anymore now that I'm away from Etherek.

Much to my chagrin, we were forced out of Etherek so that the demons could put things back together. I wanted nothing more than to stay with them, to build a life for myself there and recover without having to leave. Krell reminded me that we still have two other half-bloods who need saving. Also, until the defenses could be built up again, Etherek isn't the best place for us to gain our strength.

So here I am, stuck in the middle of the forest back in my human form and struggling to keep my emotions in check again.

Okay, the last part isn't as bad anymore. Something has clicked inside me. Even though my passions and emotions still flare up, it's much easier for me to hold them back than it was before I went to the demon kingdom.

A soft knock echoes from the door across the room. At first, I want to stay silent and pretend that I'm asleep so I can enjoy some peace.

"Hey, Kris, it's me," David's voice sounds.

And there goes all peace inside of me. Even without trying, the memory of his face so close to mine as I pull him in for a kiss comes back to me. I feel his lips on mine again, and it's impossible to stop the fluttering in my stomach. Do I regret doing that? A little. But he actually played it cool and hasn't bothered me incessantly about it. In fact, on the journey between Etherek and the elven city, he didn't mention it once. I'm sure he's thought endlessly about it though.

Sucking in a deep breath, I move to the door, count to three, and pull it open.

"Surprise," a weak voice says.

Jared, head wrapped in a bandage and using a walking cane, stands next to David with a half smile on his face.

"Jar!" I nearly scream, wrapping my arms around him and squeezing.

"Ow! Sheesh, Kris, take a chill pill," he says, wincing as I pull away from him. "I'm not fully recovered yet."

"Sorry! I didn't—you just—I thought you weren't going to make it, and—"

I stop talking and just hug him again despite his protestations. It's not like me to be this affectionate, but seeing him up and about brings me new life. I wonder how he managed to escape the eyes of the elven healers. They would hardly even let *me* go in to see him, let alone allow him to leave.

"You look like you're about to fall over. What are you even doing climbing up in treehouses just to say hi to me?" I chide. "Or did Drag-o Boy put you up to it?"

I glare at David. He puts his hands in the air and shakes his head.

"It wasn't my idea! It was your boy, Jared, who wanted to get out of there. I had to use my status to do a little ordering around for them to let him go," he admits.

"It was my idea, Kris. Don't take it out on David," he assures me. "And boy, they were not happy about it. I think David managed to make some enemies."

David sighs and rubs a hand over his face. "Once Ilvinar finds out, I'm sure I'll be in for it."

Jared laughs, then closes his eyes and wobbles a little. "Could use a sit-down though."

I rush forward and wrap my hand around his waist. David puts Jared's arm over his shoulder, and together, we hobble him to my bed. He lets out a relieved sigh when he's settled.

"Mind if I join you?" Lily pops in from the side of the open doorway, her blue skin gleaming.

What a weird girl. How did she even know they were here?

"I was just out walking and saw you two stumbling up the stairs. You could have just asked an elf to carry you, and they probably would have. These elven dudes are buff, to say the least," she says, walking fully into view. Her head has a circlet of silver affixed with green gems. The moment we arrived, her father made sure it was the first thing he did for her. What is with these kings and their traditions?

"Yeah, no thanks. As much as I want to be fireman-carried up the stairs for the whole elf kingdom to see—wait, I don't want that at all," Jared says.

Lily shrugs. "I would have taken it. It's not like you just fell over and hurt yourself. You fought a dragon and nearly got snapped in half. Nothing to be embarrassed about."

David's jaw hardens, and he looks like he wants to say something in response, but ultimately decides not to. For a moment, we all just sit there looking around the room and appreciating each other's company.

"So, here we are," David finally says. "Four of the six. We've broken the halfway point to our—um—sacrifices."

Way to kill the mood, David. I reach out and sock him on the shoulder, to which he swears and returns the punch.

"Thanks for the reminder, Dragon Breath. We just made it through our biggest battle yet, and you want to focus on the whole sacrifice angle? I, for one, am *not* ready to deal with that," I say. "Instead, we should be talking about how we're going to save the other kids. Now that we know the map trick, it should make it easier."

A breeze floats in the open window and moves the curtains in a dreamy way. A few golden and triangular leaves float in. The chirping birds pull me out of the conversation for just a moment as I appreciate the calm and relaxed nature of the forest city. Though it doesn't have the familiarity or isolated comfort of the black stone pathways and darkness of Etherek, the serenity of Terendrell is pretty awesome.

Jared looks to the window, and his eyes lose focus. "Yeah, which is great and all—but I'm not ready to travel yet. It could take weeks before I feel up to it," he says.

The idea of traveling the world without my brother sounds horrible, but in reality, the clock is ticking. We don't know what happened to Urothar and Ferona when they left, but my guess is that they aren't going to stay idle for very long. We won't have much time before the others are caught by the enemy.

"We aren't leaving you, bud," David confirms. "Even if you have to take it easy and ride on my shoulder as a mouse. I get the feeling that if we separate, it's not going to go well."

Lily nods. "I agree—to some level. Isn't it also a risk to travel as a group? I mean, Urothar wants us all for his own purposes. If we split up, we might be able to cover more ground *and* make it harder for him to catch us all."

It's actually a good point. But the idea of having to choose between David and Jared as my companion sounds like the most soap-opera-esque decision of my life. Not going to happen.

I fold my arms. "Given the fact that *we* are the ones who have to save the half-bloods, I think it makes sense to just stay together. We can move faster than the other races in the human realm. Besides, they may have run out of my blood by now. Their stone might have stopped working, which gives us an advantage. Gulran said himself that they had the problem of not having our blood to work the magic."

As the room lapses into silence, I walk over to the searching stone and pick it up, inspecting the dial in the center. It's currently set to the symbol of a music note and waves. This, I assume, is the symbol of the Siren-blooded kid, wherever they are. The stone remains dark and silent until I shift the dial to the treelike symbol, and the beam of light points toward Lily.

"Yeah, we can hope, but it still doesn't make sense to wait here too long. You could be wrong. They could have enough juice to find the next kid before us. I say we wait a maximum of two days before we phase back to our realm and get a move on," David suggests. "The faster we can get the other kids, the faster we can come back and figure out a way to save our parents."

Thoughts of Mom dance in my mind, and my chest constricts. Ever since she was taken, I can't help but be realistic about the fact that she's probably been turned into a blood teleportation stone. Still, I do have hope that she's still alive. If she is, she is more than likely being tortured.

"Wherever they are," Jared says.

Lily furrows her brow. "Your parents were taken? How did it happen?"

"Swindled by a stupid half orc. That's how," David says bitterly.

"Remind me to tell you about all that soon," Jared says, shifting and closing his eyes against the pain. "A lot has happened before we found you."

I turn the dial until it's pointed to my symbol, the beam flashing at myself. It's a set of horns surrounding what looks like bat wings. Strange considering demons don't have wings—unless my dad is keeping some wild secrets from me.

"What do you think we should do?" Lily asks.

"Like David said, we need to get out of here—as a group. You may be a guru with every weapon, but David still needs training, and I don't like the idea of you two going off on your own," I say.

David gives me a knowing look and a half smile. That's all I need to know to realize he thinks I'm saying I don't want to be separated from him because of our kiss. Dumb teenage boys. Even if that may be slightly true, it's very presumptuous of him.

I turn the dial to David's symbol, a slitted eyeball bathed in flames, and it springs to life, facing him now.

"Okay, so we stick together. That's fine. I may even have to ride along like David said, but you aren't leaving me," Jared agrees.

"Do you think we can phase back now?" I ask.

David closes his eyes and stands still, his arms hanging by his sides for a moment. Then, his eyes snap open.

"I think we've waited long enough. Lily probably can't, but I can feel the tug of our realm. We should be smart and only use one of our—um—bloodlinks, or whatever, to teleport back. Then, we can save the others. We just have to make sure we hold hands strong enough," he says. "Because we also have to find Amir and Rolinda." His face pales slightly. "In fact, that probably needs to happen before our parents. As much as I wish it didn't."

"It's not your fault that they got lost," Jared assures him. "You didn't know that would happen."

David's jaw tightens, and he punches one of the posts on my bed. "But it was my dumb hand that got loose. It *is* my fault for dragging Amir into all this, and now we have no idea where they are."

I sigh, turning the dial to Jared's symbol and watching the beam move to him.

"Don't beat yourself up about it, man. It's not going to save Amir," Jared says.

"Yeah, I know. It's just—I just—wish I knew where he was," David says, plopping on the bed next to Jared.

"The best thing we can do is find the other half-bloods. Then, we can figure out what to do about the others," I say. "I'm sure they are fine. Amir has Rolinda. She knows her way around Qotan, so it's not like he's left out to dry."

"Nice wording. Thanks a lot," David says.

I chomp my teeth, realizing the unintentional insinuation that David is the one who let Amir go like that.

"Anyway, we aren't focusing on that right now. The first thing we need to do is get ready to warp back to our realm and rush to the next half-blood. Jared, you need to get as much rest as you can in the next two days. After that, we're out of here whether you are ready or not," I say.

Lily cracks her neck and spins a knife between her fingers.

"I could use a little more practice with fighting. Being home-schooled gave me such little practice. Except maybe video games, but those got boring real fast," she says.

Jared chuckles. "You do realize that we didn't fight in public school either, right?"

Lily shrugs. "I don't know what you all did in classes. All I know is that I didn't get attacked while we were in hiding until you all showed up."

David shakes his head. "Sorry about that, by the way."

She raises her eyebrow at him. "I didn't say I was mad."

I hold up my hand to bring the attention back to me. "We're losing track. Can we all agree to the new plan?"

I look into each of their eyes, and they nod their approval.

"Good. Once we arrive back in our realm, we'll use the stone to find the closest half-blood and go from there," I say, flipping the dial until it lands on the last symbol—the one with the mountain and the axe.

A beam of light explodes from the stone, and my blood runs cold. "Uh—guys—are you seeing this?"

The energy in the room shifts from our lighthearted plan to nerves and confusion. David rushes over to the stone in my hand and follows the light with his finger.

"No way," he murmurs.

"Yeah," I whisper. "One of the kids is here, and if they're not with us—"

I remember the map my father had drafted for me. It's rolled up and stuffed in the pack laying by my vanity. Grabbing the pack with my free hand, I plop it on the bed and rummage through it until I can pull the map out. For a moment, I struggle to get the bit of twine off that holds it closed.

David rolls his eyes and does it for me, laying the parchment out flat on the bed behind Jared. My heart thunders in my ears as I hesitate to drop the stone onto the map's surface. Do I really want to know what it will say?

"Do it," David says. "Or I will."

With a death look, I slowly lower the glowing stone to the map. The moment it touches the surface, the beam of light snuffs out. A pinprick of white light appears far to the north-east. The light is extremely far away from us—smack dab in the middle of a city labeled "Orc Kingdom."

Jared's eyes are as wide as saucers, and David's hands curl into fists.

"I guess we aren't going back to our realm after all," Lily says nonchalantly.

I stare at the dot, wondering how long this half-blood has been there. How did we manage to fail them? How long had it been since I checked their location back in our realm? No matter how hard I try, I can't get rid of the images of a poor teenager being tortured by Urothar or his son.

"Change of plans," I say. "We leave immediately."

ALSO BY DAN KENNER

B ooks by Dan

www.dankenner.com

Epic Fantasy

Shielded: A Prequel to The Lightbearer Chronicles - Get the Ebook **FREE** at www.dankenner.com/free

Awakened: The Lightbearer Chronicles Book One

Transformed: The Lightbearer Chronicles Book Two

Ascended: The Lightbearer Chronicles Book Three

Young Adult

Sunfire

Dragon Blooded

Middle Grade

The Search for Silence

A Voice in The Noise

The Thundering Echo

About the Author

D AN LIVES IN RURAL Idaho where he happily lives with his wife, seven children, goats, chickens, Ginger the cow and her baby, and three cats named Wilma, Greg, and Gertrude. Aside from writing, which he'd happily do full time, Dan spends most of his time outside in the homestead he built with his wife, playing with kids, and enjoying hard work. When he's not writing, he spends his time with his nose in a fantasy or sci-fi book.

You can connect with me at https://www.dankenner.com

ACKNOWLEDGEMENT

T HIS BOOK, ALONG WITH the first draft of the next two books, came at a very difficult time in my life and the life of my family. So to have this book finally published is both an incredible accomplishment, and, admittedly, a relief to me. Not only did we have the blessing of our seventh child being born, but we also ventured into cows for the first time. Our baby was born within two weeks of our cow having her calf. Jumping immediately into milking twice a day with a two week old baby was not what we bargained for, nor was maintaining that milking schedule *and* dealing with twelve to fourteen gallons of milk each week for the next nine months. On top of that, I decided, for some strange reason, to change jobs less than a month after all this. Needless to say, there was a time I wondered if I'd ever finish another book and get it published. There was a time I wondered if I would make it through it all in one piece.

Yet here we are, and I am eternally grateful to many people for it. I am so thankful to my incredible wife, who supports me and encourages me to write my stories (and fund them, which is no small thing) even amidst the chaos of every day life. Even when she doesn't prefer to read fantasy or sci-fi stories, she is always ready to take highlighter to page to help find the mistakes that

I always miss. She even tells me she likes the story, the story of genres she doesn't normally enjoy. I am eternally grateful for her managing the home, our health (through food) and the children and their education. These things, taken care of, allow me to work not only at my job, but also on writing and building up an author business. It may not have turned into anything yet, but her continued support will only make it more possible.

I am thankful to each of my children. They love that their daddy writes stories that some have enjoyed already, and some have vowed they will enjoy when they learn to read. Hearing their excitement about another story finished is very motivating, and their love of reading and stories helps bolster my drive that writing is worth my time and theirs. They remind me the importance of clean and adventurous stories like this one. More kids need to exercise their imagination safely, so I need to get more of those stories out to the world.

I am grateful to the author community, and some of my most dear author friends, who show me and help me see daily that writing is a way of life, that success is measured differently, and that the work is always important, even if money isn't the direct outcome. Specifically, thank you to Jon Monson, Zac Diamanti, and L. Blaise Hues for being incredible examples of creativity, business, and authorship. May you continue to find success in your author endeavors.

Last, but certainly not least, I am thankful for my Heavenly Father and His direct hand in my life. Becoming an author was always a dream, never a reality in my mind, but certain people and circumstances have clearly been placed in my life to make this possible. I could have stepped back long ago, claimed that life was too busy or this was too expensive, but Heavenly Father continues to bless me with the mental creativity, time (however limited currently), and drive to bring adventure and clean, safe, stories to the adults, teens and kids of this world. His blessings have abounded, and continue to abound, which allow me to keep writing. In short, I thank Thee dearly for everything.